"Do you want to raise Mason?" Wyatt asked.

"No, I . . . not exactly. . . ." What, in her heart of hearts, *did* she want? Holly could see Mason's round little face, his blue eyes smiling up at her. "Yes. Maybe," she confessed. "I feel so protective of him," she said quickly. Her vision suddenly blurred. Shocked and embarrassed by even the hint of tears, Holly turned away from Wyatt.

"I understand. But he is your sister's son."

"I know."

"Hey." Wyatt stepped up behind her, put his arms around her, and pulled her close. "It's going to be okay," he said. "He's lucky to have you."

Holly was the lucky one. She turned toward him. Neither of them spoke; Wyatt's fingers drifted across her cheek, brushed her hair back, and grazed her ear. Holly looked at his lips, recalling the kiss they'd shared yesterday. A man was the last thing she'd had on her mind when she'd come out here, but then he'd appeared in her yard, and he was so understanding of the chaos in her life . . .

"And I'm a lucky guy," he murmured, and kissed her. His hand slid to her neck, his fingers curling softly around it, his mouth moving against hers.

ALSO BY JULIA LONDON

JULIA LONDON

a light at
winter's end

POCKET BOOKS

New York   London   Toronto   Sydney

Pocket Books
A Division of Simon & Schuster, Inc.
1230 Avenue of the Americas
New York, NY 10020

Cover illustration by Tom Hallman
Interior design by Davina Mock-Maniscalco

Manufactured in the United States of America

ISBN 978-1-61129-324-1

This book is dedicated to all the women and men who have cared for children who are not their own.

a light at
winter's end

Chapter One

The cowboy rose at dawn's first light and pulled on a pair of worn, dirty denims. "Come," he said to his dog and, scratching his bare abdomen, which had been made lean and hard by the work he did around the ranch, he padded down the hall of the nondescript redbrick ranch house and into the kitchen.

There was something sticky underfoot on the linoleum, but since the fluorescent bulb overhead was out, he couldn't really see. He sleepily made a note of it and thought Sunday, when he washed his clothes in that old harvest yellow washer, he might wash a few things around the house as well. He couldn't remember ever mopping the floor here, and figured, after a year, it was as good a time as any.

He studied the row of buttons on the trendy contraption that some would call a coffee machine and he called a pretentious piece of pain-in-the-ass machinery. It was one of the few things he'd kept from his marriage. He'd bought it for her, of course, and she'd been ridiculously pleased with it. He'd never quite figured out how to operate it correctly. Why had he kept it? He didn't know anymore. The only thing he did know was that Wyatt and Macy Clark were no more.

He punched a few buttons and the machine sounded like a locomotive steam engine. He turned away and almost tripped over his black Lab. Milo was always sneaking up on him like that, appearing underfoot, that damn tail always wagging. Wyatt had never known a happier dog, and he'd had quite a few in his life. No matter what he put the dog through, he grinned and wagged his tail and acted like he wanted more hard living.

Milo was the other thing Wyatt had kept from his marriage. Because Milo was *his* dog. Not hers. His.

His dog was hungry. Wyatt opened a sack of dog food he kept in a trash can next to the greasy kitchen wall. He scraped out two cups of chow and poured it into a dirty dog bowl. Milo didn't mind that he ate from a petri dish; he had one eager paw in the bowl as he wolfed it down.

Wyatt walked back to his bedroom and found a shirt in his pile of unwashed clothes that didn't smell too bad. Today he was going to tackle that broken fence the cattle kept trampling, and he didn't need to be clean or smelling of roses to do that. He dressed, pulled on his boots, brushed his teeth, and ran his fingers through his black hair. It had grown kind of long, and he'd taken to wearing it in a little ponytail at his nape. Never thought he'd see the day he did that—he'd always been a clean-cut kind of guy before his world collapsed—but what the hell? He lived by himself. The only person he saw on a regular basis was his baby daughter Grace, and she didn't care what he looked like. He didn't have anyone to impress, and Milo would like him if he walked around naked. Which, in all honesty, he'd done a time or two.

Wyatt returned to the kitchen. The coffeemaker now showed all green lights, so he poured himself a cup and sat down at the kitchen table. There was a neat line of stuff he used every day: salt and pepper, Tabasco sauce. A stack of paper napkins next to a stack of paper plates. And his laptop, his only real connection to the outside world. Oh, he had a television hooked up to some rabbit ears so he could get football and golf, but not much else came in over the rabbit ears.

He opened the laptop and his home screen popped up, with the news and the sports scores and his personal favorite, the Word of the Day. Today's word was *chary.*

> *Chary.* Meaning discreetly cautious. As in, *the gentleman is chary about voicing his concerns.*

Chary.

Wyatt sipped his coffee, clicked over to ESPN.com to check the baseball scores. He didn't see anything he didn't already know, and closed his laptop. He looked outside. Wyatt never bothered with breakfast. He liked getting out early while it was still cool and the wind was still. He liked the sound of the morning birds before the day got too warm for them and they disappeared into the brush.

He heard a bit of whining and looked over his shoulder. Milo had finished his breakfast and was standing at the back door, ready to go out. The paint was all scratched up where Milo would claw on it when Wyatt wasn't paying attention. Wyatt stood up, picked up his sweat-stained hat from the table, and fit it on his head.

He opened the back screen door. Milo took off, racing across the unkempt lawn with his nose to the ground. Coffee cup in hand, Wyatt moseyed on down to the barn, put his coffee cup on a shelf inside the barn next to two other coffee cups. He had three horses inside and turned two of them out to the pasture, swatting their rumps and sending them trotting to stretch their legs. He saddled the third. Troy, he called him, named for the great Dallas Cowboys quarterback Troy Aikman.

When he had Troy saddled, he led him out, whistled for Milo, and swung up into the saddle. The dog raced out of the brush and ran alongside Troy as Wyatt reined him around. He rode out into uncut land, through thickets of cedar and pin oaks and around prickly pear cactus spread as wide as swimming pools. His ranch was big for this part of Texas: about fifteen thousand acres, or a little over twenty-three square miles. That was a lot of fence to mend, a lot of ground for cattle and horses to cover. Wyatt had had an old pickup truck he used when the work warranted, but mostly he liked to ride.

He rode up on the southeast corner of the fence, where the cattle had gotten their big heads through and had busted through the barbed wire. He surveyed the damage: the wire would have to be cut out and re-strung. He figured he'd call Jesse Wheeler to come out and give him a hand. Jesse was Cedar Springs' resident jack-of-all-trades, a skill he'd picked up as he hopped from one woman's bed to another, doing odd jobs to earn his keep.

Wyatt spent the morning cutting the barbed wire from the posts. It was hot as blazes by eleven, and he paused to wipe the sweat from his eyes and take a drink from his canteen. He was standing next to Troy in the shade when he heard the cars. He turned around to see a hearse turn into the drive on the adjoining property. Another car was right behind it. And another. A funeral procession was heading up to the old Fisher cemetery. Wyatt had heard the old lady who lived there had cancer, but he hadn't heard she'd died. Frankly, between him and Milo and the big blue sky, he'd been biding his time, hoping to buy up that property when the opportunity arose.

That's what Wyatt did. Or used to do. He used to buy and sell ranch land, sometimes put a development on it. And Wyatt Clark of Clark Properties would buy up half of Texas if that's what it took to keep him from civilization. Since his wife, Macy, had left him for her first husband, he hadn't felt much like being in the world, and the more land he could put between him and everything else, the better.

He squinted at the cars as they disappeared into the cedars on the drive up to that old homestead cemetery and took another swig from his canteen.

It looked like the opportunity to make some chary inquiries had presented itself.

Chapter Two

When Peggy Fisher learned there was nothing more that could be done to save her from the cancer that was eating away at her, she set about planning her funeral with a vengeance.

It was exactly what she'd wanted, thanks to her daughter Hannah. She was buried in the blue linen suit she'd picked out herself, and per her instructions, the color of the casket complimented the suit. Her cousin D.J., a welder and aspiring singer, sang "Amazing Grace," and a funeral spray of daisies covered her grave. Mourners were kindly asked to give to the Susan G. Komen for the Cure foundation, if they so desired. Peggy hadn't died of breast cancer—hers was pancreatic—but she'd thought breast cancer would sound better in the obituary. "No one even knows what a pancreas is," she'd said, clearly annoyed that she should get cancer of an organ that no one understood.

There were only two pictures of Peggy at the funeral. They'd been blown up and placed on either side of the casket so that mourners in the back of the crumbling old limestone Presbyterian church with the sagging balcony could see them. Peggy had often lamented that she'd not done something with photos when her husband, Dale, had died fifteen years ago. He'd been out mowing the lawn one hot afternoon and had dropped dead right next to the roses he'd planted that spring.

"He never had much heart after Dale Junior died," Peggy had explained to Hannah and her other daughter, Holly, when she'd delivered the bad news. "His ol' heart finally gave out."

Holly, her youngest, had always found this idea a little odd, as Dale Junior had been born with a hole in his heart some twenty years prior and hadn't survived more than a few days after his birth. She thought it was more likely that her father's ridiculously high cholesterol was the source of his demise. But Holly didn't argue with her mother, because her mother liked things to appear a certain way to the outside world. She liked her husband to have died of a broken heart, and her daughters to be shining examples of the feminine ideal. Whatever that was.

After the funeral and the graveside service on the old Fisher homestead, where Peggy had lived forty-some years of her life, some kind soul carted her photos back to the house where family and friends had gathered to offer their condolences and to eat the food the church ladies had prepared. The two pictures were placed side by side against the dining room's sliding glass door, blocking the view of the back lawn and the rolling pasture and cedar trees beyond.

Holly studied the pictures. She'd politely refused an offer of beans, potato salad, and ham from the church ladies, but had given in and taken the iced tea, and occasionally she felt a cold drop of condensation from the sweaty glass hit her toes between the straps of her sandals. The photos of her mother didn't stir her numb head to any thought other than that it was only her and Hannah now. Holly was officially bereft of any emotion, having grieved the last painful months of her mother's life. Even longer, if she thought about it. Which she did not want to do.

Her mother had fretted over which pictures to choose, finally settling on these two. The first one, taken when she was around ten, was a blurry black-and-white image of a girl in pigtails, seated on an ancient-looking bike. It didn't even look like Peggy. "I was so happy then," she'd said with a sigh as she admired herself as a redheaded, full-lipped kid.

The second photo was taken after Peggy had become a mother. She was laughing at whoever was taking the picture, an openmouthed, spontaneous sort of laugh. She held Holly and Hannah, who was two years older than Holly, on her lap. They wore matching green sundresses. Hannah's auburn hair was cut shoulder-length, and she had bangs. Her blue eyes had a happy shine to them. Holly's strawberry blonde hair was pulled back in a ponytail, but her grayish-green eyes looked somber. Peggy's arms were wrapped tightly around her girls. *When had Peggy Fisher lost her grip of her girls? When had they slid off her lap and stopped wearing matching sundresses and ponytails?*

Holly guessed the photo had been taken about thirty years ago, when Hannah was six and she was four. Did her mother choose it because Hannah and Holly were young and free of the tension that had existed between them in the last several years? Was it taken before the comparisons began to be made, or had her mother already started making them? She had an odd flash of memory, of making biscuits with her mother, of her and Hannah wearing aprons tied up under their arms, standing on stools beside their mother. Holly could remember rolling the dough and then cutting rounds with the lids of mason jars. *Holly, look at the mess you've made. Look at Hannah! Look at how neatly she's made hers.* Holly could still see Hannah's row of perfectly formed biscuits, lined up like soldiers, spaced equally apart. And her biscuits—not quite round, not quite straight. One of them shaped like a doggie.

Why can't you do it like Hannah?

A collective cry of alarm startled Holly from her thoughts. She looked around the two pictures to the back lawn. The sprinklers, which Hannah had insisted be installed around the lawn so that Peggy wouldn't have to worry about the yard, had come on where a few people milled about with plates heaped with funeral food.

"I told Loren to turn the sprinklers off."

Holly hadn't realized Hannah was standing beside her until she spoke. She glanced at her sister, noticed how Hannah watched with weary dissatisfaction as the guests hopped awkwardly away from the sprinklers. She looked wan, Holly thought. Drawn. She never ate, she just drank tea. But Hannah was beautiful as always, impeccably dressed in a tailored black suit and a pair of killer heels. Her hair was knotted neatly at her nape and a diamond pendant twinkled at her throat. As usual, Holly felt a little dumpy next to her sister. Her shaggy hair was down around her shoulders, clipped back from her face. She wore a black sleeveless shift and a pair of nondescript black sandals she'd picked up from Payless.

"What are you going to do with these?" Holly asked, nodding at the enlarged pictures as Hannah's husband, Loren, rushed out to help people off the lawn and turn off the sprinklers.

"Throw them away," Hannah said with a shrug. "Unless you'd like some giant pictures of Mom hanging in your apartment." She smiled.

Whoa, was that a joke? Holly couldn't remember the last time her sister had joked about anything. "I'll pass," Holly said, and returned her smile. But Hannah looked as if she were bored, and an awkward silence filled the space around them. The two of them had very little to say to each other these days; their mother's illness had taken a toll on their already fragile relationship.

Holly looked past Hannah to the dining room, where the food was laid out in Corel casserole dishes. "Is there anything I can do to help you?"

Hannah shifted her expression of weary dissatisfaction to Holly. "No, thank you. Everything is taken care of," she said, as if Holly had waited too long to ask an obvious question.

Hannah was probably still mad at her. She'd asked Holly to call the nurses at Cedar Springs Memorial Hospital and tell them about the visitation, but Holly had forgotten to do it. She'd been trying to cover as many shifts at work as she could so that she could afford to be off for several days after the funeral, and she'd forgotten to call. Only one nurse came, and Hannah blamed Holly for it.

"I'm just trying to help," Holly said now.

Hannah's gaze flicked over her. "I think I'll get something to eat."

Holly tried not to be offended as Hannah walked away. Okay, it was true that Hannah had handled everything with their mother. *Everything,* from the moment they'd found out about the cancer until the very end. In spite of being the office manager at a big downtown Austin law firm, it was Hannah who found the time to check on their mother every other day, driving forty miles each way out here to where they'd grown up. It was Hannah who took their mother to every doctor appointment, to every chemotherapy session, and made sure her prescriptions were filled and that she took her meds. It was Hannah who had hired the nurse to see after Mom when she grew weak but refused to leave the home she'd known all her adult life; and in the end, it was Hannah who brought Mom into Austin to live with her, Loren, and her new baby, Mason.

No one could say Hannah Fisher Drake hadn't been the perfect daughter all her life. No one could say she hadn't been a paragon of strength and virtue during her mother's illness. Hannah was a rock; she knew just what to do in any given circumstance. She was, in Holly's mind, the mother of all control freaks.

But no one could say that Holly hadn't tried to help out with her mother, and hadn't always—*always*—tried to measure up. Only Holly couldn't drive out to check on her mom every day like Hannah. Holly was a songwriter living in a studio apartment and surviving off her coffeehouse wages and the nice bit of income she'd gotten from Austin Sound Company, or ASC, a music publisher that had bought three of her songs. Holly's life was black and white compared to Hannah's. She couldn't miss work. If she didn't show up, she didn't get paid; and if she didn't get paid, she didn't pay rent. Holly didn't have different banks with different savings like Hannah. She didn't have any cushions to fall back on. She wasn't as organized or as efficient as her sister. She'd tried to explain that when Hannah had asked her to check on Mom once, a few months before her death.

"I can't," Holly had said, feeling terribly guilty and inadequate. "I have to work. Rent is due next week."

Hannah had remained silent for a very long moment. "Really, Holly?" she'd said at last, her voice full of skepticism. "Because I have a baby, I am working fifty hours a week, and I am taking care of Mom. You really can't get out there in the next couple of days?"

"I can go Wednesday," Holly had offered.

"Wednesday is too late."

"See, this is why I tried to pick up the slack for you last week," Holly had said irritably. She was aware of her shortcomings and her inability to be a model sister or daughter. "I had the days off then. But you had it all figured out and there was no room for me, remember?"

"No *room*?" Hannah had snorted her opinion of that. "You couldn't take Mom to chemo, *remember*? So what was the point? I still had to take time off from work."

"But I could have done *something*, Hannah. Come

on, you know I don't have the same degrees of freedom as you do. I have gone out to see about Mom every chance I've been able to do it. I took her food shopping just last week. I took her to see Uncle D.J."

"Yes, I know you took her to the grocery store and to see Uncle D.J. But you did those things when it was convenient for *you*. I used to wait tables in college, so don't act like I don't know that you can switch shifts."

"But I am a shift supervisor," Holly pointed out. "I can't just switch with anyone. It has to be another supervisor. So let's hire someone, Hannah. Then you don't have to do it all."

"Are *you* going to pay for someone?" Hannah had snapped. "Look, don't worry about it. I'll handle it just like I always handle it. I should have known better than to try and count on you being there."

"I should have known better than to expect you to be anything less than a complete control freak," Holly shot back.

"Jesus, Holly, our mother is dying! Do you really want to do this now?"

"Oh, great, pull out the trump card and have the last word," Holly had scoffed.

That phone call had ended like so many of their phone calls: in an angry stalemate. There had been other phone calls, too, all with the same tone. Hannah, increasingly distant, and Holly, never doing enough.

Holly shook her head as she gazed that photo of the two girls. There was so much freezing, bitter water under their bridge now. In the last year, it had felt like rising floodwaters, moving too fast, threatening to sweep them away and pummel their relationship into nothing. And then Hannah *had* hired a nurse to see after Mom a couple of hours each day. She'd done it without consulting Holly. She'd just done it.

It hadn't always been like that between them, but Holly could no longer say when the fissures had begun to open up between them. There'd been a time when Holly had worshipped Hannah. Her sister was smart and fun and sunny. They'd played dolls and cowboys and Indians together. They'd slept in twin beds in a room at the end of the upstairs hall, where summer breezes drifted in through open windows and their dog, Tigger, would stand still to be dressed in silly outfits.

When Holly had boarded the school bus in the first grade, it was Hannah who held her hand and found a seat they could share. Hannah had walked her to her class and met her after school. Hannah helped her learn her multiplication tables and tacked up the drawings Holly had made at school around their room. Hannah was compassionate when Holly's poor performance in school was diagnosed as dyslexia, and had drilled her on the tricks for dealing with it. Not that it had helped—Holly had never been a great student.

Hannah was the first person Holly had turned to when she had her first boyfriend, and then her first breakup, at thirteen. She'd helped Holly prepare to audition for the school musical at fifteen, and when Holly had been awarded with a lead part, she'd helped her make her costumes.

When had things gotten so cold and distant between them?

At the moment, Holly could see Hannah flitting

here and there, making sure no one's plate sat empty or any glass went unfilled. She was a model hostess, and a little thing like her mother's funeral didn't throw her off her game.

Holly had moved dumbly through the day, not feeling, not helping . . . She looked away from Hannah and her gaze landed on Hannah's husband, Loren. *Ugh*. With hand shoved in the pocket of his suit trousers, one shoulder against the wall, Loren was chatting up Stella, the daughter of Holly's cousin, Renette. Stella was a pretty nineteen-year-old girl with expressive brown eyes. She was laughing at something Loren said, and honestly, Loren seemed just a little too smiley-faced, as if this were an afternoon barbecue instead of the somber occasion that it was. Holly had never cared for Loren; there was something a little too slick about him for her tastes. She'd never understand what Hannah saw in him, which had just shoved another wedge in between them.

Oh, sure, she got the obvious part—Loren was a handsome guy with blond hair and blue eyes. He was a lawyer who specialized in oil and mineral rights, and liked jetting around on oil company planes to consult. He bragged about his golf scores and his hunting, and it seemed as if every weekend he went away to do one or the other.

Hannah had met Loren at work. She was an assistant administrator at the Baker Botts Law Firm in Austin when Loren was hired. Holly had the impression that he'd immediately started hitting on Hannah, which was understandable, as Hannah was beautiful. She was toned and tan and had such pretty blue eyes. But Hannah was usually very reserved about that sort of thing, especially at work. Hannah had rules to live by. Loads of them.

Holly would never forget the day that Hannah announced that she was leaving the firm because she and Loren were officially an item. That had been eight or nine years ago. Holly and Hannah were here, at the homestead, which was what their parents had called the family ranch, just as Dad's parents before him. It was a rambling old Victorian house with a wraparound porch and lots of natural light streaming in through big windows. From every room, there was a view of pastures filled with grass, live oaks, cottonwoods, and cedar. And cows. Lots and lots of meandering, cud-chewing, bellowing cows.

The floors were wood planked and the bedrooms—five in all—had high ceilings and tiny closets. There were two shared baths upstairs and one half bath on the first floor, and a big farmhouse eat-in kitchen with a scarred table where the family had dined over the years. The living room—or, as Holly's grandmother had called it, the parlor—was small and cozy with a big fireplace as the focal point.

That Sunday, Holly's mother had baked a ham and Hannah was making her perfected low-fat potato salad in the chipped blue ceramic bowl with the little flowers that their mother had always used to make cake batter.

Holly had brought her usual contribution to the Sunday gathering—chips, salsa, and a six-pack of beer that no one drank besides her. Holly would freely admit she wasn't much use in the kitchen, no matter how many attempts her mother had made to turn her into a cook. Holly had sat on a red bar stool, watching Hannah and her mother.

Her mother was healthy then. She was a little thick around the middle, and her red hair was beginning to gray; but she'd worn it short and curly in the last several years, and when she went to church on Sundays, it looked as if she'd shellacked it into place.

"Are you still seeing that boy in the band?" her mother had asked Holly.

Holly had to think which guy her mother meant. She hadn't had much luck in the relationship department; it was a fact that musicians made for lousy boyfriends. And, Holly suspected, she didn't exactly choose well. She'd always been attracted to the bad boys: rogue cowboys she met at the Broken Spoke, or musicians who liked to drift from gig to gig.

"Which guy?" she'd asked curiously.

"Ru-al, or something like that," her mother had said, trying to jog Holly's memory.

"Raul?" He'd been the dark-eyed, sweet-lipped guitarist who had played with Charlie Sexton for a while. She'd gone out with him three or four times before he'd moved on to the next woman. Holly had walked into the Saxon Pub to catch his set, and there he was, kissing the next woman. "No," she'd said, studying the salsa. "I think he's in San Antonio now."

"San Antonio," her mother had repeated, as if she hadn't been quite sure where or what that was. "That's too bad."

"Not really," Holly had cheerfully assured her. She was over Raul. She always got over them.

"Well, as your mother, I'd sure feel better about you if you could meet a nice man like Hannah's Loren."

As if meeting a man would somehow improve Holly. And Hannah's Loren? Holly had met him a couple of times by then, and both times, he'd done a slow, casual intake of her body with his eyes. It had given her the creeps.

"Speaking of Loren, I have news," Hannah had said lightly. She was wearing a cute green cotton dress and kitten-heeled sandals, and Holly, in her shorts and flip-flops, had felt a twinge of jealousy. "It's gotten kind of serious," Hannah had said, and paused to smile girlishly at her mother, which had surprised Holly. "I am quitting Baker Botts at the end of the month."

"*What?*" her mother had cried. Peggy Fisher thought there was nothing worse than being without a job—Holly knew that better than anyone.

"Well, we're officially a couple, and Baker Botts has a no fraternization policy, so . . ." She'd shrugged. And with that pert little smile on her face, she'd stirred the potato salad again.

"You're going to *quit*?" Holly had asked incredulously. She'd been shocked that Hannah—driven, ambitious Hannah—would quit.

"Hannah!" her mother had cried, ignoring Holly. She was beaming as if Hannah had just announced she'd found a million dollars buried in the backyard. "This must mean it is *very* serious between the two of you."

"We'll see," Hannah had said coyly.

"But why do you have to quit your job?" Holly had

asked. "Where I work, no one cares who dates whom as long as everyone shows up for work."

"But you work at Whole Foods," Hannah had calmly pointed out.

Holly hadn't known exactly what that meant, but it didn't seem very flattering.

"I guess I can assume that even bigger news is coming?" Holly's mother had pressed excitedly.

"Calm down, Mom," Hannah had said laughingly. "Right now we're okay with seeing where this is going."

It had been Hannah speaking, the woman who planned everything to the nth degree. Hannah, who had known from the time they were girls where she would go to college (the University of Texas) and what she would study (business administration). She'd never done anything without a firm plan, whereas Holly did things without a plan all the time. But not Hannah; she'd never quit a job just to "see where it goes."

"I don't get it," Holly had said. "You would really quit your job?"

Holly's question had earned her one of Hannah's patently impatient looks. "Well, I can't work there and see Loren. So, yes, I'm really quitting my job."

"Why do you have to be the one to quit?" Holly had asked as she dipped another chip in the salsa. "Seems like a huge deal and you've worked really hard to get that position. Why not him?"

"*Because,*" Hannah had said, and put down her spoon to give Holly her full attention. "Because that's what we decided to do. He's got a great position there—"

"So do you."

"—And I am going to look for another job, Holly, okay? Does that meet with your approval?"

"I don't mean it like that," Holly had said, miffed. "I'm just thinking of you, to be honest. I mean, how easy is it going to be for you to find a job like the one you have now?"

"Holly, you stop that right now," her mother had chastised her. "You don't know what you're talking about."

"I wouldn't do this if I didn't think I could find another job," Hannah had said, and returned to her potato salad. "I've got a couple of really good leads and Loren knows a lot of people in town. I don't think it will be a problem at all."

"Honestly, Holly, you would do well to focus on your own job choices," her mother had tossed out there, because her mother had always enjoyed spicing up an already tense conversation.

It had worked: Holly had stilled with one chip in the salsa. "What does that mean?"

"You know very well what I mean: working at a grocery store isn't what I'd call a real job. You had every opportunity to finish college and make something of yourself, too, and you threw that all away."

They'd started down a familiar path with that: Holly had washed out of U.T., whereas Hannah had graduated with honors. Holly hadn't wanted to spend four years in school trying to figure out something that would go with songwriting, which was what she'd really wanted to do. But when she'd taken music theory and piano her first semester, her mother had threatened to cut off her college funds. So Holly had signed up for history and business administration classes, like Hannah, and had been so bored and so lost in the words that she'd lost all interest in school.

"I am guessing that grocers the world over would not appreciate you disparaging their occupation, Mom. And really, do we have to turn everything into a lecture on why I should have finished college?" Holly had asked testily.

"I'm just saying that all your life, you've flit from one thing to another," her mother had rather blithely continued. "How many jobs have you had now?"

"I've had a few," Holly had admitted, her annoyance barely contained. "But they're just jobs. You seem to forget that my life's work is music, and I've stuck with it since I was a little girl. I've had different jobs to accommodate my songwriting, Mom. *That's* what I want to do with my life."

"Well, I am entitled to my opinion, and my opinion is that you are setting yourself up for a long, hard life. You're thirty-four now, Holly, and I've never known a songwriter who could put as much as a chicken on a table," her mother had said, as if she'd known loads of songwriters instead of one. "Your sister finished college and she's been working hard all her life. I have no doubt she'll find another excellent job, if that's what she wants—and I am sure it is, because Hannah is a very focused and ambitious. So, instead of giving her the third degree, you should be looking at how Hannah has accomplished so much in her life and take a page out of her book."

As if Holly were lazy. As if she wanted to write songs because that was somehow the easy way out.

Look at your sister. Holly had been duly stung, and she'd gaped at her mother. "Do you honestly think it's a good idea that Hannah quits her job so she can see where it's going with some random guy she is dating?"

"For God's sake, Holly," Hannah had said, and brushed past her, walking to the table with the potato salad. "He's not random."

"Let me tell you something, Holly Lynn," her mother had said, pointing the knife she was using to carve the ham at her. "Loren Drake is a good man. You should find yourself a man like him."

Be like Hannah, date like Hannah. Holly, trained like one of Pavlov's dogs, had reacted without thinking. "I don't *need* a husband, Mom." She'd known the moment the words came tumbling out of her mouth that she was responding exactly as her mother had wanted, and yet she had gone on. "I don't have to have a guy to feel like my life is complete."

"No, I guess that high-paying songwriting does it," her mother had said with a snort.

It was as infuriating now as it had been then. Her songwriting wasn't some lark, it was Holly's passion, and she was good at it. She was finally starting to get somewhere with it. Moreover, she'd never asked her mother for money, she'd always made her own way, and she could not understand why her mother couldn't just . . . *support* her.

Because she wasn't perfect. She wasn't Hannah.

Holly looked across the living room to Hannah now. She looked distracted, on autopilot, as she carried empty plates into the kitchen and handed them to one of the church ladies. Holly shifted her gaze to Loren again. He'd moved closer to Stella.

She heard her nephew Mason's cry through the baby monitor on the mantel at the same moment Hannah heard it. Hannah instantly started for the stairs, but Holly intercepted her. "Is it all right if I get him?"

Hannah blinked and stood a moment as if she couldn't process Holly's question. Then she nodded curtly. "Sure."

Holly made her way up the stairs with the worn red carpet runner and down the hall to the nursery.

The shades had been pulled and it took a moment for Holly's eyes to adjust to the darkened room. The walls were still covered in the faded yellow wallpaper with the green ivy vines, and it had begun to curl away from the wall in one corner. The old braided rug was the same as it had been when Holly and Hannah were girls, but there was a crib in here now, and a changing table, and a rocker in one corner of the room that looked as if it had been picked up from a garage sale. There was also a portable Baby Einstein Play Gym.

Mason was sitting in the middle of his crib like a Buddha, his fists on his dimply thighs. He watched Holly with big blue eyes, and as Holly drew closer, he suddenly gave her a big toothless grin and gurgled.

Holly grinned and dipped under the elaborate mobile with the airplanes and helicopters and picked him up. "Hey, Mason," she whispered. She loved the almost weightless feel of Mason in her arms. She loved the smell of baby lotion and the smooth, silken feel of his skin. She eased down on the floor with him and laid him on his belly in his play gym, and watched him chew on the tail of the dolphin.

She could watch him for days, Holly mused. There was something endlessly fascinating about babies, and in a corner of her heart it made Holly wish for her own. That wasn't something she knew how to pull off with her lifestyle and income, or any practical knowledge for that matter. Not to mention a lack of a sperm donor. But she was thirty-four years old, and there were times—like now—that she ached for a Mason.

She picked him up under his arms and had him stand in her lap. He began to gurgle and bounce on his fat little legs, up and down, up and down, as he reached for her nose and her earrings. He'd managed to get the little silver peace sign she wore on a chain around her neck into his mouth when Hannah walked in with his bottle and a blue plastic cup.

"There he is," she cooed, and put the bottle aside to hold out her arms for her baby. Holly handed Mason up to her, then got to her feet.

Hannah kissed Mason's round head. She put one hand to his bottom and frowned. "Didn't you change him?"

It hadn't even occurred to Holly. "No, I—"

"Babies are generally wet when they wake up from a nap," Hannah said. She put Mason on the changing table. "My little man," she cooed as she changed him. "Did you have a good nap? Are you hungry?" When she had him in a fresh diaper, she picked him up and lifted him up over her head, giving him a playful shake. Mason kicked his legs and stuffed a fist into his mouth.

"I love you, baby boy," Hannah said, and kissed his face before settling him on her hip.

"He's growing so fast," Holly said.

"And he's got the appetite of a horse," Hannah agreed.

"What does he like?" Holly asked.

"Huh?'

"To eat," she clarified.

Hannah looked blank. "To eat?"

"You were saying—"

"The usual baby food stuff," Hannah said with a shrug, interrupting Holly. "There is nothing this kid won't eat. Isn't that right, sweet pea?" she asked, tweaking Mason's nose. Mason grasped his mother's finger and tried to put it in his mouth. "People are starting to leave," Hannah added without looking away from Mason. She was swaying now, side to side, bouncing him a little.

"Oh. Okay," Holly said. "I'll go and thank them for coming."

"If you wouldn't mind."

Holly leaned over to kiss Mason's cheek, but when she did, she thought she smelled alcohol and looked at her sister curiously. "Have you been drinking?"

"Yes," Hannah said. "It's been a trying day."

It had certainly been that. "Yes, it has been trying," Holly agreed. "Okay, Mase, here's your aunt Holly, going out to thank everyone for coming," she said, and started toward the door. She paused there and looked back at her sister. Hannah's focus was entirely on Mason; she was speaking softly to him, chattering in the language of mothers. "Hannah."

Hannah looked up.

"Thanks for taking care of everything," Holly said, gesturing vaguely in the direction of downstairs. "The funeral, I mean. You did a really great job, and I know it's been hard with your job and Mason and everything else."

Hannah didn't say anything—just stood there, staring back at Holly as Mason mouthed her shoulder.

Holly expected her to at least say *No problem.* Or even *Thanks for noticing.* Something. *Why didn't she speak?* "Okay," Holly said. "I just wanted to say thanks." Bewildered, she turned back to the door.

"It was hard," Hannah said, her voice low. "Harder than you can possibly know."

Holly looked back at her sister. She could see the stress and wondered if maybe, Hannah was actually opening up to her.

"I spent every waking hour making sure Mom had what she needed," Hannah said, and suddenly swiped up the bottle from the dresser. "I haven't had a moment to myself since she got sick."

There was an accusatory edge in her tone, and Holly steeled herself. "I know. You've gone above and beyond."

"Then maybe you can appreciate," Hannah said as she maneuvered Mason into her arms and handed him the bottle, which Mason eagerly took, "how hurt I was when Mom left it all to you."

Holly had already started nodding, but suddenly stopped. "Wait . . . What?"

Hannah's gaze was hard, her jaw tight. "You heard me."

"Yeah, I heard you, but that's crazy," Holly said. "What are you saying?"

"Don't pretend you don't know—"

"I have no idea what you are talking about!"

Hannah tossed back her head with a groan. "Come on, Holly! Are you going to tell me that you didn't talk to Mom about it in the last couple of months?"

Holly's head was spinning. "Talk to her about *what*?"

"About her will!"

"Her *will*? Are you kidding?" Holly tried to recall if she and her mother had ever discussed her will, other than to note that her mother at least had one. "It never occurred to me, Hannah. She said she had one, and I left it at that. I just assumed that everything would pass to us."

"Really?" Hannah asked skeptically. "You never wondered what Mom was going to do with the homestead? What her final wishes might have been? Do you honestly expect me to believe that?"

"I don't like the accusation in your tone," Holly said, folding her arms. "*You've* obviously thought about it. You've obviously read it, and Mom is hardly even buried. So if you have something to say, Sis, just say it."

"Mom left the homestead and all her savings to *you*."

Holly was stunned. "There is obviously some mistake. I don't know where you got that idea, but I am sure it is easily cleared up, because it is not true."

But Hannah was already shaking her head. "There's no mistake." Mason pushed the bottle away, but Hannah pushed it right back in his mouth. "She left it *all* to you, Holly. And I have a hard time believing you didn't know it."

Holly couldn't make sense of it. It was inconceivable—her mother had thought Hannah was the greatest daughter in the history of the world. "You've got something wrong, Hannah. She left it to *both* of us."

Hannah snorted and turned away. "Read the letter yourself."

"*What* letter?" Holly demanded heavenward.

"The one she left with her pastor, along with a copy of a will that I have never seen. The one where she writes that she left it all to you, to poor, helpless, hapless Holly, because you would need it worse than me, because *you* didn't have anyone to take care of you and *you* couldn't make your way in the big bad world."

That stung. Even in death, Holly's mother had found a way to criticize her. "If that is true—and I don't believe it is, but for the sake of argument, if it is—I'll give you half of everything, Hannah. I mean . . . is there anything besides this house? Whatever it is, I will give you half—"

"God, that is so like you to completely miss the point," Hannah said coldly, and put Mason in his crib with the bottle. Only Mason didn't want in his crib. He started to cry. Hannah swiped the cup of the dresser and drank deeply.

"What point am I missing?" Holly demanded. "You are practically accusing me of stealing this run-down old house! I had no idea Mom did that—This is the first I'm hearing it, and I'm telling you, we will share—"

"It's not the estate!" Hannah cried, and Mason wailed. "The point is that while you were here in Austin, slinging frozen coffee drinks and writing your songs," she said, flittering her fingers at Holly, "I was working fifty hours a week, taking care of Mason and Loren *and* Mom. Just like always! I took care of everything while you were off doing whatever it is you do, and she rewards *you*?"

Holly recoiled. "Come on. I didn't ask for it. I didn't even *know* it."

"You may not have asked her outright, but you ended up right where you wanted. You never have to work again, do you realize that? You never have to care for anything. You can do whatever the hell you want to do while I clean up behind you. *God.*"

Holly was suddenly shaking with angry frustration. The fingers of one hand curled into a fist as she worked to keep from exploding. "Don't lay that guilt trip on me, Hannah. You want to know what Mom thought of me? She thought I was stupid and useless and that I would never amount to anything because I wasn't *you*. All my life I have tried to be who I am, but it was never good enough for her because I wasn't *you*!"

"That's bullshit," Hannah said angrily. "She let you get away with murder."

Holly drew a long breath. "I am not going to do this here, today of all days. Your baby is crying and I am leaving." She walked out of the room, her head spinning with Mom's last dig at her from the grave.

Chapter Three

Five months later

Hannah ran her finger down the names of doctors in the yellow pages. *Family practice, family practice, OB/GYN*. Family practitioners were no good; they made you pee in a cup these days. OB/GYNs were the worst, all of them on some freaking crusade to save women from themselves. Orthopedic doctors were suspicious right off the bat. *Dentist,* she thought. Dentists were so trusting. They would call in a scrip and an antibiotic before you ever saw them. But if you wanted a more than a few, it was best to call on a Friday, get enough to get you through a weekend, then forget the appointment they made for you on Monday.

Hannah glanced at the clock on the kitchen wall. It was already nine. She'd taken the day off of work to take care of this. Mason was down for his nap, and she had a window of maybe an hour to get it done. An hour wasn't much time.

She pulled her sweater tighter around her and rubbed her hand under her nose. She made a mental note to call someone about the air-conditioning. It was freezing in the house, like the thermostat was broken. She'd checked it twice and it read seventy-eight. It couldn't be seventy-eight. More like forty-eight. She shouldn't be freezing in August.

Stupid pain clinic. She'd gone yesterday, but they said they had to have the clinic director sign off on her scrip, which Hannah had instantly known was trouble, because if there was the slightest delay in filling it, she would run low. And of course there had been a delay, they hadn't yet called it in, and now she was dangerously low. The incompetence of people astounded her.

Pain clinics were generally easy, but Hannah didn't like to going to them because they were full of little old ladies who needed their pain pills. Plus, a lot of the clinics would fill only one prescription—they didn't want anyone's abuse of pain meds traced back to them. Nevertheless, they never suspected her. One doctor wrote a scrip for her while he was on the phone. He never really looked at her . . . but then there was the doctor with the unpronounceable last name who had asked her if she was uncomfortable when she didn't take the pain meds. Hannah had said no, that she was fine without them, and the doctor had suggested perhaps she try physical therapy instead, and Hannah had realized her mistake.

As she was leaving that clinic, a nurse with a rose tattoo on her neck pulled her aside. Hannah had wondered, why the neck? Why not the ankle? The shoulder?

"Listen, if you need something, you can call Brian."

"Brian?" Hannah had asked suspiciously. "Who is Brian?"

The nurse with the rose tattoo on her neck had jotted down the number, and pressed it into Hannah's palm. "He's a friend," she'd said softly. "He can hook you up, sweetie."

"Excuse me?" Hannah had demanded haughtily. "Are you a doctor?" And she'd walked out with Mason.

But she'd kept the number. It was in her wallet now. Not that she would ever *call* it, no no no. She didn't use pills like that.

Hannah's phone rang, startling her. She picked it up and stared at the number. It was work. Hannah squeezed her eyes shut a moment against a pain in the back of her head. What part of *Home with sick baby* did they not understand? She punched the button on her phone and said, "Hannah Drake speaking."

"Hey, Hannah."

Great, just great, it was Rob Tucker, one of the partners. Rob was a talker. "Hi, Rob, how are you?" *Just make it short. Don't tell me about a case, God, please, don't tell me about a case.*

"I can't complain. Hey, listen, I hate to bother you at home, but I've got a little bit of an emergency this morning."

"No problem!" she said brightly. "What's the emergency?"

"You said you left the files of the candidates we are interviewing this morning on my desk, but I must be blind, because I can't find them anywhere," he said with a chuckle. "We've got four lawyers sitting in the lobby and I don't remember any of their names."

This keeps happening. The pain behind Hannah's eyes was excruciating. She vaguely remembered the files. What had she done with them? *Okay, you had them in your hand just yesterday.* "I am so sorry you can't find them," she said lightly. "I put them on your desk." This was the third time Rob had to remind her about those damn applications. Why couldn't his assistant handle routine hirings? Why did she have to do *everything*?

"Are you sure?" he asked.

"Positive," Hannah said confidently.

"I know when I saw you in the hall yesterday, you had them in your hand. But I don't remember you coming into the office."

Hannah couldn't think with her head in a vise, but she was fairly certain she'd left them on his desk, right next to the computer. "You must have been in a meeting, Rob. Do you think someone might have moved them?"

"I can't imagine who," he said thoughtfully.

The pain surged. Hannah gripped the phone, trying to stay focused.

"Oh, man," Rob said suddenly, and laughed sheepishly. "Connie just brought them in. They were on her desk— Wait. What, Connie?" Hannah could heard Connie's voice in the background. "Oh," he said. "Connie said she found them in the copy room."

"Oh?" Hannah could hear Connie talking still. Could they not have their conversation after she was off the phone?

"Well, we found them. So sorry to have bothered you at home," Rob said. "Hey, tell Loren I said hello, will you? Is he doing all right? Working on some big cases?"

"You know Loren," Hannah said with false cheer, as if Loren were always working on a big case instead of big tits. She'd recently found out about Loren's third affair in their seven-year marriage, only this time when she confronted him, he didn't buy her a diamond necklace like he had the first time, or get her pregnant like he had the last time. This time he told her it was over, and he'd walked out. That was two days ago. Maybe three. Or four. The days had kind of run together.

"He's a real go-getter," Rob said amicably.

He was a colossal ass. "Yep. So, listen, Rob, I really have to run. Mason's home sick—"

"Yeah, sure. Sorry to have bothered you. But before you go . . ."

Hannah suppressed a sigh and rolled her eyes.

"Is everything okay?"

She stilled. Her grip tightened and she closed her eyes against the pain. "What do you mean? Everything is fine. I mean, Mason is sick, but you know, babies get these fevers—"

"Yes, right," Rob said. "I don't know, it just seems you've been a little distracted lately and I thought maybe you wanted to talk. I know your mom's death must have been hard to deal with."

Living was the hard part. Dying seemed easy. Just close your eyes that last time and sink . . . "No," she said. "Everything is fine."

That was followed by an awkward moment of silence. But then Rob said, "Well, good. I'll see you tomorrow?"

"I'll be there," she said cheerfully, and clicked off. She made a face as she dropped the phone onto the bar with a clatter. "Idiot," she muttered, and reached for a tissue. Her nose was always running now.

She bent over the yellow pages again, and felt a dull pain at the base of her skull. The pain was getting worse and worse, and Dr. Blakely was obviously incompetent if he couldn't find whatever it was. She was sure it was a tumor or something like that, but no, Dr. Blakely said it was nothing worse than seasonal allergies. How was it that the world was populated with imbeciles?

Hannah turned the page to the dentists and, with her finger, started going down the list. *Cosmetic dentistry . . . cosmetic dentistry . . . general dentistry.* Harrison, DDS. Had she seen a Harrison before? The name sounded familiar, but then again, there was a Harrison at the office, too. Unfortunately, Hannah had forgotten her little notebook in which she kept her records of doctors and such at work.

One hour. You have one hour.

She picked up the phone and dialed Dr. Harrison's number. "Hi," she said brightly when the receptionist answered. "I'm kind of new to town and, wouldn't you know it, I cracked a tooth." She laughed, but realized that a person in pain wouldn't laugh. "It's really painful," she said quickly. "I don't have a dentist and was wondering if I could get in to see Dr. Harrison?"

"Have you seen Dr. Harrison before?" the woman asked.

"No. No dentist." Hadn't she already said that? Hannah rubbed the back of her neck.

"Can you come in today?"

"Ah . . . no. That's the problem. I am on my way to

the airport to catch a flight to Dallas for this huge budget meeting, and I won't be back until late Thursday. Do you have any time then?" That was two days away. That would get her some pills.

"You really shouldn't let a bad tooth go if you can help it. It might abscess."

"I can't miss this meeting," Hannah said apologetically.

"We can work you in Friday morning," the woman said. "May I have your name and date of birth, please?"

"Hannah Drake, July twenty-one, seventy-four," she said, and heard the click of the computer keys on the other end. "If there is something Dr. Harrison could give me for the pain, I'd really appreciate it. This tooth is really killing me."

"Hannah Drake?" the receptionist asked. "At forty-two oh eight Wilshire?"

Hannah's heart leaped. She abruptly clicked off and dropped the phone. She'd already seen him! *Dammit, dammit, dammit.* Her heart was pounding now, her hands shaking. What a stupid mistake! What if she couldn't get any pills? *No, no, calm down, there are pain clinics all over Texas.* She'd already been to two clinics in Austin, which made her a little anxious, but okay, if she used up all the Austin clinics, she could go to San Antonio. Then Houston—Houston was the mecca of pain clinics. And then there was Dallas. It would be all right.

Plus, there was always the Internet. But that scared Hannah. She could just picture the FBI showing up at her door. Or she could cut down on the number of pills she took by injecting them. She'd seen that on A&E's *Intervention,* and had actually tried it once with a syringe she'd stolen from a doctor's office. The pain pills had worked so quickly and powerfully that she told herself she'd only do that in emergencies. She didn't want to get addicted.

And then there was Brian. Faceless Brian, his number in her wallet. Hannah imagined a college student with glasses, picking up OxyContin and hydrocodone in Mexico during spring break trips to South Padre Island. A kid who was helping the suburban moms whom doctors wouldn't take seriously.

Dentist.

Hannah reached for her purse and fished around the bottom until her fingers gripped her makeup bag. She pulled that out, then took out a tube of lipstick and opened it. Several oblong pills emptied onto the kitchen countertop and she carefully doled out four pain pills. She usually took six in the morning, but desperate times called for desperate measures. She dug around the makeup bag and picked out a little blue pill, a Valium, and threw it in the pile to calm her nerves, because she couldn't call around town sounding like a lunatic.

She put all the pills in her mouth and washed them down with her morning coconut water, then dialed another dentist. That one refused to prescribe anything without seeing her. She phoned another dentist. This one was happy to prescribe her something until she could get in late Thursday afternoon, and Hannah almost collapsed with relief. She figured if one dentist gave her pills, maybe another one would too. Hannah called two more dentists, both of whom refused to pre-scribe anything without seeing her.

Hannah might have methodically worked her way down the list, but she happened to glance at the clock. She had maybe forty minutes to go pick up her pre-scription before Mason woke up.

Forty minutes. She'd already made up her mind she was going to go while Mason was napping. He'd had a restless night and needed his sleep, and he could get so fussy when she was in a doctor's office or at the pharmacy. What was the worst that could happen? He would wake up and cry a little, that was all.

"He won't wake up," she said to herself. "He never wakes up before ten."

Hannah glanced down the hallway of her Crafts-man house with the expensive rugs on polished wood floors and the framed pictures of Mason on the walls. Behind the closed door at the end of the hall, Mason lay sleeping.

It was such a pretty house. Loren had insisted they buy in Tarrytown—an area of Austin they really couldn't afford—because they would "look success-ful." He was like her mother had been in that regard. It had been so important to her that Hannah look suc-cessful, or beautiful, or smart, or accomplished. Han-nah and Loren's house wasn't a large one, but it had all the necessary features: wood floors, stainless appli-ances, granite countertops, and lots of interior stone-work and crown moldings. Hannah had done her best to make it a comfortable home for the three of them, but Loren . . . Loren had done exactly what her mother had done. He'd used her up, then chosen someone else.

Now she worried if she could afford this home for her and Mason.

Mason. Hannah grabbed her purse and hurried down the hall to check on her son. He was sleeping on his belly with his knees tucked up under his chest. She rolled him onto his side and made sure a bottle was within reach, should he wake up.

She hurried out to her car and, once inside, she pulled her sweater tighter around her. When she reached up to hit the garage door button on the window visor, her hand brushed against her forehead. She was surprised to find it was damp. *Damp?* She was perspiring a little. Jesus, wasn't a cold sweat with pain a symptom of some sort of disease? She made a note to tell Dr. Blakely about it, but forgot by the time she reached the end of her drive.

The dentist's prescription wasn't ready, of course, so Hannah paced anxiously in front of the pharmacy counter, watching the clock, imagining Mason waking up and crying for her. She tried not to imagine how confused he'd be if she didn't come. Would he be scared? Would he try and climb out of his crib? What if he fell? What if he was hurt and she wasn't there? What if the house burst into flames because of some gas thing and he was killed?

With her anxiety ratcheting up, Hannah banged on the little bell at the counter. The pharmacy technician, a tall, good-looking kid, appeared. "I'm waiting for a prescription," Hannah said. "I was just wondering how much longer."

"Name?" he asked pleasantly.

"Hannah Drake."

He typed that into the computer and studied the screen. He hit another button and studied the screen some more. *What are you looking at?* Hannah screamed in her head.

"I think the pharmacist is just about done. I'll be right back," he said, and disappeared again.

He returned a few moments later with the brown bottle. He looked at the label and typed something into the computer. "Any questions for the pharmacist?"

"No." Hannah's wallet was already open, her debit card in her hand.

The young man looked up, looked right at Hannah. "That will be sixty-five dollars."

Hannah handed him her debit card. *Why was he looking at her like that? What was he thinking?*

"You'll need to sign, please," he said, and handed her a notebook. *Was that a disapproving look?* Hannah looked at the blue pages with the row of tiny stickers from pill bottles and the signatures beside them. She signed by a sticker and handed the book back to the young man. He, in turn, handed her the debit card and the slender white paper bag with the vial of pills inside. Hannah didn't dare look at him again, just kept her head down and hurried out of there, certain the kid was making a note in that notebook: *pain pill junkie.*

In her car once more, Hannah swallowed a handful and washed them down with cold coffee from a mug she'd left in her car the last time she'd gone to work. She leaned her head back and waited for the pills to work their magic. First came the warmth, then the rising relief. Her body released cell by cell as the medicine cascaded through her, and she imagined landing in a vat of cotton candy, spinning around and around in the soft, wispy cloud. The walls that seemed to close in around her without the drugs began to fall away. The pain, the anxiety, life . . . all of it receded on a gentle wave. Hannah had what she needed; she could breathe again.

She glanced at the clock. Ten minutes to ten. She had ten minutes to get home. In ten minutes, she would be fine. In ten minutes, this would all be a distant memory, and Mason would wake up, and he would never know she'd been gone, and she wouldn't remember it, either. No harm, no foul.

At the exit where Hannah intended to turn right, she slowed to look left, but she didn't stop. She slid into the right lane without noticing the car in front of her had slowed to allow another car to turn.

She rammed into its back bumper.

The shock of the impact stunned Hannah, and she sat for a long, breathless, heart-pounding moment with her hands wrapped around the wheel, gaping at the car before her. *Mason.* That was all she could think of. Mason, her beautiful baby boy. *Don't vomit.*

The man driving the car she'd hit was out at once, stalking back to look at the damage, and then casting a glare at her. Hannah quickly stuffed the white bag with her pills into her purse and made herself get out of her car too. "I am so sorry," she said. Her hands were shaking. She couldn't even see the damage; she could only see Mason, alone in his crib. At home alone, only eleven months old.

The man looked at the bumper, then at her. "Didn't you see me?"

"No, no, I was looking back to see if any cars were coming, and I didn't see you had stopped."

He looked at her strangely, and Hannah realized she was nervously wringing her hands. She stopped.

"Are you all right?" he asked, squinting at her.

"Yes! Yes, I am so sorry, I just didn't see you." She realized cars were honking, trying to squeeze around them, and she nervously pushed her hair back behind her ears. It felt greasy.

"Let's pull into the parking lot and I'll call the police," the man said.

Hannah's heart plummeted. "The police?" She folded her arms tightly. "I don't think we need to do that. Honestly, I don't have time to do that. We can exchange information—"

"Lady, you just wrecked my car. The insurance companies are going to need a police report," the man said brusquely, and eyed her, Hannah thought, with suspicion.

Swallowing down a sudden surge of nausea, Hannah returned to her car and followed him into the parking lot.

After they'd exchanged insurance information, the man paced beside his car, looking at his watch every little bit, talking on his cell phone. Hannah was leaning up against her red coupe—another Loren idea—trying very hard not to hyperventilate. She'd been plunged into the middle of a nightmare. She could picture Mason hanging on to the rail of his crib, crying for his mommy. She imagined him trying to climb out and falling to the hardwood floor, cracking his round little head open. She could see blood flowing from his nose and ears. She imagined him getting stuck in the slats of the rail and suffocating, his face purple, his eyes bulging, his fat little legs kicking desperately. Hannah was beside herself with fear and desperately wanted to take another pill, but she did not dare.

After what seemed like hours to her, a patrol car eased into the parking lot. Two officers got out and strolled over to have a look at the damaged cars. One of them, a tall, good-looking young man with light-brown skin, smiled at Hannah. "Rough morning, huh?"

"It's my fault," Hannah said. She thought if she just admitted it, got it out there, maybe they could do this quickly. "I was looking back to see if any cars were coming and I didn't see that he had slowed down, and I hit him. I take full responsibility."

"You do, huh?" the officer said, and leaned over to look at the damage to her car. "Do you have insurance?"

"Yes," Hannah said, and started to fumble for it in her wallet. In her haste, she dropped it. The cop squatted down to pick it up at the same time Hannah did. "Thanks," she said. "I've got it." She grabbed her wallet and noticed, for the first time today, that she was wearing two different flip-flops. *Good God.* She quickly stood up, pushed her greasy hair from her face—*Did I comb it?* She risked a wary look at the cop. He didn't look at her feet, and Hannah realized she was being paranoid. Men did not notice shoes . . . unless, like Loren, they were platform heels that were wrapped around a shiny silver pole.

She opened her wallet and handed him her insurance card.

"License?"

She handed him that, too, and looked at the man she'd hit. He and the other officer were looking at her.

"What have you been doing this morning, Mrs. Drake?" the officer asked her.

"What?" She unthinkingly pulled her sweater tighter around her.

The officer looked at her again, only this time his brown eyes looked very directly into hers. "I asked what you've been doing this morning."

Hannah's heart was pounding so hard now that she was certain the officer could see it. She forced a smile. "Running errands."

He kept his gaze steady on her. "What sort of errands?"

"You know. Bank. Gas."

"Well, Mrs. Drake, I'm looking around and I don't see a bank or a gas station on this street."

She was going to faint. The officer would arrest her and Mason would be taken by the state and she'd never see him again, all for a few pain pills. "I had to go to the pharmacy and pick up a prescription."

He nodded. He looked a little closer at her. "It's Hannah, right? Are you okay, Hannah?"

She nodded. She could feel the tears starting to build behind her eyes and thought that crying was the worst thing she could do now. She just didn't seem to have control over her emotions these days; everything made her angry or weepy. "I'm fine."

"Have you had anything to drink this morning?"

"*Drink?*" she said incredulously, and shook her head. "No, sir," she said, and the damn tears began to fall. *Please God, please, let me out of this. Let me go home to my baby and I swear I will never do this again. I swear it.* "It's . . . My husband is going to kill me," she blurted. "We just paid the car off this month."

Please, please, please.

The officer didn't say anything to that. He stood calmly observing her. It was nothing less than a miracle that Hannah was still standing, and at the very moment she thought she would lose her composure and collapse in hysteria, he looked at the damage to her car and then at her insurance and driver's license. "I'm sorry to hear that," he said. "Remind him that accidents happen." He gestured to the squad car. "I'm going to run these. Have you given the gentleman your insurance information?"

It had worked again. Being a reasonably well-dressed middle-aged white woman had worked to Hannah's advantage again. Doctors, cops . . . no one ever suspected her. *Thank you, God!* "Yes," Hannah said.

She stood by her car and forced herself to take deep breaths. When the officer returned, he handed her the insurance card and license. "Be careful, Mrs. Drake," he said.

"I can go?"

"You can go."

It was all she could do to keep from leaping into her car. "Thank you," she said, and calmly opened the car door of her car.

Inside, she looked at the clock. It was almost eleven now. She was sweating; her entire body thrummed with fear and nausea, shuddering against the strong desire to punch the gas, to drive as fast as she could. She was on the verge of hyperventilating as she pulled into traffic and drove the speed limit to her house. But the moment she pulled in her drive, she leaped out and left the car door open as she raced up the walk.

Hannah burst through the door of her house and stood, listening. *There was no sound. No sound!* "Oh God!" she screamed, and ran to the nursery, her shin colliding with the umbrella stand as she raced to Mason's room.

She threw open the door and saw the crown of Mason's head through a gap in the bumpers of his crib. She lurched forward; Mason was on his stomach, his face turned away from her. Hannah grabbed for him, hauling him up like sack of flour. He must have been holding his bottle, because it hit the floor next to her foot. She turned him around and saw the snot on his face at the same moment he opened his eyes and screamed.

He'd been crying, he'd been crying for his mommy, and she hadn't been here. Hannah's heart crumbled. "Oh, baby," she said, and put him on her shoulder, holding him tight as he began to wail. "Oh, baby, oh, sweetie, I am so sorry. Mommy is so so sorry." She was sobbing and shaking so badly she could hardly hold him. She sank to the floor with him in her arms, laid on her side, and cried along with Mason.

What if the wreck had been worse? What if she'd been injured? What if she'd been arrested? She had risked so much for the sake of those goddamn pills, and she would never, ever forgive herself. *Never.*

The accident had scared her so deeply that she

marched to the bathroom, opened her OxyContin and hydrocodone bottles, and poured them into the toilet.

She was *done*. Never again!

But by mid-afternoon, Hannah was driving with Mason to another pharmacy to pick up the prescription the pain clinic had finally approved.

That night, after she'd put Mason to bed, Hannah wandered through her house with a full wineglass in hand. Her body was fluid; she was feeling languid and mellow. All the anxiety of the day was gone, and she was finally able to think.

She floated into the living room and stared at the state-of-the-art, fifty-two-inch flat-screen, high-definition, 3-D, cook-your-dinner television Loren had insisted on buying. And the Persian rug. And the ridiculous crystal light fixtures, like they were living in a palace instead of Craftsman house with manufactured Old Austin charm. Hannah had never liked the rug. It had been the subject of one hellacious fight between her and Loren, and she calmly turned her wineglass upside down and watched the pinot grigio splatter and pool, then slowly sink into the fibers of the rug. She dropped her glass on top of the spill. The carpet was so thick, the glass didn't break.

Hannah turned her back to the mess and moved to the Italian leather couch, collapsing onto it. She loved this feeling, this weightlessness. She toyed with the idea of taking one or two more pills. If she took two more, she'd have twenty-two for tomorrow. That was two more than she needed in a day.

Then what? That was the problem: Then what? If Hannah didn't have her pills, she got sick. It was such a struggle to find them, but she had to do it to be well enough to take care of Mason. She drew a breath and slowly released it. Just eight hours ago she'd sworn off pills forever, and here she was, already on the hamster wheel again, counting pills, doling them out in her head, planning how to get more.

I have to do something. I have to stop.

It was the first time Hannah had ever admitted to herself that she needed to quit.

She turned on her side so that she was facing the back of the couch, her head on a silk-covered pillow. *Am I an addict?* She'd never thought of herself as an addict. Abuser, okay, yes. A situational pain pill abuser who could quit right now if she wanted to. Not an addict. She wasn't anything like those people on *Intervention.* Those people didn't have jobs, but she did. She went to work every day. She was the office manager of a downtown law firm and she was damn good at her job. No one could do that job and be an addict.

The memory of Rob's phone call crept into her mind. *You've been a little distracted lately.*

Hannah quickly pushed that away, and a dozen other little things like it. She was under a lot of stress, that was all. Her asshole of a husband had just left her, for Christ's sake; her mother had died; her sister was in la-la land . . . *Yes, but when did everything spiral out of control?*

It was a question she'd asked herself many times today after she'd come so close to disaster. If she was honest, she would admit that lately, she felt as if she were floundering in a pool, unable to swim and desperately trying to reach the side.

She couldn't really remember when it got out of hand. Hannah had always liked wine. After Loren's first affair, she'd sort of leaned on it. She would wait up for him at night in this room, sipping wine until he came home smelling of liquor and women, and Hannah would drink some more. But the pills?

Mom. It had started when her mother was diagnosed three years ago. At first, Hannah would take a couple of her mother's pain pills just so she could cope. Her mother had always been a trial, but when she got sick, she was much harder to handle. Not that Hannah hadn't understood her mother's anger and anxiety; of course she had. It was hard to be any less than self-centered when one was diagnosed with terminal pancreatic cancer. Nevertheless, Hannah had been caught off guard by her mother's bitterness and, more accurately, how much of it was directed at her.

She'd wanted to be a good daughter and give her mother everything she needed . . . but there had been no end to the help her mother needed. The woman suddenly couldn't make a doctor's appointment. Hannah had had to do it. And she had had to drive her. Her mother had refused to ask questions of her doctors, so Hannah had done all the questioning for her. She would wave her hand at all the pills she was to take and say things like "It's all so confusing." It had driven Hannah to drink. Literally. She would have thought her mother would be invested in her own survival, but she'd had no problem handing it over to Hannah.

When the oncologist had explained the reasoning for a new round of chemotherapy, Peggy had sat stoically, glaring at him.

"How long will one session take?" Hannah had asked.

"Four to six hours."

"And recovery?"

"That depends on the individual."

The doctor had gone on to explain the chemotherapy process, how the drugs would be administered, what Peggy could expect. Throughout the explanation, Hannah's mother had not asked a single question. Hannah had driven her mother home and gone in with her to make sure she had the food Hannah had ordered. She'd done some research on chemo recovery diets and was trying to get her mother to change her eating habits.

As Hannah had checked on the contents of the fridge, her mother had asked, "What pills do I have to take when I come home after chemo?"

Admittedly, Hannah's mind had been on something else—a half-eaten chocolate cream pie in the fridge—or she would have paused to take from her purse the little notebook in which she'd made meticulous notes. "I don't know, Mom. I am sure they will explain it to you there." She had extracted the pie from the fridge and turned around, placing it on the bar between her and her mother.

"They explained it today," her mother had said, ignoring the pie. "Why didn't you ask what pills I would have to take when I got home? They throw so much information at you and expect you to remember it," she'd complained. "I don't know why you didn't just ask that one question. There you were, asking everything else under the sun, and you didn't ask what I thought was the most obvious question."

Hannah had paused in her perusal of the fridge contents, which was totally lacking in fiber, and looked at her mother. "Are you kidding?"

"Kidding?" her mother had scoffed. "No, I am not kidding. You know I can't keep up with everything. I'm trusting you to stay on top of it all."

"Mom, do you hear yourself? You are blaming me for not asking a question that *you* should have asked. You are expecting me to know what *you* want to ask. How can I do that? I can't read your mind, and besides, you should take a more active role in your treatment."

"Oh, *ooh!*" her mother had cried, throwing up her hands. "Ain't that a kick! Hannah Drake has to control *everything*, including how *I* handle *my* cancer!"

Hannah had been stunned. And confused. All that she'd done for her mother—all the doctor trips, the prescription fills, the errands, the shopping, the drive out here day after day—swirled around her mind.

Her mother had stalked to the pantry, thrown it open, had grabbed a bag of chips.

"Wait—where did you get that?" Hannah had asked. "And this pie? Did you buy these?"

"Holly takes me shopping," her mother had said. "Holly lets me buy food *I* like to eat."

If Hannah had had an instrument of destruction— a grenade launcher would have done nicely—she would have used it. Of course Holly would take her mother shopping. Of course Holly would find some time in her oh-so-busy songwriting schedule to show up a few times a month and undo everything Hannah had worked so hard to do. It had made Hannah crazy then, and it made her crazy today. Holly made excuses for three years: she couldn't pick up a couple of prescriptions and run them out. She couldn't hold the tray under her mother's head when she was violently ill from the chemo. She couldn't manage to help with anything, but she sure could ruin the diet Hannah had worked so hard to put her mother on.

"I can't *believe* her," Hannah had said, shaking her head, staring at the chips and the pie.

"What?" her mother had asked as she munched on chips.

Hannah took the bag from her hand. "I can't believe she would buy you all that junk. Come on, Mom. You've been feeling so good. Why do you want to mess it up with this junk?"

"It's not junk! I *like* chips! I *like* pie."

"Holly should know better . . ." Hannah had started, but Peggy grabbed the bag from her hand.

"Don't talk about your sister like that," she'd snapped. "I happen to like this food, and as *I* am the one dying around here, I guess I can have it if I want."

"I am trying to help you prolong your life!" Hannah had cried, frustrated.

Her mother had suddenly softened, almost as if she'd set out to rile Hannah, and once she'd accomplished that, she could relax. "I know you are, honey, and I appreciate it. But I also appreciate that Holly wants to help me in her way too. You should let her. She doesn't have the same capacity for this like you do."

Hannah had snorted at that. "You make her sound mentally challenged."

"Well, maybe in a way she is. God knows, she

doesn't have your brains or your skills. She's writing songs, for Chrissakes."

"Oh, yeah, she's dumb like a fox," Hannah had said with a snort. "She's dyslexic, Mom. She is not mentally handicapped. She's actually very smart."

"You need to look out for your little sister, instead of always finding fault," her mother had said sternly, pointing a chip at her.

Look out for Holly. All her life, Hannah had had to look out for Holly. All her life, she'd had to take care of everything else while Holly flitted from one thing to another. And in the end, Hannah's mother had given everything to Holly, because Holly wasn't Hannah, because Holly didn't have the brains to make it big like Hannah.

What a joke.

Through the three years of having to deal with her mother's increasingly dire illness and her general annoyance with her life, Hannah had found herself borrowing her mother's pain pills. At first, it had been just a couple here and there to take the edge off, to help Hannah tune her mother out. And then a few more. Even when Hannah had hired a nurse to check on her mother each day, she took them. She'd just explain to the nurse that her mother was losing the pain pills, and the nurse would always get her more. And when the nurse hadn't gotten more, Hannah had borrowed from her mother. Only she never had replaced what she took.

How had she become this woman?

Hannah had been valedictorian of her senior class. She had been Phi Beta Kappa when she graduated from college. She was a model citizen, an invaluable employee, a loving wife and excellent mother. How had she become *this* woman, this boozy, pill-popping nightmare?

Moreover, how did she *stop* being this woman? How did she right a badly listing ship?

Reflection made Hannah nauseous. She shouldn't have taken the Ambien. Hannah got up from the couch and stumbled into the hall bath. She sank down on her knees before the toilet and threw up.

She hated herself. Mason deserved so much better than this. Both of his parents were losers. As Hannah rested her head against the cool tiles of the bathroom floor, fighting down another wave of nausea, she thought that while she couldn't do anything to change the fact that Loren was Mason's father, she could make sure that at least *she* didn't disappoint her son.

That was something she'd have to think about, but right now her head was killing her. She needed some pills to take the pain away. But where was she going to get them? Hannah took the last few remaining pills she had, washed her face, brushed her teeth, then went in search of her wallet. She pulled out a slip of paper with Brian's number.

Chapter Four

Wyatt decided his next project was a pergola.

He'd taken a critical survey of his little red ranch house with the big picture windows and the wide front porch and decided, with an update, his house could be . . . nicer. It would never be on the Parade of Homes, that was certain, but he could at least make it a little more inviting.

He hadn't done much to it since he bought it over a year ago, other than to rip up carpet and put in hardwoods, because it didn't seem very permanent to him. He still hadn't decided if he was going to stay here. He didn't like putting down roots these days, because if roots got too deep, the only way to move them was to cut them off completely. He'd had his roots whacked off once before and wasn't looking to repeat the experience, and it seemed to him the best way to avoid it was not to commit to any place or thing for too long.

Still, he needed to replace the windows with something more energy efficient. The kitchen needed a major overhaul; the cabinets, the appliances, the flooring—all needed to be replaced with something from the twenty-first century. He'd really like to rip out the guest bath back to studs and start over as well, and if he was ever made king, he'd have a rule that people who thought pink tile was a good color for a bathroom would be shot.

But the flagstone patio he'd put in out back could use a pergola for shade on days like this. "Yeah, pergola first," he said to no one.

Milo lifted his head from his spot beneath a ceiling fan and stared at Wyatt a long moment before lowering his head again.

Wyatt could put in a pergola in a day. Maybe two. He made a mental note to price lumber next time he was in town. Right now, he needed to get the mail. He wasn't very good about staying on top of the mail.

"Truck," he said to Milo, and his dog leaped into action, racing out the open garage door to the truck and jumping up onto the tailgate. He bounced onto the bales of hay Wyatt had stacked in the bed. The dog's tail was wagging enough to fan Wyatt, and he tried to lean down and lick Wyatt's face. "Fool dog," Wyatt said, and pushed the dog back into the bed of the truck so that he could shut the tailgate.

When he had it secure, Wyatt climbed into the cab, lifting himself up and over the tear in the seat where the spring was sticking through. He really needed to put some duct tape on that; as it was, he had to sit a little off center behind the wheel. He gave the gas a couple of pumps and started the old truck. It cranked a few seconds before catching, but the next moment he was bouncing along the rutted road toward the mailbox.

Wyatt turned on the radio. He lived far enough away that he couldn't get much besides KASE 101, a country station. A song by the Court Yard Hounds was up, one that had been played into the ground on this station, and Wyatt sang along under his breath, drumming along on the cracked steering wheel. *"'What'd you think I was gonna dooooo / When you left you left all my loving toooo . . .'* Dumb lyrics," he muttered. "One might even say nescient." *Yes!* He'd squeezed in the word of the day. "Nescience," he said aloud. "Lack of knowledge or awareness, as in: *That songwriter's nescience is downright embarrassing.*" He grinned for a moment, but then the truck hit a hole and bounced hard. He glanced in the rearview mirror. Milo's legs were spread-eagle across the hay bale, but his tongue was hanging out the side of his snout and his tail was still wagging.

He drove down to the gate, opened it up, and walked out to the road to pick up his mail. There was nothing of interest to him: bills, flyers, and a big creamy envelope made of expensive paper that looked like a wedding invitation. The return address said *Asher Price.* Asher had been a client of his at one time, and Wyatt guessed he was going to marry the woman from Houston. Wyatt didn't bother to open the invitation to find out. He wasn't going.

He threw the mail into the seat next to him and started back to the house with Milo still perched on the bales of hay. When he reached his house a few minutes later, Milo bounded out of the truck and went after something in the brush. Wyatt headed inside after something to eat.

He tossed the mail on the counter and opened the fridge to stare at its meager offerings. He had a twelve-pack of beer, a pack of bologna, some bread, and some moldering hummus. He'd bought that on a whim when he was in Austin one day and had stopped by Whole Foods. Whole Foods had made him nostalgic for the lifetime he'd lived two years ago, when he'd been married and living in the gated community of Arbolago Hills in Cedar Springs, in a big damn house he'd built for Macy. Back when the most work he did was move papers from his secretary Linda Gail's desk to his own.

He picked up the hummus and tossed it into the trash, removed a beer from the fridge, and cracked it open as he walked outside to the back porch. He sat down in the rusting metal chair and propped his booted feet up on a planter. It was hot as Hades now, but in a month or so, the mornings would be nippy, the afternoons warm, and the evenings really pleasant, just right for a fire in the chiminea. Only Wyatt didn't have a chiminea. He'd had one when he'd been married, and he didn't want to be reminded of the nights he and Macy had sat around wrapped in a sarape they'd bought in Cabo San Lucas, sipping good wine and watching boats drift lazily on Lake Del Lago. That had all been before her first husband had come back from the dead. Literally. He'd been a soldier, reported killed by the Army. But the Army had gotten it all wrong, and he wasn't dead, he was being held captive, and he escaped, and he came back for Macy, his wife. Only Macy was Wyatt's wife at that point, and pregnant with Grace, and . . . Well, long story short,

Macy had chosen Finn. That's all there was to be said about that. She'd chosen Finn, and Wyatt's happy little dream marriage and great life had crumbled like a cone of ash.

So, no, he didn't have a goddamn chiminea.

He was in the middle of taking a swig of his beer when his phone startled him by going off in his pocket. He sat forward, wiped the beer he'd spilled from his jeans, and fished the phone out of his pocket. "Yo," he said.

"Wyatt?"

He settled back into his seat. "Afternoon, Linda Gail. What can I do for you?"

"You can come in and sign these checks is what you can do for me," Linda Gail said, sounding snippy. Wyatt supposed she had a right. Linda Gail was his right-hand man, and had been for years. She'd been after him for a few days to come in to his office in Cedar Springs and sign things. He knew it was bad when she called on a Sunday.

Wyatt was the primary shareholder in the new Hill Country Resort and Spa. He'd put the deal together, had overseen the groundbreaking and construction . . . well, Linda Gail had, really, because Wyatt had sort of dropped off the map after the thing with Macy. But she needed his signature to keep things moving. "I'll probably get that way next week," he said.

Linda Gail sighed. "All right, Wyatt. I asked you politely the first time. Hell, I asked you nicely the second and third time too. Now I am telling you if you don't come in and sign this stuff, I will come out there. Do you want that? Do you really want me to drive twenty-five miles out of my way and maybe have to spend the night with you?"

He had images of nightgowns and fuzzy slippers and hot cocoa, and no, he most certainly did not want that.

"I didn't think so," Linda Gail said, before he could answer. "Why you have to hole up out there like an outlaw, I will never understand. It's not healthy at all to live like you do, without people."

He really wished he didn't have to have this ongoing conversation with her. Linda Gail seemed to think that if someone preferred his own society to her, there was something wrong with him. "I have people, Linda Gail," he said gruffly. "But there is nothing wrong with a man preferring his own company."

She snorted. "Aren't you coming into town to see Grace?"

Of course he was coming in to see Grace. He did not miss a moment of his time with his daughter. "Friday."

"Then I will expect to see you on Friday, Wyatt. And if you don't come by the office on Friday, I will come to you. That's not a threat, that's a warning."

"You don't scare me."

"Like hell I don't," she said. "Have yourself a good week." She clicked off.

Wyatt smiled. Linda Gail acted as if he'd be lost without her, wandering about the brush, looking for the trail back home. Okay, maybe he would be a little lost. And he probably would have lost the considerable fortune he'd managed to amass before he'd gone AWOL. That's what he'd done after Macy left him for

Finn. He'd gotten in his big fancy truck with Milo one day and just driven. He'd ended up in Arkansas first, where he joined a group of Civil War reenactors for a couple of weeks, hiring himself out to help with the cooking. He didn't know much about the Civil War or cooking, which was why it had seemed the perfect thing to do. When he'd tired of that, he'd gone on, driving aimlessly and ending up in Arizona, where the fuel pump went out on his truck. He didn't have the heart or inclination to fix it, so he'd sold it to a Mexican-American for twenty-five hundred dollars. That was about twenty thousand dollars less than what he should have gotten.

But Wyatt had sold it and found himself in Cochise County without any transportation. An old man in a café had told him about the job on the M Bar J cattle ranch. That wasn't really a stretch for Wyatt, as he had been born and bred a rancher. He'd given it up to pursue real estate development, an occupation that had made him a rich man. But after the world had been yanked right out from under him, and he'd spun out into the blackness without Macy to anchor him, Wyatt didn't care about things like money. He didn't care about much of anything.

He and Milo had hitched a ride out to the headquarters and he convinced the manager that he knew how to sit a horse, he knew how to rope a cow, and, though he was a little rusty, he was as fresh as a spring breeze. The manager didn't need much convincing as it turned out—he needed a body. He'd given Wyatt the job, put him out in the bunkhouse with a bunch of sun-dried vaqueros, and every day for five months Wyatt had pulled on his boots and his borrowed spurs and he and Milo had worked cattle.

But then Grace was born, and he needed to be near his daughter, so Wyatt had packed up his one bag, caught a ride back to the town of St. David, and bought an old used truck to take him back to Texas. It was the same truck he drove around the ranch now.

Macy had been shocked by his appearance when he'd returned. He'd had a beard then, and he'd lost about twenty or pounds or so, and he didn't have much to say. But when he held his daughter Grace in his arms for the first time, he knew he'd never leave her again. He fell in love with that little girl with the black hair— his hair—and with her smile. Her mother's smile.

Wyatt wasn't leaving Grace, but he hadn't been ready to resume his place at the top of Cedar Springs society, either. So he'd taken a job as a pen rider at a feedlot. It was a dirty, mean job, riding through acres of penned cattle, culling out the sick from the rest of the herd. Yet, there was something about that sort of work, that mind-dulling, physical work, that gave Wyatt the strength he needed to get up every morning.

Linda Gail was the one who had told him about this place. She was handling his clients, taking leads, and she'd told him that there was this ranch between Cedar Springs and San Antonio, tucked away from civiliza- tion but close enough that he could see his daughter. Wyatt had bought it after one trip out to take a look. He'd put forty head of cattle on it, had bought a couple of horses from the animal rescue ranch that Macy and Finn had started up, and had been here since, more than a year, taking each day as it came while he mended some fences and tore down others. He avoided people and things and, most of all, he avoided his thoughts.

Wyatt finished his beer and headed for the shower. He donned a pair of lounge pants and a torn T-shirt, then settled down in an old velvet chair with some unidentified stains to watch the NFL preseason football games.

Just him, his dog, and a couple of beers. That's all he needed.

That same afternoon, in central Austin, it was muggy and cloudy with a strong scent of rain. Rain would be welcome relief to the heat, but as was often the case in August, it would probably amount to nothing more than a tease.

Nevertheless, Holly was feeling particularly creative and happy. She was comfortably ensconced in her studio apartment on Austin's Enfield Road, seated at the upright Hamilton piano she'd found on Craigslist a couple of years ago. The wood casing of the piano was scratched and dull, but Holly had had it tuned and it was perfect for her needs.

She was very excited about her latest project. After having successfully sold three songs to ASC Music Publishing—two of which had been sold to artists for recording—the company had approached Holly with a unique opportunity. They had joined forces with a young, up-and-coming singer, Quincy Crowe, and they believed Holly's music style was a perfect match for his. They had recently inked a deal under which she would collaborate with Quincy and write three original songs for him. It was decent money up front, but if the songs sold well, it was great money on the back end.

Holly liked Quincy. He was a handsome guy with soulful brown eyes and sleek, shoulder-length hair. He was about ten years younger than her and naturally talented. He hadn't studied music, but his instincts were excellent. Most important—to Holly, anyway—was that he understood the construction of a song.

That afternoon, she was working on their first collaborative song. They'd agreed on the lyrics, and Quincy liked the melody, but he thought the bridge was kind of bland and the key a bit too high.

Holly experimented by changing the key from D major to B minor. *"His heart as hard as coal,"* she sang softly. "Ack," she muttered to herself, and changed a few of the chords around.

She was in the midst of trying it again when a knock at her door interrupted her. She glanced at the clock that hung above the bar that separated her living area from the little galley kitchen. It was two in the afternoon, too early for Quincy. He was due at four, and she had a shift at half past five at the Java Hut. She put down her pencil and walked across the travertine tile floor and opened the door.

Holly was shocked to see Hannah standing there with Mason on her hip and a giant duffel bag slung over her shoulder. "Hello, Holly."

"Wow! What a surprise!" Holly said. It was the letter, she was certain of it. She'd written Hannah a letter apologizing for not helping more with their mother and wanting to bury the hatchet. She wanted her sister back. Maybe Hannah did too.

"May we come in?" Hannah asked, but she was already moving past Holly into her apartment.

"Yes, sure." Hannah had been here once before, about four years ago, when Holly had found the place, back when they at least spoke and tried to be sisters. Holly shut the door and grinned at Hannah and Mason. She noticed that Hannah didn't look quite like herself—she was so thin, and there were shadows under her eyes. Her skirt hung on her, and the zipper was off center. Her hair was down too. Holly could not remember a time she'd seen Hannah dressed for work that her hair wasn't pulled back and tucked away for the day's labor. There was a stain on the shoulder of her blouse. Mason, who was chewing on his fist, was wearing overalls and one sock. "I'm really surprised, but I'm glad you're here," Holly said hopefully.

Hannah responded by putting Mason on the floor; he instantly righted himself and began to crawl for Holly's piano. "Wow," Hannah said, looking around. "It's cleaner in here than I thought it would be." She dropped the big dark duffel bag she had on her shoulder and looked at the sliding glass door. "Isn't there a balcony out there?" she asked, and walked to the door and pushed aside the drapes. Holly's apartment overlooked the pool. "Do you keep this door locked?"

"I don't know. Yes, I think," Holly said. "Why? What's going on?" Mason had reached her piano and was trying to pull himself up on the bench. She caught it before he pulled it over on himself. "Is everything okay?"

"Everything is fine."

"You look tired," Holly remarked.

"You would, too, if you had a job like mine. So . . ." Hannah turned around, put her hands on her hips. "I need you, Holly."

That left Holly speechless. "Are you serious?"

"Would I be here if I weren't serious? Look, I have to go away. There is no one else I can trust with Mason." She scratched her arm. Hard. "I know you and I have had our differences, but I know you love him. So I need you to keep him."

Holly instantly thought of her shift, and looked at the clock again. Lucy, her boss, would kill her for calling in on such short notice. "This is . . . this is really surprising, Hannah. You want me to babysit? For how long? Like, overnight?" If she could get hold of Elliot, he would cover her shift. He was always looking for extra shifts.

"Babysit, keep him, whatever," Hannah said, and shifted her gaze to Mason. "I'm going to be a while."

Something was wrong. Hannah was not herself. She didn't look right. Her gaze seemed distant, too distant, like she wasn't all here. "What's 'a while'?" Holly asked. "And where are you going?"

Hannah shrugged. "A while," she said again. "I really don't know how long."

"Wait—I don't understand," Holly said as Hannah squatted down next to Mason. He'd found a blank page of sheet music and had put it in his mouth. "Why don't you know how long you'll be? Where are you going? And what happened to your nanny?"

"Mason, Mommy loves you so much," Hannah said, and kissed the top of his head.

"*Baa baa baa,*" Mason said, and tried to push the paper into Hannah's mouth.

"Hannah!" Holly insisted, truly alarmed. "What is wrong? How long will you be? I need to know so I can get someone to cover my shift."

"I don't know," Hannah said, and stood up. "Is that where you sleep?" she asked, pointing to the loft. "You'll need to get a gate or something."

It was like Hannah's body was in Holly's apartment but her head was somewhere else. Mason began inching his way along the furniture to the guitar stand.

Holly picked him up. "Something is wrong, obviously. You can tell me."

"I already told you," Hannah said, and pushed both hands through her hair. "I have to go somewhere for a while, okay? I *need* you, Holly. For once in your life, can you help me?"

"Hey, come on," Holly said, and moved Mason to a chair across the room. "You show up unexpected when I have to work and ask me to keep your son. I don't think I'm asking unreasonable questions." She put a pillow on the seat that Mason could grab. It made him happy; he grinned and bounced on his chubby legs.

"I don't want to argue with you—"

"Good. Me either. Did you get my letter?"

Hannah looked blank. "What letter?"

"The letter I wrote you—"

"I just need to do this, Holly," Hannah said, talking over her. "I need you to help me, and honestly, I think you owe me at least this much."

"*Owe* you?" Holly protested. "I somehow *owe* you endless babysitting?"

"It's not babysitting, It's a whole lot more than that," Hannah said, and squeezed her eyes shut a moment.

God, she was pale. She opened her eyes and nudged the duffel with her foot. "Here is his bag," she said. "His clothes and toys are in there, and some diapers. Maybe a week's worth."

"Are you out of your mind?" Holly cried. "I can't keep him a week, I have to work! I have a contract for three songs and I can't just stop everything to babysit Mason while you flit off to God knows where. You look sick, Hannah. Maybe you need to see a doctor. I can take you—"

"Like hell you have to work," Hannah said quietly, in a voice dripping with bitterness. Her hands were shaking. "You have your inheritance, remember?"

"Stop that," Holly warned her. "I don't have anything. I've told you, I don't know why Mom did that, but it doesn't matter, I will share it with you. I wrote you that, Hannah. I told you in a letter that the estate doesn't matter to me."

Hannah rolled her eyes. "Really? And what have you done about it? Have you seen a lawyer about the will? Have you even been out to the homestead?"

Holly recoiled. "Okay, so I am not as organized as you. Is that what this is all about? You're pissed about Mom's will and you're trying to take it out on me somehow?"

Hannah snorted. "Do you honestly think I would stoop to such childish tactics?"

"Honestly? I have no idea what you'd do. I don't even know you right now. You show up at my apartment for the second time in five years and dump your son on me for a week. You look like hell, you're skin and bones. Actually, you look a little crazy to me."

That seemed to set Hannah back a step. Her mouth gaped; she didn't seem to notice that Mason was crawling past her now, on his way to the kitchen.

Something was desperately wrong with her sister. "Hannah? You really can talk to me, you know," Holly said. "Just tell me what's going on."

Hannah turned her back and moved to the bar, away from Holly. "I *am* telling you. I am saying that you have to keep my baby."

"Okay, I can keep him for a couple of days—"

"Don't you get it? I am going away! I won't be in Austin."

"What?" Holly exclaimed, confused more than ever now as she followed Mason into the kitchen. He'd opened a drawer and was pulling out plastic bags. "*Where* are you going? You at least have to tell me that much."

"I can't."

"You *can't*? What the hell does *that* mean?" Holly demanded as she scooped Mason up and put him on her hip. "You're acting crazy! I'm calling Loren—"

"Go ahead. He's gone too."

Holly was starting to feel like she'd walked into the middle of some weird sci-fi event. "Where is he?" she demanded, and picked up her cell phone. "I'm calling him right now."

"He left me."

Holly stilled. She gaped at Hannah, hoping it was a joke, knowing it wasn't.

"For some chick he met on the Internet." Hannah smiled wryly. "Can you believe it? Trawling for ass on the Internet. Blond, I think—"

"Hannah!" Holly said, and put the phone down. "When did this happen?"

"I don't know," Hannah said with a hapless shrug. "A couple of weeks, I guess. I really don't remember. Or care, to be honest." She chuckled. "Do you know that was his *third* affair? Or I should say, the third that I knew about."

Stunned, Holly put Mason down again. "Oh, Hannah." She moved toward Hannah with the intent of holding her, but Hannah turned to one side and looked out the window. Holly dropped her hands. "I am so sorry," she said. "I had no idea." She did not add that she was not surprised, because she'd guessed Loren was a scumbag.

"Of course you didn't," Hannah agreed. "Not exactly the sort of thing one likes to broadcast."

"I know, but I—"

"Right," Hannah said, cutting her off. She pushed her hands through her hair again, a nervous characteristic Holly had never seen her do.

"Are you going after Loren?" Holly asked, hoping to high heaven that was not the case.

"God, no," Hannah said impatiently. "I'm glad he's gone."

At least they agreed on that.

Hannah abruptly picked Mason up and held him tight. "Mommy loves you," she said. "Never forget that Mommy loves you, baby. I'll be home before you know it." She kissed his cheek, but Mason pushed against her, wanting down. Hannah handed him to Holly. "Okay. I'll be in touch." She started for the door.

"No!" Holly cried, and darted around her, reaching

the door before her. "Look, I understand you've been through a lot, but I can't take Mason for a week."

"Let me see if I have this straight," Hannah said, folding her arms. "You couldn't help with Mom and you can't help me now. When is it you *can* help, Holly? What is a convenient time for you?"

"I have tried so many times to help you that I can't even count them anymore. But every time I try and help, you shut me down. And now that you've decided to actually let me in, I'm supposed to drop everything and jump? Look, I'm sorry about Loren. I'm sorry for a million things between us. But I cannot take Mason indefinitely." Holly tried to hand Mason to Hannah, but she refused to look at her baby. Mason began to fuss and kick his legs.

"This is ridiculous," Hannah said. "All our lives, you have done whatever you wanted to do, when you wanted to do it, and you left me to take care of everything else. Who was there to help Mom after Dad died? Who was there when Mom got sick? Where were you, Holly? You got off scot-free, didn't you? So it's really past time you pitched in and I need you to do it today. Will you please move away from the door?"

"You're acting crazy!" Holly cried. "I *have* tried to help you—"

"It was always too little and too late!" Hannah said angrily.

"Right," Holly said, just as angrily. "Like when I offered to have Mom come live with me in the end. I said, 'Hannah, let her come here,' but oh no, Saint Hannah had to take her into her home with her husband and her baby and just blew me off."

Hannah's eyes rounded. "Are you kidding? You offered to let Mom come live with you *here,* in this tiny studio apartment! Oh yeah, that would have worked."

"I told you I would get a one-bedroom apartment! It might have not been a Tarrytown palace, but it was definitely doable!"

"Please! You knew the moment you said it that it would never happen. Why didn't you offer to go live at the homestead with her? That would have worked!"

"Because of my work," Holly said angrily. "I know, I know, it's just songwriting, it's just a coffeehouse, but it is my *livelihood,* and I have commitments, and I couldn't conveniently forget them just to suit you! So if this is some sort of sick game of resentment you are playing right now, I am not going to engage."

Hannah's eyes flashed with anger. "You have no idea how deep my resentments run," she said, her voice shaking. "Get out of my way. I have to go *now.*"

"Take Mason," Holly said sternly.

Hannah glared at her a long moment. "Fine," she said, and took Mason from Holly. "Can you hand me his bag?"

Holly eyed her skeptically, then slowly moved away from the door to get the bag. She hadn't taken but a few steps when she heard the door open. She whirled around; Hannah was standing at the threshold, her hand on the knob, her gaze on Mason, who was sitting in chair, watching his mother curiously. "Take good care of him," Hannah said, her voice breaking. "I'll be back."

"Hey . . . *hey!*" Holly cried, and lunged for the door, but Hannah was already outside. "You can't abandon him!" Holly said frantically. "I swear to God, if you go, I will call the police and tell them you abandoned your baby!"

"Great plan, Holly! They'll come and take Mason and put him in foster care."

Holly gasped.

"God, don't look so shocked. Can you, just this once, do something for me? Do you really think I would ask if I didn't need you now more than ever? Just do this one thing for me, Holly. *Please*. I *will* be back, but right now I have to go. And you have to believe me when I tell you that I wouldn't do this, I would not leave—" A loud sob escaped Hannah, and she looked as if she would be sick, but swallowed hard as she backed away from Holly's door. "You have to believe me—I would not leave my son if I didn't absolutely have to."

"How can you do this?" Holly cried, and tried to grab Hannah's arm, but Hannah darted out of reach.

Behind them, Mason started to cry. Hannah looked as if she could not breathe. "I am counting on you, Holly," she said roughly, and abruptly turned and ran down the stairs as her son cried for her.

Chapter Five

The first thing Holly did was try to reach Loren, but predictably, she got no response from his cell. She dialed it three times just to make sure. She next called her manager to announce she would not be in to work today as Mason wailed in the background.

As she expected, Lucy was unhappy with Holly for ditching her shift. "It's after three, Holly. Your shift starts at five thirty. Who am I supposed to get to cover for you at this late notice? Did you at least try and find someone to cover?"

"I did," Holly said apologetically. "I called Elliot but he couldn't cover."

"Great." Lucy sighed irritably. "You know we get slammed about this time. Are you going to be in to-morrow?"

"Yes," Holly said emphatically. She would not lose another shift; she couldn't afford to lose another shift. And besides, as much as she loved Mason, he was not her responsibility. Loren the Asshole could look after his son if Hannah wasn't going to do it. "Thanks, Lucy. I am really sorry. I had no idea this was going to happen."

"Okay, fine," Lucy said crisply. "I'll see you tomorrow, but right now I need to get off the phone and find someone to cover."

"See you tomorrow," Holly said but Lucy had already hung up.

Mason, who had not yet begun to walk, but who was, Holly had discovered, quite adept at pulling himself up and moving around by using the furniture, had stopped crying and was standing next to her, his hands flat on the cabinet, looking up as if he expected her to do something.

What she was supposed to do, Holly had no idea. She picked him up. "It's okay, Mase," she said, and leaned down to pick up the duffel Hannah had left. It was heavy. Holly tossed it up onto the bar and tried to unzip it, but she couldn't do that and hold Mason at the same time and had to put him down again.

Mason howled. "Don't cry, sweetie," she said in a singsongy voice. "People will think I am beating you." She grinned as she unzipped the bag. It was stuffed full with toys and clothes and diapers. Just how long was Hannah going to be gone? "Oh, look! Look, Mason, look!" she cried, latching onto a tiger in the bag. She held it up and shook it. Mason paused in his crying and looked with wonder at the tiger.

"Hooray!" Holly said. That was it, that was all she needed, one of his favorite toys. She bent down to give it to him, and Mason instantly put it in his mouth. "Thank God," Holly muttered under her breath, and stood up again to inspect the contents of the bag. The moment she did, Mason threw down the tiger and started to cry again.

"Hey, baby, what's wrong? What's wrong with Tiger?" she asked, scooping up the stuffed toy. Mason swiped at it, trying to knock it out of her hand. "He's not your favorite toy?" She could kill Hannah for this. Poor Mason had no idea what was going on. Holly tried offering him the tiger again, but this time he knocked it out of her hand and sent it scudding across the tile.

"Are you hungry?" she asked hopefully, and stood up again to inspect the jars of baby food in the bag. Strained peas. Strained carrots. Strained peas and carrots. "Look, Mason, look!" she said, gaining his attention. "I have peas!"

Mason looked truly interested in that, and held up his fat little arms for her.

She picked him up and looked around for something small enough to feed him with. She had nothing. She rooted around in the duffel bag and found nothing there, either. She opened her cutlery drawer and examined her utensils. All of her spoons were too big for him. Holly closed the drawer. Mason was crying again, trying to reach the jar of peas. *Measuring spoons!* Holly opened another drawer and found her one set of rarely used measuring spoons. They were ceramic, and the half teaspoon would work. "We're in business, kiddo," she said confidently.

She sat with Mason in her lap on a bar chair and fed him strained peas. He seemed to like that; he pounded the bar with his palms, and once, when she was distracted by the duffel bag again, he fit his fingers into the jar.

While he smeared peas all over her countertop and

himself, Holly tried Loren again. It rolled into voice mail. "Loren, you better call me back," she said after the tone. "This is an emergency!" She called Hannah, too, in the tiny hope that Hannah might pick up and Holly could reason with her. No luck there, either. "Hannah, you are not getting away with this!" she yelled into the phone.

When Mason had polished off most of the jar of peas, he began to fuss again.

"You're supposed to be happy and full, like all the babies on TV. Why aren't you happy?" Holly asked, and tickled his belly. "Smile, Mase! You had peas—who doesn't smile for peas?"

Mason opened his mouth, revealing a half dozen perfect little teeth, and wailed again.

Holly reared back. "Okay, okay," she cooed as she wiped him down with a wet paper towel. She had forgotten to look for a bib. "Are you still hungry?" She picked up a jar of carrots, but Mason pushed it away. "What about thirsty?" Holly persisted, and searched the duffel bag to find a sippy cup. Mason didn't like that, either. He kept crying, his face as red and round as a big tomato.

Did he miss his mother already, or was it something else? Could he be sick? Holly touched his face, but he didn't seem unusually warm. Not that she would know what unusually warm was for a baby. Maybe he was just tired. Babies napped all the time, she thought. But where could she put him down to nap in this apartment and continue to work? She was living in a studio loft. She couldn't put him in the bedroom for fear that he would crawl to the railing that overlooked the room below, slip through the iron bars, and fall. She couldn't leave him down here, because the piano would keep him up.

His cries were unbearable. She tried to soothe him, and when that didn't work, she had to put him down so she could look in that damn duffel bag for some clue as to how to quiet him. But that made Mason furious. He screamed at her now, using the couch to pull himself up, then falling on his bottom and doing it all again. "Hold on, Mason, hold on," she urged him, and dumped the contents of the duffel on her couch, looking for something—anything—that would tell her why he was crying. A cascade of diapers tumbled out, and Holly suddenly remembered Hannah the day of the funeral, coldly telling her that babies needed to be changed after napping.

Holly picked up a diaper and put Mason on his back. He didn't resist her; he just rubbed his fists into his eyes and continued to cry as she peeled off his overalls and diaper. "Oh God, Mason," she said when she had them off. The poor kid was soaked, his skin raw and red. She had no idea how long he'd been sitting in urine. "Oh, sweetie, you have to forgive me," she said apologetically, and tossed the offending diaper aside.

She wiped him down, spread some diaper rash cream—which made him scream louder—and then sprinkled baby powder on him. By the time she had a clean diaper on him, he had quieted and was watching her with big blue eyes, as if he didn't quite trust her. "I don't blame you," Holly said, and stroked his cheek. "I'll be honest with you, Mase. I don't know much about babies." She leaned over and kissed his forehead before she picked him up. Mason laid his head on her shoulder and sighed.

"Yessir, it's been kind of a trying day for both of us, hasn't it? I think we both could use a nap." She managed to pull a lap rug off her couch and laid it on the floor. She put Mason on top of it and the stuffed tiger next to him. Now Mason put his arm around the toy and rolled onto his side with a sigh.

Holly sighed too. She tossed the dirty diaper into the garbage, filled a bottle she found with water—she didn't have milk—and then lay down beside him. Mason gripped his bottle and sighed again. A moment later, his eyes had fluttered shut and his long dark lashes lay against the smooth skin of his cheek.

He was exhausted. Of course he was. He'd be a year in . . . wow, in about two weeks. He surely sensed something awful had happened today. He surely missed his mother and his father. Although he knew Holly, he had to be wondering why she was here and his mommy wasn't, and why he was lying on a floor and not in his own bed, and why he was eating peas and not solid foods.

It was so unfair that the life of this perfect, precious, plump little boy had somehow disintegrated. How could anyone do that to him? And Hannah! She'd completely wigged out.

Loren, that ass. Holly was convinced that Hannah's strange appearance and disappearance was because of him.

Why didn't Hannah tell me? Had they really drifted

that far apart? It made Holly sad that her own sister didn't feel as if she could talk to her. Had Hannah known Loren was cheating? Had she been surprised by it? Had she suspected it? Holly would have been sympathetic. She would have had Hannah's back, would have stood up for her, would have helped her. Did Hannah really not know that? Had Hannah honestly believed the only way to ask Holly for help was to abandon her son here? Sure, they'd had their differences, but they were *sisters*.

Holly looked down at Mason. It was all so unbelievable. Holly told herself not to panic: Hannah would come back. She was upset with Loren, but she'd be back. Hannah was the most competent person Holly had ever known. When Dad had died, Holly and her mother had been useless. Hannah, at the age of twenty-one, had been the only one of the three of them who could hold it together and see things through. Holly was ashamed that that was true, but she'd been so attached to her father, and she hadn't been able to cope with the reality that he was gone. Her father had never criticized her like her mother had. When Holly had wanted to pursue things different from what Hannah was doing, her father had been her biggest cheerleader, no matter what it was. The sudden death of her ally had left her reeling.

Mason moaned in his sleep and rolled onto his back. He looked like Loren, Holly thought. He'd be a cute kid, a handsome man. She just prayed he didn't inherit any more of his father's traits.

Hannah had always taken care of Loren too. Regardless of how often Holly's mother would say Loren was a good man, Holly had sensed the truth almost from the moment she met him. He was a user, and he'd wanted a trophy wife. Hannah had proven to be an excellent one. They'd bought the house in Tarrytown, and Hannah had made it the showplace Loren had wanted. Holly had never heard Hannah say an unkind word about all the hunting and golfing that kept Loren away from home each weekend. Hannah had just continued to plan the gourmet meals she made for him during the week on the heels of working ten- and twelve-hour days.

Hannah was a strong woman, there was no debate about that. Too strong, perhaps. So strong that she had refused to ask for help and then reached the point where she had to dump her son on her sister.

Mason's plump lips were slightly open; he was breathing deeply, fast asleep. Holly eased herself up off the floor, grabbed her phone, and stepped into her bathroom to call Loren.

"Hey, Holly," he said, answering on the second ring.

Holly was so startled that she didn't respond at first.

"Holly?"

"Yes, I am here," she said. "I've been trying to get hold of you."

"You've got me. What's the emergency?" he asked.

Holly leaned against the bathroom counter. "I heard you left."

"I figured that was what this was about," he said with an impatient sigh. "Look, let's cut right to the chase. It was a long time coming. You know your sister, how she is."

"I know she is entirely devoted to you and Mason—

that's how she is, Loren. And what do you mean, 'It was a long time coming'? For who? Not for Hannah. Not for Mason."

"God," he muttered irritably. "I really don't expect you to understand—"

"You're right," she interjected angrily. "I have never understood what can lead a person to cheat on the one person they have vowed to be faithful to, and I have definitely never understood *you*, Loren. Hannah was so good to you. She did everything you ever wanted. She was the perfect wife—"

"I thought your message said there was an emergency," he said curtly.

"Just a bit," she said sarcastically. "I heard about your cheating only today, when Hannah dropped Mason off at my apartment, unannounced, and then took off. You need to come get your son, Loren. He is not my responsibility and I'm not getting in the middle of this thing between you guys."

"What do you mean, she took off?" Loren demanded angrily, as if Hannah had no right to take off, as if he were the only one who had the right to leave.

"She left! She said she had to go somewhere and she wouldn't say when she'd be back. But judging by the amount of clothes and diapers she left, Mason might be a teenager before she comes back."

"She'll be back," Loren scoffed. "She just needs a break."

"This was more than just needing a break," Holly argued. "I've never seen my sister like this. Something is definitely wrong, and I'm worried about her."

"Wrong? There's nothing *wrong*."

"She wasn't herself."

"Was she lucid?" he snapped.

"Lucid! Yes, she was lucid."

"Well, then *what*, Holly? Do you think she is going to try and hurt herself?"

"What? No!" Holly cried angrily.

"There is nothing wrong," he repeated. "She's just being a drama queen."

Holly's pulse was racing now. "You need to come and get your son," she said evenly. "Do you know that he is sleeping on the floor of my apartment right now?"

"I can't come get him," Loren shot back, as if that were the most preposterous thing Holly had ever said. "I've got too much going on right now."

"Loren!"

"He'll be fine with you," Loren said. "Hannah will be back soon. Trust me, she dotes on that boy. She's probably off doing something to make my life hell."

"I can't take your son! I have a lot of work to do, and my apartment is so small that he can't escape the music! So please come and get him."

"Holly, you're not listening: I can't take care of him right now! You're just going to have to do your best until Hannah comes back. Mason is not going to bother you or impede your ability to write songs," he said in a tone that suggested he didn't think there was much to the art of composing.

"Have you heard anything that I've said?" Holly cried. "Can you imagine *any* scenario in which Hannah would abandon Mason? Do you even care that the mother of your child is having some sort of crisis right now?"

"If she doesn't come back, call me. But I am not going to change my plans because Hannah is throwing some jealous fit. That's what this is, you know. It's been over a long time, and she knows it, but she's still throwing a tantrum. She didn't have the guts to try and confront me, so she's trying to manipulate me through you. I have to go. Call me in a few days if she hasn't shown up."

Holly heard the click of the phone as Loren hung up. She gaped at her cell phone. "What an asshole!" she cried, and sank down onto her haunches, pushing a hand through her hair. How had Hannah stayed with him so long?

What was she going to do? She didn't have food for Mason. She didn't have a bed for him. She didn't even have a car seat! And she had to work. She *had* to work. She was not going to blow the opportunity of a lifetime because of Hannah. But Holly had a very bad feeling about this—so bad, she was suddenly having a little trouble catching her breath.

This was a crisis, and Holly's life had been so blissfully free of crises that she had no idea what to do, where to turn.

Check on the baby.

Holly left the bathroom and walked back into the living area. Mason was still asleep. He'd rolled onto his stomach and had the bottle clamped in his mouth. He looked like a little angel lying there, like one of the babies they used in ads for toilet paper and fabric softener.

The enormity of what was happening was beginning to sink in. "Okay," she whispered, and rubbed her palms on her faded jeans with the holes in the knees.

She just had to think logically. What would Hannah do? Hannah would say something about taking the first step. Okay, the first step. *What is the first step, Hannah?*

Food. He couldn't live on strained peas forever. And a bed—she needed someplace for him to sleep. But to get a food and bed, she needed to go to a store, and to go to a store, she needed a car seat. Or a babysitter.

Holly climbed onto her brown suede couch and sat on the back of it, thinking. None of her friends had babies. Some of them had kids, but they were past the baby stage. She couldn't think of anyone who had a car seat.

She was pondering how, exactly, she was going to do this when she heard a knock at her door. *Hannah! Oh, thank God, she couldn't do it, she's come to get Mason!* Holly hurried to the door and threw it open, expecting to see her sister.

It was not Hannah. It was Quincy, with a guitar slung over his shoulder. He grinned. "Ready to work, beautiful?"

She had completely forgotten about their work session.

"What's the matter?" he said, his smile sliding off his face. "Did you forget?"

She grabbed his hand and pulled him inside. "I need a favor."

"Sure," he said easily as he removed the guitar from his back.

"Can you babysit for about an hour?"

Quincy laughed. When Holly didn't laugh, he blinked. "Babysit what?"

"Not what. Him," Holly said, and pointed to Mason on the floor. Mason rolled onto his back and looked at Quincy.

"Wow." Quincy pushed his hand through his long blond locks. "Where'd he come from?"

"He's my nephew. It's kind of a long story, but I have to run and get some food and a bed, but I don't have a car seat, so I can't take him."

Quincy blinked again. "Okay," he said hesitantly. "But I don't know about babies."

"They aren't hard," Holly lied. "Look, he has a bottle. And here," she said, diving for the duffel bag. "Here are some animal crackers."

Mason rolled onto his side and his hands and knees, then stalled, as if he weren't certain where to go. Quincy grinned. "He's a little ball of blubber, isn't he?"

"There's a Target just down Mopac," Holly said quickly. "I won't be long. Please, Quincy? I'm kind of in a bind here."

"Yeah, sure," Quincy said and walked across the room to Mason. He dipped down and put his hand on Mason's head. "Hey, little man. Want to play some tunes?"

"Thanks, Quincy. I owe you one," Holly said, and grabbed up her purse. "You've got my number if anything happens, right?"

"Right," Quincy said as he tried to give Mason his bottle. Only Mason was more interested in the guitar on Quincy's back. "We'll work on the song when you get back. Right, little dude?"

But when he turned around for Holly's response, she was already gone.

Chapter Six

Wyatt saw the cloud of dust rising up on the road of the Fisher property for the third day in a row, a sure indication that something was going on; there hadn't been anyone around over there for a couple of months or more. Wyatt knew this, because he'd driven over there one afternoon with Milo in the bed of his truck to make acquaintances. He figured it never hurt to meet one's neighbors, particularly if one wanted to acquire said neighbor's property. But the place had been locked up tighter than Guantánamo Bay.

If he had to bet, he'd say that someone in the family had finally come to clean out the old lady's things, and paid no more attention to it as he went about his work.

Later that afternoon, he was down near the Fisher property, patching a section of fencing in the cattle chute. Some cow had gotten a hind leg on it and kicked it clean through. He finished up, surveyed his work, and paused to take his hat off and drag his sleeve across his brow. He seated his hat back on his head and put his hands on his waist. The afternoons were getting milder now, the days shorter. He liked this time of day. It was still—just him and nature and a patched cow chute. There was no sound of traffic, no phones, no televisions—nothing but the call of mockingbirds that were thinking of bedding down for the night, or the occasional bellow of a disgruntled cow. That afternoon, it was so still that Wyatt could hear the horses over at the Russell place, whinnying for their supper.

He squatted down to gather his tools, and as he slipped the hammer into his tool belt he thought he heard something.

Wyatt paused, straining to hear it. There it was again: it was music. Someone, somewhere, was strumming a guitar. Out here, sound carried so far, he couldn't detect exactly where it was coming from, but it sounded like it was coming from the Fisher place. It was a breezy tune that sounded like Spanish guitar, one of his favorite music genres. Whatever it was, he'd never heard it before, and he liked it. He liked it a lot. He sank down onto his knees, listening.

The music ended abruptly, and just like that it was gone. Wyatt remained in one spot, waiting for it again. When a minute or two had passed, he picked up his tools and walked back to his truck, wondering who that was, playing the guitar out here in the middle of nowhere.

He'd forgotten about it the next day when he and Troy rode out to check on the cattle.

The cattle had moved to the northeastern corner, which butted up against the Fisher homestead. As he neared the herd, Wyatt could see a thin tail of smoke above the tops of the trees, coming from the general vicinity of the Fisher house. It wasn't enough smoke to be a fire—or not a very big one—but Wyatt was unaccustomed to seeing any sign of life there at all.

The cattle were unconcerned. They came lumbering toward him, hoping for hay, as he rode into their midst. "Shoo," he said to them, as Troy slowly pushed through. Milo barked at a pair that got too close, and they darted into the brush.

Wyatt kept on until he reached the fence that separated his property from the Fisher homestead. Below him, he could see the old house. The smoke was coming out of the chimney. Looked like someone had lit a fire and found the birds' nests, he guessed. All the windows had been cranked open. He heard a baby cry, and squinted in the direction of that sound. He spotted the baby then, sitting on a quilt spread out in the yard, facing the house.

Milo heard the baby, too, and slipped under the barbed wire and went racing toward the house.

"Don't do that," Wyatt groaned, and dismounted, climbed over the fence, and started striding down the hill after his dog.

Milo was eagerly sniffing the baby's diaper. The baby regarded Milo curiously, but then Milo put his snout in the baby's neck, and the baby opened its mouth and screamed.

A woman raced out of the house as Wyatt reached the edge of the overgrown yard. *"Get away!"* she screamed at a tail-wagging Milo, and threw something—a shoe, Wyatt thought—at the dog, then snatched the baby up as if she were snatching it from the jaws of a wolf. Milo, who had never been one to take criticism well, slunk away, running up under the wraparound porch with his tail between his legs.

"Sorry about my dog," Wyatt said.

The woman—maybe mid-thirties, he thought, with a peasant blouse and a pair of jeans that fit her pretty darn good—gasped with surprise when she saw him and clasped the crying baby's head to her shoulder like she feared Wyatt would yank him right out of her arms. "Where did *you* come from? What are you doing here?" she demanded breathlessly, and looked around as if she expected Ninjas to leap out of the bushes at her. "I have a gun."

Wyatt almost laughed at that. "Hopefully, you won't need it. I'm your neighbor," he said.

"Neighbor!"

"Look, there's my horse," he said, and raised his chin toward Troy, who was munching contentedly on some grass by the fence. "I live right over that hill."

She looked at Troy, then at Wyatt, her expression full of suspicion.

Wyatt sighed. He took his phone from his pocket and tossed it at her feet. "Call nine-one-one if you need to."

She looked at his phone, then peeked up at him. "You should keep your dog on a leash," she said, her voice calmer.

"Keeping him on a leash would be impractical out here," he said, thinking that was painfully obvious. "And besides, he's a good dog. He wouldn't hurt your baby." The baby was missing a shoe, and Wyatt noticed it in the grass and bent down to pick it up. "I'm sorry we scared you. I saw the smoke and thought you might need help."

"The smoke?"

Wyatt pointed to the chimney.

She twirled around and stared up at it. "Oh my God," she said, and sighed loudly at the smoke pouring out of her chimney. When she turned back to Wyatt, her expression had softened. She had a pretty face, he thought, with gray-green eyes and a smattering of freckles across her cheeks and nose. Her shoulder-length hair was a strawberry blonde, more blond than red, and shaggy. She was, he couldn't help noticing, a nice-looking woman. Cute. "I didn't know it was smoking that bad," she said, looking embarrassed.

"Yes, ma'am." He handed her the shoe. She stooped down to fetch his phone and handed that to him. Her fingers were slender, he noticed. No manicure, the nails cut short.

They both looked up at the smoking chimney a moment.

But then she locked those gray-green eyes on him. "Why are you here?" she asked, eyeing him curiously, taking in his dirty jeans, his sleeveless chambray shirt. He'd cut the sleeves off with a knife and supposed it looked a little untidy, and he knew his jeans had seen better days. Well, hell, he hadn't expected to meet anyone today.

"Did you come here for a reason?" she asked curiously.

"Fence needed fixing."

She looked up at the fence. The baby began to squirm in her arms, but she held him tight. She was obviously expecting a different kind of neighbor. She looked back at him. "Mind if I ask your name?"

"Wyatt Clark," he said obligingly. She didn't so much as blink, which said to him she obviously hadn't heard about him around town. Wyatt knew people talked about him. Two years ago, he'd been a story too juicy to ignore: completely in love with his wife, trying for a baby, and then her first husband came back and made Wyatt the most pitied guy in all of Cedar Springs. In all of Texas, for that matter. Maybe even the United States.

"I'm Holly Fisher," she said, and extended a hand.

Wyatt hesitated a moment before taking it. Her hand was soft and slender, like her fingers. "I was sorry to hear about your mother," he said. In truth, he hadn't been sorry to hear about the old lady's death at all; it had just been news. But it seemed the right thing to say, as she softened considerably.

"Oh. Thank you."

Wyatt was aware that his own hand was rough and callused, quickly dropped hers, then shoved his in his pocket. "What's his name?" he asked, looking at the baby.

Holly suddenly smiled at the restless baby, a pretty, glowing smile. "This is Mason," she said, and put him down on the quilt. Mason didn't seem to like that; he started to cry, his little fists on top of his knees. "And Mason is not himself today. He's been very fussy. Maybe because I smoked up the house." She seemed amused by her observation.

Mason leaned over on his hands, placed his feet flat on the ground under him, and tried to stand, but fell over on his butt. That made him cry harder. His shirt-front was covered with drool and his jeans—the kind that snapped between the legs—had spots of saliva on them also. Mason suddenly stopped crying and used Holly's leg to hoist himself up, then clutched her as he wobbled on his fat legs.

Wyatt smiled. He liked toddlers. He wished he could be like a toddler, discovering something new every single day, his only concern eating and sleeping. Mason looked to be about the same age as Grace, and she'd just started walking about a month ago. Now he couldn't keep her in one place.

Mason fell on his rump again.

"Glad to see someone is here to take care of the place," Wyatt said.

"Oh, I'm not here," Holly said, and shook her head so quickly that a silky strand of hair fell across her face. "I mean, I'm here for the time being, but I'm not really *living* here," she said, as if she found the idea reprehensible. "Just temporarily. I live in Austin."

"Ah." He wondered how long she was going to be here, and hoped it was at least long enough for him to make a discreet inquiry or two about buying the place. He looked up at the smoking chimney. "You need help with your chimney?"

"No, thanks." She hooked her hands in her back pockets. "I couldn't get the flue open, and I smoked the whole house; and then I got it open, but the wood is green I guess, and *whoosh*—all that smoke went out the chimney. I don't think it's been used in a while." She smiled sheepishly. "I'm not exactly Rhonda Rancher, but I've got it."

Wyatt nodded. The baby used her legs to haul himself up once more. He stuck his head between her legs and blinked big blue eyes up at Wyatt. But when he tried to move through her legs, he fell again and helped himself to a stick on the edge of the quilt. Holly took the stick from him before he put it in his mouth, and Mason wailed.

Wyatt subscribed to the theory that you let kids experiment. That's how they learned. But Holly picked him up, as if she suddenly feared he'd eat all the sticks in the grass—and there were plenty, as the yard hadn't been tended to in a long while—and the baby cried harder. She sighed again and put him on her hip, bouncing him. "I don't know what's wrong with him."

"Looks like he's teething," Wyatt observed.

"I don't know," she said, frowning at the baby. "I gave him a teething ring and he threw it down."

"Freeze a wet washcloth and then let him chew on that," Wyatt suggested.

Holly Fisher laughed, the sound of it light and disbelieving. "I am not going to give him a washcloth to chew on. He could choke on it."

Wyatt shrugged. It sure had worked for Grace. "Just an idea. Well, Miss Fisher, I'll let you get back to your chimney. Probably just a buildup of creosote."

"Of what? What's that?"

"Fire residue. Builds up and prevents a good draw of air." He shrugged a little. "It can be a fire hazard if you don't get it cleaned out."

Holly's eyes widened.

Great. He'd just made her think she was going to burn her house down. He suppressed a sigh. "Want me to take a look?" he asked.

"Ah . . ."

"I wouldn't want you to burn the whole county. I've got cows depending on the grazing around here."

She blinked, then smiled at his jest, and Wyatt found it to be a very enchanting smile. Almost as pretty as Macy's. That he could even think that without feeling a jab in his heart was a pretty good sign for him, because his heart had been living in the dead of winter for a long time now.

"I hate to be a bother," she said.

"No bother." Just annoying.

"Okay," Holly said. "Thanks." She started toward the house, walking across the yard to the porch steps, Mason riding along on her hip. Wyatt tried not to look at the sway of her hips, but those jeans rode just right, and it was . . . hard not to watch.

He followed her inside, stepping cautiously over the threshold and doffing his hat. The house smelled musty. The green plaid living room furniture was worn, and the lace curtains looked yellow to him, but other than that, everything was nice and neat. It looked as if she'd just arrived. Her purse was lying on the couch, and there was a playpen in the middle of the living room. Several baby toys were scattered about the rug, and a guitar case was propped up against the wall next to the door. He remembered the music he'd heard last night and wondered if she was the one who had been playing.

Wyatt could see evidence of Holly and the baby but no one else. No man, specifically.

"Would you like something to drink?" Holly asked, and put Mason in the playpen. He began chewing on the rail.

"No, thank you," Wyatt said. He felt restless. He didn't want to be in this house. It felt too . . . close. He wanted to be outside, away from an attractive woman and her baby. This all felt very weird, very déjà vu, even though he'd never been in this house before this moment.

Wyatt walked over to the fireplace and went down on one knee to look inside. The fire had never caught, and the wood she'd tried to burn was so green, she could probably bend it. "Do you have any wood besides this?"

"Mmm . . . I don't know," she said. "I'm not sure where it would be."

Wyatt held his breath and stuck his head in the fireplace, craning his neck to peer upward, looking for daylight. The opening was so narrow, he could barely make out the light filtering in from above. He pulled himself out and stood, brushing his hands against his jeans.

"You should have this cleaned before you try and use it," he said. "I know a guy who will do it for a small fee. I can send him around next time he's working at my place." He put his hat on his head.

"That's okay," Holly said apologetically. "I shouldn't be building fires anyway. Obviously." She smiled again, and Wyatt felt a little warm. "I'll just . . . I'll just use the heating."

"Got propane?"

She blinked. "Propane," she repeated.

Lord. Rhonda Rancher apparently had shipwrecked herself out here without any survival skills. "I'll check it on the way out," he offered. "I'll let you know if you need any."

"Thank you," she said sheepishly.

Determined to get out before he was checking

the plumbing, Wyatt walked to the screen door and pushed it open.

"Thank you, Wyatt. I really appreciate it."

"Yep," he said, and stepped off the porch. "Milo, come," he called in a low voice, and the dog bounded out from under the porch. Wyatt walked around to the side of the house to the propane tank and checked the gauges. She had enough propane for the time being, thank God. He started up the hill to where Troy stood waiting at the fence.

"Oh, hey, Wyatt?"

Wyatt paused and looked back. Holly had walked out onto the porch with Mason. "You just put a washcloth in the freezer?"

He honestly thought every mother knew that trick. Macy was the one who'd told him. "Yes." He touched his hat and walked on, climbed over the fence, unwrapped Troy's reins from the fence, and hoisted himself up. He glanced back down the hill before he rode away and saw Holly Fisher on the porch with Mason, holding his hands out, helping him to walk. He could hear her encouraging him, her voice lilting in her praise.

A curious prickle went up his spine.

Wyatt figured he'd make another trip over here in a day or two and see if she was still around, maybe bring her some firewood. If she was, maybe he'd ask her about the Fisher place and what they intended to do with it. He felt a sale in his bones.

Providential. Relating to or determined by Providence. As in, *he'd just made a providential acquaintance in Holly Fisher.*

Chapter Seven

Holly's life was utter chaos, and now she had Hop-along Cassidy riding the fence line, peeking in. He probably thought she was a lunatic, anyway, because really, who tried to burn green wood?

Someone who was desperate for a little heat, that's who. Holly wasn't exactly an expert in building fires, and while she knew green wood was hard to burn, she didn't know it would smoke up the entire county.

She shouldn't have come out here. It had never occurred to her that the house might need things, like wood. Or propane! She didn't even know where one acquired propane.

She certainly had not *wanted* to come here. In fact, she could say confidently it was the last place she'd wanted to be. There were a lot of memories within these walls: Her mother's cancer was still fresh, like a new coat of paint. And lurking beneath that were older, painful memories of her teen years.

Plus, she was impractically far from Austin—so far that she might as well be in New Mexico. None of her friends was going to come out all the way out here just to hang out. One of her best friends, Ossana, had made that painfully clear. "Do they even have a Starbucks there?" Ossana had asked when Holly told her she was moving out here for a while. Ossana, like Holly, enjoyed her creature comforts.

But Holly had run out of options. She'd had Mason for a little over three weeks now, and everything she'd known—her lifestyle, her work, her friends—were floating off into the ether, and Holly couldn't seem to grab any of it back.

The first twenty-four hours with Mason had been a nightmare. Holly loved Mason, but she knew so little about babies. That first night it seemed she would sleep only minutes before he would begin to cry, and cry so loudly she worried he would wake the neighbors. She had had no idea what was wrong with him. She'd changed him, she'd tried milk, she'd walked the floor with him, and nothing had calmed him down. She'd worried that he was missing his mother—that a hole was forming in his little tiny heart and growing deeper with every moment of Hannah's absence.

By morning, she and Mason were lying on their stomachs in her bed, both exhausted from the sleepless night.

By mid-afternoon of the following day, Holly had discovered baby poop in her hair and cereal on the shoulder of her new white T-shirt. But by the end of the second day, Mason had stopped crying. He'd banged her bar with a measuring cup, completely delighted by the sound of it, and Holly could not help but be delighted with him.

Nevertheless, having to care for a baby was exhausting in a way Holly had never known she could be exhausted. Mason wasn't walking yet, but he was definitely mobile, and she was constantly chasing after him to remove things from his hand and mouth, and to block access to things such as electrical outlets and floor lamps and the cords around her musical equipment, which attracted him like chocolate attracted her.

Unaware that her life had been so dramatically altered, Holly's friends had called, wanting her to come out. Ossana had called twice that first week. "Ry Cooder is playing at Stubb's Bar-B-Que. You know him, right? See if you can get us in," she'd suggested excitedly.

"I can't," Holly had said as she peeled dried SpaghettiOs from her shirt. "I am keeping Hannah's baby."

"Who?"

"Hannah. My sister."

"Oh," Ossana had said, sounding disappointed. "How long?"

That was the sixty-four-thousand-dollar question. "A few days," Holly had said.

When Ossana had called again later in the week, Holly had accepted the fact that Mason would be around at least for a while, and told her it would be indefinite.

"I don't understand. Is your sister sick?" Ossana had asked.

"Yes. She's sick. Really sick," Holly had responded with conviction. Sick in the head at the very least.

Ossana had seemed confused by it all, and Holly had been too embarrassed to tell her friend more. At that point, she'd still believed Hannah would come back.

By the end of the week, however, Holly had had to quit her job at the Java Hut. Just as she had sworn to Lucy, Holly had tried very hard to find a babysitter. She had. But she'd not admitted to Lucy that she'd actually found a sitter but was too afraid to leave Mason when it came right down to it.

That sudden surge of maternal instinct had surprised Holly. Until that point, she had been showering with Mason in his playpen in the bathroom with her, her eyes full of tears because suddenly her life was no longer her own. She had woken up each morning as the sun rose—an hour she'd not seen in many years—listening to the happy chatter of a drooling toddler. She had been exhausted, emotionally spent, and angry.

She'd alternated between fear of what had happened to Hannah and anger with her sister for completely uprooting her life. Hannah had essentially tramped all over it, as if Holly's life weren't worth her consideration when she'd gone off to do whatever the hell it was she was doing. It was grossly unfair, and Holly was so determined not to let Hannah win, in fact, that she'd dressed a happy Mason in a little University of Texas Longhorns tracksuit and, armed with a small bag of animal crackers, had marched down to the offices of the apartment complex where she lived.

"Hi, Holly!" the manager, Barb, had chirped when Holly entered, carrying Mason. "Oh, who is *this*?" she'd exclaimed delightedly at Mason.

"This is my nephew, Mason."

"He's a cutie!" Barb had trilled. "Look at those big blue eyes. How old is he?"

"Ah . . . he'll be one soon." Next week, she'd realized. Surely Hannah would be back for that. Who missed their child's first birthday?

"Is he walking?" Barb had asked.

"Not yet."

"He will be any day now," Barb had said with all the authority of an oracle, and Holly had felt another tic of panic. She'd imagined him tottering around her apartment and things crashing on the floor behind him.

Holly had asked Barb if she knew anyone at the complex who could babysit.

"Lemme see," Barb had said thoughtfully, obviously wanting to be helpful. "I think the Hernandez girl babysits for her mother. Let me call them."

Ten minutes later, as Holly had stood looking out the office window, a girl came loping across the interior lawn, with a pink swath through her hair, her pants riding low and tight, and some chains of some sort hanging from them. Her belly was exposed and spilling over the waist of her jeans.

As the girl strode up to the office door with her cell phone clipped to her jeans, Holly had looked at Mason and could not imagine leaving him with a stranger—not after what he'd just been through. Not for a single moment.

Barb had been perplexed when Holly had suddenly announced that Mason was not feeling well. If the Hernandez girl cared, she certainly hadn't given Holly any indication. She'd merely shrugged and loped back home, the cell phone pressed to her ear and the sparkly design on her pockets catching the sunlight.

Holly's problem of what to do, exactly, with Mason was only one of her accumulating problems that presented themselves in that first week.

There was the problem of Quincy, who was eager to work on their songs. Holly was too. She and Quincy had tried to work in her apartment, but Mason had wanted to play the piano, and when Holly tried to put him in his portable playpen, he'd howled. It had been impossible to hear the music, much less to compose.

"Maybe we ought to wait until your sister picks him up," Quincy had suggested after they'd aborted their session. He'd been on the floor, playing with Mason, who had squealed with delight every time Quincy hid his face behind a pillow then surprised him.

"I'm sorry, Quincy."

"Hey, it's all good. When is she picking him up?"

"Ah . . . I'm not really sure," Holly had said, and Quincy had looked mildly perplexed and annoyed by her answer.

There was the issue of Mason crying. The boy cried a *lot*. Holly was always trying to figure out if he was hungry, or wet, or tired. Without the benefit of nine months to read up on babies, and at her wit's end, Holly had called her friend Belinda, the wife of a musician Holly knew. Belinda and Mike had two kids who were now in elementary school.

Belinda hadn't believed Holly when she'd explained her situation. "What do you mean, she left him indefinitely?"

"I mean, I'm not certain when she'll be back," Holly had admitted.

"What sort of mother does that?" Belinda cried. "You should call the police."

"Yeah," Holly had said, but she had no intention of doing that. She feared they really would take Mason from her and put him in foster care, and she could not abide that. "What do I do, Belinda? He cries all the time."

"Schedule, Holly," Belinda had said sagely. "Schedules mean everything to babies. Get him on a schedule for feeding, naps, and play. But take him to a pediatrician and make sure he's not lactose intolerant or maybe has an ear infection."

"An *ear infection*?" Holly had exclaimed.

"Yep. Very easy for them to get. Could be gas, too. You never know. But get him on a schedule!"

Holly's head had spun. "But how do I know what the schedule is?" she'd asked helplessly.

"Oh, honey, you really *are* dumb about this," Belinda had said sympathetically, and had given Holly a schedule and had advised her, "Get a book about babies and their development."

Holly had taken Belinda's advice. As she had no idea who Mason's pediatrician was, Holly had taken Mason to the People's Community Clinic, where she'd waited three hours for someone to see Mason, her imagination working overtime all the while. People and the babies who belonged to them had surrounded her, but she had nothing that said Mason should be with her. What would they make of that? Would they call the police?

As it turned out, the nurse practitioner who saw Mason wasn't the slightest bit concerned with why

Holly had Mason. He'd been too perturbed that Holly didn't have Mason's shot records. "Are you certain his vaccinations are up-to-date?" he'd asked more than once.

"Yes," Holly had said, but wasn't certain at all. She just knew Hannah, and knew that she'd have Mason in for his shots the moment they were due. But then again, *that* Hannah would never have abandoned her baby.

After babbling on about the importance of keeping vaccination records, the practitioner had pronounced Mason perfectly fine.

"Really?" Holly had asked. "He cries a lot."

The man had given her an impatient look. "Babies cry when they are unhappy," he'd said, then marked something on a clipboard and left her and Mason to gather their things.

Schedule. Holly had left the clinic and headed for the bookstore, where she found a whole array of *What to Expect* books. She selected two and left the bookstore feeling armed.

But that trip to the bookstore had pointed up another issue for Holly: Mason was not inexpensive to care for. Holly was furious about that; it seemed to her that if someone was going to abandon their baby at one's doorstep, they ought to at least leave the things one would need for the baby. In the giant duffel Hannah had left, there were diapers and a few changes of clothes that looked as if they'd been grabbed from the dirty-laundry pile and tossed in without regard to how many shirts and pants and pajamas there were. Hannah had also included a very strange mix of toy parts, such as the rubber workbench without the rubber hammer.

Hannah had left nothing useful with Holly, no emergency numbers, nothing about what to feed him or what to put in his bottles. Certainly no car seat or bed. Holly had coughed up two hundred and sixty-five dollars at Target for those things and more essentials. How in the hell did people afford babies?

To add insult to injury, it had taken her a good half hour to get the portable crib she'd bought out of its Fort Knox–like box and then get it to stand up on its own. It was supposed to snap into place. The picture on the side of the box showed a smiling mommy in capris and a blue shirt assembling it without breaking a sweat while her happy baby sat nearby. It had taken Holly thirty minutes and a miracle of physics to get the thing to work.

When she was certain that the portable crib would not collapse, she'd put Mason in it and sat cross-legged on the floor, exhausted but fascinated as she watched him. Mason had grabbed on to the rail and laughed with ridiculous delight as he bounced up and down. He'd inched his way around the perimeter like a drunken sailor, stepping on his own feet and pausing now and then to chew on the railing and talking happy gibberish as he went.

He was, Holly had thought dreamily, perhaps the most adorable baby on the planet. It was a tragedy that both his parents were losers.

Exhausted, and her creative juices at an all-time low, it had enraged Holly that neither of Mason's parents would answer the phone. At Hannah's workplace,

she'd gotten "She's not in; may I take a message?" At
Loren's she'd gotten "Mr. Drake is not accepting calls
this afternoon."

Nevertheless, Holly had called them continually as
her life had steadily fallen apart. She had been breathless with anxiety, the tears of frustration constantly
burning in her eyes, and she had been slowly eating her
way through a mountain of chocolate.

Holly had finally reached her limit. She'd put Mason
in his brand-new car seat and driven to Hannah's
house. She hadn't actually believed she'd find Hannah
there, but she hadn't really expected to find her sister's
Tarrytown bungalow deserted, either. The yard hadn't
been cut, and a clutter of newspapers littered the walk.
Holly had picked them up and tossed them into the
garbage cans that were on the street, then pulled the
garbage cans up to the garage. She'd found the front
door locked, so she'd held Mason and walked into the
backyard and to the back porch and tried that door.

"Ma-maw," Mason had said, surprising her. It was
the first thing he'd said that actually sounded like a
word.

"That's right, Mase. Mama is supposed to be here,
but I don't think she is." Holly had given the door a
good yank, but it was locked. She'd put Mason down
and cupped her hands around her face and peered inside. She couldn't see anything but two brown pill bottles on the kitchen table. Everything else had seemed
in place. Nothing out of the ordinary. Just a normal,
hyper-clean Hannah house.

But it had seemed almost too clean, even for Hannah. It looked as if she'd literally walked out of her

own life. At that point, Holly had had enough of this strange little saga and left Tarrytown confused and feeling like she needed a big dose of bourbon. She didn't even like bourbon, but if she'd had a bottle, she'd have drunk it.

With Mason dozing in his car seat, she'd driven downtown to the Baker Botts Law Firm where Loren worked. She'd had to wake Mason to carry him inside just so that she could confront Loren. Exhausted, Mason had cried, his face red and gaping open, but Holly would not stop until Loren told her what the hell was going on.

At the reception desk of Baker Botts—a polished, expensive furnishing with chrome trim and leather seating in the waiting area—Holly had asked the man behind the desk for Loren Drake.

"Is he expecting you?" he'd asked pleasantly.

"No, I am sure he's not expecting me," Holly had said as Mason screamed in her ear. "Please tell him that Holly Fisher is here with his son, and if he doesn't come out, I'll walk these halls until I find him."

The young man had blinked and almost smiled, as if this were the most exciting thing to have happened to him in ages. Then he'd picked up the phone. "Hi, Kendra," he'd said a moment later. "A Holly Fisher is here with Mr. Drake's son to see him." He paused a moment and glanced up. "Mr. Drake is in a meeting."

"I don't care," Holly had said firmly. Mason had cried louder, and Holly had tried to put him down, but he'd clung to her. "Tell Mr. Drake that his son needs a nap, but he's going to sit in the lobby screaming until his father comes out and talks to me."

The young man had nodded and said into the phone, "Kendra, we have a situation. Mr. Drake needs to come to the front as soon as possible."

Loren had appeared a few minutes later in shirtsleeves and holding a file. He'd glared at Holly, as if she had no right to seek him out, as if she were completely out of line. "What are you doing here?" he'd asked, looking self-consciously at the receptionist. He'd clearly been embarrassed by Holly, and that had made her fury soar.

Upon hearing his father's voice, Mason lifted his head from Holly's shoulder and reached out his arms for Loren. He'd cried for his father, a snot-filled wail, and Loren had taken him from Holly. "Hey, big guy, what's the matter?" he'd asked, kissed Mason's forehead, then said to Holly, "Follow me."

He'd led her into a small conference room directly behind the reception area, shut the door, then glared at Holly. "What the *hell* do you think you're doing?"

"Are you kidding?" Holly had exclaimed breathlessly, her pulse ratcheting up.

"What makes you think you can come into my workplace and disrupt things like this?"

"Don't pretend I've done anything to *you*. Hannah dumped your son on me, and I have a right to know what's going on!"

Loren had sighed. He'd sat with one hip on the table, Mason in his lap, and with his foot had kicked out one of the leather chairs for Holly. She'd ignored it. "Your timing couldn't be any worse, Holly," he'd said, conveniently forgetting that she was there because she couldn't get him or Hannah on the phone. "In three hours I'm catching a flight to California for a week, and when I get back, I have two days before I have to turn around and fly out to San José, Costa Rica. We're opening a satellite office there, and I am going to be away for at least six weeks."

"*What?*" Holly had demanded, incredulous. "Jesus, do you ever listen to your voice mail? I am trying to *find Hannah*. I've had Mason for over a week, and my life is going to hell as we speak. I can't compose, I lost my job at the Java Hut, Hannah has disappeared, and you act like this is some great imposition on *you*. I am so worried about her, Loren!"

"She hasn't disappeared," he'd said dismissively.

"Oh yeah? Do *you* know where she is?"

"Not exactly," he'd said with a shrug, "but I've spoken to her." He'd nudged the chair again. "Come on, sit down."

Holly had sat just because she didn't think she could stand any longer, and she'd bent over, her head in her hands, trying to catch her breath. It had felt as if her lungs would not open.

"Look . . . Hannah had to take care of something very important," Loren had said while extricating his tie from Mason's grip.

"What?" Holly had lifted her head. "Where?"

"I can't tell you that, but she has my full support."

Holly had never trusted Loren, and she certainly didn't then. "Support for *what*? Why can't you tell me?"

"Because she asked me not to," he'd said impatiently. He was not the sort of man who liked to be questioned. "She wants to tell you herself when she's ready. She's going to call you."

"No"—Holly had shaken her head—"no way. I won't leave until you tell me—"

"She's in rehab, okay, Holly?"

Stunned, Holly had reared back. She couldn't even make sense of that word in relation to her sister. *"Rehab?"*

"Yes. Rehab," he'd said tightly, seeming almost embarrassed by it.

"For *what*?" Holly had exclaimed. "And *why*? *When*?"

Loren had sighed. "She'll explain it to you. The point is, she's fine, she's not lying in a ditch, but she needs some time."

The news was more than Holly could digest. It had seemed as if the walls were moving closer to her as she tried to make sense of what Loren was saying. She'd thought of Hannah the last few times she'd seen her—the distraction, the smell of alcohol on her breath at her mother's funeral. Was that it? Was she a drinker?

"So you need to buck up here," Loren had added, as if it were somehow Holly's job.

"Are you kidding?" she'd gasped. "Are either of you the least bit concerned that my life is falling apart because of this?"

"Don't be ridiculous," Loren had said impatiently. "That's the problem with you, Holly. You can't handle *anything*. This is the one time you need to step up. You're pampered with some pie-in-the-sky ideas, and the one time life gets a little hard, you fall to pieces."

Holly hadn't been able to even think of what to say to him. He'd acted as if he bore no responsibility to his son, that it was all Holly's.

"Hannah has obviously been through a lot, and if you can't help your sister in her darkest moment, you're selfish."

"Oh my God, you are so unbelievable," she'd said breathlessly. "He is *your* son."

"Look, I can't take Mason right now," Loren had doggedly continued. "The office in San José is very important to this firm, and I have to be there to launch it if I have a prayer of making partner here. Which means providing for Mason's future, if I have to spell that out."

"But he is your *son*, Loren! You haven't even called to check on him! It's like he doesn't even exist to you!"

"That's not true!" he'd said heatedly. "I haven't called because I've been out of town, and frankly, Holly, I knew if I did, you would give me the load of shit you're giving me right now," he'd snapped. "I *know* he is my son and I love him, but he's a baby, and I can't take on a baby right now. Think about it! I can't take him to Costa Rica! What am I going to do with a baby in Costa Rica?"

Holly's heart had pounded so painfully that she'd bent over again. This could not be happening.

"When I get back, if Hannah isn't . . . through," he'd said awkwardly, "I'll deal with it then."

"And what the hell am I supposed to do in the meantime?" she'd demanded in disbelief. "I don't even have a job now, thanks to you and Hannah. And I have a contract to deliver three songs. I can't afford to just sit around and wait for you or Hannah to show up and take your kid!"

"You can do it," he'd said, but he'd avoided her

gaze and looked at his watch. "Millions of people do it every day. They work, they take care of kids. Look, I've got to get back." He'd handed Mason to her, and Holly had taken him, suddenly wanting Mason as far from his narcissistic father as she could possibly get him. But Mason had reached for his father again.

Oblivious, Loren had pulled his checkbook from his pocket. "I'm not saying I don't know this isn't unusual and somewhat of a pain," he'd said as he dashed off a check, "but divorce is painful for all the parties involved. It's probably best for Mason that he's away from all that negative energy anyway." He'd torn the check out and passed it down the table to Holly. "That should more than take care of his needs."

Holly hadn't even looked at his damn check. "This is insanity, you know. You and Hannah are treating Mason like a dog that needs a good home. It's unconscionable, really. I always knew you were a colossal asshole, Loren, but this is the cake topper, even for you."

"I don't need any lectures from you of all people," he'd said. "I'll call you in two weeks. But stop calling my cell phone every ten minutes." He'd run his head over Mason's crown, then kissed his cheek. "You be a good boy for your aunt Holly, and Mommy will be home soon," he'd said, and walked out the door.

Mason had screamed. He'd cried so hard he began to hiccup.

Holly had felt dizzy with despair and incredulity. She'd shoved the check into her purse and held Mason tightly as she walked out.

She'd gone back to her apartment that day in a state

of devastation. There'd been no escaping it—her life had been irrevocably changed, and she'd had no say in it. And as for Hannah . . . Holly couldn't even begin to wrap her head around the news that Hannah was in *rehab*. How was that possible?

That night, she'd lugged the Pack 'n Play up to her bedroom, wedged it between her bed and the wall, and put Mason in it. He had fussed a little but fell asleep. Holly had lain on her back in that darkened loft, her arms and legs spread wide, staring at the ceiling, still unable to manage anything but shallow breathing, tears falling silently, soaking one big spot on her pillow. Holly had had a meltdown, had just melted into nothing. How would she ever manage this? How would she juggle her songwriting career around a baby? And what about Mason? How long could one baby be confined to a Pack 'n Play because she was too afraid he would get hurt in her child-unfriendly apartment?

When she was all cried out, and her breathing had returned to normal, Holly had decided to think logically about it. Hungry, she'd gone down to the kitchen to eat and think.

First, this space wouldn't work for Mason. It was about as safe for a kid as playing in the middle of the street. Second, she couldn't work like this. She did not want to rush the creative process; she had a real shot at something big, and she didn't want to risk ruining the opportunity by rushing through it. Holly needed time and space to work.

In the course of making herself an enormous sandwich, Holly had heard Mason sigh.

It was a small sound, but so sweet, and it had occurred to Holly again that this might be a nightmare for her, but her nightmare was actually a blessing for Mason. Where would he be right now had Hannah not brought him here? Foster care? Maybe Holly was meant to be home that afternoon. Maybe she was meant to do this. Maybe she had to make herself believe it so she could deal with it.

That's when Holly had decided to come home. She'd stood over the sink, munching her sandwich, and decided it was the only option. The last place she'd wanted to be was the homestead, but she'd had to admit, it was big enough that she'd have the space she needed to work. It was childproof and definitely child-friendly. And honestly, it was time she did something about her mother's will and the homestead anyway. Hannah was right—she'd let it go too long.

It had taken a few more days for her to get things squared away. She'd given Barb a check to cover the next month's rent, then had called Loren and left a message that he would be paying the rent on her apartment until Hannah came home. Next, she'd called Quincy and explained her situation. Quincy had seemed confused about how they would possibly finish their songs, but Holly had promised him they could make it work. She'd had no idea how, but she'd promised that she'd have something for them to work with in a couple of weeks.

Then she'd called her uncle D.J., who had made a point of going by to check on the homestead from time to time, and told him she and Mason would be there for a few weeks. Uncle D.J. was old and didn't get around as well as he used to, and as she'd guessed, he'd been happy to hand off the responsibility for the place to someone else. "You and Hannah make sure that gate is locked when you're not there," he'd said.

Holly had assured him they would and let him believe that she and Hannah would both be out there, that all was well with Hannah.

Then Holly had called a few friends to tell them she'd be out of touch for a while. She had told them she was working on her music.

"No way!" Ossana had said when she told her she was going out to the homestead.

"You can come out and see me," Holly had suggested.

"I guess I could. Yeah, maybe I'll do that when I have a weekend off from work," Ossana had said. But Holly knew she wouldn't. Ossana enjoyed the nightlife in Austin too much to be poking around some ranch on the weekend.

And with that, Holly had packed her guitar, her music files, her bags. She'd strapped Mason into his car seat between the portable crib and the giant duffel that now held Holly's clothes and she had headed home, composing a song in her head as she drove:

Packed her bags and drove all night
Couldn't get his image from her sight
Came back to the place she was supposed to be
Surrounded and steeped in misery
She'd come home, ooooh, ooooh, she'd come
      home.

Maybe, Holly had told herself on the drive out, maybe this could work. She'd tried to recall the last time she'd been left alone to really work on her music—when she hadn't been interrupted by her job and friends—and she had not been able to recall one occasion in recent memory. So maybe this was just what she needed to get the creative juices really flowing.

She'd arrived at dusk. The gate Uncle D.J. was so concerned about locking had a new combination lock on a chain that wrapped around the gate and the fence post. Holly had memorized the combination, but when she'd lived out here, they'd never shut the gate—it had always been open, because none of them had liked having to get out of the car to unlock it and then lock it again after them.

She had driven up to the house and looked around. The old windmill, which hadn't pumped water in years, still squeaked something awful. The yard had become overgrown and the house needed a coat of paint.

Holly had found the key to the house under the welcome mat where they'd always kept it. The house had smelled musty when she opened the door, and it was cold too. She'd forgotten that it really cooled off at night out here in the sticks, and insulation had never been a top priority. She'd vaguely remembered Hannah saying something about turning off the utilities a few months earlier, but Holly hadn't wanted to think about it then, and held her breath when she tried the lights. They were still on, and Holly had pretended that miracles really did happen.

"Well, Mason, say hello to your home away from home," she'd said, putting him down next to the old plaid couch so he could inch his way around while Holly dragged a couple of bags inside.

She'd spent the next day dusting and washing bed linens, running into town for supplies, and playing through a couple of song ideas, but she hadn't been very pleased with what she'd come up with.

She'd been looking forward to working more today, but then Wyatt Clark had come riding up to her fence with those vivid blue eyes. Lonesome cowboys always made for good song material, she mused. Who knew? Maybe he'd be her muse and she would actually write a Grammy-winning tune or two.

Chapter Eight

A week after her return to the homestead, Holly was sitting at the Formica-covered breakfast bar, going through some of her mother's papers. Mason was playing with cars on the on the linoleum floor—which, Holly noted ruefully, she needed to mop.

Okay, all right, she could admit it: she wasn't exactly a go-getter. Hannah was right that Holly had a tendency to flit from job to job and from guy to guy. The only constant in Holly's life was music and a burning desire to create it. Melodies and lyrics were constantly running around in her head, and when she was composing, Holly felt the most at peace, the best version of herself.

But she realized now, as she sat in her late mother's kitchen with her sister's child, that she was thirty-four years old and her last job was working at a coffeehouse. She hadn't had a meaningful relationship in a couple of years . . . or longer. Holly didn't know why nothing seemed to last with her, but there had been times in her life that it seemed easier if she just moved on instead of trying to make a bad situation better.

She was fortunate that she had managed to score the contract with ASC. She truly believed she could make it in the music industry if she kept at it, and had long ceased caring if anyone else believed it. Most people she knew would have given up if success hadn't come to them by now, but Holly was more persistent than that. Slow and steady progress, she told herself. And she had an unflappable belief in herself. How she'd managed that, Holly could not say, because most of her other beliefs were pretty flappable. But not this.

For a long time, she'd tried to make her family understand that. She looked at the empty chair at the kitchen table, near the window, her father's chair. He'd sat there every meal that Holly could remember, and she could still see him leaning over a plate of eggs, buttered toast, and crispy bacon. He would put the salt and pepper on the edge of his rubber place mat in case he needed to re-up in the course of the meal. Her father had believed in Holly's talent. He would listen to her songs and applaud. He would brag about her to his friends. "That's my little songbird right there," he'd say, pointing proudly to Holly. "She might sing at the Opry someday."

Holly's mother, on the other hand, thought Holly was a flake and was hiding behind her dream of being a successful songwriter. "People get jobs," she'd say when she lectured Holly, which had been regularly. "Hannah knows that. Hannah applies herself. Why you don't, I can't begin to understand. I don't know what we're going to do with you, Holly."

Her mother had never accepted that things didn't come as easily to Holly as they did to Hannah. For starters, dyslexia had made school hard for Holly—her grades had been solid Cs and never better than a B. Except in music. In music class, she had excelled.

Holly had never measured up in her mother's eyes, and moreover, somewhere along the way, she'd begun to fear she *couldn't* measure up, that maybe her mother was right; maybe she really wasn't as smart as Hannah. Well, she was determined to make this contract work, and to use this time at the homestead to write some great songs. And someday, when she heard her songs playing on the radio, she'd look up and smile and say, "See, Mom? I told you I could do it."

Later that morning, Holly put Mason down for a nap under a blanket and wandered about the house. She hadn't really looked around yet, other than to pick up toys and vacuum a little. She hadn't been out here since her mother had died. That was something else that had made Hannah angry, that Holly had not been helping with the property, or done anything to probate the will. When Holly had tried to explain to Hannah how difficult it was for her to come back here, Hannah had dismissed her feelings as irresponsibility. Okay, she'd own up to some irresponsibility, but she really had found it painful, and she wished her big sister understood that.

Holly opened the door to her mother's room. It had been left like it was the last day she'd lived in it, except that the bed had been made. Empty pill bottles were still standing like soldiers on her vanity, and there was a selection of books on her nightstand by her favorite authors: Carl Hiaasen, Robert Ludlum, and Debbie Macomber. It was weird to see her mother's clothes still hanging in her closet, as if she would be back to wear them sometime soon. Her shoes were scattered on the closet floor as if she'd just kicked them off. Someone really needed to do something about her things.

The blinds had been drawn and the drapes pulled, but her mother had always liked them open, so Holly opened them.

She walked on, to the room she'd occupied through high school. Her mother had converted it to a sewing room when Holly had left for her short-lived stint in college, so it didn't really resemble anything in Holly's memory. There was a daybed shoved against one wall with a few bolts of material stacked neatly on one end.

In the closet was a stack of her school yearbooks and the dress she'd worn to Hannah's wedding. She'd hated that dress. It was green with poofy sleeves, exactly the type of thing Hannah would love and Holly would hate. In a moment of frustration with Hannah, Holly pulled the dress down from its hanger and tossed it on the bed. Someone needed to do something, and it occurred to Holly that the someone was her.

Through a door next to the closet was the bathroom she'd shared with Hannah. It had an old claw-foot tub and a black-and-white-tiled floor. The vanity mirror was chipped and tarnished, and the twin sinks looked like big clamshells. Holly could remember the school mornings she and Hannah had stood side by side, brushing their teeth and trying not to laugh at each other. The bathroom was as spotless as it had been in their youth. Holly guessed Hannah had stayed here a night or two after the funeral and had kept it nice and neat.

Another door adjoined Hannah's room to the bathroom. Of course Hannah had been granted the best room with the window seat. Holly had always loved this room with its high Victorian ceilings and its bay windows and its yellow wallpaper with tiny little green vines and white flowers trailing up to the crown molding. Her mother had given Hannah this room because, she'd said, Hannah kept her room so clean and her grades high, whereas Holly hadn't been quite as neat, and of course there were those pesky Cs that had determined her privileges.

Holly was sleeping here now, however, as it was next to the nursery.

The rose-colored bedspread matched the drapes. On the dresser was an assembly of Hannah's school awards and trophies. She'd been second in tennis, first in track, and first in debate for three years in a row. And there was the tiara that she'd worn as homecoming queen her senior year.

Holly put it on and looked at herself in the mirror. The day after Hannah had been named homecoming queen, she'd put it on Holly's head. Holly had been so thrilled that she'd danced around with it, being silly. But then she'd made the mistake of wearing it down the stairs, her arms extended, queenlike. Her mother had walked out of the kitchen to see her, and her face had darkened. "Take that off," she'd said ominously. "That belongs to Hannah. You aren't ever going to be no homecoming queen, so take it off."

"Mom, I gave it to her," Hannah had said from behind Holly.

"Take it *off*," her mother had said again, and Hannah had wordlessly accepted the crown from Holly and retreated upstairs. Holly's mother, apparently satisfied that Holly would not usurp the throne of her favorite daughter, had walked back into the kitchen. And Holly? She wasn't entirely certain, but she thought she'd written a song in three-quarter time: *The summer night feels heavy when the flashing lights come round to say / Mom ain't coming home tonight, no, Mom ain't coming home* . . . Holly laughed softly at her teenage self. If you can't beat them, kill them off in a song.

She took the crown off her head, gathered the rest of Hannah's trophies and medals and symbols of success, and walked back through the bathroom, depositing them all on top of the bridesmaid's dress on the daybed. Today was feeling like a good day to clean house.

Holly walked on to the nursery where Mason was sleeping. She'd moved the crib away from the toy boxes her father had built, which still held their Barbies and other dolls. When they were girls, Hannah and Holly had spent hours playing in this room. They'd been the best of friends, inseparable, playing Xena, Warrior Princess, commanding armies of dolls.

When did we lose each other? How did I lose you now? Where are you?

She moved quietly down the hall and downstairs to the kitchen, where she found a box of big black trash bags. She went back upstairs and walked into her mother's room and closet, and began to take her clothes off the hangers, one by one, pausing to put her mother's favorite sweater to her face.

It was time.

She stuffed the clothes into the trash bags. And it was time to stop letting the past define Holly, to stop allowing Hannah's many successes to shine over her. It was time to do something with the homestead, starting with a good cleaning of this house, top to bottom.

She'd put all her mother's clothes and shoes into bags, and had piled them on the bed to be hauled downstairs, when a sound caught her attention. Holly stilled; it sounded as if someone were on the porch. Her heart leapt; she checked on Mason, then hurried to her room to grab her cell phone and the fire poker she was keeping at her bedside. She cautiously headed downstairs, her finger poised to hit 911 in an instant if she needed to.

Wyatt had just pried his muddy boots off his feet—the result of trying to fix a spigot at a stock tank—when his phone rang. He eyed the caller ID suspiciously. He didn't recognize the number, and unknown numbers were never good news. It was usually someone wanting money or some good-hearted woman wanting to "check on him."

Then it occurred to him that it could be someone about the latest batch of checks he hadn't gotten around to signing, and it would be just like Linda Gail to give out his personal number. Wyatt answered it.

"Hey, Wyatt."

Wyatt recognized Sheriff Pickering's voice immediately. He and the sheriff were friendly due to a few sizable donations Wyatt had made to Pickering's reelection campaign. Wyatt didn't have any political leanings anymore—that would require more thought than he had in him—but he figured the donations would be good for something. "Sheriff Pickering, how are you?" he asked. "What's up?"

"I'm good. But I got an emergency call from your neighbor up there."

"Who, the Russells?"

"Nah. Someone out at the Fisher place. Seems like your cows got out again and they've wandered up to the house. I guess one of them was feeding on some plants she had on the porch and she thought it was a burglar."

"A burglar," he said, thinking that was about the dumbest thing he'd ever heard. A burglar worthy of his profession would not make the sort of noise a cow made. But never mind that—Wyatt and Jesse had fixed that fence this morning, and this news annoyed Wyatt. He'd never had so much trouble with a fence as he was having on that northeast side. Fortunately, Jesse Wheeler was still here, rummaging around in Wyatt's kitchen like he lived here.

"I sent a deputy out there, but she's holed up inside while your stock grazes the yard."

"I saw that yard earlier. I'm doing her a favor."

Pickering chuckled. "Just get your cows out of there, will you?"

Wyatt sighed. These were the moments he wished for a good cow dog instead of the lump of black lying on the floor, head between his paws. "I'll head over there. Thanks for letting me know." He hung up, pulled on his boots again, and looked at Milo. "Are you going to help me? Or are you going to make matters worse?"

Milo lifted his head and thumped his tail against

the floor. "That's what I thought," Wyatt groused, and walked on to the kitchen. "That was the sheriff," he announced to Jesse, whose head was in the fridge. "That fence didn't hold. The cows are out."

"No way," Jesse said, and stood up. He had a sandwich in one hand, a beer in the other.

"Help yourself," Wyatt said.

Jesse grinned. "Thanks," he said, and bit off half the sandwich.

It was easy to see why women of all ages fell for Jesse Wheeler. He had movie-star good looks with that honey-streaked brown hair and soft green eyes. His grin was irrepressible and a little infectious. If Jesse could act, he could make some money with that face and that build. Too bad he couldn't act.

"No way that fence busted out again," Jesse said thoughtfully through a mouth full of bologna sandwich. "That doesn't make sense."

"No, it doesn't. Last thing I want is to drive back over there, but I've got cows grazing the lawn of the Fisher house and need to round them up. Can you give me a hand?"

Jesse glanced at his watch and then winked at Wyatt. "I guess Kourtney can wait another hour." He guzzled the beer, took another bite of sandwich, and threw the rest at Milo, who caught it in midair and wolfed it down. "Let's roll," he said, and brushing his hands against his jeans, he walked out of the kitchen.

They put the tools in the back of the pickup and barreled up the caliche road to the Fisher house. Cattle were standing on the road and in the yard, grazing contentedly. A patrol car was parked on the drive and the deputy was leaning against the hood, chatting on his cell phone as casually as if he were in a lounge chair by the pool.

Wyatt parked the truck; Milo jumped over the side and went trotting through the cows, his nose to the ground. Absolutely no help at all, that dog. Wyatt and Jesse got out and surveyed the scene.

The deputy closed his phone. "These your cows?" he asked.

"Yep."

"Can you take it from here?"

"Yep."

"Great." The deputy waddled on back around to the driver's side. The car listed when he got in and kicked up a cloud of dust as he sped up the road.

"Let's go have a look at the fence," Jesse said.

They started up the hill to where the fence could not be mended, and there it was, a huge hole where the damn cows had marched through like they'd been invited to dinner. Jesse crouched down and studied the wire. "Someone's messed with this," he declared, and pointed to where it looked like there was a clean cut through the wire.

"You sure we didn't do that?" Wyatt asked, squinting at it. They'd cut some wire today as they restrung the fence, but this was cut in an odd place.

"Sure of it." Jesse stood up. "Now, who'd want to come cut a newly strung fence, I ask you? That's just all kinds of wrong."

Wyatt agreed, but they had the more immediate problem of getting the cattle through the fence and back onto his property. "Let's get the cows," he said, and turned back to the house and his truck. When he did, he noticed that Holly Fisher had come out on her porch with her baby boy. She was wearing a dress, a short blue thing with thin little shoulder straps, that skimmed her thighs. A nice pair of thighs at that. Holly Fisher had an attractive set of legs on her.

Beside her, Milo was laying on the porch like he lived there, his pink tongue hanging to the porch slats. The baby was grabbing up handfuls of him and pulling his ears, but Milo just panted. Wyatt saw the reason why—Holly Fisher was holding what looked like a generous-sized cookie in her hand.

"Well, now, who have we here?" Jesse asked, and pushed back the brim of his trucker hat to have a better look.

Wyatt didn't answer; he was striding down the hill. Holly's strawberry blonde hair was clipped to the back of her head. She was wearing a necklace around her neck, and Wyatt was surprised that now he was noticing that she had a very nice neck, because his radar for all things feminine had been dead for a long time.

"We meet again," she said cheerfully when Wyatt and Jesse walked up to the bottom step of her porch. She took a bite of the cookie.

Wyatt didn't say anything. He'd zeroed in on the fact that the necklace, which was hanging just above a fairly enticing cleavage, was the yin and yang symbol. Why did people have to announce their spiritual beliefs? *Taoism, noun. Chinese philosophy advocating humility and religious piety.* Whatever. That sort of thing meant nothing to him anymore. He had no belief system.

"I sure haven't had the pleasure," Jesse said, and shifted slightly, knocking Wyatt with his elbow.

"This is Jesse," Wyatt said, hooking a thumb at his friend. "Sorry about the cows. Got a bad fence up there. Milo, get off the porch."

"He's okay," Holly said. "And I gathered as much about the cows." Her baby gurgled happily at Milo and grabbed his ear. "I'm Holly Fisher," she said to Jesse, and smiled like all women smiled at Jesse, yet Wyatt detected something a bit tired about her smile.

"Pleasure to meet you," Jesse said.

"I'm sorry I called nine-one-one," Holly said. A strand of her hair had escaped the clip and was drifting down her temple. "I heard something awful and thought someone was trying to break in." She smiled self-consciously and took another bite of the cookie.

"If there's any damage, I'll take care of it," Wyatt said. "Milo, come off that porch." Milo wasn't going anywhere. He rolled onto his side and held up one paw, like he thought the baby was going to rub his belly for him.

"I can't imagine there's any damage to this old place," Holly said, and bent at the waist to look around the side of the porch before popping the last bite of cookie into her mouth. "I think one of them ate a couple of dead palm trees."

"*Ba ba baaaaAAA,*" the baby said.

Jesse crouched down beside the steps. "Hey, kiddo," he said, grinning at the baby. The baby grinned right back and slapped his palms on Milo's side. Even that little stinker was captivated by Jesse's charm. "What's his name?" Jesse asked Holly.

"Mason."

When she spoke, Mason looked up at her and gurgled. Holly smiled in a way Wyatt wished every child got to see from someone.

"So, where did you come from, Holly Fisher?" Jesse asked.

She smiled and folded her arms. "Venus."

"Venus," Jesse repeated, nodding. "Did you just fly in?"

Holly grinned. "Limped in is more like it. Actually, I came in from Austin, but I grew up out here."

"Oh yeah?" Jesse was undoubtedly wondering why she wasn't in his database of women. "Where'd you go to school?"

"Cedar Springs."

"Get out," Jesse said, and shifted forward, propping one foot on the bottom step of her porch. "I went to Cedar Springs. What year did you graduate?"

"Ninety-five."

"No kidding? I graduated in ninety-eight. You know what? I remember you."

Holly laughed at that. "I don't think so."

"Tennis, right?" he said.

"No."

"Basketball?" Jesse asked, undaunted.

Holly giggled; she was enjoying it. "No. Band." Jesse's face fell, and Holly laughed roundly. "That's right, I'm a band nerd." She seemed kind of proud of it. She had a very easy way about her that Wyatt liked.

What the hell? What was with all this noticing all of a sudden? It made Wyatt feel uncomfortable. He was ready to be done with this job and get back to his porch and his beer and his word of the day. "We'll get the cows out of here and get the fence fixed. Milo, *come*," he said sternly, and Milo hopped up, toppling the baby on his rump in his eagerness to run down the stairs. Wyatt started for his truck.

"Oh, hey, Wyatt," she said.

He paused and glanced over his shoulder.

"Thanks for the washcloth tip. It worked!"

Of course it did, but she said it like the mystery of the universe had been revealed. He nodded, gave her a short wave, and walked on.

"Thanks!" he heard Holly call again.

Wyatt got a pair of long sticks out of the bed of the truck to herd the cows, one for him, one for Jesse. When he turned around, Jesse was standing there, frowning disapprovingly. "What?" Wyatt asked, and handed him the stick.

"Where'd you go to charm school, anyway?" Jesse asked as he took the stick.

"What the hell are you talking about?"

"You know what I am talking about. I'm talking about how you talked to your neighbor back there. Or *didn't* talk. Just stood there looking annoyed."

Wyatt frowned and waved him off. "I *am* annoyed. We came here to get the cows off her lawn, not to stand around and chitchat. So, are you going to stand there chitchatting some more or are you going to help me?"

"Man, you are an old grump," Jesse grumbled as he walked away.

Once they got the cattle up the hill and back through the hole in the fence, they set about repairing it. Jesse was a talker, that Wyatt knew, but usually Jesse was talking about himself, and Wyatt could easily tune it out. Not today. Today Jesse was analyzing him. "I'm honestly amazed that you don't have a line of single women right up to your door, Casanova."

"Shut up," Wyatt said.

"Look, Wyatt, it's none of my business—"

"You're right, it's none of your business—"

"—but it's been a couple of years now since Macy left."

Just hearing the words made Wyatt cringe inwardly.

"What are you going to do, live up here all by yourself with a FedEx box and a volleyball for a friend?"

Wyatt paused and glanced curiously at Jesse. "Come again?"

"You know," Jesse said impatiently, "that movie where Tom Hanks gets stuck on a deserted island."

"Oh. Right." Jesus, now he was talking movies. Wyatt turned his attention back to the fence.

"My point is, you're not getting any younger," Jesse continued. "Especially living out here all by yourself."

Wyatt did not care to be reminded that he was getting older; he'd be forty in a few months. "Now, when did you go and get your license to hand out free advice?" Wyatt asked. "I seem to recall a time in your life that you weren't exactly sociable."

"Hey," Jesse said, pointing a finger at him. "That was a bad breakup with Molly. You know how bad that was."

Wyatt smiled wryly. "Oh, I know. Which is why I find it a little odd that you're feeling so good about things now that you can weigh in on *my* life."

"I guess because I know what I'm talking about,"

Jesse said amicably. "I'm just saying, you're wasting some of your prime daylight pining away for someone who's never coming back."

Wyatt bristled at that. He wasn't waiting for Macy; he was just trying to live without her, that was all. It didn't help that when he went to pick up his daughter, he had to see Macy looking so beautiful and happy and, God help him, pregnant again. Pregnant women did something to him, pushed a little button that made him feel all gooey inside. "I know she's not coming back. And if I need any more advice, Ann Landers, I'll give you a call."

"I wouldn't mind that call one bit," Jesse said. "And even though you've been plain hateful to me on occasion, I'd be happy to take you out on the town and buy you a couple of beers at the Rawhide," he said, referring to a gin joint on the edge of Cedar Springs. Jesse picked up the tools and tested the barbed wire once more. "Nothing's getting through here," he said, and the two of them started down the hill. "I'm not kidding, Wyatt. I'd be happy to help you get back to living again."

"Will you please put a cork in it? I'm fine. I don't need your help or your advice. I am perfectly happy."

"Now, see," Jesse said, pointing at him, "you're acting like that because you know I'm right—well, look here. She just couldn't keep away from that charm of yours, could she?"

Wyatt looked up. Holly had come back outside without the baby. "Hi," she called as she walked down the steps of the porch. "I forgot to tell you that the cows were coming in from over there, too." She pointed down the fence line.

Wyatt peered past the windmill and water tank. He could see a bit of barbed wire curling away from the pole. *Damn it.* He stalked forward to have a look, skirting around the tank. The wire had in fact been cut here, too. He pivoted around and walked back to the drive. "Anyone been out here lately?" he demanded, and noted, for the record, Jesse's withering look.

Holly looked surprised. "What do you mean? I've been here—"

"Besides you."

"I think my friend is asking if anyone has come out to work around the fence," Jesse explained politely.

Holly shook her head, and that strand of golden hair drifted across her cheek and eye. "Just the Russells."

"The Russells," Wyatt repeated, and looked at Jesse.

"Melissa Russell was a friend of my mom's," Holly said, and brushed the strand of hair with the back of her hand away from her cheek. "She and her sons were here the same day you were here."

Jesse suddenly smiled at Wyatt, clearly delighted to hear he'd been here before.

Wyatt ignored him. "I think we should go have a chat with the Russell boys," he suggested.

"Just as soon as we fix that hole," Jesse agreed, still smirking a little.

"What . . . you think they cut the fence?" Holly asked, her pretty green eyes widening with astonishment. Why did women have to do that? Why couldn't they all be as jaded as Wyatt was? "Why would they do that?"

"Well, now, we don't know if they did," Jesse said. "But it's kind of hard for a fence to get busted out more than once a day, and definitely not in two places. And honestly, Miss Fisher . . . the Russell boys have a reputation around here."

She stared at Jesse. She blinked. And then her brows dipped. "Then you might want to look at the fence down the road a bit. When I was out with Mason this morning, I noticed another hole."

Wyatt gritted his teeth. He was going to kill those kids. Right after they fixed his fence and spit-shined his shoes. "We'll get it fixed," he said, and looked at Jesse. "Let's go." He turned back to his truck.

"What Wyatt means to say is, thank you," he heard Jesse say. "He hasn't been quite himself since that horse kicked him in the head."

Wyatt rolled his eyes, pretended he didn't hear, and got in the pickup. Milo hopped into the bed and Jesse appeared a few minutes later, tossing their tools in the bed with Milo. He climbed in the passenger side, perched his elbow on the seat back, and looked at Wyatt. "Wyatt, I'm going to tell you what no one else in town has the guts to tell you, except for maybe Linda Gail."

"Do you want a job?" Wyatt asked gruffly.

The question startled Jesse. "What?"

"A job. You know, where you get up and go somewhere and work for pay—and not on your back."

"I am not going to be offended by that," Jesse said amicably. "What sort of job?"

"Helping me," Wyatt said. He backed the truck up to turn it around. He saw Holly Fisher walking back to the old house. She was talking to the baby on her hip.

There it was again, that gooey feeling. Wyatt wondered why she was here with that baby. It seemed strange to him, out of place. She didn't even know if she had propane.

"I'm listening," Jesse said.

"This isn't a one-man operation anymore. I could use some help. I'll pay you twenty bucks an hour, but there is one condition: no talking. I mean it, Jesse. You can talk about work, but nothing else. I don't want to be hearing your opinions on every goddamn topic under the sun. Can you do that?"

Jesse laughed. "Of course I can. If you want, I won't talk at all."

"I want," Wyatt said.

"What about football?" Jesse asked. "Can we talk about football?"

Wyatt rolled his eyes. He might live to regret this, but Jesse was a good hand. He glanced in his side-view mirror and watched Holly walk up the steps and across the porch and disappear inside of that run-down house.

Yep. Those were some nice legs and, as long as he was looking, a nice, curvy rump. Wyatt was reminded of what it felt like inside to really notice a woman. It was a sudden rush of blood, a bona fide thrill, and he could feel that physical itch deep inside. It felt kind of odd to him now, he thought, as Jesse began to prattle about the Cowboys' chances this season. But his thrill felt a little off center. Wyatt used to be like Jesse, dating as many women as he could, enjoying female company like a healthy man ought to do. Then he'd met Macy, of course, and everything had changed. His life had changed. *He'd* changed. He'd fallen so hard for Macy that he'd never been that guy again. He'd quit running around and he was entirely devoted to his girl, who became his wife.

Now, two years after having his whole world smashed with life's giant wrecking ball, Wyatt was pretty sure he would never be that guy again. He sure as hell wouldn't feel that way again. These days he felt nothing but . . . old. To have this little nudge of attraction was more bothersome than inspiring, but he figured it was nothing that a beer or two wouldn't dull.

As they turned down the ranch-to-market road toward the Russell spread, Jesse was chatting enough to power a windmill, clearly ignoring Wyatt's rule. The sun was beginning to sink into the edge of the earth, and Wyatt thought of the Fisher house, which now had plenty of cow patties for that little boy to avoid. Maybe he'd go around tomorrow with some decent firewood and clean that up. That seemed a fair way to apologize for his cows grazing her grass.

Even if he had done her a favor by getting that lawn mowed.

Chapter Nine

Mason was not sleeping through the night. Holly guessed it was because he'd been bounced out of his comfortable home to strange new surroundings, and she hoped he would settle soon. But in the meantime, it was making for some very long days. A sleep-deprived baby was an unhappy baby.

Holly was exhausted, emotionally, mentally, and physically. She'd spent yesterday moving furniture around to make the house more accessible to an increasingly mobile Mason. Holly's mother had been freakishly fond of knickknacks, and Mason was managing to get his hands on each and every one; she'd ended boxing them up and hauling them out to the barn.

She'd tried to work on her music for a while, but Mason had found her sheet music again, and it was still scattered all over the front room. She was up twice with him overnight, and then was awakened at the crack of dawn by a flock of damn mockingbirds. Holly had never noticed birds chirping in Austin, but out here a full-blown chorus lived in the tree right outside her window.

Mason was still sleeping. Oh, sure, he could sleep through that ruckus, but if she played a single chord, he awoke crying.

Holly got up and made her way down to the kitchen. The flour was still sitting out on the counter from the batch of cookies she'd made a couple of days ago. She decided she would make some more. A small voice in the back of her head reminded her that her clothes were getting a little tight, but Holly didn't care. There was something about a major personal crisis that demanded a few batches of big, fat chocolate chip anti-anxiety pills.

She'd found the recipe in her mother's red-checkered Betty Crocker cookbook, her mother's kitchen bible. Stuffed in between the pages were recipes torn from magazines and written on old index cards. In those pages, Holly had found the family favorites: chili, meat loaf, chicken-fried steak, fried tomatoes, English pea salad. And then there were the sweets: banana pudding, coconut cream pie, cinnamon rolls, strawberry cake, and cherry pudding pie. All of them memories.

Holly could still see her mother in the kitchen with the cookbook, her flour-dusted finger running down the list of ingredients, her apron stretched across her belly. As Holly had never been much help in the kitchen, she felt strange being the one to wear the apron now, but she'd strapped it on like armor and started with the homemade chocolate chip cookies.

It was odd how the life she'd known was disappearing a little more each day, and in its place was Mason. She was flustered by him, frustrated by him . . . but she also marveled at him, delighted in him, and realized the afternoon when she'd made her first batch of cookies and watched him pick up the pieces with his fingers and push them into his mouth, that she was falling in love with the little guy. Of course she loved him. Mason was her nephew and she'd loved him from the beginning. But she hadn't loved him like this—not in the way that her every waking thought included him. Not in the way that made her want, above all else, to make him happy, to see him smile, to hear him laugh. She felt protective of him. Loren was way too self-centered to ever pay attention to Mason. And Hannah? Holly didn't know what she thought of Hannah anymore. She recognized that with her increasing love for all things Mason, her fury with Hannah was slowly fading.

Holly was worried about her sister. The more Holly was with Mason, the more impossible she believed it would be to leave him behind; it seemed to her that as Hannah did leave him behind, she must have been in really bad shape. *What was it?* What was it that had sent Hannah into rehab?

Holly couldn't think about that all the time. It brought her down, messed with her head, and made her music that much harder to create. And besides, she had more pressing issues, like a meeting with a lawyer this afternoon. She'd gotten the name from Melissa Russell. "If Jillian Harper doesn't know about wills, she'll know someone who does," Melissa had said.

So Holly had finally made the call she should have made months ago. And just as soon as she was through with her meeting, she'd head to the grocery story, because there was baking and cooking to be done. She made a grocery list. She needed diapers. When did kids learn how to use a toilet, anyway? Was she supposed to be doing something about that? She made a mental note to look that up.

Groceries. Milk for Mason. Peanut butter for her. More flour, more chocolate chips. And ingredients for her mother's red velvet cake—she'd been craving that. And her mother's Mexican pie casserole. Holly looked at the list and frowned. Her days of shopping at Whole Foods for organic were temporarily suspended due to her location. She would need to find an Internet café in town to check her bank balance, because there was no Internet connection here on Mars. That was because her mother had not been a fan of computers. "People spend way too much time on them," she'd said dismissively, but Holly knew she'd been intimidated by the concept of computers and the Internet. Her mother had not been the sort to own up to her fears—even the fear of dying. Peggy Fisher was always too concerned about how she appeared to the world, and a fear of dying would be perceived as weak. Holly had asked her one day if she was afraid. "Of what?" her mother had scoffed with a flick of her wrist. "Everyone has to die."

Yes, but most people didn't know when that was going to happen.

The grocery list made, the cookies baked, Holly dressed and got Mason up. She fed him baby oatmeal, which he did not like. When she'd managed to stuff as many spoonfuls down him as she thought she could get, she put him in the living room and picked up her guitar. Mason was in the living room with the train set

Holly had found in the nursery, so she got out a blank sheet of staff paper and started playing around with a melody and lyrics that had been in her head for a while.

You'll remember me the way I used to be
And you'll wonder if we could have made it work.
You'll remember me the way I used to be
Only now it won't have to hurt.

She'd just found the rhythm she was wanting when the sound of the piano startled her. Mason was standing with one foot on top of the other—one shoe missing again—and his hands on the keys, banging and laughing. He was a little round ball of drooling happiness. Holly smiled and put down her guitar. She wondered, as she stood up to fetch him, if Hannah thought about him. Did she wonder if he was okay? If he was eating? If he was walking or talking? Holly thought of all the other abandoned babies out there, all of them as cute as Mason. It was gut wrenching to think about, and for the umpteenth time Holly was glad she'd been home the day Hannah had lost her mind.

Mason banged again, then put his mouth on the keys.

"Okay, no eating the piano. Aunt Holly doesn't like touching slobber when she's working," she said lightly. "Anyway, I've got something for you right here," she added, and fetched one of seven washcloths that were in the freezer. Hopalong Cassidy had been right about that—frozen washcloths worked brilliantly for teething.

Hopalong Cassidy was a handsome muse for such a cold fish, she thought idly. She had a mental image of him standing at the bottom of her porch steps, his black hair pulled back into a little ponytail—which, much to her surprise, she'd found incredibly sexy on a Texas cowboy—and his vivid blue eyes locked on her, the shadow of a dark beard on his tanned face. He was a big man, tall and lean and muscular. He looked like he could lift the cows he was so mad at and toss them over the fence.

The first time Holly had met him, she'd been wary of him: he'd hardly said two words and had looked at her like he couldn't quite figure out who or what she was. She remembered that his jeans were so worn that they looked as smooth and fit as well as a leather glove. He could have stepped out of a Marlboro ad.

The second time she'd met him, she'd wondered who or what had planted a stick so firmly up his butt that he could hardly even speak. He'd kept staring at her, his gaze flicking over her, then looking away. Then back again. Thankfully, he'd had Jesse along to do his talking.

Jesse . . . Now, *there* was an attractive man, the type of man who would have Ossana doing backflips. But Jesse was *too* cute. Holly knew Jesse; she'd known dozens of Jesses. She'd danced with them, drunk with them, and dated more Jesses in her life than was reasonable, even for someone as perpetually single as she was. They were always drop-dead gorgeous, always charming, and always bad for you in the end.

Holly pulled Mason away from the piano and put him on the floor and handed him the frozen washcloth.

Mason bit down on it but then tossed it aside and pulled himself up on the coffee table. "Da," he said. "Da da da da." He let go of the table and stood on his own two feet, his hands out.

Holly laughed. Mason had been doing this for a couple of days now, pulling himself up and standing all by himself. And he was so proud of himself! He grinned, and Holly squatted down, holding out her arms to him. "Come on, Mase," she said. "Come on, come over to Aunt Holly."

Mason wobbled. Almost casually, he put one foot in front of the other and stepped away from the coffee table. He stood there a moment, looking almost alarmed by what he'd done.

"You can do it!" she gleefully encouraged him. "Look at you, you're doing it! You're a big boy, Mason!"

He teetered for a moment, wavering between planting himself on the worn carpet or walking, and suddenly took several steps toward Holly before falling on his rump.

"*Mason!*" Holly cried with delight. She grabbed him up and fell onto her back, holding him above her. "Mason, you *walked*! You walked, you *walked*! I am so proud of you!" She gathered him to her in a big bear hug. Mason giggled and tucked up under her arm as she rolled around the floor with him.

Holly sat up and put Mason on his feet, letting him hold on to the tips of her fingers before slowly pulling one hand away. She hopped up and was backing up, pulling that last finger away from him, when someone knocked at the door. The sound of it knocked Mason off his game; he fell onto his rump. "Bubby dee," he said.

"Bubby dee is right," Holly said, and leaned around to look out the window. Speaking of the Marlboro Man, there he was on the porch, his weight on one hip, his arms folded across his chest as if he didn't want to be on her porch at all, and his dog standing by his side. "Why?" Holly muttered, and walked to the door. She opened it and stared through the screen. "Hello, Wyatt. Are the cows out again?"

"No. I'm sorry to bother you, and I won't keep you. But I brought you some firewood."

"Firewood?" Holly didn't know what to think about that. "You brought me firewood?" Curious, she opened the screen door a little to see him better. He'd been working, obviously. A sheen of perspiration covered his skin.

His dog instantly stuck his muzzle into the crack, sniffing in the direction of Mason. "Milo, sit," Wyatt said sternly, and the dog sat. But his tail was wagging furiously, and he was grinning at Mason. "You don't have any," he said, his gaze still on the dog.

"Pardon?"

"Firewood," he said, and lifted his gaze to hers.

His eyes really were an unusual color of blue. Cobalt blue, she thought. *His eyes the color of a blue jay's breast, his smile as warm as a soft caress . . .*

"You said you didn't have any, and that green wood might have smoked you out of your house. I've got plenty, and we were heading over here anyway, so I stacked it by the shed. It's probably enough to get you through winter."

He'd brought her enough wood for winter? Someone had been stacking firewood outside and she hadn't known it? That didn't exactly make her feel warm and fuzzy; it made her feel entirely too vulnerable. First cows, now this.

"Wow," she said. "I didn't know anyone was around. I didn't hear anything. I wonder what else I haven't heard out here."

"Hard not to hear things out here," he said. "Sound carries." He pulled the tail of his shirt from the waist of his jeans and used it to wipe his face. Holly saw his abdomen, lean, with a row of tight muscles.

Wyatt paused to give her a look.

Holly realized she was staring. *Whoa.* "That's right neighborly," she said in an exaggerated Texas accent. "But you didn't need to go to any trouble." Mason suddenly stuck his head through her legs, and Milo began to whimper, wanting at him. Holly picked the boy up.

"It wasn't any trouble," Wyatt said. "You'll need it in a few weeks, and anyway, we brought the Russell boys down to fix the fence, so . . ." He shrugged and tucked his shirt into the waist of his jeans again.

"You brought the Russell boys here?" Holly asked, and looked past Wyatt as Mason started to squirm in her arms. A whole army had been tramping about outside and she'd been oblivious. Holly could see Jesse down by the windmill, leaning up against the truck. Two younger men were working on the fence. Mason pushed against her shoulder. "Da," he said, and Holly put him down. "So it really was the Russell boys?" she asked as Mason crawled away.

"It was them," Wyatt said, and glanced back over his

shoulder where they were working. "Dumb kid stuff," he said, which she supposed was his explanation for it. "When I'm done with them, they won't be bothering the fences out here or anything else out here." His gaze flicked over her body, taking her in. She'd dressed in jeans, a white T-shirt, and an old bomber jacket she'd found at a thrift shop. She'd pinned some of her mother's old costume jewelry brooches on it. "Mrs. Russell, she's a nice lady, but she's got two of the orneriest boys in Cedar County. They're going to fix a few fences, and then they're going to clean up the cow dung from your yard, and then they are going to clean my boots."

Holly laughed.

Wyatt didn't. "You think I'm kidding."

She grinned. "No, actually, I'm quite sure you're not."

His gaze flicked over her again.

"Hey, can I ask you something?" she asked. "Do you ever smile?"

He looked surprised.

"You know . . . just smile," she said, smiling playfully at him.

"Not much," he admitted.

"Didn't think so." She chuckled.

Wyatt appeared completely disconcerted and looked down at his feet.

"Thank you for the firewood," she said. "That was really nice of you."

He nodded. "Hey, there, buckaroo," he said.

Mason had returned, this time with the washcloth he'd thrown down earlier. He was standing at the door with one hand on the frame, the washcloth in his mouth. Holly smiled sheepishly. "See? I told you it worked. It's really been a lifesaver, so thank you for that. It's funny, isn't it? You've been all kinds of help to me this week, and I don't even remember your last name."

"Clark," he said, and winked at Mason.

Mason grinned. "Bah."

"Do you have any kids, Wyatt?" Holly asked, opening the door a little more, suddenly curious about him.

"Stay," Wyatt said, and the dog, quivering with self-restraint, remained seated, his eyes trained on Mason and the washcloth, one long string of drool hanging from his muzzle. "I've got one, like you."

Like you. Holly didn't have any kids; she had Mason, who wasn't even remotely hers, although he was feeling more like hers each day. *Like you.* Those two words, so innocently spoken, made her feel oddly guilty, as if she were lying to this man. How she would ever tell anyone the truth? How long would this go on before Mason really *was* hers?

"How old is Mason?" Wyatt asked, and squatted down beside the dog before Mason.

"He, uh . . . he turned one a few days ago." She felt another pang of guilt. She'd bought a cupcake. There was no cake, no birthday balloons, nothing to mark the first year. Holly didn't know how to mark it. Balloons for a party of one seemed so sad.

"Bah bah bah bah bah," Mason said.

Wyatt grinned at that, and Holly was startled by how easy his smile was. It creased his face and made his eyes shine; he looked like a different man altogether. He looked like a man who was used to smiling instead of the aloof stranger she'd thought him to be up until this very moment. "Well, now look at that. You *do* smile."

He glanced up at her. "On rare occasions."

"And a joke!" Holly laughed. Her muse was suddenly becoming more interesting, and as his smile deepened she saw a very attractive and approachable man. "Hey . . . you want a cup of coffee?" she asked.

He shook his head. "No, thanks. Gotta make sure the boys are working."

"Are you sure? I've got cookies," she said.

He looked like he was about to shake his head again, but the word *cookies* gave him pause. "What kind?"

She grinned and held open the screen door. "Chocolate chip. My mom's recipe. Mexican vanilla is the key, you know."

"I didn't know that." He glanced back at the men, then at her, and shrugged lightly. "Okay. Thanks," he said, and looked down at his dog. "Stay," he commanded him, and stepped across the threshold.

He looked around the living area, cluttered with toys and music. Holly's guitar case was open on the couch, and various Little People figures were lying like fallen soldiers on the blue velvet. The train set had been dismantled and reconstructed in a way only a one-year-old could. Wyatt doffed his hat and held it in both hands.

"How old is your child?" she asked, gesturing to the kitchen and moving that way.

"Grace," he said, and his smile was automatic and irrepressible. "She's fourteen months."

Holly grabbed two mugs from the cabinet. She

poured two cups of coffee and slid one across the breakfast bar to Wyatt, then placed the last of the cookies in front of him. "Toddlers are so . . . exhausting," she said.

Wyatt smiled. "They are certainly that." He picked up a cookie.

A question that had been nagging Holly suddenly presented itself in her thoughts. "Are kids supposed to have vaccinations when they are one? Or have they had them all by then?"

Wyatt said nothing at first, but slowly lifted his gaze to hers and looked at her strangely as he munched the cookie. Upon seeing his expression, Holly realized that she'd revealed too much and laughed self-consciously. She should know the answer to that question. "Yes, that was a dumb question," she said, and waved a hand. "Sorry." She picked up a cookie.

Wyatt put down his coffee mug and regarded her dubiously, and she didn't blame him. "Mason has a pediatrician, doesn't he?"

"He does," she said, nodding with confidence she did not feel. "The thing is . . . Mason is my nephew," she said, trying to sound nonchalant. "And I don't know for sure what shots he's had."

Wyatt looked at Mason, then at Holly, but his expression had changed. He looked suspicious.

"My sister . . . who is his mother . . . she had to go away unexpectedly. She left Mason with me." That sounded even worse. Holly's mind was whirling, her thoughts a confused mess. She hadn't exactly worked out how to explain her situation to strangers. But she saw something in Wyatt—something in his gaze—that made him seem oddly approachable. "You want to know the truth?"

"I would," he said.

"Okay." She drew a breath. "My sister didn't just leave Mason with me, she actually . . . sort of abandoned him." Her voice sounded bitter to her own ears, but at the same time something was opening up inside her. Maybe it was the need for someone, anyone, to understand she'd been dealt a very unfair hand. Maybe it was just the presence of an adult. Whatever it was, words were suddenly tumbling out of her mouth. "It wasn't 'sort of.' She dumped him. She dumped him and didn't tell me where she was going or how long she'd be gone, much less if he needed vaccinations, or what he ate, or anything else for that matter, and I . . . I was just wondering." There was no way to sugarcoat it, no way to make it sound less dysfunctional and repulsive than it was.

Wyatt looked shocked. His gaze moved searchingly over her, looking for signs, she imagined, that she was a true nut job. *I eat my steak with a big fat spoon, wait till dawn and bark at the moon . . .*

"That sounds . . . intense," he said. "Are you . . . are you okay?"

"Yes," Holly said. It was remarkable that this man she hardly knew was asking if she was okay, when her own sister hadn't bothered to check in. "And thank you for asking. We're both okay, me and Mason, but my sister obviously has some issues that I didn't . . . I didn't see." She still didn't see them. She wasn't sure she'd ever understand Hannah's issues. "But I wasn't sure about the vaccination thing."

Wyatt looked at Mason. "Yes. Babies need more vaccinations when they turn one."

Holly was afraid of that. "Then I guess I better do something about it," she said, sounding more chipper about it than she was. "Mind if I ask which doctor your daughter sees?"

"Martin," he said. "But surely you can find out who's been seeing Mason."

"Well, that's the other thing," she said, frowning a little. "Mason's father is in Costa Rica, and I don't have anyone to call to get that information. And besides, I should have a doctor out here. I was living in Austin in a small apartment when this happened, and it wasn't big enough for me and Mason, so I came out here where we'd have space, and I think I'll be here a little while because I really need to do something about this old homestead." That was the first time she'd actually admitted it to herself. She could be out here for a long time.

"What do you mean?" Wyatt asked. His deep blue gaze was intent on her now, and it gave her a funny little shiver.

"Just that it's been sitting here empty since my mom died," she said. What he must think of her! Mothers dumping babies, aunts living off peanut butter, and wondering when babies got vaccinations, and hoping to sell off the birthright.

But Wyatt didn't seem particularly appalled, just curious. "What do you want to do with it?"

"Sell it," she said. "I don't think Hannah has any more desire to live out here or take care of it than I do." At least she'd thought that. She had no idea what Hannah desired anymore. "Hopefully I can get enough for it to take care of Mason for as long as I need to do that."

"You'd get quite a lot for this place," he said as he polished off his cookie.

"Really?"

"I'd guess millions," he added, and picked up the coffee mug and drank.

Holly gasped. *"Millions? Are you kidding me?"*

He smiled at her surprise. That was two Marlboro Man smiles in one day, which made the day a whole lot sunnier. "Austin is growing in this direction. People want land. You could probably hold out for as much as six or seven million. Or you could avoid putting it on the market and sell it to a willing investor for a little less."

Holly gaped at him. She had had no idea the land was worth so much! She'd heard her father complain about what a money sink it had been for so many years that she'd just assumed it was a financial drain. *"Wow."* Hannah would be shocked . . . or maybe Hannah knew. Maybe that's why she was so angry when their mother had left it all to Holly.

"Thanks for the cookie and coffee," Wyatt said. "I've got to get back to work." He picked up his hat from the counter.

"Bubbadi bubbadi," Mason said. He'd made his way around to Wyatt's leg. *"Bubbadi bubbadi."*

Wyatt smiled down at him. "You're gonna make a good cowboy someday, just like Gracie," he said, and started back through the living room.

"That's a pretty name," Holly said, following him. "Hey, here's an idea . . . Maybe we could have a play date sometime," she suggested. "I could bring Mason over to play with Grace."

Wyatt hesitated at the door. "Gracie doesn't live with me."

"Oh."

Wyatt opened the door.

"Wait," Holly said. "We could at least exchange numbers. You know, in case your daughter comes to visit. I'll jot down my number."

Wyatt seemed reluctant. He looked out to where the Russell boys were working. "I don't have Gracie out here much."

"Listen, I'm not going to stalk you or anything," Holly said with a lopsided grin. "But Mason and I are stuck out here, and if there is ever a time we might let them play, that would be great, that's all. If not, that's okay, too . . . I mean, I totally understand, but it would be great if Mason could have some social acquaintances." She was begging, she realized, but she couldn't let even a hint of a play date for Mason go without at least trying.

Wyatt looked down the road again. He looked antsy.

"I'll just jot down my number," she said again, and hurried to the little desk where her mother's bills were neatly stacked.

"Dubby dubby dubby day," Mason said from his place at the couch. "*Dubbydubbydubbyday,*" he said more earnestly.

Wyatt looked back at him.

Mason must have liked Wyatt because he suddenly let go of the couch and waddled three steps toward Wyatt before falling on his bottom.

"Mason!" Holly cried with delight. "You did it again!"

"He'll be everywhere in a few days," Wyatt said. "Do you have a baby walker?"

Holly shook her head, but she was adding that to the shopping list. "I need to get some of those gates, too—you know, the kind to block doors."

Wyatt smiled a little at that. "I know," he said, and held her gaze a moment.

"Here," Holly said, and handed him a yellow Post-it with her cell phone number written on it. "Just in case," she said again, and wished she'd stop repeating herself.

Wyatt slipped the Post-it in his pocket. "You have a good day," he said, and opened the screen door. He walked outside, whistling for his dog.

Holly watched him walk down the porch steps. "Thanks for the firewood!" she called after him. He gave her one of his little waves behind his head and sauntered down to where the boys were working, Milo trotting alongside him.

Holly slowly closed the door, peeking out around the edge of it once more to see him. When she turned around, Mason had her purse. She grabbed it from his hands and looked inside for one of his favorite things: her car keys. As she might have guessed, they were gone.

The intriguing cowboy was forgotten for the moment.

Chapter Ten

Her number burned a hole in Wyatt's pocket all afternoon. He wished he didn't have it; he didn't like even thinking about it. In fact, having it made him so annoyed with himself that he worked the dog out of the Russell boys and turned a deaf ear to their protests at picking up cow patties.

"You're in a mood," Jesse observed casually.

Wyatt glared at him and moved on to the next task. He kept picturing the Fisher house with the baby stuff and the sheet music scattered about. He'd heard the guitar when he'd walked up to the house and had been mildly captivated by the melody. She was good. She was really good. He had been thinking about how good she was and then she'd opened the door and the smell of cookies had assaulted him. It was definitely an assault—he hadn't had a good chocolate chip cookie in about a hundred years.

Jesus, God, and Mary, it annoyed him to no end that he had been lured inside by a chocolate chip cookie.

At home, after a chattering Jesse had taken his mouth and driven off in his big Ford one-ton and left him the hell alone, Wyatt took Holly's number out of his pocket and looked at it. She had an artistic hand. The six was a lot bigger than the other numbers, and he wondered idly about the significance of that. He put the number on the kitchen table next to the salt and pepper and his laptop, stared at it for a moment, then decided he'd probably lose it if he left it there. So he moved it to the old white Frigidaire and tacked it up with a magnet.

It was the only thing on his fridge, a stark square of yellow against faded white: *Holly 555-2609.*

Holly.

He thought about Mason. That fat, happy little boy was about as cute as he could be, and Wyatt couldn't help but wonder about the mother who had left him. He tried to imagine a circumstance in which Macy would do that, and thought that even if she were drawing her last breath, she wouldn't let Grace out of her sight.

The good news for the day was that Wyatt had learned that Holly intended to sell. And she was apparently clueless about property values. He could probably get that place for a great deal and she'd feel like she'd hit the jackpot. That alone was as good a reason as any to get the kids together. Yeah, he could get them together to play, maybe whip up some of his famous chili. *Was his chili famous anymore? Did his friends remember it? Did Macy?* Maybe steaks.

Wyatt looked at Milo. "What do you think?" he asked. Milo sighed and sank down to the floor, his head between his paws.

He thought of Grace, the most beautiful little girl

in the world. She had black hair like him, and light brown eyes that reminded Wyatt of caramel. She said *no-no* and *Dada* and *kitty*. She liked bouncy toys and Thomas the Tank Engine and Minnie Mouse.

Grace did *not* like shoes—neither did Mason, Wyatt had noticed—or the ribbons her mother insisted putting in her fine hair. When Wyatt had Gracie, she pulled them out and let them drop from her fingers as she tottered away. She left a trail of flotsam wherever she went, little Gracie droppings of shoes and ribbons and toys.

Wyatt loved that little girl something fierce.

He could picture her leading Mason around. He looked at the number on his fridge and saw an attractive woman with strawberry blonde hair and laughing gray-green eyes. *Holly.*

Wyatt picked up his phone and punched Macy's number. She picked up on the second ring and said breathlessly, "Wyatt? How are you?"

Every time she asked him that, he had to resist the urge to shout, *How do you* think *I am?* "Good. Did I catch you at a bad time?"

"What? No, no. We're . . ." She paused. "Right there, honey," she said to someone else. "I'm sorry, Wyatt. No, we're having a little get-together out here with some friends."

His jaw clenched tighter. That had been him and Macy once, hosting dinner parties on the boat or on the deck of the house he'd built for her in Arbolago Hills. He'd sold it when she'd chosen Finn. He could hardly stand to step inside of it then.

"So, what's up?" she asked cheerfully.

"I was wondering if I could have Gracie this week-end," he said. "I've been missing the little squirt."

"Sure, Wyatt, of course. Want me to bring her to the office Friday?"

That was their normal arrangement—Macy brought Grace, and he checked into one of those hotel suites for business travelers with a little kitchen and living area. It was easier than trying to babyproof this old house, and closer to Austin and Cedar Springs and all the things for little kids to do. "Ah . . . no," he said. "I was thinking of bringing her home."

"Where? Do you mean your ranch house?"

"That's right. My house."

Another long pause. "Are you sure? You always seem so reluctant—"

"I'm sure. I'll come pick her up—"

"No, no, you don't need to do that," Macy said. She at least understood how difficult it was for Wyatt to see her and Grace at the house she and Finn had reno-vated. They ran an animal rescue ranch specializing in larger animals. It had been written up in all the big city papers. Finn had written a book about his ordeal as a captive of the Taliban, and they'd made enough to turn that place into a little Hill Country paradise.

"I'll bring her out to you," Macy said.

"That's too far out of the way."

"It's not at all. Friday?"

"Saturday morning," Wyatt said.

"Saturday morning," Macy said. "I'll see you around nine."

"Great." He wanted to ask her how she was, how her pregnancy was coming along. "See you then," he said, and hung up. He'd learned a long time ago it was best not to ask Macy anything, because it just opened wounds that never seemed to heal.

He looked around the kitchen and living area. Yeah, he'd need to do a little work around here before he could set Gracie lose. Move stuff up out of her reach. He'd have to move the lumber for the pergola he'd started, too; or, better yet, just finish it up. He could put Jesse the magpie to work on that in the morning. Maybe that would shut him up.

Oh, who was he kidding? He didn't think even an act of God could keep Jesse Wheeler from talking.

At Daisy's Saddle-brew Coffee Shop—Cedar Springs' answer to Starbucks—Holly struggled through the door with Mason, her laptop, and the diaper bag. She made her way through the boutique part of the coffee shop: a round rack with paperbacks; a couple of counters with hand-beaded jewelry, silk scarves and embroidered linen shirts, lotions and handmade soaps; and a rack of greeting cards. On the other side of the room were some tables and chairs and big, plush armchairs where a couple of young men were sitting with their laptops open.

Behind the counter, a woman about Holly's age smiled at Mason. She had dark hair piled up on her head and held in place with a pencil. She was wearing a tank top and, over that, an apron with dancing coffee cups. "Hey, there, kiddo," she said to Mason. "Coffee, black, right?"

Mason looked away and she laughed. "What can I do for you?" she asked Holly.

"He's going to stick with juice, but I'll have a vanilla latte and, hopefully, some free Wi-Fi."

"You're in luck on both counts," the woman said. "We just got free Wi-Fi. What size latte?"

"Grande," Holly said.

"Coming up." The woman rang it up and suggested that Holly have a seat. "It's so slow, I'll bring it out to you. There's actually a play area in the corner," she said, pointing. "We've got to compete with the Baby Bowl, which just opened up."

Holly had seen that place down the street. It was one of those indoor playscapes with a bouncy castle.

She made her way to the far corner of the store, where a section had been blocked off with plastic fencing about two feet high. Inside were some big plush cubes and a table with an elaborate train track. Mason picked up a train.

By the time the woman brought the latte, Holly had checked her bank balance.

"Are you from around here?" the woman asked pleasantly, perching on the arm of one chair.

"I grew up here," Holly said. "But I've been gone for a while."

"Then welcome back! I'm Samantha Delaney, by the way," she said, and extended her hand.

"Nice to meet you, Samantha. I'm Holly Fisher. That's Mason."

"Fisher? Any kin to Peggy Fisher?"

Holly blinked with surprise. She couldn't imagine that her mother had frequented a coffeehouse. "Peggy Fisher was my mother. Did you know her?"

"Oh, I'm sorry," Samantha said. "No, I didn't know

her, but I know Hannah. She must be your sister."

Holly's heart skipped. "Hannah? Have you seen her? I mean recently?"

"Not in a few weeks. Not since she was working out here."

Working out here? When had Hannah ever worked out here? "You mean when my mom was alive," Holly suggested.

"Well, really after that," Samantha said. "She was working on the house, I think. You know . . . taking care of things that needed to be done."

Holly didn't know.

"I had the impression she was working on the actual house, like sprucing it up." She laughed. "She always looked like she'd been dragged through the attic when she came in here. I mean, you know, she's so pretty and neat, and to see her when she'd been working was funny."

What was she talking about? When had Hannah ever worked on a house? "You're talking about Hannah Drake, right?" Holly said. "About my height? Auburn hair?"

"Right," Samantha said. A man in a suit walked in the door and moved briskly to the counter. "Okay, back to the grind," she said, and winked. "No pun intended." She jogged to the counter.

Holly knew Hannah had taken care of some things—all of their mother's important papers were neatly stacked and rubber-banded together on the desk in the living room. But Holly hadn't seen signs of any other kind of work—certainly not the type that would make Hannah look like she'd been dragged through the attic. Her mother's things were just like they'd been when she'd left that homestead and gone to live with Hannah. So, what could Hannah have been doing out here?

Affair. The thought popped into Holly's head. Maybe she'd turned the old place into a love shack. Maybe that's where she was right now, in another love shack, beating Loren at his own game. Nothing would surprise Holly anymore.

Holly sipped her coffee and used the little time she had to answer some e-mails. She made arrangements to meet Quincy a week from Tuesday and made the completely outrageous promise that she'd have the first song for him then. She assured Ossana she was *not kidding,* that she really could not accompany her to The Shady Grove on Saturday night to hear Guy Clark.

When she'd finished with her e-mails, it was time to head to the attorney's office, and she gathered up her things and Mason.

The Harper & Preston Law Firm in Cedar Springs was a little less opulent than where either Hannah or Loren worked; for starters, the offices were in an old Victorian house that had been converted to house three lawyers. The reception area was in what had once been the front room. There was a desk and some up-holstered chairs that looked as if they'd been snagged from government surplus.

The receptionist sat a few feet away, perusing a Web page that looked to be about romance novels. She had a stack of them next to the computer.

Mason was making a game of waddling from one chair to the next. He was walking more and more each day. He was still unsteady, and Holly thought it must be impossible to teeter about on such tiny feet. But teeter he did, laughing every time he reached a chair, then squealing with delight when he started for the next chair.

She heard Jillian Harper before she saw her, her heels striking a decisive staccato on the porch floor before the door burst open and a woman strode through. She was tall and lean, with sharp elbows and hair pulled tightly back into a chignon. She looked to be around fifty, and was smartly dressed in a sleek, form-fitting lavender dress and carrying a black clutch that matched her black pumps. She paused at the desk to pick up a stack of pink messages.

"Your two o'clock is here," the receptionist said, and nodded in Holly's direction.

The woman turned around and gave Holly a quick once-over.

Holly smiled. She wished she'd had something a little more professional than the jeans, tunic, and boots she was wearing. She'd toyed with borrowing one of her mother's dresses, but she wasn't quite ready to take on the nineteen-seventies housewife look.

"Holly Fisher, glad to meet you. I am Jillian Harper," Ms. Harper said, marching forward, her hand extended. Her gaze drifted to Mason for a moment, then back to Holly.

"Thank you for seeing me," Holly said, and rose to her feet, hopping over the diaper bag to shake the woman's hand.

"We can go to my office," Ms. Harper said, and stood back, gesturing in that direction.

Holly scooped up Mason and the diaper bag and followed Ms. Harper down the narrow hallway to a cozy office with bay windows that looked out onto a manicured lawn. Ms. Harper had a floral couch and a hooked rug, and the room smelled rosy. The office was completely incongruous with the woman who strode around to her desk—this office was too soft for Jillian Harper.

"Well, then," Ms. Harper said as she donned reading glasses and picked up a pen, poised to write. "Tell me what brings you here."

Holly handed her a will and her mother's last handwritten letter, in which she'd left everything to Holly, and explained the circumstances of her mother's death.

Ms. Harper perused the documents. "The letter is different than the actual will in that it leaves everything to you," she said. "Is anyone going to dispute that this is authentic? Siblings? Relatives?"

Holly thought of Hannah, and of Hannah's anger over the letter. "No. I told my sister that regardless of what our mother wrote in the letter, I will split it all with her."

Ms. Harper's eyes narrowed slightly. She frowned at the letter. "We can proceed on the assumption that she won't contest it, but I think you should know that there are few things on this earth that bring out the family claws like money."

"I don't think there is enough money for her to care about," Holly said confidently.

"You just never know," Ms. Harper said shrewdly. "We will have to have this probated, of course. Do you know what that means?"

"Not exactly."

"It means that a court of law is going to have to deem this will and this handwritten codicil are valid. And then there is a period where we wait to see if there are any claims against the estate."

"Okay."

"That usually takes a little time."

"How much time?"

Ms. Harper shrugged. "I'd say two or three months, but maybe longer, given the discrepancy between the letter and the will."

"Two or three months?" Holly looked at Mason, who was sitting in her lap, chewing on her keys. She groaned.

"Is that a problem?"

"Yes," Holly admitted. "I need to access my mother's bank account." That sounded perfectly wretched. "I don't mean it like that," she said. "I have—had—a job and an income, but I got caught in a situation . . ."

Ms. Harper arched a brow. "That sounds ominous."

Holly looked at Mason. "This is my nephew," she said, and described her situation to Ms. Harper, including Hannah's resentment about the will. She told her about Loren, and how Hannah had appeared at her apartment with Mason and had left him, saying she'd be back, then had disappeared, and how Loren was out of the country. She explained that she needed money for her and Mason until Hannah came back, and to make some repairs to the house.

Ms. Harper listened to it all, nodding and making notes. When Holly finished telling her everything, Ms. Harper leaned back and tapped the end of her pencil against her lips. "I'd say we need to get this will probated before your sister decides she wants to make trouble over it."

"Trouble?"

"You said she was angry about the will. If she's getting drug treatment, she will come out with a clearer head and might have a different opinion of what she wants to do about your inheritance."

Holly thought about that and shook her head. "I honestly don't think so. I mean, she doesn't need the money."

"Need rarely has much to do with it," Ms. Harper said. "Have you filed a missing-person report?"

Holly winced. "No. I should have, I know, but I feared they would take Mason from me and give him to his father."

Ms. Harper shrugged. "At this point, you'd need a judge's intervention to place him back with his father."

"I don't know," Holly said skeptically. She couldn't take that risk. "Loren is a high-powered attorney in Austin."

"Well," Ms. Harper said with a shrug of her shoulders. "My advice is the same—file a missing-person report. It will protect you if there is any trouble in probate court later. And you need to get the will probated."

"Let's just go with probating the will for now," Holly said.

"Just out of curiosity, what do you intend to do with the property?" Ms. Harper asked as she jotted down another note.

"Sell it, I think," Holly said. "My neighbor said

I could get a lot." She laughed at that. "I think he's overly optimistic, but maybe I can get a decent price."

Ms. Harper shook her head. "All of those old farmers believe that," she said. "How much did he say you could get?"

"He said five to six million."

Ms. Harper snorted. "Who is your neighbor?"

"Wyatt Clark."

Ms. Harper stopped writing and looked up. "Wyatt Clark? That's different. Wyatt knows what he is talking about. Of course, even at that price, the government is going to take a huge chunk of it, but you ought to come out good. And if you do get that, your sister is definitely going to want a piece of it."

"What?" Holly asked, skipping right over the part about how much she'd get. "You know Wyatt?"

"Oh, I know him," Ms. Harper said with a laugh. "He was married to my daughter, Macy."

Holly was shocked. Obviously, Wyatt had been married, but the coincidence was too much. "I . . . I didn't know that. Does your daughter live around here?"

Ms. Harper smiled a little. "She lives out at the Hill Country Animal Rescue Ranch. You know where that is, right?"

Holly shook her head, and Ms. Harper's eyes widened a little. "Honey, do you know anything about Wyatt Clark?"

"No. I've only met him a couple of times."

Ms. Harper put both of those sharp elbows on her desk and leaned forward. "Let me tell you something. Wyatt Clark is a good guy, and if he says you can get that for your ranch, listen to him. Better yet, let him sell it for you. He'll get you the best deal to be had."

"Wyatt Clark," Holly said.

"Wyatt Clark, the one and only," Ms. Harper said. "He doesn't get into town very often, but if he tells you that land will bring millions, you can bank on it. He was a developer for a very long time. One of the best."

"Ah," Holly said. She was shocked that the reticent cowboy who had shown up with firewood was a developer. Almost as shocked as she was that her family home could bring so much money. She was learning all sorts of surprising things today.

"Let me give you some things to look at," Ms. Harper said. "Here is the contract I use with my clients and my fee schedule. I take it you don't have the money for a retainer, so we'll work something into the agreement that I'll be paid from the proceeds of the probated will."

Holly took the papers that Ms. Harper shoved at her. She said she would call the next day after she'd looked everything over. She thanked her, picked up Mason, and left. Her mind was not on the windfall she'd just learned of, but on Wyatt Clark. He was suddenly even more interesting to her.

After a quick trip to the grocery—Holly was dying to bake her mother's red velvet cake—she headed back to the homestead. It was a twenty-minute drive from Cedar Springs, twenty minutes of miles and miles of fences and grazing cattle and dizzying thoughts of a cowboy who was much different than he appeared. And Hannah's secret life.

Holly turned in through the open gate and onto the pitted caliche road, which desperately needed to be graded, and bounced up to the house. She opened the car door and stepped out. It was one of those clear and mild fall days when there was no sound but the steady creaking of the windmill.

And Mason fussing in the back of the car.

She took him into the house and sat him in the middle of the playpen to chew on a frozen washcloth while she hauled the groceries in and put them away. When she'd finished, she looked around. What had Hannah been doing out here? The kitchen, like the rest of the house, was exactly as it had been all the years Holly had lived here. She opened some of the cabinets to assure herself of that. There was the plastic spice rack with the red tins of odd spices that Holly guessed were at least as old as she was. There were the everyday Fiestaware dishes, orange and blue and green, from which they had eaten pancakes and meat loaf and chicken-fried steaks. There were the red plastic tumbler glasses and the matching red plastic pitcher.

What were you doing, Hannah? Nothing had changed but that neat stack of papers. There was nothing else, nothing to indicate that Hannah had spent any appreciable time here after their mother had died, much less engaged in something that made her look like she'd been dragged through the attic.

Holly shrugged it off. Samantha's memory was wrong, that was all. She had Hannah confused with someone else.

Mason started to cry, and Holly put him down for a nap. She returned to the kitchen and boiled water for tea, then picked up her guitar and carried it and her tea into the living area to work on her song. She made good progress and felt good about how it was developing. She really had found her vibe out here, and thought Quincy would be pleased with what she had.

The chorus was the only thing that didn't seem right, and she messed with it awhile, finally hitting on the right cadence. When she did, she fell back on the couch in a moment of gleeful relief and promptly knocked her forgotten teacup from its precarious perch on the couch's arm. It fell to the wood floor and broke, splattering tea everywhere.

"Great," she sighed, and put aside her guitar to clean it up. She picked up the pieces and wiped up the tea, but decided, after considering the wood floor, that she really should mop. While she was at it, she'd mop the kitchen floor too. In the utility room, she opened the closet where her mother had kept the vacuum and mops and remembered that she'd thrown out the old mop head. But her mother had always kept a stack of them. Right, the storage closet on the porch. Holly went outside to check that closet.

She opened the door to the closet . . . and took a step back. There were definitely mop heads there, and bottles of bleach and laundry detergent. But there was also a litter of wine bottles. Most were empty, some partially empty, and all of them tossed haphazardly into the closet.

She stared at the bottles. It seemed absurd to her that they were here. Her mother had hated alcohol, having lived under the thumb of an alcoholic father Holly had never known. Was it hereditary? Had Hannah inherited some alcoholic gene?

However it had happened, Holly felt a little ill at discovering the evidence of her sister's addiction. The smell was overwhelming. Had Hannah driven all the way out here just to drink? And if she had, what had she done with Mason?

The Shania Twain ring tone of her cell phone startled her; she shut the closet door and ran inside to grab it up off the breakfast bar before the song woke Mason. "Hello?"

"Holly. This is Wyatt Clark," said a masculine voice with a slight drawl.

Holly was surprised to hear from him, but even more surprised by how sexy his voice was on the phone. It took a moment for her to gather her wits.

"Your neighbor," he added, as if he thought her silence indicated that she didn't know who he was.

"Yes, yes, of course! I'm just . . . How are you, Wyatt?"

"Good, thanks. As it turns out, I'm going to have Gracie this weekend. I thought maybe you could bring Mason over on Saturday."

His invitation, so unexpected, gave her an absurd little rush. "That's great. Thank you! Should I bring anything?"

"Just the boy," he said.

"Are you sure? I could make something."

"Well . . . maybe some of those cookies."

Holly grinned. "You'll be doing me a favor by taking them off my hands. What time?"

"Two," he said. "Gracie will have had her nap."

"Sounds perfect."

He gave her directions to his house and Holly hung up, ridiculously pleased that he'd invited them. She thought about his smile, how it made him look so attractive. A developer! Who would have guessed it? She wondered how often he saw his ex-wife and what their relationship was like now. Actually, she was thinking a lot about Wyatt Clark, which was a little surprising in and of itself, because a week or so ago she had thought he was about as enticing as a fence post. Holly was smiling at that when she went back outside, but her smile faded as she began to clean the wine bottles from the porch closet, counting them as she did.

Chapter Eleven

M acy was late.
    She'd called and left a message on Wyatt's cell while he'd been out feeding the horses, something about a llama needing medicine. She showed up at his place around one thirty on Saturday.

"Hey!" she said cheerfully as she climbed out of her Jeep. She was wearing jeans, cowboy boots, and a turtleneck sweater under which he could see the swell of her pregnancy beginning to show. Her hair was clipped back, away from her face. She looked to him like the spokesperson for the benefits of fresh air and sunshine, and his heart clenched a little.

"I am sooo sorry we're late," she said, stepping backward to the door to the backseat. "I told Finn I don't want any more llamas. It seems like there is something wrong with them all the time." She opened the door and ducked in to get Grace. A moment later she emerged holding Wyatt's daughter, and he could feel his smile all the way down to the tips of his toes. "Hey, baby girl," he said.

Gracie frowned at him and looked away, over her

mother's shoulder. She'd obviously been sleeping—the neck of her clothing was wet from drool. Macy had dressed her in a pretty little pink dress with bloomers, an outfit that was inappropriate for a ranch. He had some overalls he'd put her in just as soon as Macy left, and then he'd take that bow from her head and pull her hair back in a ponytail so it would stay out of her eyes.

"She's had her nap," Macy said. "But she's probably hungry."

"Come here," Wyatt said, reaching for his daughter. Grace stretched her arms out to him. When Wyatt took her from Macy, Grace laid her head on his shoulder.

Macy dipped into the backseat again and retrieved a Hello Kitty overnight bag. She smiled at her daughter and brushed a wisp of hair from Grace's eyes. "She has a new toy in her bag," she announced, smiling proudly at Grace. "A doggie. She likes to sleep with it."

Wyatt didn't tell her that when Grace was with him, she got to sleep with the real McCoy. Milo liked nothing better than a wet diaper and wouldn't think of sleeping anywhere but by her side. "Noted," he said.

Macy put her hands on her waist and peered up at him. "You look tired. What have you been up to?" she asked, as if they were nothing more than old friends. High school acquaintances, college classmates. Not husband and wife once. There was a time she'd known him better than anyone else.

"I've been mending fences," he said.

She eyed him skeptically. "Are you sleeping?"

"Macy—"

"I can't help it," she said with an apologetic smile.

"You know I worry about you, Wy. You're all alone out here. You could fall off your horse and break your neck, and who would know?"

"I'm not going to fall off my horse," he said, and despised the urge he had to touch her face just now.

She looked past him, then bent to her right and peered around him. "Wow," she said, looking around. "You've really cleaned the place up. Is that a pergola?"

"I've done a little." So he had mowed and trimmed the shrubbery. What was the big deal? "Yes, that is a pergola. I needed some shade."

"So, are you finally going to renovate this place and then sell it for a bajillion dollars?"

"Maybe."

She grinned at him. "You know, I wish you'd get into town more. People ask me about you all the time."

He just bet they did. *Gee, Macy, do you ever see that pathetic second-place finisher?* "You and Jesse Wheeler both missed your calling at being social directors," he said, and shifted Grace to his waist. "Da da da da," she said, and put her hand in his pocket.

"Jesse Wheeler?" Macy said, peering up at him now. "What's he got to do with anything?"

"Nothing. He likes to think the world doesn't turn unless he's doing the cranking. And he's doing some work around here for me."

"You're kidding!" Macy cried, and laughed. "Jesse Wheeler, what else?" She laughed again, and then nodded her approval. "Good move, Wyatt. You and Jesse will do each other a huge favor. He'll be here to haul you in if you fall off your horse, and you will keep him out of Laru's bed."

Laru Freidenburg was Macy's aunt. She was a good-looking woman in her late forties with an appetite, and it wasn't for food.

"Emma says they're an item again," Macy added. "But you know how Emma is—very good about imagining things and stating them as fact."

Emma was Macy's younger sister, and Wyatt knew exactly how she was. He knew everything about Macy and her family—he'd made them *his* family, so happy to be part of one. He was an only child whose parents spent their time traveling the country in an RV. They'd been older when they had him, and while his father had been a rancher, most of Wyatt's childhood memories were filled with quiet evenings reading books and the scent of Bengay permeating everything. Macy's family had been alive and full of laughter, in spite of their own troubles, and yes, he knew how Emma was.

"Bye-bye," Grace said, and squirmed, wanting down.

Wyatt put her down. "Well, now that you can rest easy that someone will find my carcass—"

"All right," Macy said. "I'm going, I'm going."

But as she turned away, the sound of another car caught their attention. A little red car was driving entirely too fast up the road to his house. Great. She was early.

"Who is that?" Macy asked curiously. When Wyatt didn't answer, she looked back at him.

"A friend."

"A friend? What friend?"

"My neighbor. Look, Macy, if you don't mind—"

It was too late. The red car was practically screeching to a halt in the drive, and Macy was walking toward it, her curiosity aroused. When she saw the woman inside, Macy turned around fully, her eyes wide and bright. *"Seriously?"*

"Go home, Macy," Wyatt said. "Seriously."

But Macy was grinning at him. "Are you kidding? I'm not going anywhere till I meet her."

"It's none of your business," Wyatt said.

"Oh, I know," she eagerly agreed as Holly got out of her car.

Holly looked at the two of them uncertainly. "Ah . . . hi."

"Hi," Wyatt said. She looked good. She'd worn jeans, too, the tight-leg type that rode low on her hips. She had on a long-sleeve shirt with some artsy design of crosses tucked in to her jeans and belted with a vintage-looking leather belt. She wasn't wearing boots but some funky blue sneakers.

"Well, hello," Macy said, as if she were Wyatt's mother, and walked forward, her smile big. "I'm Macy Lockhart."

"Nice to meet you. I'm Holly Fisher, and I . . . I need to get a baby out of the backseat."

"Please!" Macy said, and gestured with both hands to the car. When Holly dipped into the backseat, Macy twisted around and beamed at Wyatt, then mouthed the word *Cute.*

Go home—Wyatt mouthed right back at her.

"Baby," Grace said, grabbing on to her mother's leg and looking up at her. "Baby."

"That's right, honey, it's another baby," Macy said as Holly hauled Mason out of the backseat.

"So, who is this little guy?" Macy asked brightly,

and tickled Mason's belly. Mason did not look amused. "He's adorable!"

"Thank you," Holly said, smiling proudly. "This is Mason, and he's here for his play date."

"Oh, a *play date*," Macy said, looking meaningfully at Wyatt. "Grace will love that."

Grace would have no idea she was involved in a play date, Wyatt figured. Fourteen-month-old kids were more interested in themselves than in others.

"Baby," Grace said, pointing up at Mason. Mason leaned over Holly's arm to take a good look at Grace.

"So . . . where did you two meet?" Macy tried to sound casual, but Wyatt knew she was about to bust with excitement. He knew she'd never stopped caring for him—was no longer in love with him, maybe, but she cared—and she had made it known on more than one occasion that she hoped he would meet someone and get past their ill-fated marriage.

But Wyatt didn't need his ex-wife vetting his play dates. "Good-bye, Macy," he said, moving next to her and touching her elbow with one hand as he pointed to her car with the other. "Don't you have a llama that needs attention?"

"No, I really—"

"Yes you do," he said firmly.

"Okay, all right, I'm leaving," Macy said cheerfully. "Call me when you are ready for me to pick up Grace. Very nice to meet you, Holly."

"You too," Holly said.

Macy kissed Grace good-bye and climbed into her Jeep. She backed away from the house and started down the long drive to the county road. Holly and

Wyatt watched her drive away. When the Jeep had dipped out of sight, Holly looked at Wyatt.

"Ex-wife," he said.

"So I gathered." She gave him a sympathetic smile but then looked at Grace, who was crouching down to pull some grass from the yard. "So this is Grace!" she said excitedly, and squatted beside her, putting Mason on his feet. The little soldier's balance had improved greatly in the few days since Wyatt had seen him, and he took several steps before he, too, crouched down to help Grace pull grass.

"I like your house," Holly said.

Wyatt didn't, not today. Today, as he looked at it through Macy's eyes, he could see just how much work it needed. "I am making some improvements," he said. He was glad that he and Jesse had at least finished the pergola.

"Hey, I brought cookies," Holly said. Mason had begun to crawl toward the drive, and Holly skipped behind him to pick him up before he reached the gravel.

"I'll get them," Wyatt said.

"In the back!" she called after him as he walked to her car, and chased after Grace, who, Wyatt noted with a smile, had already pulled the bow from her hair and let it drop in the yard. He opened the door to Holly's backseat and saw a box filled almost to the brim with some of the thickest chocolate chip cookies he'd ever seen. There were dozens, and he idly wondered how long it took to whip up a batch or twelve of them. He grabbed the box and the diaper bag, and as he was removing himself from her little car, he noticed the guitar case in the front seat.

With the diaper bag slung over his shoulder and the cookies balanced in one hand, Wyatt bent down and picked up Grace. "Come on in," he said to Holly.

She followed him inside with Mason, through the open garage door and the utility room and into the kitchen. Wyatt put the cookies down on the stained Formica counter, which was peeling in one corner. He could guess what she was thinking about the place; he'd cleaned it up, but there was no disguising the fact that it was terribly outdated.

He had an electric stove he'd used maybe twice. There was a brand-new microwave on the kitchen counter next to the old white fridge, which looked more green than white under the harsh glare of the fluorescent lighting overhead. In the breakfast nook was his table with the condiments he could not live without.

Holly looked around. "Well," she said, smiling easily. "You can certainly tell a man lives here."

"How's that?" he asked as he deposited Grace on the floor and watched her totter off.

"Not a lot of furniture," she said, putting Mason down as well. "Not a lot of kitchen stuff."

Holly walked around the kitchen bar and into the living room. Wyatt had a big leather lounger in front of a small TV, and an old couch that had once been in his office on which he occasionally took a Sunday afternoon nap while watching football. He really had no room for more than one to sit comfortably, a fact that Jesse had complained about recently. Wyatt had no inclination to get seating for Jesse, but he found himself wishing he had a nice chair for Holly to sit on.

If she was bothered by it, he couldn't detect it. She looked out the sliding glass door. "Oh, wow, that's a great view."

It was definitely a great view: miles of raw land looking out over the rolling hills of the Hill Country. He'd put in a flagstone patio and the pergola, and this week, he'd finally gotten that chiminea. There had only been one rusted metal lawn chair until last night, when Jesse, in a snit, dragged the other one from the barn, helped himself to Wyatt's beer, then proceeded to wax ineloquently about the sorry economy of Cedar Springs.

"There's one thing I wish I had at the homestead," Holly said, folding her arms as she looked out the sliding glass door.

"The what?"

"The homestead." She laughed. "I always thought that sounded like we just drove into town and staked a claim. But that is what my parents and grandparents always called our ranch, and the name stuck. And that old house doesn't have a view of anything but cows."

"Would you like a beer?" he asked and opened his fridge. There was nothing in it but some butter, some eggs, a twelve-pack of Fat Tire ale, and a fruit-and-cheese plate he'd picked up at the local grocery. He showed her a bottle of Fat Tire, and Holly grinned with delight.

"My favorite," Holly said. "How did you know?"

Well, now, there was a mark on the pro side of the pros-and-cons chart—a woman who appreciated a good beer.

Mason and Grace were at the couch, standing side by side, banging on the cushions. Wyatt figured the allure of that wouldn't last too long and grabbed the beers and the box of cookies and pointed to the back porch. "We can sit out there. There's enough to keep them occupied but not much trouble for them to get into."

"Great idea," Holly said.

"I'm going to put Gracie into something a little more ranch-friendly," he said. "If you don't mind . . ." He handed her the cookies and beer, fumbling a little, his hands catching hers to keep from spilling things.

"We'll meet you outside. Come on, Mase," she said cheerfully.

When Wyatt and Grace returned a few minutes later, Grace was dressed in corduroy overalls and a plain white T-shirt, her hair in a little ponytail. Holly and Mason were examining the underside of a rock with Milo's eager assistance. Grace squealed when she saw Milo and tottered forward to join them. Her cries of delight caught Mason's attention, and he started toward her, taking two or three steps before falling and bending over double in order to get up and try again.

"He's walking pretty well," Wyatt observed.

Milo happily rolled onto his side, his tail beating the ground, sniffing the babies as they alternately pounded him and grabbed his fur.

"Aren't you a little worried about the dog?" Holly asked, wincing when Grace caught Milo's ear and pulled hard enough to make him squeal.

Wyatt shrugged. "I figure if he doesn't like it, he's

smart enough to get free of them. Would you like to sit?"

"Thanks." She followed him to the lawn chairs. "I'm so happy Mason actually gets to play with another kid," she said as she took a seat. "I read that socialization is so important at this age."

"Doesn't he have a few friends?" Wyatt asked curiously. Gracie was a little social butterfly, always off on play dates.

"I don't know," Holly said, and shrugged self-consciously. "I assume so, but my sister and I have drifted apart, and I don't know nearly as much about Mason as I would like." She didn't look at Wyatt, but at her belt, fidgeting with the end of it.

"It must have been a great shock to you," he said quietly. "The way Mason came to you."

Holly snorted. "You have no idea. It knocked me off my feet."

Wyatt certainly empathized. "I know what that's like."

"Really?" Holly asked, looking at him dubiously. "At first I thought it would be easy, you know? I mean, he's a baby, and I figured, how hard could it be? But he was crying, and I didn't know why, and I finally figured out it was his diaper." She shook her head. "So dumb."

Wyatt smiled. "That's nothing."

"No, I was clueless. You should have seen the poor kid's rash."

"A few months ago, I had Grace for about three days. She was fussy, really unlike herself. I thought it was growing pains. I found out later she'd had an ear infection."

"Oh no," Holly said, her eyes widening. "Did she have a fever?"

"Hell if I know," Wyatt said. "Not that I ever noticed. But the point is, these kids don't come with manuals, yet it's amazing how many babies and parents survive. So will you and Mason."

"Thanks for the vote of confidence," she said with a grateful smile. "Here's something else I didn't fully appreciate—Mason requires a *lot* of attention."

Wyatt chuckled. He could hardly watch a football game when he had Grace. Or rather, he could, but he was always a little surprised by the carnage he found when the game was over. He never did figure out how she'd managed to pull the carpet up in the hotel where they were staying. "Yep. If you don't keep an eye on 'em, it's like turning your back on a hurricane."

"Exactly!" Holly said, laughing.

"But you seem to be weathering the storm."

"Yes, shockingly, I am." She looked across the yard to Mason and her smile deepened. "Funny how they can get under your skin, isn't it? One happy gurgle, one smile, and I melt."

Wyatt knew the feeling. He had no doubt Gracie would have him completely wrapped around her finger when she grew up.

"Mind if I ask what's going to happen with Mason?" he asked curiously.

"Happen?" She was sitting with her chin propped on the palm of her hand, her legs crossed, watching the kids.

"I mean, are you going to keep him?"

The question clearly flustered her. "Oh," she said,

and abruptly straightened up. "*No.* I mean . . . Hannah will be back. Sooner or later, she will be back."

"You don't sound so certain of that," he said.

She blinked. She worried the end of her belt again, the frown still on her brow. "I honestly don't know what is going to happen," she said. "I still don't know how my sister and I got to this point. It's all so surreal."

"Was she always . . ." He tried to think of an inoffensive word. "Irresponsible?"

"God, no, the opposite. Valedictorian. She was the one who has always taken care of everything. She was the one who took care of my mother when she was terminal. She was the last person who would dump her baby and drink herself into . . . rehab." She glanced away, avoiding his gaze.

That was a surprise. He'd guessed a flake, an affair. "Is that what happened?"

Holly nodded. "Mason's father told me, that she's in rehab. And I . . ." Whatever she was going to say, she seemed to change her mind. She pushed her hair from her eyes and smiled at him. "And it looks like I brought all the family's dirty laundry to air," she said with a sheepish smile. "Do you have brothers or sisters?"

"No," he said, shaking his head. "I'm an only child."

"Ah," she said. "Well . . . I never in my wildest dreams thought my sister could do something like this, and I am having a hard time accepting that she has. But in the meantime, I'm digging having the little guy around. And now that I've figured out how to squeeze work in, it's much less stressful."

"What is your work?" he asked curiously.

"Well . . . I'm a songwriter."

She said it almost as if she were apologizing for it. He'd always had a great appreciation for people with God-given talents, like writers and artists and musicians. He had nothing like that in him; in fact, he left most of the business writing to Linda Gail, having suffered through a period of inferiority after she told him one afternoon that he was using too many split infinitives. "Just do it yourself, then," he'd said gruffly, rather than admit he didn't know what the hell she was talking about.

To Holly he said, "That's a very cool occupation. Good for you."

"Thanks! Most people seem to think it's an expensive hobby," she said with a flick of her wrist.

"A hobby? Do you make a living at it?"

"Yes," she said, sounding more confident. "I'm not making a huge living, obviously, but it's enough for me, and it's starting to get better."

"Then I'd say it's more than a hobby."

Holly smiled gratefully at him, and it made Wyatt feel a little tingly inside. He took another swig of beer. He supposed he'd been out here on the ranch so long that he'd forgotten what it felt like to have an attractive woman smile at him. Macy didn't count. He got a different kind of feeling when she smiled at him, and it wasn't good. But Holly's smile felt nice.

"Right now I'm contracted to write three songs for Quincy Crowe. He's an artist whose star is rising."

Wyatt's beer froze halfway to his mouth. "Quincy Crowe?" He knew Quincy Crowe. They played his music on the one radio station he could pick up out here. "I know who that is."

Holly's pretty green eyes widened with surprise. "You *do*?" She eagerly leaned over the arm of her chair. "Are you kidding? He's just starting out, so not a lot of people know about him. You've heard him?"

"Yeah—they play him on KASE. I like that kid. I like his style."

"Me too!" she exclaimed, as if they'd just discovered they were the only two people in Texas who liked brussels sprouts. "A music publisher in Austin thought we'd be a good fit and put the deal together. I'm co-writing three songs with him."

Wyatt's curiosity was definitely piqued. "That sounds like a whole lot more than a hobby. And it sounds like a helluva a good time. How's that going?"

"It was going *great*," Holly said, and looked at Mason.

Wyatt did too. Mason had tipped the flowerpot over, and Gracie was putting rocks on top of it.

"I love that kid to pieces," she said, "but Mason makes it really hard to write. It is getting better, though, especially now that we are out here. Like I said, I've learned how to work around him."

"Play something," Wyatt said.

She laughed and blushed appealingly. "No way," she said, and helped herself to a cookie. He watched her take a bite. "Ooh, these are my best yet," she said with a wink, and offered him one.

Wyatt took the cookie. "Come on," he urged her. "I'd love to hear your music."

"Nope. I have a rule—I don't share my work until the song is done. Or if I have one too many beers." She laughed again and took another bite of the cookie.

"Anyway, I'm a songwriter, not a singer. You should thank me, really, because my singing is painful."

"Well, then you leave me no other choice. I'll have to go for too many beers." He winked at her and took a bite of the cookie. Damn, but the woman made a good cookie.

Holly laughingly waved him off. "Don't even think of trying. I'm an old pro at dealing with men and beer," she said. "You can't write music and hang out in live-music venues and not be."

Holly was a very attractive woman with a warm, inviting smile. That and a beer was all a guy needed. It was damn sure all he'd need. And look at that, he was holding a beer. "Do you know any other musicians in Austin?"

"Quite a few. I sat in with Patty Griffin once," she said, and proceeded to rattle off the names of some of the biggest names in country and folk music around Austin. She'd played with Patty Griffin. The Court Yard Hounds had bought and recorded one of her songs. She'd collaborated with Guy Clark, Bob Schneider, and Kelly Willis. She seemed very connected to the Austin music scene.

"It must be hard to be out here and away from all that," he remarked.

"It is. But it's been really nice having some time to myself and learning new things. Like how to make chocolate chip cookies. Is it just me, or are they really good?"

"They're really good," he confirmed. "Do you ever hear your songs played?"

"Yes," she said proudly. "A couple of them."

Wyatt was fascinated by that. It was an experience so far beyond him. "Tell me," he said. "Tell me how you write a song and then hear it performed. It must be a rush."

"Oh, wow, it is." She sighed up to the sky. "It's amazing. Incredible. For me, a song starts when I hear a phrase or a few words in my head that spark the idea. And then the melody follows," she said, fluttering her fingers. "For a few days the pieces of the melody come to me, and it all kind of steeps. Then I start playing around on the piano or the guitar, trying different chords, different keys, different cadences, and sooner or later I have a song." She looked at him. "But when I hear it performed by a band, it's amazing. I hear all those parts, and little pieces come together, and I can almost feel it, because it's part of me." She smiled. "It's magical. But it's hard to explain."

Wyatt held her gaze. He could feel himself smiling too. "I think you explained it pretty well." He was utterly beguiled. He hadn't even realized how much time had passed until Mason interrupted them with a wail.

Mason was on his bottom, and Gracie had the flowerpot. Holly jumped up from her seat and hurried over to Mason. By the time she reached him, Milo was there, too, licking the tears from his face, which only made him cry harder.

"Dee-eeee!" Grace sang, and gave Holly a rock.

"Thank you," Holly said, and stuffed the rock into her jeans as she picked Mason up. She kissed his cheek, held him tightly, caressed his back. "Are you all right, buddy?" she cooed.

"I've got something for Mason," Wyatt said, and

put down his beer. He went to his shed, returning with a rusted old toy lawn mower. He set it down before Mason, wrapped Mason's hands around the handle, and gave him a push. Mason was off and walking around the yard, delighted with it. "Be *be*!" he cried as he went.

Grace's gaze was riveted on Mason. She began to run toward him. Wyatt intercepted her, catching her around the waist and lifting her up onto his shoulder. "Let Mason have it, sweetheart." Grace was unhappy with the change in direction and cried. Wyatt picked up a few rocks. "Look here," he said, and put one in Grace's hand.

Just like that, all was right in his baby's world. She chattered as she handed him a rock. Then another. And another and another, and Wyatt was reminded again that there was nothing in the world that made him feel quite like Grace did. She was the one thing he'd gotten right in his life.

They played with the kids like that for a while, Wyatt allowing Grace to push rocks into his pockets and Holly darting around to remove obstacles from Mason's path before he plowed into them, until Holly announced that a diaper change was needed.

"This way," Wyatt said. He led her into the house and back to the room he and Milo shared. There wasn't much there but windows on three walls, his bed, and a dog bed in the corner on the hardwood floor. He'd covered his bed with a quilt he'd found in the Arbolago Hills house that he thought had once belonged to his mother. There was a nightstand with a book of crossword puzzles and a lamp. He didn't have an alarm clock; his body woke with the sun's first light.

Holly paused as she crossed the threshold with Mason and the diaper bag. "On the bed?" she asked, and at his nod she moved ahead and made quick work of changing his diaper.

"You look like an old pro," he said as he kept Grace from helping.

Holly laughed. "Necessity is the mother of mothering." She tickled Mason's belly, and Wyatt felt a strange little twinge in his heart. He knew the emotion on Holly's face, because it was the same thing he felt when he looked at Grace.

"It takes a remarkable person to take in a child," he said.

"I'm not remarkable," Holly replied as she buttoned Mason's pants. "It's not like I wanted him—I *didn't* want him. I didn't want to take care of him; I didn't know *how* to take care of him. I was shocked, I was furious, and I felt trapped. No, it wasn't remarkable, Wyatt. I just had no choice. I didn't know how to get out of it."

"You had a choice," Wyatt pointed out. "You could have handed him over to authorities or to another relative."

She shrugged. "I wasn't going to send my nephew into foster care. And we don't really have any other relatives. Believe me, I racked my brain trying to think of one. So, just like that, in the space of an hour, my whole life was turned on its head." She looked at him. "I felt cheated, if you want to know the truth. I cried. I wanted out. I even went to Loren's office—"

"Loren?"

"Mason's father. I went to his office and made a *huge* scene," she said, throwing her arms wide, and groaned to the ceiling. "I guess I thought histrionics would free me of the responsibility."

"Wait . . . you spoke to his father, and he didn't take Mason?"

Holly snorted. "No. He was on his way to Costa Rica. Can't disrupt work for a little thing like his son."

Wyatt was astounded by that. He couldn't imagine any circumstance in which his work would come before Grace.

"I was trying to avoid the responsibility," she said, as if it had been her responsibility to begin with. "I always do that. Like the homestead . . . Do you know that my mom has been gone six months, and I haven't done anything about the will? But you know what? Sitting in that conference room, when I realized just how incredibly selfish Loren is, I couldn't get Mason away from him fast enough. I had visions of Mason being totally neglected. But it wasn't until that very moment that I could agree to even consider disrupting *my* life to save him."

"He wasn't your responsibility to save, Holly. You shouldn't have had to disrupt your life."

"Maybe," she said, nodding. "But that baby was in crisis and I was thinking of me. So . . . don't say I'm remarkable." She self-consciously pushed her hair behind her ear.

Wyatt smiled. He lifted his hands. "All right. You are officially unremarkable," he declared, and Holly grinned.

But that didn't keep him from thinking it.

They went back outside and fed the kids juice and grapes. When they were refueled, Wyatt brought out the big, round, brightly colored balls he'd bought for ninety-nine cents apiece at the dollar store in Cedar Springs and threw them out on the lawn. "There is nothing little kids like better," he said, and like puppies to kibble, Mason and Grace exclaimed with delight and tottered after the balls.

"Wow," Holly said with a shake of her head as she watched Mason pick up a ball and fall with it. "What I don't know about babies is astounding. I thought grapes would choke them. And these balls? Genius, Wyatt."

He chuckled. "It comes with time," he said. "I had nine months to get ready for Grace's arrival, and four-teen months to figure out what she likes. You'll start to know these things too. You want another beer?"

She looked up at a clear blue sky. "Yes . . . but I think we should go. It's time for his nap."

"He can nap here," Wyatt suggested quickly, sur-prising himself. He was having a great afternoon and he did not want her to leave. He couldn't remember the last time he'd enjoyed the company of a woman, just hanging out with a woman. *Talking.* He guessed the last time he'd been this comfortable was with Macy.

"I don't want to impose any more than I have," Holly said. "I practically twisted your arm for this play date as it is."

"No you didn't. The opportunity presented itself," he lied. "We'll put them down for a nap together."

Holly grinned. "You talked me into it."

Together they barricaded the kids with pillows on Wyatt's bed, staying around long enough to assure themselves the kids would sleep. "I'll grab a couple of beers," Wyatt said softly as Holly pulled the door of his room partially closed.

He fetched the two beers and put them on the counter, and through the window saw Holly standing on the patio, her weight on one hip, her reddish-blond hair glistening in the late-afternoon light. She was talking on her cell phone.

She was pretty. Not just pretty, but *really* pretty. Of course, he'd noticed her good looks the first time he'd ever seen her, but today she was even more attractive to him. It was her smile, her mannerisms, her laugh, the shine in her eyes—full of warmth and genuine earnestness.

Wyatt liked Holly Fisher. A lot. The thought gave him one of those strange little electric shivers that made him feel rusty. He hadn't liked being around anyone—male or female—in a long time. He'd spent the last two years merely tolerating people and hadn't wanted any complications in his life. He'd wanted to be left alone. He'd especially wanted women to leave him alone.

Wyatt had been, as he liked to think of it, "off" women. Yes, there had been that afternoon with Samantha Delaney, the woman who ran Daisy's Saddlebrew Coffee Shop. She'd been Macy's best friend, and he guessed he and Sam had both wanted to hurt Macy for all that had happened that summer. That had been his first and last taste of revenge sex. It had been awful, too. Worst sex he'd ever had. He hadn't felt avenged;

he'd felt cheap and low when Macy had discovered them in bed together.

After Sam there had been Adelita in Arizona. He'd met Adelita in a bar, of course, and had followed all the clichés down to the dotting of the *i*. He'd been a little wasted and a lot turned on by her shiny black hair and soulful brown eyes. Somehow they'd ended up in her dingy apartment under a window AC in her bed. Wyatt had spent a week there, feeding his body physically and emotionally. He'd even fantasized for a couple of days that he and Adelita would get an Airstream and head out, destination unknown. But he didn't speak Spanish, and English wasn't exactly her first language. And then, mid-week, he'd figured out the little girl who showed up with some woman was actually Adelita's daughter. He'd finally awakened from that fantasy and moved on.

Adelita had not seemed particularly sad about it, either.

There hadn't been anyone since Adelita. He'd spent the last eighteen months living alone. But then he'd met Holly, and she'd caught his attention not just with her looks but in unusual ways. The music coming from her house. Her playful nature. Her ease with him. Her cookies. Mason. Telling tales about musicians he really admired without the slightest bit of pretense in her.

Yeah, he liked her. He liked her so much he hadn't even thought of her property today.

He popped the plastic top off the fruit-and-cheese tray, grabbed the beers, and went back outside.

"Great!" Holly said. "I'm starving." She helped herself to some apple slices.

The day was turning cooler, and Wyatt decided to fire up the chiminea for its inaugural run. They sat in the rusty chairs, sipping beer and munching on the fruit-and-cheese tray, and Wyatt felt more relaxed, more content, than he had in a very long time.

"This looks new," Holly said, pointing at the pergola.

He looked up. "Yep. Put it in this week."

Holly gasped. "*You* put it in?"

Wyatt laughed. "Don't look so shocked. I can be kind of handy."

"I'm not surprised, I'm impressed! What else are you going to do?"

"I'm not sure," he said. "Redo the kitchen, definitely. The bathrooms. After that, I don't know. Maybe nothing."

"Why don't you know?" she asked.

He shrugged. "I don't know if I am staying here."

She paused in her examination of the cheese cubes to look at him. "Really? You'd leave that view?"

He looked at the view before them. Would he? "I don't know if I belong here," he said, and was a little surprised he'd actually said that out loud.

But Holly didn't look surprised. She nodded. "That's really important, isn't it? If you don't know where you belong, you don't feel settled."

An understatement if ever he'd heard one. "Do you know where *you* belong?"

She smiled. "I do—I belong in the moment," she said with a wink, and laughed.

He gazed at her face and smiled. Yeah, he liked this girl.

"Hey, I was in Cedar Springs at Daisy's Saddle-brew

Coffee Shop, right?" she said. "And I saw a flyer for a holiday carnival next month. Do you know anything about it? Do you think it would be something Mason and Grace would like?"

The mention of Cedar Springs flattened Wyatt's fizzy feelings. If they went to Cedar Springs, how long would it be before someone told her? And then how long would it be before he saw in her eyes what he saw every time he was in town? *Poor Wyatt Clark to be caught in that love triangle. How sad that he'd lost the love of his life when the love of Macy's life was returned to her.*

"Dunno," he said.

"Sounds like fun," she said.

There wasn't anyone in Cedar Springs who wouldn't bring it up at the first mention of his name. *Where are you living, Holly? Out on Deadeye Road? You must know Wyatt Clark, that poor, pitiful man.*

"Maybe we could take them," she said.

He could just picture the two of them walking down Main Street during the carnival. The tongues would be wagging, wouldn't they? *Who's that with Wyatt Clark? Oh, I hope he found someone . . .* "Maybe we could," he said. "Are you hungry?"

"Hungry?" Holly glanced down. "Well, let's see. I've eaten about a dozen cookies, a brick of cheese, and about three apple slices. Yep. I'm hungry."

He laughed. "I like the way you think. I've got some steaks that have been waiting for an audience." He stood up. "And it beats the hell out of peanut butter."

Holly stood up too. There wasn't room between the two chairs; they were standing only inches apart and he could see the tiny flecks of dark gray in eyes that were shimmering up at him. This was dangerous territory—he could feel a little army of Wyatts lining up haphazardly, ready and eager to conquer if called upon.

"Don't knock peanut butter," she said softly, her gaze on his mouth. "It's gotten me through some very tough times, right out of the jar."

His rusty, unused engine was coughing to a start. His gaze drifted over her face, lingering on her mouth. He didn't think much when he put his hand on her cheek and bent his head to touch his lips to hers. All those little Wyatts, starved for sex and a woman's touch, took the proverbial bull by the horns. The softness of her lips stirred his blood, the feel of her cheek beneath his fingers stoked fire into him.

The sensation—primal and deep—startled him almost as much as it surely startled her. Wyatt lifted his head and stepped back. What had possessed him? "Holly, I'm—"

Holly didn't let him finish. She went up on her toes and kissed him back. He felt her hands go around his neck, her fingers tangling in his hair, the warmth of her body seeping into his. He felt the Wyatts cheer, felt himself turn hot and fluid, desire sluicing through him like a flash flood.

Then she faded away from him. When he could focus again, she was smiling. "Curiously, I am starving now." She started for the house.

Curiously, hell. As he watched her go inside, Wyatt figured Holly Fisher had no idea what starving really meant.

Chapter Twelve

Hannah received her four-week sobriety pen in a group meeting. She accepted it with a smile, thanked her sponsor and the others in her group, and resumed her seat. She kept smiling, but inside she was dying.

Four weeks sober meant nothing to her but that she could call Mason. Four weeks meant four weeks she'd not been his mother, had not smelled his skin, had not seen his smile, had not fed him or bathed him or changed his diaper. Four weeks of not holding him or knowing if he was walking, or talking, or even if he was okay. *Was* he okay?

Francine Goldberg had the floor. "Hi. My name is Francine, and I'm an addict," she said into the microphone.

"Hi, Francine!"

Hannah didn't care if Francine was the president of the United States. Francine, who liked a lot of attention, was one of the inmates here—Hannah couldn't look at them in any other way, as all of them had come here by court order or family order or the order of God. Francine had something to say at every meeting. "Didn't you think about your baby?" She'd asked Hannah that question in group one day. This, from a woman who drove a car through the plate-glass window of a neighborhood grocery and seriously injured an elderly man waiting for his blood pressure medicine.

Yes, Hannah had thought of what she was doing to Mason. But she couldn't seem to stop herself. She now knew that avoiding withdrawal by feeding her addiction had been more important than her own son.

Hannah had had the opportunity to call him at two weeks, after detox, but she'd been such an emotional wreck, she couldn't face Holly. She'd felt like she was drifting in and out of sanity as it was. A mother cannot walk away from her baby and expect to stay sane.

Dr. Bonifield, her shrink, had helped Hannah set a new goal for calling Mason: her four-week sobriety checkpoint.

That was today. She was sick with nerves, ashamed of what had happened, lacking confidence to speak to her sister. Sick.

Dick, the group leader, was talking to her, Hannah realized. "Do you have anything you want to say about your journey thus far?" he asked, and nodded toward the new guy. Jeff something. Meth. They were the worst, Hannah thought. The craziest. She looked at Jeff, who stared at her with hollow eyes, daring her to hand him some hackneyed message of hope.

But Hannah stared at him blankly. She felt wrung out. Emotionally and physically spent. She had nothing, nothing to offer this man. "No," she said. "Sorry."

"Okay," Dick said, nodding nervously. He didn't like it when people didn't share. "Okay. Rayshon? How about you?"

"Why me?" Rayshon asked. "She's been here longer than me."

Rayshon was a drinker, and Hannah had heard detox wasn't as hard for them as it was for OxyContin or meth or heroin. Detox had been very painful for her, that was certain. Thankfully, she didn't remember that much about it. She'd come to the center after a weekend spent drinking and drugging in a Hilton Garden Inn hotel room, where she'd waged an ugly battle with herself to actually go through with the treatment. It had seemed so impossible at the time.

Rob Tucker had arranged it all for her. After the worst day of her life—the day Hannah had skipped work and called Brian, the mysterious college kid Brian—she'd actually driven with Mason to a dilapidated apartment complex off Rundburg Lane in Austin. But Brian wasn't a college kid. Brian was a fat man with a missing tooth. He'd sold her thirty OxyContins from the trunk of a banged-up Lincoln. The whole thing had scared Hannah so badly that she'd called Rob Tucker and asked him to meet her at a Starbucks near the office.

While Mason had tried to push a chair around, Hannah had told Rob the truth. She didn't know why she told him, or why she felt compelled to unload everything on him. It seemed as if once she had started talking, the floodgates had opened and it all had come tumbling out. She'd told Rob about Loren and the affairs, and her mother, and the homestead, and how she had been taking the pills just to cope. She'd even told Rob how she had gone to meet this guy Brian. Rob had looked shocked, but he hadn't said a word.

When she'd finished—when her body had been completely drained of words—Rob had picked Mason up and set him in his lap, then reached across the table and put his hand on Hannah's and squeezed it tightly.

"We're going to fix this, Hannah," he had promised her.

He'd meant it too. Rob had sprung into action after that afternoon. He was the one who had called the Watershed Addiction Treatment Program in Palm Beach, Florida, and set up Hannah's admittance. He was the one who had figured out how to make Loren pay for it too. He'd arranged for her leave of absence, and he'd suggested she find a safe place for Mason to reside while she was away. Hannah had lost all her friends, but it didn't matter. The only person she could even think of taking Mason to was her sister Holly.

Hannah didn't remember most of detox, other than they'd taken all her things, and found the pills in her luggage and her emergency stash in her lipstick tube. She remembered that she had been so sick, and her whole body had raged with such pain, and she'd wanted to die. But every time she'd opened her eyes, she had seen the picture of Mason she'd put at her bedside, and she'd gritted her teeth and told herself just to make it to the end of the day. To the end of just one day.

She'd done it. She was still getting the massive withdrawal headaches, but she'd done it, she'd detoxed, and had made it a whole month now without a single pill, without a drink. She'd gained seven pounds, and she'd actually been hungry this week. And she'd earned her call to Mason, if she didn't disintegrate with nerves first.

"Is there anything you can offer Jeff, Rayshon?" Dick asked.

"Oh, I got plenty to say," Rayshon said, and began to talk.

Hannah didn't think she was like the others in her group. She couldn't relate to their tales of mean streets and abusive homes. She didn't feel as if anyone understood the sort of stressors she'd been under, either.

At least Dr. Bonifield understood Hannah. She'd told Hannah on the very first day of detox, when Hannah had felt so sick and had hurt so bad from withdrawal, that this was the most important thing she'd ever done for her son. "I know it is hard," she'd said as Hannah retched into the toilet, "but spending a few weeks away from Mason to get yourself well will give Mason his mommy back to him. If you'd kept going down the path you've been on, Mason wouldn't have a mommy at all. Think of that, Hannah. Think of what it would be like to grow up without a mother. What you did by coming here is not only the hardest thing a person can do in his or her life, it is the bravest thing you can do."

Dr. Bonifield was right about that. Nothing was harder. Not detox, not facing her demons, not reliving, in excruciating therapy sessions, how her mother had been a head case and Loren was a shit bag. All of that paled in comparison to having abandoned her son.

Hannah looked at her watch again. In fifteen minutes she would walk down to Dr. Bonifield's office, and

Dr. Bonifield would be waiting with her graying blond hair and her reading glasses perched on top her head, and Hannah would call Mason.

God, she hoped Holly answered. If Holly didn't answer, Hannah didn't know if she could go the rest of the day.

Rayshon stopped talking. Garret, a heroin addict, talked next. Dick said something, *Blah, blah, blah-di-blah,* then said they were through and everyone applauded. This was it. This was the day she'd speak to her son. Hannah stood. She smiled and nodded as group members congratulated her on her four-week sobriety pin, but she was moving, because if she didn't move, she'd lose her nerve.

She walked past the dining hall with its industrial tables and weighted chairs that could not be picked up and thrown, past the classrooms where clients were expected to figure out all the reasons they were addicts in sixty to ninety days, and then past the admin offices. Dr. Bonifield's was at the end of the hall. The door was closed; Hannah knocked.

The door swung open, and Dr. Bonifield stood there, a full head shorter than Hannah's respectable five feet seven inches, smiling up at her. "I figured you'd be here right away."

Or lose her nerve. "May I call him now?" Hannah asked.

"Yes. Come in," Dr. Bonifield invited her. She waited until Hannah was seated on the couch, then picked up the handset. "Remember what we talked about, Hannah. Holly wouldn't be human if she didn't have some anger. Just be honest with her."

Holly. For some reason, when Hannah thought of her lately, she thought of the chubby freckle-faced kid with the bouncy golden hair. That Holly had worshipped her. "Right," Hannah said.

"Good luck," Dr. Bonifield said kindly, and handed Hannah the handset. "I'll be back in half an hour." She touched Hannah's cheek in a maternal manner that her own mother had never possessed, and walked out of the room, leaving Hannah on the couch with the phone in her hand.

Hannah's belly churned. Thinking of Holly—the pretty grown woman with the cute, shaggy haircut and the warm smile—made her nervous. Holly probably despised Hannah now, and who could blame her? But Holly had Hannah's son, and although her heart was starting to beat like a kettledrum—big, reverberating thumps—Hannah dialed Holly's cell phone number.

It rang once. Twice. Hannah's heart went from thumping to racing. *Third ring.* Hannah could feel a hole opening in her, a big black hole where Mason should have been, where emotional shit went in and nothing came out.

Holly wasn't there.

Or wasn't answering, which was a distinct possibility. The phone rang a fourth time, and Hannah's eyes began to fill with tears of disappointment. She'd waited so long, and she needed this so *badly*—

"Hey!" Holly said into the phone. She sounded happy and out of breath.

Hannah gulped. "Ah . . . Holly, it's me," Hannah said. Her voice was shaking. "It's Hannah." That was met with a hard silence. Hannah waited a moment, then asked, "How is Mason?"

Still, Holly didn't speak right away. When she did speak, her voice was low and dark. "Where *are* you?"

"How is he, Holly?" Hannah asked, her voice pleading. "Is he okay?" Tears were falling, *she* was falling. She hadn't even said hello and she was already falling apart.

"Are you kidding me?" Holly snapped. "You don't ask questions this time, Hannah. You do the answering! You've been gone, what, a month now, and this is the first you are calling? You don't care how Mason is!"

Holly's words were knives plunging into Hannah's heart.

"Where the hell are you? Are you really in *rehab*?"

Holly said it as if she were asking if Hannah were really lying in a gutter. "I . . ." Hannah wiped the tears from one cheek. "Yes. I'm in rehab. In Palm Beach, Florida," she added.

"*Why?*" Holly cried. "Rehab for *what*?"

Dr. Bonifield had warned Hannah of this. She'd said that Hannah could not rid Holly of her anger—only time and Holly could do that—but Hannah could be truthful and attempt to explain that what she'd done had been the best for her at the time. "*Vital*," Dr. Bonifield had reminded her. "You might possibly be dead today had you not taken these very important steps."

"I've, ah . . ." Hannah faltered and pushed her hair back from her face as she searched her pickled brain for the right words. "I've had a . . . a problem for a while, I guess." She herself hadn't realized just how long until she'd begun intensive cognitive therapy.

"And it got way out of hand when Mom died, and . . . here I am."

"For wine?" Holly asked, sounding confused. "All those wine bottles in the porch closet at Mom's house were yours, right? You're in rehab for *wine*?"

Hannah squeezed her eyes shut. She'd forgotten about the accumulation of wine bottles through the last couple of years of Mom's illness. And after. "Ummm . . . yeah, those were mine. I do drink. A lot," she added self-consciously. "But my addiction is mainly pills."

"*Pills*," Holly repeated disbelievingly. "*What* pills?"

Hannah drew a breath. "OxyContin. Vicodin. Ambien. Xanax." She drew another breath. "There are others, but those are the main culprits."

Silence again. Hannah waited for Holly to speak. She knew her sister must be overwhelmed by what she was saying, and that made her feel even worse. No one wants to tell their little sister they are a pain pill junkie. Hannah could feel the tears again, always the goddamn tears. When would they stop falling? When could she walk through an entire day without crying about every little thing?

"Do you honestly expect me to believe this, Hannah?" Holly asked, her voice shaking. "Don't you think I would have noticed if you were drunk or wasted on Xanax? How would I, or anyone else for that matter, have missed it? How could you even hold down a job? I don't believe it."

Dr. Bonifield had warned her about this, too. People close to addicts felt guilty for not saving the addict from themselves. "No, Holly, you wouldn't have noticed, because I was really good at hiding it. And I . . . I've been past the point of being high for a couple of years. I needed them just to be normal."

"I have no idea what you are talking about," Holly said, sounding very confused. "That makes no sense— you took them to be normal? I don't believe you! How can I believe you? And if it were true, why didn't you tell me? Why didn't you get help? Why didn't you *tell* me?" she demanded.

"Because I was ashamed," Hannah said. "But I am telling you now," she added, meaning it sincerely. "I should have told you, I know I should have, but I wasn't thinking straight. At the time, the only thing I could think of was where was I going to get my pills. That's it. Addiction is . . . it's really a hideous thing—"

"You want to know what's hideous?" Holly angrily interjected. "When your sister dumps her baby on you without regard for *your* life and takes off. When your sister's husband is more interested in fucking his new girlfriend and making partner than taking care of his son. *That's* hideous!"

"Holly, please," Hannah pleaded. "You have every right to be angry with me, and I have a lot to explain to you, I know. A *lot*. But right now . . ." Hannah pressed her palm flat against her howling heart. "Right now, I can't breathe until I know how Mason is. Could I talk to him? Could I please just talk to him?"

"He's fine. No thanks to you or Loren, he is *fine*."

Part of Hannah wanted to hear that Mason had been despondent without her. Another part of her was so relieved that he was okay. "Is he walking?"

"Yes, of course," Holly said. "He's walking and

he says *no* and *bye-bye,* and he waves." In the background, Hannah heard Mason, and Holly said, "Bye-bye, boo-boo. Bye-bye."

Hannah sucked in a painful breath. She could picture Mason's happy smile, that dark bit of hair on his head, like his father. "Please, Holly," she begged. "Please let me talk to him."

Holly responded with a sound of impatience, but in the next moment Hannah heard Holly's voice at a distance. "Say hi to Mommy, Mase. It's Mommy!"

"Bye-bye," Mason said into the phone, and Hannah's heart clenched.

"Mason! Mason, it's Mommy! Mommy loves you, baby, I love you so much!" She was blubbering now. "I am so *so* sorry I'm not there, buddy, but I am going to be home soon. Mommy is going to be home soon and I promise I will make this up to you—"

"He's gone now," Holly said coolly. "He saw his truck and went after it."

Hannah rubbed her hand under her nose. "Thanks, Holly. Thanks for letting me talk to him. And thank you for taking care of him."

"What am I supposed to do with that, Hannah? One thank-you and then I should say it's all okay? Because it's not. It's not okay on so many levels, I can't even begin to name them. What you did was cruel to both me and Mason. And now you tell me you're an addict? I can't even wrap my head around it, and honestly? I am so angry right now I don't think I can talk about it rationally. How long are you going to be there, anyway?"

It felt as if she'd been here for a lifetime already.

"Ah . . . another sixty days," she admitted nervously. "And then ninety days in the transitional housing—"

"The *what*?"

"Transitional housing. You, ah . . . you live in a place with counselors and support groups to help you with the stress as you resume your life. It's to support your transition back to life and help you manage the temptation to use."

Holly gasped. "Jesus. Does Loren know?"

Hannah couldn't help a snort. "He knows I'm in treatment, but I haven't told him everything yet."

"But you *are* going to tell him, aren't you?"

Hannah chafed at the notion that she had to tell that lying, cheating scum anything, but she was not in a position to argue with Holly, and part of her treatment and recovery was to come clean with everyone who had ever mattered to her. Loren had mattered to her at some point. Loren had mattered more than anything in the world at one point. "Yes," she said tightly. "I am going to tell him. Have you heard from him? Has he seen Mason?"

"Are you kidding? No, I haven't heard from him! He's in Costa Rica, setting up an office."

Hannah didn't say anything, but she was relieved by the news. She would much prefer her son to be with her sister than with Loren.

"Do you know I'm at the homestead, Hannah? Do you know that I had to quit my job because I didn't have day care for Mason? And that I have a contract with ASC and I am currently behind schedule because I have to work around Mason's schedule?"

Hannah didn't know any of that, of course, but she

wasn't surprised. In the long nights she'd been here, she'd realized there was nothing else Holly could do but go home. "I know this is a horrible thing I've done, Holly, but I couldn't leave him with anyone else—"

"I will never understand how you *could* have left him. But I do understand this—you cannot just call up several weeks later and expect everything is going to be A-okay, that you can just come tripping back into his life."

"I didn't expect that," Hannah said.

"Then what *did* you expect?"

Hannah couldn't answer that. She had no expectations. Every day was such a blank slate for her. "Listen, I'll be out in two months—"

"I honestly don't care," Holly said. She sounded on the verge of tears. "I really don't. All I care about is making sure Mason is okay. After what you and Loren did to him, that's the best thing I can do. I can't just blithely hand him over to either of you."

Hannah's heart stopped beating altogether. "What do you mean?" she asked. "What are you saying?"

"What am I saying? I don't know," Holly said, her voice breaking. "I only know that I am only now learning that my sister is a . . . a serious addict, and she is in some pretty intense treatment, and she's going to live in some . . . some transitional house so there will be people around to make sure she doesn't *use* again, and I'm wondering what happens when those people *aren't* around anymore, and Loren is more interested in his job than his son, and I don't know what to do with either one of you! But right now I am expecting company, so I really have to go. Good-bye, Hannah."

"Holly, please don't hang up—I have to earn my calls."

"I have to go, Hannah."

She hung up.

Hannah stared at the phone. This was such a mess, such an unholy mess. In a moment of frustration, she threw the phone, hitting the edge of Dr. Bonifield's desk.

A moment later Dr. Bonifield opened the door and walked into the office. She looked at Hannah's tearstained cheeks, then at her desk. "Well," she said, and quietly shut the door. She stooped down to pick up the phone. "We knew it wouldn't be easy."

Hannah buried her face in her hands and sobbed. She suddenly felt so fragile. "I can't do this!" Holly was right—if Hannah weren't locked up in this awful place, she would be popping pills right now. Handfuls of them.

"But, Hannah, you *can* do it," Dr. Bonifield said soothingly. "You've *been* doing it." She touched Hannah's back, and Hannah felt her spirit collapse like a cone of ash.

Chapter Thirteen

Wyatt woke up with Grace's feet in his face. His own feet were hanging off the side of the bed, because Milo had taken up the real estate at the foot. It was too damn crowded in this bed . . . but he liked it.

He got Grace up, bathed her, and put her in a pair of denim pants and a red sweater, a pair of Keds, then tied her hair up in little pigtails. But he was all thumbs when it came to that, and they stuck straight up from the top of her head. His daughter spent the morning darting about his living room, squealing with delight at the strangest things: a couch pillow, the lamp cord. A cow-breeding magazine, which she slapped with her hand and said, "*No no no,*" over and over again.

Wyatt picked up around the house and fed his dog. He checked the word of the day but promptly forgot it: *advise, advice,* something like that. He pulled the portable playpen into the bathroom, wedged it in between the sink and the linen closet, and set her in it with some toys, then stepped into the shower. Grace was content for all of two minutes, then spent the better part of his shower holding on to the railing, crying loudly.

When he'd cleaned himself up and set his little prisoner free, he dressed in a white-collared shirt and a clean pair of denims and pulled on his boots. He thought of the days when he used to wear expensive Italian leather loafers without socks. He'd been married to Macy then, and dressed like the other hip movers and shakers in central Texas. Now he was more comfortable with his foot in a boot, the better to kick ass when the need arose.

When he was ready to go, he tossed a dog biscuit into the yard and watched Milo chase after it before locking the back door. He picked up Grace like a bag of flour and draped her on his shoulder, which delighted Grace to no end, and walked out to the shed, which looked like it was leaning a little to the right. He adjusted Grace on his arm and, with one hand, he thrust the rotting door up. Inside was a brand-new Ford F-150 Platinum SuperCrew truck.

"Truck!" Grace said, pointing.

"That's not just any truck, sweetheart," he said proudly. "That bad boy has the advanced trailer sway control, the polished cast-aluminum wheels, and the 5.4-liter V-8 engine."

"Truck!" Grace said again.

This was the truck Wyatt used to carry himself the fifteen miles into Cedar Springs on those occasions he needed to sign checks or pick up some groceries. It was the only thing he'd bought in over a year. In the backseat of the SuperCrew was a car seat, and he deposited his daughter into it and buckled her up. He climbed into the cab and backed the truck slowly out of the garage, then pointed it toward Cedar Springs.

He'd decided, somewhere in the middle of the night, in one of his many instances of waking, to go into town and pick up a few things to bring to Holly's house for the afternoon. A good bottle of wine, he thought, perfect for a cool day. Maybe some gourmet cheeses and crackers. Maybe even some flowers. He didn't like to think that he'd turned into some flower-toting guy after one kiss, but the fact of the matter was, he hadn't been able to get Holly Fisher off his mind all night. He kept seeing those laughing green eyes, that inviting smile. And his body, which had lain dormant for a couple of years, aroused only by the scent of food, had spent a restless night as well. He was craving more than a kiss, craving like a dying man craved water.

In Cedar Springs, the choices for wine shopping were limited to the local H-E-B grocery and the CVS pharmacy on 281. He pulled into the H-E-B parking lot, stuffed Grace into a basket, then gave it a good push and jumped on, rolling along with her while she laughed.

In the grocery, he was surprised to find an almost decent selection of cheeses and crackers. He tossed hummus into the cart, too, and a pair of cucumbers.

The wine selection was surprisingly good for this little town in the middle of Texas. He found a serviceable Malbec with a chair on the label and put it in the basket. He rolled past the flower section and debated whether or not flowers were too much, and while he thought they were, he picked some up all the same. Then he wheeled over to the toy aisle and picked up two little pull toys that made music. Grace was beside herself with joy.

He wheeled the basket up to the only checkout lane open, and while Grace chewed the handle of the little pull toy, Wyatt examined the contents of his basket.

What in the hell was he doing?

He hadn't shopped for this kind of stuff in so long that he felt a little foolish. He wasn't the Camembert-loving wine-drinking snob he'd been with Macy. He didn't cater to women anymore: that regrettable tendency had died with his marriage. He tried to tell himself that he was being a good neighbor, but seeing the contents of his basket announced to him, in froufrou glory, that he'd been smitten.

"Gracie! What a surprise!"

Wyatt's head jerked up at the sound of his ex–sister-in-law's voice. Emma Harper, Macy's younger sister, was standing behind the register wearing the H-E-B red polo, her face lit up like Rockefeller Center. "Wyatt, good night, I haven't seen you in ages!"

He felt his face warming. He frantically thought of how he could back out of this aisle, just get his baby and walk out of the store, but Grace had begun to babble and was trying to climb out of her seat to see her aunt.

"Stay there, sweetie, I'll come to you," Emma said, and marched around the checkout to his basket.

"What are you doing here, Emma?" Wyatt demanded. "I thought you were working at the paper."

"God, Wyatt, I did that while Macy was out on maternity leave. I haven't worked there in months. Hi, Baby Grace!" she trilled as she took Grace out of the basket. "What are you two doing here this morning?" she said, wiggling Grace's hand.

Wyatt glanced down at his basket. What he was doing now seemed so patently obvious, he might as well be standing there naked. And when Emma realized what he was doing, the whole town would know. With a huff of disgruntlement, he began to toss his items onto the conveyer belt.

"Pretty flowers," Emma said as she carried Grace around to her station to scan Wyatt's items. "Finally sprucing the place up, are you?"

"What makes you think my place needs sprucing?" he asked, eyeing her.

Emma, with her fair blond hair and deep-blue eyes, was the sort of woman who was not easily embarrassed. She certainly wasn't embarrassed by the fact that she'd held nothing but odd part-time jobs since losing her position in a big New York finance firm a couple of years ago when the economy went south. "Macy told me," she said unabashedly. "She said it was like you were living in a Quonset hut."

"A Quonset hut, huh?"

"That's what she said. So I figured you were sprucing up— Oh, hey . . . nice wine," she said, examining the bottle. "Have you had this before?"

Wyatt glanced back over his shoulder. An elderly gentleman had rolled in behind him. "Do you think you could just ring stuff up without commenting on each item?" he asked gruffly.

"No, I don't think I can. Yum, olives. And gourmet cheese and crackers? Wow, Wyatt, if I didn't know you were a hermit, I'd think you were having a party for two." She laughed, as if that were patently ridiculous.

It *was* ridiculous—Wyatt had indeed made himself into a hermit, but he didn't like the fact that Emma was so certain that he was. "Just ring it up, Emma," he said impatiently, and jiggled his wallet out of his back pocket. He opened it up, taking out one of several one-hundred-dollar bills.

"Where's the dessert?" she asked. "Don't you need a little whipped cream?" She laughed again and kissed Grace's face.

Wyatt shoved the hundred-dollar bill at her. "I like olives. I like cheese. I like wine. And I especially like it when you mind your own business."

"Touchy, touchy," Emma said cheerfully. "That's thirty-eight sixty." She handed Grace to him over the conveyor belt, took his one hundred dollars, and made change. While he stuffed the bills into his wallet and returned it to his back pocket, the coins going into a front pocket, she put his items into a paper bag and handed it to him as he was preparing to leave. "Good to see you, Wyatt."

He smiled a little. He'd always liked Emma. "Are you doing all right, squirt?"

"Well . . . I am still living with Mom, so that should answer your question."

He grinned. "It sure does. You should try the Malbec: it might make it go a little easier with Jillian. I'll see you later," he said, and started for the exit.

But Emma wasn't ready to say good-bye quite yet. She put a hand on his basket. "So? Who is she?" she asked, her eyes sparkling mischievously.

"Don't kid yourself," he said.

"Come on, Wy. It's been so long since you were . . .

you know, sociable. It's good that you're getting out and around again." She smiled pertly.

"Can't a man like his cheese and wine without you jumping to conclusions?"

Emma winked at him. "Okay. Whatever you say, big guy." She stepped back into her little checkout stand and waved her fingers at him before turning back to her job.

Wyatt could already hear the tongues wagging at the Saddlebrew. *Wyatt Clark finally found himself a girl, bless his poor old heart.*

They could kiss his ass.

Chapter Fourteen

Holly could not picture it. Try as she might, she could not picture her sister as some pill-popping, strung-out housewife. She stood in the kitchen staring blindly out the window at the windmill, trying to understand it, racking her memory for something she had noticed that might have tipped her off. There was nothing. Sure, she'd seen Hannah get tipsy on a couple of glasses of wine. But they all had done that, Holly included, as well as friends. She'd never seen Hannah drunk or high.

How did someone end up in rehab for *ninety days?* That wasn't the result of a binge; that had to be the result of a very serious addiction. How? Where had Hannah gotten enough pills to be addicted? She'd heard about a bartender she knew only vaguely who was addicted. He'd had surgery on his leg, and they said within two weeks he had become hooked. Was that Hannah? Had it happened that fast?

What had happened to Hannah? What horrible thing had made her turn to booze and pills? And had she, Holly, Hannah's sister, been so self-absorbed that she hadn't been there when Hannah needed her? That was a painful thought. Holly and Hannah had their differences, but Holly didn't want to think that had made her blind to Hannah's troubles. But it had, apparently. She'd been so busy proving to her family that they were wrong about her that she hadn't seen her sister was suffering a crisis.

How tragic that someone like Hannah would be reduced to such an incredible state of dependence. Holly was angry with Hannah for what she'd done to her and Mason—nothing could excuse that—but Holly was sad, too. She felt bad for Hannah. She couldn't imagine the sort of pain her sister must have felt that she'd tried to medicate herself to such an extreme.

But still . . . what about Mason? Could Holly, in good conscience, give him back to Hannah, knowing what she knew now? Shouldn't there be some sort of wait-and-see approach? What if Hannah fell off the wagon? If she did, what would happen to Mason?

But that meant Mason would be with her . . . did she want to *keep* Mason?

The thought was startling, but it was not entirely surprising. The truth was that Mason felt more like hers each day. He wasn't hers, and nothing could ever make him hers—she understood that—but somewhere in the last weeks she'd crossed a line from being inconvenienced by him to unable to imagine her days without him. Mason had grounded her. He'd made her feel needed and capable on a level she'd never believed of herself. He was entirely dependent on her for his care. He'd learned to walk and was beginning to talk. He laughed and he loved trucks and he liked to dance when she played piano . . .

Maybe Holly could suggest to Hannah that Mason should remain with her until Hannah . . . until she was *sure* she would never take drugs again. Was that so unreasonable after what had happened?

The sound of Wyatt's truck on the road down to her house shook her out of her thoughts. *Okay, shake it off, pull it together,* she told herself. She was not going to let Hannah ruin this day, and tossed her phone into her purse. She looked at herself in the mirrored planter and smiled, thinking of yesterday.

How strange that before yesterday, when Holly had thought of the play date, she'd tried to picture herself with the Marlboro Man while the kids played. She'd imagined a lot of awkward silences, she'd expected tedium, but the day had been anything but. It had been extraordinary.

She remembered looking at him across his kitchen table with his black hair pulled back and his square jaw and dark blue eyes. She'd looked at the lonesome Marlboro Man who listened to song lyrics and built pergolas and brought firewood to his neighbors, and thought that she'd never met another man like him.

And then, of course, there had been that kiss. That spectacular, unplanned-for, unanticipated, unlikely, out-of-the-blue kiss. That kiss was chocolate soufflé, it was expensive champagne, it was a warm fire on a snowy winter day. Wyatt had seemed shocked by his own actions. He'd stared at her when he'd lifted his head, clearly stunned by what he'd done, and she'd felt him retreating, felt him pulling away, cobwebs and all, and she'd grabbed him back, had kissed him back. *That* kiss had been a gold strike, a summer thunderstorm, New Year's Eve fireworks. Spec. Tacular.

There hadn't been another kiss after that, not after the kids were up and running around. But that didn't mean Holly wasn't intensely, acutely aware of him. All of him. She'd examined his back and his shoulders as he grilled steaks, and how the muscles moved beneath his shirt, how big his hands seemed next to the steaks. She was aware of his hips, lean and tight, and his thighs, made thick by gripping a saddle . . . or so she'd fantasized.

As he cleaned the kitchen while Holly kept the kids occupied, Wyatt had kept looking around for her, giving her that lopsided smile. Something had clicked; a door had opened and waves of balmy attraction had begun to shimmer between them. It had been real. It had been exhilarating. It had been so palpable that Holly had asked if he and Grace wanted to come to her house the following day to play in the big tire tubes that someone had left in the shed.

"That depends," he'd said, his eyes sparkling in the light of the chiminea.

"On what?"

"On how many of those cookies you're going to force me to eat. I don't have a belt large enough to handle it."

She'd laughed. They'd said good night, and at her car he'd said, "Keep that guitar handy." He'd taken her hand, letting his fingers tangle loosely with hers. " 'Cause I won't be leaving until I get a song. Fair warning."

Fair enough. Holly tried to remember the last man she'd been this excited to see. She had to go way back,

Julia London

and that man had worn a red coat, had had a long white beard and six reindeer to guide him.

Wyatt honked as he pulled up to the house.

"*Doo-ey,*" Mason said when he saw Wyatt and Grace coming up the porch steps. He was standing at the old heavy wooden coffee table with his two toy trains, rolling them around, crashing them into each other.

"Hi!" Holly said, and stepped aside, making room for Grace, who entered dragging two pull toys behind her. Holly smiled up at Wyatt. She was astonishingly happy to see him, especially after Hannah's phone call. "Hi," she said again.

"Hello." A smile creased the corners of his eyes. He stepped across the threshold with a paper bag in one hand, flowers in the other, and a brisk wind at his back. "Grace, you have to share."

Grace apparently didn't think she needed to, because she started running with the pull toys, which played an almost maniacal version of "Pop Goes the Weasel."

"That sounds like hours of entertainment," Holly mused.

"That sounds like I might lose my mind," Wyatt said, frowning slightly. "They didn't sound quite so loud in the store."

Holly glanced at the flowers he was holding in one hand. "Are those for me?"

Wyatt looked down as if he'd just realized that he had them. "Yes," he said, and held them out to her.

Holly smiled broadly and brought them to her nose, inhaling their fragrance. "Thank you. Come on in," she said, and walked into the kitchen. Mason and Grace followed in her wake like minnows. She gave them each an animal cracker and shooed them out with their toys. Wyatt put his bag on the kitchen bar, shoved his hands into his pockets, and watched the kids a moment, then glanced around the kitchen. He looked uncomfortable. A little nervous, maybe. She couldn't imagine why a man like Wyatt would be nervous around her. *She,* on the other hand, was very nervous. She wasn't entirely sure why. Maybe because she really, desperately hoped she hadn't imagined everything yesterday.

"So," Wyatt said. "This is where you grew up?"

"Right here in River City." Holly opened a cabinet and pulled out a vase. The glass was cloudy, probably from sitting in this same dreary cabinet for many dreary years. "I lived here until I was seventeen." She picked up a cloth to clean it with.

"Seventeen? Then what?"

"Then I moved to Austin." She smiled at the memory of her teenage self, with her big hair and tight jeans. "I loaded up my Volkswagen Beetle with my guitar and a few clothes and off I went in search of fame and fortune."

"Really?" Wyatt said, looking interested. He moved deeper into the kitchen but kept one eye on the children. "That's a big step for a seventeen-year-old. Where did you go?"

She laughed wryly and shook her head. "To the trailer park on Barton Springs Road, next to the Shady Grove Restaurant." She glanced back at him. "Remember that little park under the pecan trees? It was sandwiched between all the restaurants."

Wyatt nodded.

"Well, I met a guy who played in a band, of course, and he lived there with a couple of the band members." The truth was that she'd hardly known Zach. He'd played in a swing band on Saturday nights at the old Rooster Dance Hall, the dive on the edge of Cedar Springs. He had had long blond hair and would drape himself over his guitar as if he could feel the music coming from it. Holly had thought it was very artist-like; she'd been completely captivated, falling in love with him almost instantly.

Zach had been happy to have her adore him, in spite of their eight-year age difference. He'd encouraged her to come to Austin. "You'll never get anywhere out here," he'd scoffed.

So Holly had packed her things. Hannah had warned her she was making a mistake. She'd stood there at the door of Holly's room, her arms folded, watching stoically as Holly rifled through her clothes, picking some and quickly discarding others. "You know that if this guy really cared about you, he'd come and get you and talk to Dad himself," she'd said.

"He cares," Holly had insisted. "You don't understand. He's an artist, a musician."

"Being a musician doesn't mean he shouldn't come here and get you if he's really into you," Hannah had persisted. "I know that kind of guy, Holly, and I'm afraid you're going to be really sorry."

But Holly hadn't listened to her sister. She'd had visions of great things happening to her. Love. Freedom to be a musician. Stardom.

Hannah had been right in the end, as it turned out.

Not two weeks later, Holly was rooming with a waitress from a beer joint whom she hardly knew. Her soulful artist had turned out to be a major pothead. He'd been draped over his guitar, not because he was feeling the music, but because he was stoned. He had no money, no plan for his future, and worse, he hadn't been nearly as interested in creating music as Holly was.

"Your parents couldn't have been happy about that," Wyatt said idly, bringing Holly's attention back to the present.

"Oh, that is putting it mildly," she said with a laugh. "My dad was very unhappy." In fact, he'd ignored Holly's note that she'd gone to pursue music and had made Hannah tell him where she was. Holly would never forget opening the door of that Airstream trailer and seeing him standing there. He'd made her come home. Holly's adventure had only added to tensions with her mother, which seemed to exist like permafrost between them, unchanging, unyielding. "Now all of Cedar Springs will think we're trash because we couldn't keep our own daughter home," her mother had said.

"It was a dumb thing to do, but at the time I was convinced I had to leave or stay out here and get married. Are you from here?" she asked.

"Burnet County."

"Aha," Holly said, nodding. Burnet County was just like Cedar County—steeped in ranching and football. "Then you must have felt the pressure to hurry up and pick a girl and marry too."

"Nah," he said, with a shake of his head. "I felt the pressure from friends to have a good time and date as many girls as a I could."

"I'm sure that wasn't a problem," Holly said, smiling at him over her shoulder. "I bet girls were launching themselves like grenades at you." He smiled back a little self-consciously, but he didn't deny it. "Where'd you go, U.T.?" she asked, referring to the University of Texas in Austin.

"Yep. You?"

"Same here," she said. "For one and a half years. I wasn't exactly college material."

"That's because you had a different path," he said. "I don't think musical talent can be learned in a classroom."

"That was my argument with my mother. I stayed long enough to learn music theory, which helped me a lot. But honestly? I went to college to get away from home." Her smile turned rueful.

"I'm sure you weren't alone," Wyatt said. "I'd bet half your class was there for that very reason. Gracie, no," he said through the doorway to the next room, and walked out of the kitchen.

Holly filled the vase with water and unwrapped the flowers, then set them in the vase. Wyatt returned with both kids, one under each arm. "I thought, with two identical toys, we might have a little harmony, but apparently I was wrong."

"Dada," Grace said.

Wyatt put them down. "Play nice," he said to them, and watched them toddle back to the living room.

Holly put a plate of cupcakes on the kitchen bar and smiled proudly. They were perfectly formed, perfectly iced. "Red velvet," she said.

"Wow." He nodded appreciatively.

"I used my mom's recipe. They are the best."

"You weren't kidding about turning yourself into a cook."

"Which surprises the hell out of me. It was always a joke in my family that I didn't know where anything was in the kitchen except the refrigerator." She opened the bag of things he'd brought and gasped with delight. "Malbec! That happens to be a favorite of mine. And hummus! Yum." She placed the items on the bar.

"Shall I open the wine?" Wyatt asked.

"Yes, I'd love for you to. Look at this! Olives and cheese and crackers too?" Holly beamed at him. She had an inkling that perhaps that kiss had meant something to him, too. "This is going to make my low-rent tuna casserole look a little more uptown. It was my mom's specialty. Hope you're okay with that."

"I am . . . definitely okay with tuna casserole," he said, his gaze on hers.

Holly felt it again, that electric shiver coursing through her.

They searched for a corkscrew—an item that was not handy, given her mother's dislike of alcohol, but one Holly thought she might have found more easily, given the eye-opening number of empty wine bottles in the closet. They found an ancient one in the back of a utensil drawer. It looked hidden to Holly. Was she imagining things now?

Wyatt had to work it but got the cork out.

They joined the kids in the living area, and as they drank wine they chatted about everything and nothing, about life, about diapers and walking and the important graduation from bottle to sippy cup.

Wyatt loved music and was very interested in her career, which thrilled Holly. She felt validated, that she had a career that was not just a hobby but a true and worthy profession. She told him that songwriting had always appealed to her, in part, because she found words fascinating. "It's really hard for me to choose the right words to convey a lot of emotion in a few lines," she'd said. "I can't help but think of all the things I've said or didn't say, and of all the ways I might have said them better, you know?"

He stared at her. She was afraid for a moment that he thought she was nuts. But then he said, "Yes. I know. I know how much words and their meanings matter. The wrong words can ruin a song. The right words can convey a lot of emotion."

"Give me an example," Holly challenged him.

"Okay." He leaned back, thinking. "Paul Anka, 'Having My Baby.'" He sang off key: "'Havin' my baby / What a lovely way of sayin' how much you love me . . .'"

"Ack, stop!" Holly cried, and laughed so hard that the kids paused in their playing to stare at her.

"See?" Wyatt said, grinning. "That's some bad lyrics right there." His eyes were shining. "Top that."

"Okay," Holly said, ready to accept the challenge. "'MacArthur Park,' Donna Summer, 'Someone left the cake out in the rain . . .'"

Wyatt laughed a deep, rich laugh. He was amazingly different from the man she'd previously thought—he was *fun*. Imagine, that gruff cowboy, fun! "Yeah, those are some bad lyrics," he cheerfully agreed.

"Tell me some good lyrics," Holly asked.

"Easy," he said. "Patty Griffin. Great songwriter. 'Long Road Home' is the song. You know that one?"

"I do," Holly had said, beaming at him. "Tell me what you like about it."

"I like that she makes you think. Give me a minute," he said, and put down his wineglass. "Okay, here goes: *'Forty years of things you say you wish you'd never said / How hard would it have been to say some kinder words instead . . .'*"

Wyatt stopped there and smiled self-consciously. "I don't think that's the right tune, but you get the idea."

"*'I've had some time to think about you / And watch the stone set like a stone . . .'*" Holly finished quietly.

He held her gaze again, a pregnant moment of silent anticipation that simmered in Holly's veins. "That's the tune," he said. "And you have a very pretty voice, Holly."

"Thank you." She was feeling quite warm all of a sudden, and removed the scarf draped around her neck. "Are you hungry?"

Over tuna casserole, they covered a range of topics, such as the Dallas Cowboys' chance at making the play-offs (Wyatt seemed a little surprised that Holly was a knowledgable fan) and the greatest vacation spots. He'd traveled much more than Holly. "Cabo San Lucas," he said. "You can't beat it for ambience or things to do."

"I've never been," Holly said as she handed Mason his sippy cup of milk. "I have always wanted to go to Scotland," she said dreamily.

"Love Scotland," he said. "I played golf there a few years ago."

Holly laughed. "You *golf?*"

He chuckled. "Yes. Why?"

"I don't know," she said, eyeing him. "You don't look like a golfer."

"Oh yeah? What do I look like?"

Holly smiled and took a bite of casserole, studying him.

Wyatt leaned across the table. "What do I look like, Holly?" he asked again.

Those blue eyes could entice a woman to do just about anything, she thought. "Rodeo," she said.

"Rider? Or clown?"

Holly laughed. "Rider!"

He sat back, apparently satisfied with that.

After the meal, Holly put the kids down for a nap. When she came downstairs, Wyatt was nowhere to be seen. She walked to the sliding glass door her father had installed in place of the old double screen doors and looked out, but she didn't see him. Overhead, thick gray clouds were sliding down from the north, squeezing the sunlight from the day.

"I think we need a fire."

Holly turned around; Wyatt had come in the front door with an armful of wood.

"What about the creosote? You said I could set the house on fire."

"I told you that to keep you from trying," he said with a smile. "You didn't exactly exude an air of confidence."

"You're a smart guy, Wyatt." She poured the last of the wine into their glasses as Wyatt went down on one knee before the fireplace and built the fire. Flames instantly shot up; the fire grew and began to crackle. Holly handed him his wineglass and they stood a moment, watching the fire. "Nice job. I don't think I could have achieved that effect without a gallon of lighter fluid."

"I know," Wyatt said, and smiled at her, and it suddenly felt as if the air between them was crackling as sharply as the fire. He was looking at her so intently that Holly felt compelled to step back to catch her breath. She took a seat on the couch, and Wyatt joined her there, sitting so close that she could feel the heat from his body against her arm.

"I like building fires in the chiminea," he said. "You can see a whole word in the flames, and I could stare at it for hours. In fact, I think I have."

"Sounds kind of lonely," Holly said, and imagined him sitting in the old metal chair, one booted foot propped on the other chair, a beer dangling from his fingers.

"It's a game for one."

"How long have you been one?" she asked curiously, and felt his body stiffen.

"Two years."

He offered no more than that, so Holly said, "She seems nice."

Wyatt glanced curiously at Holly. "You haven't heard, have you?"

"Heard what?"

"About the poor schmuck who lost his wife."

"What do you mean?" She put aside her wineglass. "The only thing I have heard about you is that you are a developer. Your ex–mother-in-law is help-

ing me probate my mom's will, and she told me that.
Why? And why would anyone think you were a poor
schmuck? "

His expression darkened. "Because I was the loser."
Holly stared at him, and he shrugged self-consciously.
"I've never really talked to anyone about this. Well,
that's not true," he amended. "I told a woman once . . ."
He studied the arm of the couch. "But she didn't speak
much English."

"You are confusing me," Holly said. "What have
you not talked about?"

"How my marriage ended."

Holly twisted around on the couch to face him. "Are
you going to tell me?"

Wyatt's smile was sad. He pushed her hair off her
shoulder, touched her chin. "Yes," he said. "I met
Macy a little more than four years ago. She was a war
widow," he said, and told Holly how hard he'd fallen
for her. He'd seen a sad and vulnerable woman, but
love had developed between them.

"I loved her very much," he said quietly. He told
Holly that he'd built her a big house in Arbolago Hills,
a tony suburb of Cedar Springs. "Do you know that
community?"

Holly nodded. Everyone knew Arbolago Hills,
where million-dollar homes perched on the side of the
hills overlooking Lake Del Lago.

"She really loved that house," he said, looking at
his wineglass. "It was perfect for us both. We wanted
to have kids . . ." He gave her a lopsided smile. "I've
always wanted a whole houseful of kids, I'll be honest.
I don't know if Macy wanted as many as me, but she

wanted kids, and we were working hard on that when Finn came home."

"Who?" Holly asked.

Wyatt sighed and glanced away. "Finn Lockhart. Her dead soldier husband," he said. "He was serving in Afghanistan. He'd been reported dead by the U.S. Army, but in reality he was being held captive by the Taliban. The Army had made a huge mistake with some dog tags, and then Finn escaped and came home. I guess he thought he was coming back to the world he'd left behind, but Macy . . . she'd mourned him, and she'd moved on. Or so I thought."

"Oh my God," Holly said, shocked. "I heard about that guy."

"I'm sure you did. He was a big news story at the time." He shook his head. "Macy, bless her, she tried. But she was twisted up inside, especially when she found out she was pregnant with Grace. She loved me, I guess. But she loved Finn more. And she chose him in the end." He picked up Holly's hand and threaded his fingers through hers. "And that is how yours truly became the poor schmuck of Cedar Springs."

"Who would think that? It's an extraordinary story, Wyatt."

"Well, I kind of wigged out," he said. "I went off on a binge. Hooked up with some hippies, drank myself silly. Stole some land from Finn—"

"What?"

"Not stole, exactly," he said, waving a hand at her. "But yeah, it was a dirty deal." He chuckled as he looked at their hands. "I felt so bad about it that I sold another piece of land and donated the proceeds to their large animal rescue. That's what they do now, they run a big large animal rescue farm. Horses, llamas, I don't know what all." He shrugged and looked down again.

"That . . . is an amazing story," Holly said.

He smiled. "It was amazing all right. An amazing kick in the ass."

"It sounds to me like a remarkable chain of events with no easy answers," Holly said carefully. "I think you must be the most . . ." She tried to think of the right word. ". . . *chivalrous* man I have ever met."

That remark brought him up off the couch. "This is not something I like talking about, but I won't let you turn it into something romantic. It was way out of my hands. I didn't have much of a choice. And I did some things I am not proud of."

"You had a choice," Holly said. "You could have fought it. You could have kept your money instead of making the donation to their wildlife ranch."

"You don't understand," he argued. "I tried to fight for Macy, but what was the point? She was in love with someone else. That's all there is to this little tale. My wife loved someone else more than she loved me." He looked down at his hands, spreading his fingers wide, and clenched his jaw.

How painful it must have been for him; how painful it seemed yet. Holly rose to her feet. "Oh, Wyatt. I am so sorry. But I do know how it feels to think you have no choice when your life—your good, happy life—is completely uprooted and you can do nothing but be dragged along with the wreckage."

Wyatt looked up from his hand to her. "I know you do."

"It's so frustrating, and the sense of injustice can be so overwhelming," she said, and took his hand, pulling him back to the couch. "I'm glad you told me. We're a pair, you know? Both of us hit by that goddamn freight train." She smiled. "Don't you think it's interesting that of all the people in the world we should meet, we each met someone whose life had been shaped by events so far beyond their control?"

"I guess it is," he agreed, and pushed his hand through his hair. "I guess I ought to count my blessings. I didn't have to take care of anyone but myself. And I always knew where Macy was."

Holly's belly did a queer little dip. "Yeah . . . Guess what? Hannah is in Palm Beach, Florida. She called me this morning."

The news obviously surprised Wyatt. "She did?"

"Yep. She's in rehab for drugs. Pills. OxyContin. Xanax . . ." She shook her head. "I don't even remember them all."

Wyatt didn't even know Hannah but he looked stunned. He was probably running through all the images that had played in Holly's mind, images of people strung out on drugs in alleys, shooting dope. Dirty, toothless, used-up drug fiends. Holly would have helped Hannah if she'd known. She was almost certain she would have . . . but then again, she'd let Hannah do all the heavy lifting with their mother, had abdicated all responsibility with the excuse of too much work and costly transportation. The truth was that she would have done just about anything to avoid dealing with their mother. Was that when Hannah became an addict? When Peggy was dying and Holly was avoiding it?

"How long is she there?" he asked.

"She said she had another sixty days. And then . . . sixty days of transitional housing or something."

Wyatt's expression was full of sympathy.

"I don't know what to do about Mason," she muttered. She suddenly pictured Hannah strung out and Mason forgotten, crying for her attention. It made her gasp softly.

"What do you mean?"

"His mother is an addict," Holly said. "I know she's in rehab and she's trying to get well . . . but isn't this very serious? Can she really just quit taking pills or drinking? I found a closet full of her empty wine bottles. How can I know she won't fall off the wagon? She could hurt him, you know, or put him in danger."

"Holly?" Wyatt said, his eyebrows dipping into a puzzled frown. "What exactly are you saying?"

"I don't know," she replied, shaking her head. "I really don't know what I *am* saying, but I don't know how I can put him back in that situation."

Wyatt studied her a long moment. "I don't know what the alternative is here, baby," he said gently, and Holly flushed at the soft endearment. "Mason is her son."

"I know, but I thought maybe . . ." Holly felt herself stepping out on a limb. "I thought maybe I could convince Hannah that he should stay with me until she's better. A whole lot better. You know, after some time has passed and we all know she's okay."

Wyatt put his hand on her knee and rubbed his thumb on her skin. "Do you want to raise Mason?"

"No, I . . . not exactly, but after talking to her . . ."

What *did* she want? What, in her heart of hearts, did she *want*? She could see Mason's round little face, his blue eyes smiling up at her. "Yes. Maybe," she confessed. She could see the doubt in Wyatt's blue eyes. "I feel so protective of him," she added quickly. "He deserves stability."

"He does," Wyatt agreed. "But that's a big step."

"I know, I know . . . but I can't imagine him in a bad situation. I would never live with myself if something happened to him after I gave him back." Her vision suddenly blurred when she thought of that wonderful little boy. Shocked and embarrassed by the possibility of tears, Holly turned away from Wyatt.

"I understand. But he is your sister's son."

"I know," she said, with a flick of her wrist. "I don't know what I'm saying. I'm just talking out loud."

"Hey," Wyatt said, then leaned closer, put his arm around her, and pulled her close. "It's going to be okay," he said.

"How can it ever be okay for Mason?"

"Because it will. Kids survive much worse. They're resilient."

She hoped that was true, but she wished Mason didn't have to "survive" anything. He should wake up every morning to sunshine and bluebirds and new discoveries, to love and laughter and parents who loved him and wanted only the best for him. Not to a mother who was stoned and an absent father.

"He's lucky to have you," Wyatt said. "He's a lucky little boy."

Holly was the lucky one. She turned toward him. Neither of them spoke; Wyatt's fingers drifted across her cheek, brushed her hair back, and grazed her ear. Holly looked at his lips, recalling the kiss they'd shared yesterday. A man was the last thing she'd had on her mind when she'd moved back here, but then he'd appeared in her yard, and he was so understanding of the chaos in her life . . .

"And I'm a lucky guy," he murmured, and kissed her. His hand slid to her neck, his fingers curling softly around it, his mouth moving against hers.

Holly swayed into him, pressed her body against his, wanting to feel his strength, the power of his arms around her. She slipped one arm around his waist, the other sliding up his chest. She felt light-headed with desire, felt herself starting to float with want, anchored only by her hold on him. She had an insatiable need to be with him, to feel him.

When his hand moved to her shirt and slipped under it, his palm against the bare skin of her back, Holly had a nudge of conscience and leaned back. "What are we doing?"

His gaze drifted to her mouth. "*I'm* doing what I've wanted to do since the moment I saw you," he said. "What are you doing?"

There was something sinfully sexy about the way he had said it, and Holly melted. "What about the kids?" she whispered as his lips touched her cheek.

"They're asleep."

"But I—"

"Don't overthink it," he murmured, and teased her earlobe with the tip of his tongue.

She was not going to overthink it. It felt too good and too perfect on an overcast, blustery day with two babies sleeping upstairs and a very nice fire crackling in the living room. And she needed him. She was caught off guard by the strength of her need. He was the one person in a very long time who had accepted her as she was, and Holly had an insane desire to cling to that just now.

He pulled her down onto the living room rug and kicked off his boots at the same time that he moved over her to kiss her, his hand on her waist, sliding up under her shirt to her breasts. A lusty warmth spread through Holly; her arms went around his back, her hands splayed on his shoulder blades. He was hard and muscular, and she was aroused in a way she had not been in a very long time. When he filled his hands with her breasts, he made a sound of pleasure that fired her blood; she sat up, pulled her shirt over her head, tossed it aside, and watched Wyatt's gaze rake over her body. His dark and shining eyes were full of desire, of reverence, of gratification, and there was nothing, absolutely nothing, that could arouse Holly more. She felt herself so damp and eager for just a touch from him. Her arousal was powerful; she'd not been moved this way by a man in so very long. If ever.

He stroked the inside of her thigh, lowered his head to her bra, mouthing her breast through it. Holly dug her fingers into his arms and pressed against him. She hadn't realized how starved she was for intimacy, but nothing seemed more urgent. He slid down her body with his mouth and hands in one excruciatingly pleasurable move.

With his thumb, he popped the buttons of her jeans, one by one.

Pure instinct took hold of Holly; somehow her jeans came off. Somehow his shirt came off, and her hands were on his bare skin, feeling the muscles in his chest and abdomen move, then they slipped into the waist of his jeans, her fingers skating over his hips, his erection hot and thick in her hand.

"I've been wanting you something awful," he said, his voice low, his breath hot on her skin. A moment later they were naked on that old worn rug before the fire, and his hands, his thick, callused hands, were stroking her everywhere, and Holly's heart was thudding in her chest.

Delicious, consuming desire seared her as they explored each other's bodies, fingers trailing over hot, damp skin, mouths warm and moist on each other's flesh. This felt right to Holly; it felt as if she'd been waiting for this very moment. Wyatt locked his eyes on hers, watching her reaction and pleasure as he slowly slid into her.

Holly closed her eyes and allowed him to push her out into a deep pool of sensation. He was so hard, so hot, so thick inside her; his heart was beating as rapidly as hers; his breath was ragged. He was attentive to her, sensing her climax and riding along with her as she burst, falling like glitter into the ecstasy of it, falling still moments later when he withdrew with a strangled cry at the moment of his climax. He pressed his forehead to hers and stroked her hair, catching his breath, and then slowly moved to her side. "I'd forgotten how good it feels," he said in a low voice, and took her hand in his.

Holly felt remarkably content. All the trauma and

chaos that had swirled around her was distant noise. In his arms, she felt safe from that. It was a moment of utter peace. She stroked his bare hip and flank.

He opened his eyes, bent one arm behind his head to use as a pillow, and smiled at her. "You're something else, Holly Fisher."

She softly kissed his shoulder. "The feeling is entirely mutual, Wyatt Clark." She was on the verge of telling him that that had been some of the best sex she'd ever had, but the sound of a baby crying reached her ears, and they both stilled.

"Sounds like Grace," he said, and sat up.

"I'll go," Holly said, and grabbed the nearest item of clothing—Wyatt's shirt—and pulled it on as she darted upstairs. She walked down the hall, pushing her tangled hair back from her face, and then paused outside the door of the nursery, listening. She heard nothing. She slowly opened the door, wincing when it creaked, and poked her head around the edge of it.

Mason and Grace were lying side by side in the playpen. Grace was turned toward Mason, her arm draped over his neck. Mason was sleeping with his mouth open. How peaceful the two babies looked. Holly tiptoed over and removed Grace's arm, but neither toddler stirred. She waited a moment to make sure neither of them were waking, then went out, quietly closing the door behind her.

Downstairs, Wyatt had donned his jeans and was sitting on the couch, one arm resting across the back of it, his bare feet propped on the coffee table. He grinned when she walked in. "Everything okay?" he asked, indicating she should sit next to him.

"They're fast asleep." She crawled onto her knees on the couch beside him.

Wyatt put his arm around her shoulders and kissed the top of her head. "You look like a kitten in a bowl of cream, you know that?"

"I feel like a kitten who has been *swimming* in cream," she said, and put her hand on his abdomen. It was firm, the sign of a man who worked hard for a living. She liked that he used his hands and his body in addition to his head to run his ranch. She liked that he wasn't sitting in some air-conditioned office somewhere.

"I didn't intend this, Holly."

She looked up. "Intend what? Sex?"

He gave her a sheepish look and playfully pulled her ear. "Is that all it was? Sex?"

"No. It was ridiculously good sex."

Wyatt smiled. "I guess in my clumsy way I am trying to say that I didn't want you to think that I came over here today with sex on my mind. I mean, it probably *was*," he said apologetically. "I'll be damned if I know how to get it *off* my mind. But not like that. I'm not a player. I've made mistakes in the past, but on the whole, I don't generally make love to a woman for the sake of sex. There has to be something more for me."

"So, what are you saying?" Holly asked curiously, and idly brushed the hair from his forehead. "Is there more here? Are we seeing each other?"

Wyatt honestly looked confused for a moment. "Are we?" he asked uncertainly.

Holly couldn't help but laugh. "Let me tell you how I see it," she said as she laid her hand against his bare chest. "I see two people who weren't looking for a relationship but, through some miracle, met, and they were attracted to one another, and had ridiculous sex, and now they are contemplating seeing how things go."

He gave her a lopsided grin. "Funny. I see the same thing."

She kissed him on the mouth.

Wyatt's hand instantly went to her back, holding her there. "Great analysis, but you are forgetting something."

"What?"

"I haven't heard your music," he said, and tucked her hair behind her ears. "If you and I are seeing each other, I want to hear you play."

"The babies are going to wake up . . ."

"They're going to wake up one way or the other. Come on, now, Holly. Lots of other people—strangers—have heard your songs. If we're seeing each other, I think that ought to be one of my perks."

"So what's *my* perk?" she asked.

"Want me to show you again?" he responded with a wicked grin.

"Yes!" she said eagerly, and kissed him.

"Uh-uh," Wyatt said against her mouth, and laughingly pushed her back. "Play first."

"Okay," she said, cheerfully giving in. She got up from the couch, picked up her guitar from the mantel—she had to put it there to keep it out of Mason's reach—and settled into a chair, her bare legs daintily crossed. She strummed a few chords, thinking.

Wyatt laughed at her. Holly strummed a few more

chords, finding the right key. "You're amazing," he said, teasing her. "That song is amazing."

She grinned, settled on an up-tempo song with basic chords, and winged it. "Okay, here goes:

"Met him on a dusty fall day
Learned the man had little to say.
He's a tall drink of water, smiling at me.
Thought I was the bother, but now he won't leave.
Beware those lonesome cowboys, girl, beware those
* lonesome cowboys."*

She finished it up with a flourish on the strings, then smiled at him.

Grinning, Wyatt applauded, and Holly bowed over her strings. "You play very well," he said. "But I knew you would." He held out his hand to her. "Come here."

Holly put the guitar aside and took his hand. Wyatt yanked her toward him and she landed on his lap.

"I won't leave, huh?" he asked, and smothered her laughter with a very stirring kiss.

Chapter Fifteen

The next few weeks swirled around Wyatt, speeding past him, sweeping him along and settling him into the cooler days of fall. It seemed as if his life had turned some imaginary corner. He spent a lot of time with Holly and Mason and, on his allotted days, with Grace, too. After that incredible first weekend when he and Holly had come together, Wyatt would stop by her house at the end of his workday. After a few days, when she discovered he existed on TV dinners, she began to cook for him. Once she learned how to make a crust, she made pies, too, such as apple, rhubarb, and pumpkin.

Wyatt hadn't eaten that well in years.

He became attached to Mason, a happy little cherub of a boy who would laugh with delight when Wyatt put him in the saddle before him, anchoring the toddler to his belly with one arm, and let Troy meander along a trail across the pasture next to the Fisher house. It wasn't long before Mason was shouting, *"Hors-ey, hors-ey,"* when Wyatt appeared at the fence line on Troy's back.

When Wyatt began the renovation of his house with the guest bath, Holly wanted to help. He was reluctant to let her at first, but as it turned out, she was pretty good with a sledgehammer. It didn't hurt that she wore a tight T-shirt and yoga pants that fit her butt like a glove when she worked. He liked admiring her as much as he appreciated the help.

Sometimes in the evenings Wyatt would play with Mason for an hour so that she could work on her music. She'd sit at the piano, her brows knitted in a thoughtful frown, erasing notes with a pencil and adding new ones. She had a quirky little habit of fluttering her fingers before she touched the keys, and when she played the guitar, she would slide her fingers along the strings before playing the first notes.

On weekends when Wyatt had Grace, the four of them piled into his good truck and headed to Austin, where they would do a little shopping for the week— Holly insisted he put more in his fridge besides beer— and take the kids to a coffee shop that Holly knew of that boasted an indoor toddler playground. While the kids played, Holly would check her e-mail and catch up with her friends, and he'd work on the daily crossword.

It might not have seemed like much to the average observer—he and Holly didn't go out a lot, or dine at fine establishments, or catch movies—but it was everything to Wyatt. This was the sort of life he'd always imagined he'd have, and it was really nice after the deep hole he'd found himself in after Macy left him.

He was in such good spirits as the days moved toward the holidays, he was thinking of developing a strip of land he owned along Highway 281. It was the first time in more than a year he'd had a fire in his belly to make a deal.

He didn't even mind Jesse's nosy questions.

"Why do you always look like a choir girl about to sing her solo?" Jesse had asked Wyatt early on one afternoon as they were building an enclosed storage unit for hay. "You look like you could hit all the high notes."

"I don't know what you're talking about," Wyatt had said congenially. "I'm just building a metal box here."

"Bull," Jesse had said, then put his gloved hands on his waist and had stared skeptically at Wyatt. "Honest to God, I haven't seen you smile this much since you won that golf tournament a few years back."

Wyatt hadn't thought of that golf tournament in ages. He used to love to play and would be on a course every weekend. "What'd I shoot, Jesse?" he'd asked curiously. "Three under par? And what was the closest score to mine? Two over?" He laughed. "Good times."

"Come on, what is up with you?" Jesse had demanded, and Wyatt had just laughed.

But Jesse was a determined cuss, and he'd leaned back against the truck, folding his arms. "I bet I can guess. I bet you've been mending some more fences down by the Fisher place."

Wyatt had snorted. "What's the number one rule, Jesse? As I recall, it's no talking, just work."

"She's cute," Jesse had said. "I would have thought you'd go for a more professional type, like a lawyer, but I like Holly. Good for you, Wyatt. It's about time."

"You think you know something you don't know," Wyatt had said.

"Well, then maybe you've taken to wearing bras under your shirt—I don't know. I'm not a man to judge that sort of thing, but I sure hoped it belonged to Holly."

Wyatt had straightened up then and looked curiously at Jesse. "What bra?"

Jesse had grinned. "A blue bra in your bathroom."

Wyatt had suddenly remembered the bra in his bathroom and his gaze narrowed. "What were you doing in my bathroom?"

"What do you think I was doing? You busted up the other one, remember? Come on, pal, you can tell me," Jesse had said.

Wyatt had sighed then, knowing he'd been discovered. He wasn't going to hide it. "Okay. You're right. I've been seeing her and I like her."

"Praise be to Jesus!" Jesse had said dramatically, shaking his hands to the heavens. "I was starting to think you'd die alone out here. I can stop worrying about you now."

"I still might die out here alone," Wyatt had retorted. "And don't make a big damn deal out of it. We're just seeing each other."

But Jesse had grinned. "Yet, you have bras hanging in your bathroom. Take my advice—"

"God, please, no, don't give me advice," Wyatt had said, and started for his truck.

"Spruce things up around here," Jesse had blithely continued, following along behind Wyatt and Milo. "I like that you've started on the bathroom, but this place could use some paint, and you should definitely put some flowers on that patio. It's as bare as a washed-out gully. And by the way, since you've been living like a hermit, I've got a couple of nice places you should take her."

Wyatt had happily prayed for patience as he got in his old truck.

Jesse wasn't the only one who had it figured out. A few days later Wyatt went into the office to sign checks, and Linda Gail pushed back so hard in her office chair that she rolled right into the filing cabinet. She folded her hands over her abundant midriff and glared at him.

"What?" Wyatt asked, thinking he'd forgotten to do something he'd promised.

"Were you going to tell me, or just let me hear it all over town?"

He knew right then he was in trouble. Linda Gail didn't like being the last to know things. "Hear what?"

Linda Gail snorted. "Don't do that, Wyatt. Everyone is talking about it. I had to hear it from Sam Delaney of all people, and she seemed a little smug about it."

"So," he said, folding his arms, too, "Cedar Springs is all atwitter at the prospect of Wyatt Clark having met someone?"

"I'd say that's about the size of it," Linda Gail agreed.

"Now listen here, Linda Gail," Wyatt said sternly. "I am not going to abide a lot of talk. I've had enough of that." He started walking past all the plat maps and boxes of files that filled their little two-room office, ignoring Linda Gail and her impatient glare.

"Don't go getting your back up with me, Wyatt

Clark," she shot right back. "We're all rooting for you. Everyone in this two-bit town is rooting for you. Especially *me*!"

He paused at the door of his office and looked back at Linda Gail. She'd been with him for fifteen years, since he'd started as a cocky twenty-something with bigger ideas than sense or money. She'd been a housewife looking for some time away from three kids, and she knew how to work a computer. Linda Gail had been more than loyal. She'd stepped up and protected Wyatt and his interests when he had fallen apart after Macy left him. He'd be nowhere without Linda Gail.

"And if I was the only who'd heard something, I'd still want to know, because I care about you, you dumb-ass cowboy."

Wyatt almost laughed. Linda Gail was like a bossy older sister, annoying and irresistible at once. "Well," he said, leaning against the door frame, "I imagine you already know who she is."

"I don't know for sure," Linda Gail said with a shrug. "One of the Fisher girls would be my guess."

"That would be a good guess. The younger one. And that's all we need to say about it, okay?" He grunted when Linda Gail whooped with glee.

Wyatt didn't like the fact that the whole town seemed so interested in what he was doing, and under the normal circumstances of the last two years, it would have pushed him deeper into isolation. He'd been humiliated before all of Cedar Springs when Macy had left him for Finn. His own actions hadn't helped him any—especially sleeping with Samantha Delaney—but for a man who valued his standing in the community, to have his personal hell be so public had been a huge blow.

But now he didn't care. The only thing he cared about was what he and Holly were having for dinner that night, or when they were going to Austin again so that she could work with Quincy Crowe.

Holly often spoke about how worried she was that she couldn't find time to work with Quincy because she didn't have child care for Mason. She fretted aloud over it, talking more to herself than to him, which he was learning was a funny habit of hers. She worked whenever she managed to find the time, but Mason, cute little rascal that he was, was her biggest obstacle. He was an active toddler, into everything, and he, like Wyatt, craved Holly's attention.

"I adore him, you know I do," Holly had said one night when they lay in bed at her house. He had Grace for the weekend, and they'd spent the two days together playing with the kids while Holly experimented making dressing in preparation for Thanksgiving. It had been a great time. Holly had made lasagna and sautéed some fresh green beans she'd picked up in Cedar Springs. Wyatt could imagine coming home every night, to a pretty woman in his kitchen, to laughing babies, to a good home-cooked meal, to excellent sex. The hallmarks of a life well lived.

"I adore him but, man, he makes it hard to work," Holly had sighed to the ceiling.

"I can fix that, you know," Wyatt had said, and rolled onto his side to look at her. He'd traced his finger over her bare breast, laid his hand on the flat plane of her abdomen. She had a lush figure that made his mouth water. Curves in all the right spots; soft, fragrant skin. He had to say, the lovemaking had been fantastic. Holly had freed him from inhibition; he'd worried less about whether or not she was having a good time because Holly's response to him was so lusty and real. With her mouth and hands and those green eyes shining down at him, she did that to him. It was all instinct, all very primal. Wyatt was a healthy man, and after two years of his spirit wasting away, he couldn't seem to get enough of Holly and her body.

"How can you fix it?" she had asked. "Are you going to write my songs?"

"No. But I can take him a couple of afternoons a week so you can write them."

Holly had laughed softly and shifted closer to kiss him, cupping his chin, brushing her fingers over the stubble of his beard. "Thanks, Wy . . . but you have a job, remember?"

"Jesse can cover for me a few hours a week. I could use a break from all that talking anyway." In the light of the clear, starry night filtering in through the windows, Holly's eyes had shone up at him.

"You'd do that for me?" she'd asked, sounding surprised.

"Of course I would. Haven't you ever had a boyfriend before?"

"Yes, silly," she'd giggled.

"Who?" he'd asked curiously.

"What do you mean, *who*? You don't know them."

"So tell me about them."

"There's nothing much to tell. I've had a couple,

but not in a while. Musicians make for horrible boy-friends."

"Why's that?"

"Well, for starters, they work at night, so you don't see them as often as you might like. They go on the road and forget about you. They are surrounded by women who want to sleep with them, and sometimes they do . . ." Holly had shrugged. "See? Lousy boy-friends."

"I see," he'd said. "So there's been no one besides a couple of musicians? No great love of your life?"

She'd pondered that a moment. "There was one—Po." She had smiled. "Po was short for Poor Richard. He was a bass guitarist. I dated him for about two years."

"So, what happened to Po?" Wyatt asked.

"Ah, Po," she'd said, staring up at the ceiling. "He was a sweet guy, and he was a great musician. He really helped me develop my skills, I have to give him credit for that."

"But?"

"But . . . he wasn't the type to settle down. He liked drifting from gig to gig, and one day he sort of drifted out of my life," she'd said, and made her fingers walk up Wyatt's arm.

Wyatt had suddenly become very interested in Po. The thought of Holly loving someone was . . . disturb-ing in an abstract way. "Did you love him?"

"Yep," she had said without hesitation. "I loved him. But I didn't love how much work he was." Then she had suddenly looked up at Wyatt. "So, are you my boyfriend, Wyatt?"

"I better be," he'd said, and kissed her again, a slow, easy kiss that had stoked the fire in them once more.

That had been a memorable night. And it was how he'd come to be sitting at a table in an Austin bar in the middle of this afternoon, nursing a beer while Mason played with a truck at his feet. Quincy Crowe had arranged to use the Hole in the Wall bar down by the University of Texas campus early one Monday afternoon for rehearsal.

This was the first time Wyatt met Quincy Crowe, and he had to admit, he felt a little like a fan boy. Quincy was a good-looking young man with a warm personality. Wyatt had to acknowledge a little twinge of jealousy at the easy way he and Holly bantered as they set up mikes and tuned their guitars. Quincy would have to be blind not to see how radiant Holly looked in the black skirt that flounced around her knees. Or her black and turquoise cowboy boots, or her denim jacket and scarf wrapped artfully around her neck. She'd put her shaggy strawberry blonde hair in a ponytail, but strands of it had worked their way free and danced around her face. She was about the most appealing thing on earth to Wyatt, aside from Grace.

The bantering stopped when Holly handed Quincy the second song she'd written and they began to go over it. Holly had been really proud to finish it, hopping from one foot to the other when Wyatt had come over one evening. He'd come through the door, and Mason, in his OshKosh B'Gosh overalls, had run for him. "*Wy-wy!*" he'd cried, and Wyatt had swept him up, tossing him a little and catching him again. "How's the best boy in Texas?"

"Wyatt!" Holly had cried, and run out of the kitchen in jeans and a faded T-shirt that said *Shady Grove* across the back. "Look! I finished it. Only one more, and then Quincy goes to the recording studio!"

They'd both been so happy to see him, and Wyatt had felt so good that evening, like he really had a place to belong.

Quincy played the first few verses and the refrain, but Holly stopped him. "Ugh," she said. "Let's change key."

"D?" Quincy asked.

"Hmmm . . . let's try B minor," Holly said, and they started again effortlessly in the new key, making a subtle change in the melody that—to Wyatt's ears, anyway—was much better.

He watched with fascination as the two of them worked on that song. When Holly didn't think the sound suited her on the piano, she'd pick up a guitar, and vice versa. She changed tempo and what she called the chord variations. She seemed to be lost in her own little world, listening to Quincy sing the song she'd written with the lyrics she'd penned, stopping him occasionally to suggest a different musical interpretation.

God, the girl was gifted. Wyatt could see that she was, even with his pedestrian ears and his knowledge of music coming from the one radio station he could get on the ranch. But he knew good music when he heard it, and he had a gut feeling that Holly Fisher was going places.

Quincy Crowe seemed to think so too. "You ever think of going to Nashville?" he asked Holly when they finished work for the day.

Holly looked surprised by Quincy's question. "Ah . . . I don't know. Maybe someday."

Nashville. Wyatt found the notion a little disquieting.

"Maybe now," Quincy said. "You could make some big money there, Holly. I can hook you up with my manager. He knows all the top producers."

Holly stared at Quincy. "For real?" As if she thought he was playing a joke on her.

"Yeah, for real," he said. "Of course for real."

"Wow, that would be great. I—" She hesitated and looked over at Wyatt and Mason. "Maybe after we finish this contract we can talk."

"Sure," Quincy said. "Just let me know."

Mason ran to the edge of the stage. "Lala," he said. "Lala." That was what he was calling Holly these days. Holly scooped him up and kissed his cheek. "Just make these songs a big hit, will you, Quincy?"

"I'll do my best," he said congenially. "So . . . next Friday?"

"Next Friday," Holly promised. "I'll have the chorus worked out and, hopefully, a draft of the third song."

On the way home, they stopped by Holly's apartment so she could pick up a few things. Wyatt was surprised that she had such a small loft. It was nice enough, he supposed—tile floors, granite countertops, stainless appliances—but very small. Room for only one.

"So," he said, examining her beat-up piano. He touched a key. "Nashville, huh?"

"Oh, that," Holly said, waving her hand dismissively. "Quincy is a nice guy, but . . . you know."

"No," Wyatt said. "I don't know."

Holly smiled indulgently. "Nashville is a big deal, Wyatt. I mean, the best songwriters in the world struggle to make it there."

"And? What's your point?"

"And . . . and I'm not that." She seemed ill at ease even mentioning her talent. "I'm not ready for Nashville."

Wyatt cocked his head to one side. He thought it odd that she seemed almost ashamed by the mere suggestion. She shifted her gaze away from his and picked up Mason.

"Holly, you are amazingly talented." Surely she knew that. Surely she didn't need *him* to tell her.

"Wyatt—"

"I'm serious. I may be some cowboy from the sticks, but I know a good song when I hear it, and I know you could make it in Nashville. So does Quincy."

She looked surprised and hopeful at once, and Wyatt almost felt sorry for her. "Tell me how a woman as bright and talented as you doesn't know how bright and talented she is?" he asked, touching her cheek.

Holly glanced down, but Wyatt caught her chin and lifted her face to him. "How is it that you don't know that?"

"I . . . I don't know."

"Didn't anyone family tell you? Your teachers? Other musicians?"

"Some," she said, shrugging a little.

"Your family?"

Holly looked at Mason, who was trying to pull the scarf from her neck. "That was a tough sell," she said. "My father loved my songs, but my mom . . . She thought I was wasting my time."

Wyatt studied her face. There was more there, he could sense it. "No disrespect to your mother, but she was wrong." He bent down, kissed her lightly.

Holly smiled sheepishly. "Thanks, Wyatt. I appreciate that. Okay," she said, and shoved Mason into his arms. "I think I've got everything."

She did not speak of it again, but on Thanksgiving Day she finally told him a little about her family.

They'd planned the holiday together, joking about how they had to be the only people in the world without family. That wasn't entirely true: Wyatt's parents were in Florida. They were in their eighties and seemed content to trailer around America and settle in Florida during the winter. His conversations with them usually were along the lines of weather and politics.

Holly's sister was in a rehab facility, of course, but she had an aunt and uncle who had invited her to accompany them to Houston to share Thanksgiving with their daughter. Holly had declined. Her friend Ossana had also called, trying to entice her to Austin.

"She wants to do the Turkey Trot," Holly had said, laughing. "I have run once that I can remember, and that was in middle school. Five times around the track for talking. And Ossana thinks I am going to get out there and run with her on Thanksgiving morning?" She'd laughed. So it was set: they would celebrate Thanksgiving together with their children.

As luck would have it, Wyatt had Grace for Thanksgiving this year; Macy would have Grace at Christmas. "So," Macy had said when he'd picked Grace up, "what are your plans?" She had an overeager look on her face.

"Why?"

"Come on, Wyatt," Macy had said. "Are you going to have dinner with your girlfriend?"

He hadn't liked the way Macy had said it, as if she were very excited for him to have a girlfriend—as if he were her kid brother instead of the husband she'd once promised to cherish forever, then left. "What's it to you?" he'd asked sharply.

Surprised, Macy had blinked her big brown eyes at him. "Wow. I didn't mean to pry."

"What do you want from me, Macy? You act as if we're old friends."

"I just want you to be happy. Is that so bad? And when I hear you're dating someone, I hope that you are happy. That's all."

"I think you hope that you don't have to feel guilty anymore," he'd said. He hadn't even realized he'd been harboring that thought.

Macy had gasped. "What's that supposed to mean?"

"You know exactly what it means. You feel guilty, and you fall all over yourself trying to be nice to me."

"That's not true. I happen to care about you, and last I checked, that is not a crime," she'd said, then kissed her daughter good-bye and flounced to her car.

Wyatt hadn't exactly meant it that way, but he knew he was right. Since he had come back from Arizona, Macy had been tiptoeing around him like a fragile piece of glass. He didn't owe it to her to live a happy life. In fact, he'd worked pretty hard to make sure he didn't have one.

But he had one today. He was looking forward to the day with Holly and the kids. He'd bought the ingredients for the meal, and Holly was going to cook. "If I can make a turkey, I can make anything, right?" she'd reasoned.

He didn't know about that, but he was glad she was willing to try.

She'd found some holiday decorations in a closet. A large paper turkey that was missing one wing graced the center of the table. Wyatt had made little corncob turkeys for the babies to play with. They were a big hit, judging by the squeals of delight from the two rowdies as they beat them on the coffee table.

"Guess who called me yesterday," Holly said.

Wyatt managed to stop Grace from beaning Mason on the head with her turkey as Mason pulled the feathers from his. "Who?"

"Mason's dad, Loren. He said he wanted to see Mason today."

Wyatt gaped at her. That bastard of a father hadn't even bothered to check on Mason and now he wanted to see him? "What did you say?"

"I told him he could kiss my ass," she said, and laughed at Wyatt's expression. "Okay, not very ladylike, but really, he thinks Thanksgiving rolls around and suddenly he wants to be surrounded by family?"

"And?

"He said he'd been paying my rent and gave me money for Mason, and he had a right to see him. I told him he was a sorry excuse for a father, and if he wanted to see Mason, he could get a lawyer, and he'd have to explain how he'd abandoned his son with me, and that

I would have a lawyer who would not allow him to come waltzing back into Mason's life just because it is Thanksgiving." She paused in lighting candles at the table and looked at Wyatt. "I don't really have a lawyer. But Loren is a lawyer, and of course he believed it."

Wyatt did not smile. He worried that Loren would try to take Mason from Holly. She was completely and utterly attached to the boy. "What did he say to that?"

"He had a few choice things to say, starting with 'Wow, Holly, when did you get a backbone?'" She mimicked the way Loren spoke. "'What happened, did you suddenly grow up?'"

"What the hell is *that* supposed to mean?" Wyatt was agitated and would have liked nothing better than to personally kick Loren Drake's ass.

"What—that?" Holly held up her hand as if she were taking an oath. "Okay, true confession . . . I have not been known in this family as a high flyer." Wyatt must have looked puzzled because she said, "You know . . . an overachiever. A go-getter." She gave that a fist pump.

He had quite the opposite impression of Holly. It seemed she was constantly engaged with one thing or another, such as probating her mother's will, and looking for group play that she could enroll Mason in once a week. Her music for heaven's sake. "I don't know why you would say that."

"Because it is true," Holly said cheerfully. "Hannah was always the star, and I was always the slacker." A bell in the kitchen sounded and Holly jumped. "My first turkey!" she cried.

Wyatt made sure the kids were occupied and followed her into the kitchen.

Holly had the turkey on the stove and was poking it with a fork. "How can you tell if these things are done?"

Wyatt pointed to the thermometer button. It had popped up. "Why would you call yourself a slacker?" he asked again.

"Because I am. When we were growing up, Hannah was the one with the best grades. She was valedictorian, did I tell you that? And I . . . I wasn't so great in school. I am dyslexic, and on top of that, I have the attention span of a gnat. When I think of high school, I think of long-haired boys and guitars." She looked curiously at him. "What do you think of?"

"But how does that make you a slacker?" he asked, ignoring her question for the time being.

"I didn't mean literally. It's just that everything I did was compared to Hannah, and I never measured up, and somewhere along the way I started not to care. I dropped out of high school, I went back, then I tried college and I dropped out of that . . ." Her voice trailed off as she examined her turkey. "But look at me now. I made a turkey. A *turkey*! My mother is probably rolling over in her grave right now."

"Holly . . . I don't want to tell you how to manage things, but . . . don't you need a strategy for handling things when Loren or your sister want to see Mason?"

She gave him a halfhearted shrug as she basted the turkey.

"What are you going to do?"

"I don't know exactly," she said. "But I am not going to pretend that everything is okay and they can come walking into his life when they feel like it." She carefully maneuvered the turkey onto a platter.

"But they will come back into his life," he said quietly.

"Wyatt . . ." She smiled. "It's Thanksgiving. Is it okay if we talk about it later?" He looked at the turkey, and she gave him a nudge. "Dad always carved."

"So did mine," he said, and picked up the turkey and took it to the table.

While Wyatt carved, Holly brought out the rest of the food—green bean casserole, English pea salad, sweet potatoes, and apple pie. She rounded the kids up and put them in the high chairs she'd found at Goodwill, laid out their dinner on their trays, and poured wine for her and Wyatt.

He let the phone call with Loren slide for the time being, and they spent the meal chatting about their favorite dishes. When Mason and Grace had stopped eating and turned to smashing peas on their high-chair trays and on themselves, Wyatt and Holly put them down to play. Together they cleared the table, put the food away, and washed the dishes. Holly talked about the things she'd noticed that needed to be done to the place. "Mason put his socks down the toilet in my mother's bathroom and then broke the handle trying to flush them," she said. "The plumbing must be one hundred years old. And the house needs paint, and new carpet, and dozens of little repairs, like missing door hardware and peeling wallpaper," she said. "I'll have to do all that before I sell it, won't I?"

Wyatt reached around her to put a dish away, his body grazing her back. "Not if you sell it to me."

"What?" She laughed. Wyatt put his hands on the sink on either side of her, hemming her in. Holly twisted around to face him. "Are you serious? *You* want this old place?"

"I want the land," he said, his gaze falling to her mouth.

"Why?"

"Because I like a big spread. I can put more cattle out here. And eventually, when Austin moves all the way out, I can develop it."

He leaned down to kiss her, but Holly stopped him by pressing her hand to his chest. "So *that's* why you came loping over here on Troy the first time I met you," she said. "And all this time I thought it was me and my cookies."

"Those cookies were definitely a lure," he said, and nipped at her lips. "But I came loping over here because there was a god-awful lot of smoke pouring out of your chimney. I stayed because . . ." He kissed her again, his arm going around behind her back, pulling her into his chest.

"Why?" she asked against his mouth.

"Because you were so damn cute."

Holly bit his lip. Wyatt jerked his head back and put his hand to his bottom lip. "Ouch! That hurt!"

"You're a liar," Holly said, and slid her arms around his neck, pulling his head down to hers. "You didn't think I was cute, you thought I was going to be a needy neighbor. It was written all over your face." She kissed him again. A much gentler, arousing kiss.

"Okay, okay," he said, laughing, when she lifted her head. "I confess, you looked pretty needy."

"Why'd you come back the second time?" she asked.

"Because of you."

This time Holly grabbed his ear and squeezed. "Nope. That's not true, either. You came back because your stupid cows were dropping bombs all over my yard. And you wanted to buy this place."

He grinned at her.

"So if you want to buy this land, cowboy, tell me when you really came back because I was so damn cute."

Wyatt cupped her face with both hands. "The third time," he admitted. "And I kicked myself for taking so long." He kissed her hard then, before she could ask more questions.

He was happy, Wyatt thought as their kiss turned more ardent. He was as happy as he thought he could ever be, out here in the middle of the Hill Country in a run-down house.

A little hand grabbed his jeans; he and Holly looked down at the upturned faces of Grace and Mason. "Who wants to go for a ride on Troy?" he asked.

"Toy, Toy!" Grace cried.

"Then saddle up, little dogies," he said, and reached for both of them at once.

Yep, he'd found a little tiny patch of heaven, where he existed with Holly and two babies, and he could honestly say he was the happiest he'd been in a long, long time.

Blissful. Extremely happy; full of joy. As in, *the blissful couple watched their two babies brain each other with corncob turkeys.*

Chapter Sixteen

Wyatt didn't seem quite as excited about the toddler group Holly found at the newly opened Baby Bowl on the square in Cedar Springs. The indoor gym had a series of classes with programmed activities designed to develop the thinking and physical skills of one- to three-year-olds. The classes were held Thursdays at four. On the other side of the two-foot gate and fence that bounded the indoor gym was a seating area for parents. They could sit on stuffed leather lounge chairs and gaze out the big, plate glass windows at the traffic in the square or train their eyes on a wall-mounted flat-screen television.

Because there was free Wi-Fi, Holly convinced Wyatt he could work there.

"I won't get any work done," he argued. "People will stroll by and want to chat. I've lived here a long time and I know a lot of gum-bumping goes on in this town."

Holly narrowed her gaze. "Wyatt Clark, if I didn't know better, I'd think you didn't want to be seen with me."

He clenched his jaw and looked down at the palm of his hand a long moment. "You might be right."

"What? *Why?*"

"Not because of you, baby," he said, gathering her in his arms. "Never you. I just like to keep my life private."

"There is private, and then there is caveman," she said crossly.

Holly won the argument. Wyatt announced to her a day or so later that he'd asked Macy if he could enroll Grace, and Macy had agreed.

They'd been here a few times now, and Holly had come to love Thursday afternoons. Holly would bring coffees from the Saddle-brew—black for Wyatt, a latte for her—and a notebook so she could work on the third and final song for Quincy. Wyatt brought his cell phone. He called clients and contractors, speaking to them in that low, even voice of his. Even when he was discussing problems, Holly had a hard time believing they were very big issues, because he always sounded so calm.

Holly loved that they were so comfortable together. She'd never really had a relationship like this; she'd never sat in leather chairs and just existed with another person. Wyatt was a great guy, there was no doubt about it. Holly didn't know Finn Lockhart, but she couldn't imagine that he was the bigger, better deal compared to Wyatt Clark, no way. But Macy's loss was her gain.

Wyatt was a thoughtful man. He did little things for her, such as repairing the door on the shed, which she'd once complained was driving her nuts. He'd shown up one afternoon while she was in town and fixed it.

Early one morning she was awakened by the sound of metal on metal. When she looked out the window, she saw Jesse, Wyatt, and the Russell boys working on the windmill.

She'd bundled up in her father's old canvas barn jacket, pulled on her Ugg boots, and padded down there to see what was going on. Milo loped up to her, pushing his snout into her hand. "What on earth are you doing?" she'd said as she walked into their midst, petting Milo's head.

"Repairing it," Jesse had said cheerfully. "Apparently, it needs to be repaired right away. Before we drop hay for the cattle, even."

Wyatt was standing in the middle of the windmill structure with a pair of pliers. "Oil this gear box and that will put an end to the squeak."

"See?" Jesse had said, grinning at Holly. "Right away."

"Wow. Thanks, Wyatt," Holly had said.

He'd looked down, the brim of his hat hiding his face. "We didn't mean to bother you. We'll get in and get out."

"Are you kidding?" Jesse had laughed. "We'll be lucky if we're finished by noon."

"Perfect," Holly had said. "That gives me enough time to make some homemade cinnamon rolls."

"You don't need to do that," Wyatt had said.

"Yes I do." Holly had started back to the house before he could argue, and as she walked, she heard Jesse say to Wyatt, "Dude, do you have to do that? I mean, really, what's wrong with a homemade cinnamon roll?"

Around noon, while Mason tortured Milo on the porch, Holly had waved at Jesse and held up a plate of freshly baked cinnamon rolls. Jesse had instantly started toward her, the two Russell boys following him.

Wyatt had reluctantly followed. By the time he reached the porch, Jesse and the two boys had helped themselves. "Sorry, Holly," he'd said apologetically as he'd walked up the porch steps and stooped down to tousle Mason's hair. "You didn't need to go to any trouble. I know you've got work to do."

"Well, for pity's sake, Wyatt, if you didn't want to bother her, why would you come over at eight in the damn morning?" Jesse had complained, and had reached for a second helping.

Wyatt had grinned sheepishly, and Holly, unable to resist him when he was embarrassed like that, kissed him.

"Come on, boys, we've got work to do," Jesse had said, and hustled the two boys off the porch and back to the windmill while Wyatt kissed Holly back.

Holly couldn't ask for anything more in a relationship, and the fact that Mason and Grace were happy playmates—as happy as a pair of toddlers could be, anyway—made this relationship a dream. She smiled as she thought of them rolling their little trains back and forth on the coffee table. It felt almost as if she had been destined to come here, as if some celestial force had guided her here, where she'd found the support she needed for her and Mason in this difficult period of their lives.

In the last few weeks, Holly had tried not to think

about Hannah. Thoughts of her sister only upset her and filled her head with questions and, surprisingly, a fair amount of guilt. Holly felt dumb—how could she have seen Hannah with their mother and not known her sister was stoned? And the questions of how and why haunted her. No matter what had happened between them, Holly loved Hannah, and she worried about her. Especially after Mason stuffed the socks into the toilet and broke the handle. Holly tried to fix the handle and, in doing so, had opened the tank. There she found a baby food jar with the pills weighted down in the water. Twelve pills, she counted, white oblong tablets. Hannah was so sick she was hiding pills in jars in toilet tanks.

She burned the pills along with the trash that afternoon.

But inevitably, when Holly thought about Hannah, she thought of Mason, and her stomach would clench. She didn't know what she would do when Hannah came back for him. Holly loved Mason so much. She couldn't believe how much she loved him. It was as if some primal, maternal bond had bloomed in her, and in some ways she believed she loved him every bit as much as if she had given birth to him. She hadn't realized how much she'd come to love him until one afternoon when she took him for a nature walk around the house. She watched him squat down, the sunlight gleaming in his dark hair, the air filled with his baby chattering. He picked up a leaf, pressed it to Holly's lips. She pretended to eat it, and Mason laughed with delight and did it again.

Her heart felt so full that day. She hugged him

tight, kissed him. She was aware that day how much she wanted to protect him, to guide him. She couldn't imagine not seeing him every day. She couldn't imagine ever walking away from him, and if she had—if that had been her instead of Hannah—she would be clawing her way back to him now.

When would Hannah show herself? She had said she was in a ninety-day treatment program, but it had been more than ninety days since she left Mason with Holly. Yet, the days continued to slide by, and there was no sign of Hannah, no word from her.

In the meantime, Holly's love for Mason grew, as did her desire to shield him from any harm. How she would finesse that with Hannah was the question that burned in her heart. Holly had almost finished her work on Quincy's third song. Jillian, her attorney, said the will would be probated in a couple of months. Holly could feel change bearing down on her. Yet if she allowed herself to worry about the future and all that she would not be able to control—like Hannah's return—she would make herself crazy.

Even her feelings for Wyatt were not simple. She didn't know exactly where their relationship would go. It was too soon, the feelings she was experiencing too fresh and new and exciting. Holly was a strong believer in fate and, moreover, in tempting fate, and she worried that if she tried to define what was happening between them—to put words or emotions to it or to project too far into the future—she would jinx one of the best things that had happened to her in a very long time.

All of these doubts seemed to hover around Holly,

waiting to drag her down, so she took each day as it came.

It was Holly's idea to go the Holiday Festival of Lights in Cedar Springs. Everything they did was Holly's idea. If Wyatt had his druthers, they'd live in bed, on his patio, and in the kitchen. Throw in an occasional Dallas Cowboys game, and he would be a very happy man.

But Holly thought the kids needed stimulation and social interaction, and even though he'd argued and decried the holiday pageantry as too commercial, before he knew what had happened, he'd set up the double stroller and strapped in Mason and Grace and marched out to Main Street. But he didn't like it.

Wyatt knew he was a reticent ass about some things. Holly was unfailingly cheerful in the face of it. He supposed she recognized that he was having a hard time adjusting from being the guy who'd gone off to lick his wounds to being the guy who was part of a couple and all that entailed. Like compromise.

What was bothering Wyatt was the feeling of exposure. Maybe he was perceiving things that weren't entirely rational; that was not outside the realm of possibility. Nevertheless, he felt like every time he showed up in Cedar Springs, people were looking at him, looking for the cracks that he'd suffered when he'd broken apart after Macy left. Cracks he'd tried to patch and paint over.

He didn't think he was entirely wrong—he got a vibe from Linda Gail that a lot of folks were holding their breath, hoping and waiting to see if this thing with Holly took. He could not begin to express, even to himself, how that galled him. He'd been a mover and a shaker in this town and, before Macy, a sought-after ladies' man. He'd been a confident, well-dressed, drinks-on-the-house kind of guy. He did not like being thought of as a broken man, no matter how broken he'd become. That's what made him reluctant to come to Cedar Springs. He didn't want speculation about his life, and he damn sure didn't want people thinking he was somehow deserving of their pity.

But he had to admit, as he and Holly and the babies strolled across the square, he was glad they had come. The night was crisp but not too cold, and Christmas lights adorned every storefront and every tree around the courthouse. There were Christmas trees and candy canes, blow-up Santas, snow globes, snowmen. He marveled at the industry that produced these enormous inflated Christmas figures.

Holly had dressed Mason in a red sweater with Rudolph on the front, complete with a blinking red light for his nose. Wyatt had dressed Grace in jeans and a pink sweater. The idea of holiday-themed wear had never crossed his mind.

With the kids tucked into the stroller under a blanket, they neared a real estate office. A Christmas tree with gifts at its base and falling snow had been painted on the windows, and a sign announced that they were serving hot apple cider. "Cider!" Holly said excitedly. "I can't remember the last time I had that. Let's get some!"

In they had gone, maneuvering the stroller inside, standing in line with everyone else in Cedar Springs who couldn't remember the last time they'd had cider.

With their ciders, they continued their tour, Wyatt pushing the stroller, Holly's arm linked in his. She was in a very happy mood and looked brilliant in a knit cap and a funky-looking cape that reminded Wyatt of his college days, her jeans tucked into the Ugg boots she liked to wear. She chatted about how many people were out tonight, and how much work must have gone into putting up the decorations. She reminisced about the Christmases of her youth, the carols she had loved. She hummed along to the carols that were blasting across the square.

They stopped to look at a display in a storefront that had automated Santa's helpers. When they turned to go, Wyatt wheeled the stroller around, coming abruptly face-to-face with Macy and Emma.

"Hello, Wyatt," Macy said, and smiled at Holly. "Hi again."

"Hello, Macy," Holly said.

"Do you know my sister Emma?" Macy asked.

"No." Holly introduced herself.

"Your son is beautiful," Emma said. "What's his name?"

For a moment Holly froze, her smile too bright. "Mason," she said after a moment, and smiled down at Mason.

Macy smiled slyly at Wyatt. She rested her hand on her belly; her pregnancy was really showing now. As much as it pained Wyatt to see that, he was aware that it wasn't as painful as it had been in weeks past.

Grace started whining and holding her hands out for her mother, which, fortunately, drew Macy's attention from Wyatt. She dropped down on one knee in front of the stroller. "Hi, sweetie," she cooed.

"So, do you and Mason live in town?" Emma asked Holly.

"No, in the country. We're living out at my family's homestead. My mom died a few months ago, and I'm . . . I'm taking care of the place."

"Oh, I am so sorry," Emma said. She let a moment pass, then asked, "Where were you before you came here?"

"Austin," Holly said obligingly. Mason started to fuss, and Holly squatted down beside him to ease whatever was bothering him. She and Macy were now side by side. It was so surreal that Wyatt began to wonder if the cider had been spiked.

"I guess we better think about wrapping this up," he said stiffly. "The babies are tired."

"It's only seven, Wyatt," Macy said, and stood up. "And if you haven't walked down Pecan Street, you've missed the whole reason for coming out tonight. The lights are fantastic this year."

"I'd like to see that," Holly said, and stood up too.

"So, what do you do, Holly?" Emma asked.

"I'm a songwriter."

"A songwriter!" Emma said excitedly.

Wyatt didn't hear what else Emma said to that, because Macy was peering up at him like she used to do when she knew something was on his mind. There was a time he'd thought it was a special thing that she could read him so completely, but tonight he merely found it annoying.

"You look happy," Macy said softly.

Wyatt sighed.

"I know what you're thinking—"

"I don't think you do."

"That's all I am going to say," she said, lifting her hand as if to swear to it and glancing sidelong at Emma and Holly, who were engaged in conversation. "You just look happy, Wyatt. Happier than I have seen you in a very long time."

She meant since she had left him, of course, because he'd been as happy as a clam up until then. Well, he *was* happier. He just didn't need his ex-wife validating it for him.

"Wyatt, we should go," Holly said a moment later. "The kids are getting restless."

"Right."

"*Mamma,*" Grace said, and kicked the stroller. Macy leaned down and grabbed her daughter's hand, giving it a playful shake. "Holly, I am so glad Gracie has your son to play with."

Holly blinked. "He is . . . he loves Gracie," she said.

Macy smiled. "We'll let you two go. Bye-bye, sweetie," Macy said, leaning down to kiss her cheek. "Bye-bye. You're going with Daddy now."

"See you, Wyatt! And, Holly, it was very nice to meet you!" Emma said.

Wyatt said good night and walked on. When they'd put a little distance between them and the Bobbsey Twins, Holly puffed out her cheeks, then released her breath in one long woosh. "I wasn't expecting *that*," she said. "I had no idea what to say, especially about Mason."

"Why didn't you tell them that he was your nephew?" Wyatt asked.

Holly looked startled. "Well, he's obviously more than that," she said shortly.

"I know he is. But he is your nephew, and I think you can say that without feeling like you need to explain it," he said, and put his arm around her shoulders, drawing her close as they walked toward Pecan Street.

But Holly's mood had changed. She was looking down instead of at the lights, her brow creased.

"Don't let them ruin the evening," he said.

"It's not them. Honestly, they seem very nice. It's just . . . it's just that before we met them, we were walking around the square and I was feeling like . . . like this was real," she said gesturing at the babies. "You know, like we were this little family—"

"In a way, we are," he agreed. He did not want to sour the evening. Dammit, this was exactly the reason he didn't like to come to town.

"But not really," Holly said, and looked up at him. "He's not mine, Wyatt. He will never be *mine*. I can pretend all day long, but he's not—"

"Yes he is," Wyatt said, and pulled her closer. "Part of him will always be yours. Do you think because you didn't give birth to him that he's not yours in some way? Giving birth is not what makes a mother, Holly. A mother is someone who puts her child first, above all else. You've done that far better than anyone else. He will always be in your heart, and you in his."

Holly shook her head. "I have no legal right to him. If they came back for him tomorrow, what would I do?"

He wished he could help her, but Wyatt didn't know what would or could happen. "If those two cared about their son, they would have come back long be-fore now," he groused. "But maybe you should talk to Jillian about it and see what your rights are."

Holly suddenly looked at him with an expression of hope. "What are you thinking? That maybe I can keep him?"

The question, so earnestly asked, startled Wyatt. "I wasn't thinking that," he said carefully. "But neither do I think they can walk in after four months and take him away from you. I think you need to talk to Jillian."

Holly seemed disappointed in his answer.

"Holly?" Wyatt asked, drawing her attention back to him. "Do you want to keep him?"

"Of course I do. I love him," she said. "I'd have to be really coldhearted not to want him."

Wyatt frowned a little. "Wanting him and keeping him are two different things. I know you love him, baby, but are you being realistic?"

"I didn't say I was going to keep him," she said curtly. "But is it realistic to give a baby to someone who is just out of rehab?"

Wyatt studied her expression. She impatiently re-turned his gaze. "Talk to Jillian," he urged her again.

Holly looked away. "Macy and Emma seem nice," she said, obviously changing the subject.

Wyatt said nothing to that. He didn't want to dis-cuss his ex-wife with Holly. He wanted it to be just like this, the four of them, strolling around under Christ-mas lights. "Look, Gracie, there's Santa," he said, and dipped down, pointed to the big inflatable Santa teth-ered to a croquet bracket in the ground. Mason and Grace stared at it with wide eyes.

When Wyatt straightened up again, Holly was studying him. "What?" he asked self-consciously.

"Do you still have feelings for Macy?" she asked bluntly.

The question startled Wyatt. "Why are you asking me that?"

"Because you will not discuss her. Come on, Wyatt, I'm a big girl. I can take it. Do you still have feelings for her?"

Did he still have feelings for Macy? He'd tried for so long to bury whatever he felt for her that he didn't think about it. But he thought about it now, and he was privately surprised that he felt only disappointment. No regret. No pangs of love. No feelings of a loss so deep that the gashes of it festered inside him like a rotten wound. He stroked Holly's cheek with the back of his hand; her skin was cool to the touch. "No. I don't."

But Holly's eyes narrowed skeptically. "Really? Because she is beautiful, Wyatt. And it wasn't as if anything went wrong between you two. I think it must have been worse for you because there *wasn't* anything wrong."

"Holly . . . don't analyze it," he said, and smiled as he tugged her hat down a little. "You asked me a question. I answered it truthfully. I can honestly say that for the first time in four years . . . I don't have any feelings for Macy. Not those types of feelings, anyway. The only person I have *those* feelings for is you."

Holly's eyes widened. And then a slow smile shaped her lips. She cocked her head to one side. "Really?"

He touched her chin, lifting her face. People were

moving past them, stepping around them, and he didn't care. "Really."

Her smile deepened. "You're not the only one, you know."

"Meaning?"

"Meaning," she said as she shoved her hands into the back pockets of her jeans, "that I think I could be falling in love with you." She held her breath, watching him warily, almost as if she were steeling herself to be rejected.

"Could be?"

She bit her lower lip. "Could be."

Wyatt smiled. He laced his fingers with hers and pulled her close to him. "You're not the only one, you know," he muttered, and wrapped her in his embrace and kissed her, right there for all of Cedar Springs to see.

Chapter Seventeen

As Christmas rushed toward them, Holly could almost believe that Mason was hers and that life would always be like this. She'd finished up the last song for Quincy, who had begun the work of recording them.

"I think it could be huge," she'd gushed to Wyatt one night after working in the studio with Quincy. They were sitting on the floor at his house with the kids, playing with giant Legos. "I couldn't believe how great it sounded in the studio. Quincy thinks so too."

"I have no doubt that it is," Wyatt had said as he poured more wine into her glass. "That's a great way to arrive in Nashville."

Holly had laughed and playfully punched him in the arm. "If I didn't know better, I'd think you were trying to get rid of me."

"I'm serious, Holly. You've got a golden opportunity here. Why don't you plan a trip to talk to Quincy's manager?"

Holly couldn't even imagine it. Nashville had always seemed so unattainable, such a pipe dream. "Maybe someday. I've got lots to do here. Besides, I'd have to find a place to stay and all that . . ." She'd given the notion a dismissive flick of her wrist. "And anyway, what about you?"

"Baby, I'd be along for the ride," he'd said, and had grabbed her up, rolling with her on the floor to the delight of the kids, who'd piled on top of them.

Holly liked daydreaming about it. She pictured herself as the force behind a huge country-western hit song, arriving in Nashville with Wyatt, Mason, and Grace in tow. *She came to town with a two-bit guitar, / But when she left Nashville she was a star* . . . For a few days, after working with Quincy in the studio, it had seemed almost as if it could happen.

"My manager wants to meet you, Holly," Quincy had told her when they'd wrapped for the day.

"Really?" she'd asked, terribly pleased by it. She couldn't wait to tell Wyatt.

But then Loren had texted her and Holly had been sent crashing back into reality.

I want to see my son.

That was his first bone-jarring text that had made Holly's heart leap painfully. She hadn't heard from him since sometime before Thanksgiving. She'd stuck her phone in her purse, tried to ignore it. But Loren had texted again. And again.

It made no sense for her to be so panic-stricken. She told herself that Loren's wanting to see Mason and wanting to *take* Mason were two different things entirely. Mason was still a bother to Loren. She guessed Loren was trying to mitigate whatever guilt he felt.

But still, Holly didn't want to do it. She wanted to

keep Mason safe from the two people who had failed
him so completely, and her anxiety and fear about her
ability to do that turned to acid.

"What should I do?" she'd asked Wyatt.

"Take him," Wyatt had said. "Trust me, this guy
isn't any more ready to be a father today than he ever
has been. My guess is that he wants something else.
Maybe information about your sister."

But Loren said nothing about Hannah when he had
finally gotten Holly on the phone. He'd only demanded
to see his son. "It's been four months since Mason was
left with me, and a month since you even attempted to
contact him," Holly had said to him. "So now you start
thinking of Christmas and how *you* would feel better if
you found your conscience somewhere?"

"Jesus Christ, don't start with me," Loren had
snapped. "Do you have any idea how much work is
involved setting up a satellite office?"

"Do you have any idea how much work is involved
raising your child?" Holly had shot back.

She could hear Loren's deep, angry breathing. "Listen to me, Holly Fisher. I could make real trouble for
you. Don't think you can go up against me on this. I
want you to bring Mason to Austin so I can see him. I
want to see my son!"

Wyatt was worried about her going alone. He'd
stood at the door of the utility room as she folded
laundry. He'd looked incredibly sexy propped against
the jamb, arms folded over a shirt that was filthy from
the day's work. "I don't like it," he'd said simply when
she told him about the conversation.

"I don't, either," she'd said. "But what can I do?"

"He's full of shit," Wyatt had said angrily. "If he really wanted to see his son—if he really *wanted* him—he would have driven out here a long time ago and taken Mason without a lot of people standing around to see it."

"God, don't even say that," Holly had said, pressing a hand to her abdomen.

"He isn't going to take Mason—I'm just saying. But I am coming with you all the same."

Holly wanted to believe Wyatt, but her stomach was in knots. If, by some strange miracle, Loren had decided to be a father and tried to take Mason, Holly would kill him. Mason would never understand what was happening. Who knew if Mason even remembered his father? She felt ill imagining Mason's utter confusion if Loren took him from her.

But Holly truly did fear what Loren would do if she didn't bring Mason to him as he'd practically commanded. She should have called Jillian before now, she knew, but she'd had the idea in her head that she could somehow bargain with Hannah for Mason and had let it go, safe in the life she and Wyatt had created. *Stupid, Holly.*

Jillian was on her way to court when Holly called, and Holly quickly explained the situation.

"Tell him you have an attorney," Jillian said. "He'll know that a court would intervene, given the time that has passed since either of them saw their son. That should put him off until after the holidays, but if he gives you any reason to think otherwise, call me," she instructed Holly. "I can't talk more than that right now, but come see me after the holidays. Merry Christmas!"

Armed with that, Holly and Wyatt went to Austin. When they reached the parking lot of Central Market where they'd agreed to meet, Wyatt hugged her tightly and kissed her. "Don't worry."

"Where will you be?"

"Around," he promised her, then got Mason out of the car, handed him to Holly, and draped the diaper bag over her shoulder. "Hey," he said, stroking her arm. "Go in there like you run the joint. Don't let him see you looking like that."

"Like what?"

"Scared."

Loren was waiting for them in the picnic area of the Central Market. He was wearing a suit, as if he'd just come from the office, and leaning against the railing, studying his cell phone. When he saw her and Mason, he checked his watch.

"There he is," Loren said, holding out his arms for Mason. "There's my big boy." Mason looked out his outstretched hands, then looked to the playscape, where dozens of children were climbing and jumping and running under the shade of live oaks. Loren's expression turned dark. "Give him to me."

It was all Holly could do to hand Mason over, but Mason, bless him, didn't want to be handed to a father who was essentially a stranger to him now. He grabbed at Holly's shoulder and began to cry. "It's all right, Mason. It's Daddy," Holly said, managing not to choke on the word. "Daddy wants to say hi."

Mason studied Loren's face a moment, then looked back at Holly. "Lala," he said. "Lala."

"He's gotten big," Loren said as he studied his son.

"Yep." Holly bit her tongue from pointing out that four months is a very long time in Babyland.

"Let's go feed the ducks, son," Loren said, and began walking without saying anything else to Holly. She followed Loren through the crowded play area like a pack mule.

In the park, he walked down to the water's edge and set Mason on his feet. "Duck!" Mason cried happily, and pointed to some swans floating on the opposite end of the lake.

"Do you have anything we could feed ducks?" Loren asked, turning to Holly with his hand outstretched.

Was he kidding? "I thought you had something," she said, and Loren wiggled his fingers at her. She sighed, opened the diaper bag, and handed him a box of animal crackers. Loren spent a few minutes showing Mason how to throw crackers out into the water for the ducks, but Mason was used to eating animal crackers and ignored his father's example. After a few minutes of that, Loren sighed and pointed Mason toward a play area beneath an enormous old oak.

He and Holly didn't speak for several minutes; they stood a few feet apart, watching Mason. The silence was killing her. She told herself to keep her mouth shut, to wait another fifteen minutes and then tell Loren it was time for Mason's nap, but sometimes Holly was her own worst enemy.

"Let's walk up to the playscape," Loren said. "Come on, buddy," he said to Mason, holding out his hand. Mason waddled past the outstretched hand and squatted down to look at some rocks.

"Have you talked to Hannah?" Holly asked.

Loren kept his gaze on Mason. "A couple of times."

The answer stunned her. Hannah had talked to Loren, but not her? "You *have*? Why didn't you tell me? What did she say?"

"We talked a lot about what had happened."

He said it so casually, as if it were expected, as if he'd always known what had happened to Hannah. But it was surely not what Holly had expected, and she turned to face him fully. "And?"

"And? And we talked," he said, sparing her a glance as he moved after Mason. "Frankly, a lot things were explained."

"What things?"

"Things you wouldn't understand," he said dismissively. "Things between me and Hannah."

"Is she okay? Is she still in treatment?"

"She's okay, Holly. She's getting the help she needs, and that is the most important thing."

He sounded a little too sanguine and reasonable for Loren, and Holly was suspicious. This was a guy who didn't care about anyone but himself, and if he thought of the problems of others, it was because he was concerned about how they would affect him. "So . . . did she say when will she be back?"

"When she's had enough time to work through the issues that brought this on." He looked at her. "The best thing you can do is support her in this."

"Oh, really? And how are *you* supporting her, Loren?"

Loren looked at Mason for a long moment, the muscles in his jaw working against the clench of his teeth. "Here's another piece of advice: Dial back the attitude. Hannah and I are going to get back together."

Holly gasped. Loren could not have stunned her more if he'd said he was the pope. "You can't be serious."

"I am very serious," he said coldly. "I see now that she made mistakes, but so did I. We are both optimistic that we can work through it."

"Do you honestly expect me to believe that Hannah is going to welcome the serial cheater home with open arms?" Holly scoffed, but her stomach was already churning. Hannah had taken him back at least twice before.

"Why am I not surprised that you want to throw stones from the peanut gallery?" Loren said. "What do *you* know about marriage, Holly? It's a hell of a lot easier to sit there and criticize when you never get out and take chances, isn't it? Marriage isn't a cakewalk. Sometimes it hits a rough patch. But Hannah and I love each other enough to work at it."

"If that's what you call a rough patch, I'd hate to think what constitutes a full-blown crisis. I don't believe you," she said, her voice shaking.

"Don't be so sure of yourself." He glanced at his watch. "I've got to get back to the office." He dismissed her again by striding forward to where Mason was playing with rocks. He picked his son up and hugged him, then walked back to where Holly was standing and handed the baby to her. "I want to see him during the holidays," he said gruffly. "I'll call you and arrange a time."

With that, Loren walked on, leaving Holly standing there, holding Mason tight.

"You okay?"

The sound of Wyatt's voice sluiced warm through

her; she turned and smiled gratefully. "Where did you come from?"

"I was here all along."

"Wy," Mason said. "Wy-wy."

Holly gladly handed Mason to Wyatt, and Mason reached for Wyatt's nose.

"Hey, there, little buckaroo," Wyatt said to Mason. He glanced again at Holly. "Everything okay?"

Okay? Holly was floating in a strange dream. "Yes. Yes, I'm okay. Just confused," she said, and shook her head.

Wyatt held out his hand to her. "Come on. Let's go get a bottle of wine and talk while Mason acquaints himself with a jungle gym." He wrapped his fingers securely around hers.

Holly and Wyatt drank wine and nibbled from a plate of cheese while Mason played on the enormous playscape. She told him what Loren had said.

"Interesting," Wyatt mused. "Do you think it's true that they are getting back together?"

"I don't know," Holly answered honestly, and looked at Mason. "But what if it *is* true? Then what?"

Wyatt shrugged. "Together or apart, there are a still a lot of issues."

"Right," Holly said, but she wasn't certain that was true. Hannah and Loren would be a united front against her.

"Talk to Jillian," Wyatt urged her again.

Yes, she would talk to Jillian.

But the troubling thought that Loren and Hannah might reunite, and all the implications of that, continued to swim around the edges of Holly's thoughts.

That night, when the house was silent and Mason was sleeping, and Wyatt had gone home, Loren loomed large in Holly's mind once more.

The very idea of Hannah and Loren starting over made Holly ill with anxiety. She honestly couldn't guess if Hannah would take him back. *What about Mason?* Holly rolled onto her side and squeezed her eyes shut. They had abandoned him, they had let months pass without even checking on him regularly. Who would give this child back to them? Someone, somewhere, would side with Holly.

The next day Holly called Jillian again, only to learn she was already out for the holidays.

Holly tried to keep her mind off of it by planning for Christmas Day. It would be only her, Mason, and Wyatt, as it was Macy's turn to have Grace. She flipped through her mother's cookbook looking for holiday recipes and stumbled on one for apple turnovers. The page, yellowed with age and stained in one corner with what looked like coffee, bore her mother's handwriting.

Holly stared at the card; a host of old Christmas memories began to swirl about in her head. Usually, when she thought of her mother and growing up here, she thought of how miserable she'd been. But there had been some good times, too, particularly when she and Hannah were little girls, too young to care about which of them was prettier or smarter.

They'd had apple turnovers every Christmas morning. Holly could almost smell them.

They'd always had a real Christmas tree, too, because Peggy Fisher believed it wasn't really Christmas if the tree was anything less than real. A week before Christmas, the four of them would pile into the Oldsmobile that was still in the barn gathering dust and drive down to the vacant lot next to the hardware store, where, once a year, big tents were set up and trees magically appeared.

Holly's father would strap the tree they'd selected on the hood of the car and they would drive it home, where he would set it up in the window of the living room and string the blinking lights while Mom made hot chocolate and sugar cookies shaped like Santa hats and Christmas trees.

Holly and Hannah had the task of decorating the tree, and took great care to evenly distribute the Popsicle ornaments they'd made at school among the shiny balls and glitter-covered Nativity scenes their mother bought every year during the after-Christmas sales. The crowning glory was the star of Bethlehem, which, no matter how many attempts they made, always sat crooked on the top of the tree. The clumps of tinsel— which Holly and Hannah threw on, as their mother suggested, so that it would look like real icicles dripping from the boughs of the tree—looked about as natural as clumps of shiny synthetic silver could look.

Yet, to Holly, their Christmas trees were beautiful. The blinking red, green, and blue lights mesmerized her. She would lie on the floor of the living room, staring up at the tree, imagining the packages that would begin to accumulate at its base. The magic of the season had existed in this house. It was filled with anticipation: of new toys, of the Christmas pageant at the Presbyterian church, of Christmas morning and apple turnovers.

Was her memory correct, or had Holly's mother truly been happy then? Holly could remember her sitting on the couch next to her father, a cigarette dangling from her fingers, laughing and exclaiming as Holly and Hannah opened their gifts. There wasn't tension then that Holly could recall. When had it all started to change?

Holly wondered if Hannah remembered Christmases here . . . if she remembered the trees and the apple turnovers and the hot chocolate, and how Grandma and Grandpa had come later in the afternoon, and how Grandma always smelled a little like Listerine. She wondered if Hannah knew when things began to change, when the tension had crept in to their lives. When Santa had stopped coming to visit.

Maybe Holly could bring Santa back to this house. Starting with a tree. She and Mason had to get a tree!

That week, Holly found the old Christmas decorations in the dusty attic crawl space. Some were brittle, others broken, but there were enough to adorn a small tree. She enlisted Wyatt and Grace's help, and the four of them drove to town, to the tent next to the hardware store, and picked one out.

At home, Wyatt put the tree up in the window, and they decorated it while carols played on the old CD player, and the toddlers played with plastic Nativity figures. Between Milo's wagging tail and the four little hands, the tree ended up being decorated about halfway up, but Holly thought it was a beautiful tree.

For the space of a few hours, anyway, Santa had come back to the homestead.

Chapter Eighteen

Christmas morning dawned gray and cold and wet. The rain had started sometime in the night, and Milo had seen fit to crawl onto the end of Holly's bed and make himself comfortable. Downstairs, Santa had brought a standing easel with washable markers and a child's table and chairs. One would think that the items would be easy for Santa's helpers to assemble, but that was not the case. They required an Allen wrench of a size Wyatt did not have in his truck box of a thousand tools, and he had to make do with a knife.

Holly and Wyatt drank spiked eggnog while they worked—a Holly specialty, she said, giggling—and laughed uncontrollably when they realized they'd assembled the easel upside down. When they finally had the gifts arranged, they fell on the old couch in front of the fire that Wyatt had built and stared into the flames.

"What was the best Christmas gift you ever received?" Holly asked Wyatt.

This night. "Bike," he said. "Banana seat. Apehanger handlebars."

She laughed. "I know those ape hangers must have been important."

"You have no idea. What was your favorite gift?"

"Guitar. It was red, and it had blue strings, and I loved that thing."

Holly stood up and gathered up their cups and the detritus of putting together Santa's gifts and carried them to the kitchen trash. When she returned, she said, "I'm exhausted. Can we go to bed now?"

Wyatt stood up, too, and swept her up into his arms. "Girl, anytime you want to go to bed, you need only point the way." Holly laughed and pleaded with him to put her down, but he wouldn't do it. He carried her upstairs to her bedroom and lay down beside her. As did Milo, who never understood when to make himself scarce.

They had to wake Mason that morning. Predictably, he was more entranced with the paper and packaging than his gifts. He liked hiding beneath the mounds of wrapping paper and then springing up, laughing with delight when Wyatt pretended to be surprised each time.

Wyatt missed Gracie. Macy had sent him a video of Gracie opening the gift Wyatt had given her—a big box of Legos—and it made him miss her even more.

Holly made fresh apple turnovers that were the best Wyatt had ever tasted. When he'd stuffed himself full of them, she fetched a box from beneath the tree. "I have something for you."

"You shouldn't have, but as long as you did, let me have it," Wyatt said with a wink, and held out his hand.

Holly grinned and stepped over paper and toys to

sit cross-legged beside him. He tousled her deliciously unkempt hair, then ripped into the wrapping paper like a pro. He was a firm believer in getting things done.

In the box was a black leather belt. Wyatt was very happy. It had been so long since anyone had given him a gift that he didn't care if it was a box of chocolates. He lifted it out of the box and examined it.

"It's hand-tooled leather," Holly said. "And the silver belt buckle is handmade too. Ossana and I found it in Fredericksburg."

"That is one cool belt," Wyatt said. "Thank you." He slipped his hand around Holly's nape and pulled her forward to kiss her. She tasted like apples and cinnamon.

"Car," Mason said, holding out the truck Wyatt had given him.

"Son, that is no car. That is a two-ton truck with a Hemi engine," Wyatt corrected him, and wound the belt around his hand and put it back in the box.

"Wait!" Holly cried. "There's more in there."

Wyatt peered into the box and spotted the white envelope. "What's this, a pink slip?" he asked.

"Right," Holly said, and wrapped her hands around her mug of coffee.

Wyatt opened the envelope. Inside was a music score. He was puzzled by it until he began to read the lyrics:

Short on words cuz he'd been hurt.
She thought he was a little curt.
She didn't care cuz she'd been there.
She knew that kind of pain,

How hard it was to love again.
He didn't say he loved her but she saw it in his
*   smile.*
She asked how long he'd been alone, he said it's been
*   awhile.*
She didn't care cuz she'd been there.
She knew that kind of pain,
How hard it is to love again.

She knew the kind of man he was,
He was her lover and her friend.
He was her light at winter's end.
She knew the kind of man he was,
He was her lover and her friend.
He was her light at winter's end.

Wyatt stared at the paper.

"It's a song," Holly said. "I wrote it for you."

"I see that." He swallowed. He was moved by it in a way he'd never felt before.

"Oh my God," Holly said. "I've offended you. I am so sorry, Wyatt. I thought it would be—"

"Holly," he said, catching her hand. He brought her fingers to his lips and kissed them. "This is the best gift I've ever received. Ever. Thank you."

"You haven't even heard it."

"I want to hear it," he said.

She smiled and untangled her hand from his and stood up. "You will not appreciate the full effect of this song, of course, because I will be singing it. But wait till you hear Quincy sing it. Come here, Mase," she said, and hauled Mason up from the paper and handed him to Wyatt. "I won't be needing your help on the piano," she said, and kissed the top of his head as she took the music from Wyatt.

She sat down at the piano, glanced over her shoulder at him, then began to play. It was a beautiful melody, a slower tempo than the music he'd heard her create with Quincy. It sounded more like something Carole King would sing, not the country-western style she'd been writing. Whatever one called it, Wyatt was moved. He could feel something grow inside him as she sang. Something with very deep roots.

When she'd finished, Holly twisted around on her stool. "Well? Do you like it? I know it's a little slow," she said, "but I can change the tempo—"

Wyatt stood up and, carrying Mason, walked to the piano. He kneeled next to her and cupped her face. Mason grabbed the lapel of her robe. "That is the most beautiful song I ever heard," he said. "It's a hit, Holly. That song is a hit."

"I don't know about that . . ."

"I do. Thank you." He kissed her tenderly. "I have something for you, too," he said, and handed her Mason so he could fetch the gift.

Holly let Mason slide off her lap. Her box was small, but she opened it eagerly. Wyatt had given her a Tiffany charm bracelet. He'd noticed she was always wearing bracelets, and he'd found this one with a little diamond-studded guitar hanging from it.

"It's gorgeous!" she cried with delight, and fastened it onto her wrist. She held her arm out, shaking it, making the charm dance for Mason. "Thank you, Wyatt. I adore it. I can't wait to show Ossana."

"That's not all," Wyatt said, and from the pocket of his lounge pants he pulled out his own envelope. He'd come up with the idea because of Jesse, of all people. "You have to get her something that really matters to her, bro," Jesse had offered one afternoon—without being asked, naturally.

"Thanks, Jesse. I will remind you that I have dated many women and have even been married. This ain't my first rodeo," Wyatt had calmly informed him. "Can you please get back to work?"

"I know," Jesse had said, although instead of working, he'd propped his arm on the top of the post digger. "But you are in sad shape, Wyatt. You could use a reminder of how this works. Sexy lingerie is nice for you, but she's gonna need something that means something to *her*. You know, something she wouldn't get for herself."

Wyatt had rolled his eyes. "Thanks again for sharing yet another chapter from *Jesse Wheeler's Dating Tips*. Come on, we've got holes to dig."

But Jesse was right. Wyatt was out of practice, and he hadn't really thought about this gift until Jesse had opened his big mouth.

"Wyatt!" Holly said, laughing as she held up the envelope. "You wrote a song for me!"

"Something like that," he said.

Holly opened the envelope. Inside was a plane ticket to Nashville.

"It's open-ended," Wyatt said as she pulled it out and stared at it. "You can go anytime." Part of him found it quite difficult to say that out loud. He'd bought the ticket, but he didn't want Holly to go to Nashville. He wanted her to stay right here, in this run-down old farmhouse, with him and Milo and Mason and Grace.

But the bigger, better part of him knew that if she didn't go, she'd never know what she could achieve. Holly had been right when she'd told him that she wasn't a go-getter. She needed prodding. She needed someone who believed in her to help her take that step.

Holly seemed stunned by the ticket. She kept turning it over, as if she would find some magic words written on the back, some prediction of the future.

Wyatt cleared his throat and added, "I called in a favor from a client. He's got a condo in Nashville he uses on occasion, but he's willing to give it up for a few months until you get your feet on the ground. And once your mother's will is probated, I'll buy this property so you'll have something to live on until your music starts to earn you the kind of living I think it will."

When Holly looked up at him, her eyes were glistening. "I can't believe you did this."

"You need to go. You can't waste your talent, Holly."

"All my life I have been hearing how I need to give it up and get a real job. You are the first person who has encouraged me to go and do it."

"Because I truly believe in you." He didn't understand how anyone could hear her music and not believe in her. It had to happen . . . with or without him.

"What about *you*?" she asked as Mason crawled under the coffee table, pulling wrapping paper with him.

Wyatt chuckled. "I'll be hoping for an invitation."

"I love you," Holly said suddenly, and stood up from the piano, clutching the plane ticket. "Do you know that? I love you. I can't imagine being in Nashville without you and Mason and Grace."

There were, obviously, some complications with that, but Wyatt wasn't going to spoil the moment by pointing it out.

"I love you, Wyatt Clark, and I think you love me too."

He didn't say that he did, but he didn't deny it, either. There was a wall there, one that he realized he was too afraid to scale just yet. But as he gazed at Holly this Christmas morning, he couldn't imagine being without her, either.

When Holly put Mason down for his nap, she shooed an unhappy Milo out onto the porch, and took Wyatt by the hand, and led him up to her room, where she proceeded to push him down on the bed and crawl on top of him. "You know what I hope?" she asked as she raked her fingers down his bare chest. "I hope that this never ends, that we are always like this."

Oh God, he hoped the same thing. This was what Wyatt had always wanted—a house like this, babies sleeping in their cribs, ornery cows bellowing for their hay, dogs sniffing around the porch. He wanted apple turnovers on Christmas morning and cranky old windmills and a woman who looked and tasted and smelled like Holly. He wanted to come home to her after a hard day's work, and he wanted to lie with her in bed when it was raining outside and make love just like this. He wanted all that, and if she happened to be the hottest songwriter in Nashville, well, that was okay too.

The steady rhythm of rain sounded on the roof and

the patio as Wyatt and Holly lost themselves in each other's arms. But the rain faded from his conscience as he covered her body with his and moved inside of her, filling her up with all that he wanted and hoped and dreamed.

And then he lay beside her, breathing hard, his body warm and moist, his heart beating with gratitude. "It hasn't been easy for me," he whispered into her hair.

Holly didn't speak but turned on her side so that she was facing him.

"What you wrote in that song is true. I am afraid to love again. I'm afraid of that kind of pain again."

She kissed his throat.

"I may find it hard to say, Holly, but the truth is lying in this bed between us. I love you."

She smiled. "I know," she whispered, and kissed him before pressing her cheek to his shoulder.

"Well, you don't have to be so smug," he said, and brushed the hair from her face as she giggled. He wrapped her in his arms, pulling her close. "All right. Be smug. I don't care." But he was grinning up at the ceiling.

They napped in each other's embrace. Wyatt was having a dream about Troy's saddle being broken, and a crack in the leather so wide that he could feel cold air. It took him a moment to realize the air was cool because Holly was up. She was pulling on her jeans.

"Where are you going?" he asked sleepily. "Come back here."

"Someone's here," she said as she hastily pulled her hair back into a ponytail while she stuffed her feet into her Uggs.

Wyatt sat up, propping himself up on his elbows. "Who?"

"I don't know," she said. "I have to get Mason."

She hurried out of the room. Wyatt jumped up and pulled on his jeans as he looked out the window. All he could see was the top of a black car.

Chapter Nineteen

There were moments like this in which Hannah felt as if she were standing high above the earth on a wire, and the smallest gust could push her off into a pool of pills and alcohol.

It didn't help matters at all that she knew there were pills stashed in her mother's bathroom, hidden away for emergencies. With the gravity of this moment weighing down on her, she was having trouble keeping those pills from her mind.

She was shaky, unsteady on her feet and in her head. If it weren't for Mason, she wouldn't be driving out here, especially in the rain. But that huge black sinkhole Mason had left in her had burned hard this morning. She'd awakened in the transitional house, her pillow wet from the tears of missing her son, and she'd decided today was the day.

"Why haven't you gone to see him?" That was the first thing Loren had asked her when she'd come back to Austin.

Loren had been surprisingly forgiving when she'd called him from Palm Springs and confessed her drug and alcohol use and her part in their failed marriage. She'd expected threats and sneers, but Loren had offered her understanding and a willingness to help. They'd talked like they hadn't talked in years, about their marriage, about when things had started to fall apart. Loren even seemed to feel guilty that he hadn't been more aware of her problems. "I could have helped you," he'd said. "I'm sorry, Hannah. I could have helped you."

Hannah had been overwhelmed by his selflessness . . . until she came back to Austin and realized he was hoping for reconciliation. That would never happen, but Hannah didn't mind letting him believe it was a possibility. She would let Loren think whatever he needed to think until she had Mason back. Then she'd file for divorce.

Mason . . . her heart, her soul. She ached with missing him.

Loren told her the baby was good. "He seems happy," he said to her. "I never thought I'd say this, but Holly seems to have stepped up."

Hannah had never had any doubt of that, but then, she knew Holly better than anyone. When they were girls, Holly had loved baby dolls. She'd had three or four, with beds for all of them lined up on one wall of the nursery. She'd had clothes and diapers and bottles. Moreover, she was forever catching lizards and horned toads, which she had kept in boxes—she called them houses—in the barn until Dad made her let them go. And there had been an endless parade of feral cats Holly was always trying to adopt.

No, Hannah never had any doubt about Holly. The only doubts she'd ever had were in herself.

"Why haven't you been to see him?" Rob Tucker
had asked her that, too, when she'd come back to Austin. Rob had met her plane, although Hannah had told
him it wasn't necessary. "Are you kidding? I'm not letting you come back with no one to meet you," he'd
said gruffly, and there he'd been, standing in the baggage claim area, smiling as she came down the escala-
tor, flowers in hand. He'd been wearing khakis and a
polo shirt, his sunglasses on top of his head, and Hannah had thought it was kind of odd that she'd never
seen him in anything other than a suit, and yet they'd
become so close over the last four months.

He'd smiled and held out his arms to her. "Welcome
back to the land of the living."

She should have known that Rob was a recovering
alcoholic, and that that was the reason he'd been able
to detect her abuse. She'd found out during the many
phone conversations they'd had while she'd been in
Florida. "Been sober seventeen years," he'd proudly re-
affirmed over dinner the night she returned to Texas.
Hannah would be eternally grateful to him for not fir-
ing her and, moreover, for helping her get treatment.
He was her only friend now, her mentor, the one person
who called to check on her every day. He'd arranged
for her stay in the tony transitional house in Westlake,
where professional counselors and support staff helped
people like Hannah—on reentering a world in which
they used to do drugs all day just to cope—to remain
sober and learn new coping mechanisms.

"When will you go and see your son?" he'd asked
her two days ago.

"The time has to be right," she'd said, and felt the

flush of shame spread up her neck and into her cheeks. She could hardly speak of Mason without feeling the incredible burden of her guilt and despair.

But Rob had reached across the dinner table and taken her hand. "The pain is never going to go away. Nor is the guilt or the fear. It'll all just get bigger and bigger until you confront it. I know what I'm telling you, Hannah. My daughter was four."

She knew he was right—he was so right—but Hannah was so fearful. She used to think God couldn't keep her from her son, but she'd learned that fear was a pretty powerful force. She'd worried that Mason would be forever damaged because she had abandoned him, but Dr. Bonifield assured her that children Mason's age could overcome quite a lot as long as he'd had a stable environment and someone to love him in her absence. "It's the children who don't have that who have trouble attaching later in life," she'd explained.

That sounded like some textbook statistic to Hannah, and she wasn't convinced that Mason wouldn't always hate her for being his mother. Who could blame him? What other fifteen-month-old had lost his mother to drug treatment? Hannah could picture the moms in her old neighborhood, the ones who scheduled play dates and cooked vegetables into their kids' treats and didn't allow television. She couldn't picture any of them losing their grip to drugs so completely as she had.

She feared seeing indifference on Mason's baby face. Or, worse, seeing no recognition at all on his face.

The thought that Mason might not know her made Hannah physically ill. Once, during her first few nights in the transitional house, she'd dreamed Mason could speak, and he told her he couldn't talk to strangers. She was the stranger. Hannah had awakened herself by groping for the imaginary pill bottle on her nightstand.

Or perhaps her worst fear was the one she deserved most of all: seeing Mason look at Holly with the love he would have had for his mother if she hadn't screwed everything up. Seeing him run to Holly, want Holly, smile at Holly.

But when Hannah was feeling good, she had a whole other set of reasons why she'd not yet been to see Mason. She didn't want to upset his secure little world again until she knew what she was doing. What if . . . what if he *did* know her and wanted to be with her? What if Holly wanted him to go home? Hannah could hardly bring him home to live in a transitional house. She had to be on her feet, able to take care of him fully.

Until she'd come back to Austin, she hadn't even been certain she had a job. But Rob had made sure her job was still open, and Hannah was starting back to work after the first of the year.

Hannah had given herself her own little deadline for having everything ready for Mason. She had roughly two months yet to do in the transitional house. She felt a little stronger every day, one step further away from the grip of addiction. Hannah didn't kid herself—she was an addict, and she would always have to be on guard. But she was finally feeling capable of living without drugs.

In March she would have a new job and a new house, and she would have Mason. And on Christmas

Day—today—she couldn't stand it another minute. She decided it was time to reacquaint herself with her son.

The old homestead looked exactly as it had during those long months when her mother was dying. The same days Hannah would exist in a fog drinking and eating pills like candy.

Hannah's gut was churning; she couldn't relax. Her hands hurt from gripping the wheel of Rob's car. Her legs were stiff from the tension of her knees being locked.

A wisp of smoke was snaking up out of the chimney, and the lights of the kitchen were shining warm on this cold, wet wintry day. In the backyard Hannah could see a smattering of toys, including a red car with a yellow top. When she'd last she seen her son, he was crawling. Now he was riding in a kid's car.

Around by the shed was Holly's little car. There was also an old pickup truck. That made Hannah's stomach dip again—someone else was here. So much for the quiet scene between sisters that Hannah had desperately prayed for.

She had no idea how long she sat looking at the house and the cars and the toys, trying to summon her courage. She began to imagine backing up and driving back to Austin. "No," she said, and abruptly opened the car door. Once it was open, she couldn't go back. She had to get out. She had to walk. And she had to see—*had* to see—Mason.

Clutching the gift she'd bought her child—a truck, because she had no idea what else to give him—Hannah trudged up the walk and up the porch steps. Someone had fixed the sag in the middle of the second step with new plywood. She stepped onto the porch and made herself knock on the door.

Hannah heard the footsteps on the stairs, heard voices, and pleaded with herself not to be sick, not to crumble, not to weep.

The door swung open and Holly, her sweater on inside out, stood before her. She looked angry, which, Hannah thought, was not entirely unexpected. She hadn't called in so long, not even to say she was coming. "Merry Christmas," Hannah said softly.

Holly just stared at her in disbelief. "What are you doing here?"

"I'm back," Hannah said. "I told you I'd come back. I came to see you."

"Today?" Holly said. "Just like that, you show up?"

"Lala."

Hannah heard Mason's voice from inside the house. It wrapped around her heart and squeezed the blood from it. She gasped for air, put her hand against the house to hold herself up. Holly was standing in the door, blocking her sight of him. "May I see him?" she asked her sister. "Holly . . . please. May I see him?" Her voice was full of desperation.

"No," Holly said.

"Holly . . ." The man's voice behind her sister was soft and low. "It's okay, baby."

Whoever the man was, Holly listened to him. She was glaring at Hannah, but she stepped aside.

Hannah saw him then. Mason was standing a few feet behind Holly, hanging on to the man's leg. He was wearing a red sweater with Santa on the front, and little sweatpants, and there was the red mark of something on his cheek, impressed into his flesh while he slept. Mason took a few steps forward, peering at the door.

Holly opened the door wider, and Hannah tried to step across the threshold, but she fell to her knees instead, her eyes locked on her baby. He'd grown so much! He stared at her curiously and moved cautiously forward to wrap one plump arm around Holly's leg as he stared at Hannah.

"Baby, it's me. It's Mommy," Hannah said, her voice breaking. Mason leaned his head against Holly's leg.

He didn't know her. Hannah's worst fear had come true—he'd forgotten her. Hannah thought she would never be able to get up, not under her own power. She would stay here, all the blood and life leaking out of her. "You're my baby boy," she said, vaguely aware that tears were sliding over her cheeks. "You're my best and special boy, did you know that? Mommy loves you, Mason. Mommy loves you so much."

God smiled at Hannah then. He smiled at her through Mason, because her baby smiled at her and said, "Go." He said, "Go," and walked forward to Hannah. She wrapped her arms around him and leaned back, lifting him off his feet, holding him close. She closed her eyes against the tears that were now pouring out of her. "*Mason*," she whispered, "my baby."

But Mason began to squirm, wanting down. Hannah reluctantly let go of him and he ran back, ran to Holly and wrapped his arms around her legs. Holly leaned over and picked him up. "Come in," she said to Hannah, and when Hannah looked up, she saw the tears on Holly's cheeks, too, before her sister turned away and walked deeper into the house, carrying Mason.

By the time Hannah had managed to get to her feet, Holly had put Mason at the coffee table, where he stood, rolling a toy truck on the surface.

"Want me to take that?" Holly asked.

Hannah followed her gaze. She'd forgotten the gift she was holding, the paper torn and soggy where she'd held it so tightly.

Holly took it from her and handed it to the man. Hannah noticed him for the first time. He was tall and handsome, with longish black hair and vivid blue eyes. "This is Wyatt Clark," Holly said, and glanced at the man. "And as you might have guessed, Wyatt, this is my sister Hannah."

Hannah self-consciously pushed her hair behind her ears. "Hi," she said. Mason blithely made a sound like a motorboat as he moved the truck around the table.

"I need to get his milk," Holly said, and walked out of the living room.

Hannah glanced nervously at Wyatt Clark. He was regarding her curiously, like an oddity. No doubt Holly had told him everything.

She averted her gaze and walked around to the front of the old plaid couch, stepping over new toys and settling on her knees beside the table. "Mason, what have you got there?"

Mason held up the truck. "Car," he said.

"Truck," the man muttered.

Mason brought it around and set it down in front of her. "Thank you," she said, smiling at him. She ran her hand over the top of his head. His hair was longer now, and darker than she remembered. He'd grown so much. So tall, turning from baby to boy.

"Car," he said again.

"Oh, Mason." Tears were blurring her vision again, but Hannah picked him up and sat him on the table before her. "Look how big you are!"

Mason responded by pulling on the button of her jacket. "Bah bah bah bah."

"If you don't mind, it's time for his snack," Holly said.

Hannah hadn't even heard her come back, but she didn't resist as Holly took Mason from the table and put down a sippy cup of milk and some Goldfish crackers and grapes sliced in half. Mason picked up a grape and shoved it into his mouth with his palm, then slammed his palm on the table. "Bah."

"I should have called—"

"Yes. You should have," Holly said curtly.

"Please, Holly," Hannah said low. "I will answer all your questions. But I had to see him."

"I don't think you've earned the right to see him," Holly said. "Do you really think you can show up on Christmas Day with a gift and everything is all right?"

"No. Of course not." Hannah could see fear in Holly's eyes. She knew that fear; she felt it in her marrow.

"Then what are you doing here?" Holly demanded.

"I told you, I came home. Finally." Hannah eased herself up high enough to take a seat on the end of the couch.

"What does that mean, you 'came home'?" Holly asked. "Are you through with the treatment?"

"I'm through with the inpatient treatment. I'm in a transitional house now. And . . . and I will always be in a twelve-step program."

Mason returned to her with another truck and put it in her lap. "Car," he said.

Hannah smiled. "Pretty car." She leaned over to kiss his cheek, lingering on his soft skin. He smelled like baby lotion. Mason went back to his snack.

Holly's arms were tightly folded across her chest. Her armor, Hannah thought. Wyatt Clark was standing in the arch between the living room and the dining area, his hands in his pockets. He was barefoot, Hannah noticed. He was standing over Holly and Mason, she realized. He had that look about him, that protective, don't-mess-with-my-family look.

"Will you sit down a moment, Holly?" Hannah asked. She noticed her own hands were balled into fists and pressed tightly into her knees.

Holly's gaze flicked over her; she pressed her lips together but then sat on the opposite end of the couch from Hannah.

Hannah smiled a little. "I've been sober for one hundred and fourteen days now."

"Okay," Holly said uncertainly.

Hannah had often wondered how she had become such a raging addict and Holly had escaped that fate. "I signed a contract that I would stay in a transitional house so I can learn how to resume my life and not succumb to stress." That was what the literature called it, *succumbing to stress.* A very polite euphemism for using again. "I've been in two weeks and I have seventy days to go there."

Holly said nothing; she watched Hannah impassively.

"Doggie," Mason said, and put a stuffed doggie in Hannah's lap. She smiled warmly and shook the little dog at him. He reached for it again.

"He looks great, Holly," Hannah said. "He's beautiful. You've taken such great care of him."

"Are you surprised?"

"I'm not. If I'd had any doubt of it, I never would have . . ." Hannah hesitated; she couldn't think of an appropriate word.

"Dumped him?" Holly finished for her.

That was the right word. Hannah looked down. In the course of her treatment, she had promised herself that she would at least be honest with herself about what she'd done. Owning up to it was part of the program, no matter how painful.

"I am going back to work after the first of the year," Hannah said, soldiering on, past the pain, past the truth.

But Holly responded to that by suddenly burying her face in her hands.

"Holly?"

Holly looked up; her expression was desolate. "Why are you telling me this? What am I supposed to do with it? How am I supposed to react to you showing up out of thin air?"

"I . . . I thought you'd want to know," Hannah said uncertainly.

"*Why*, Hannah? You didn't seem to think I needed to know that you were taking drugs, or hiding them in the toilet, or stacking your empty wine bottles in the

319 *A Light at Winter's End*

shed. You didn't seem to think I needed to know that your husband was cheating on you. But here you are, on Christmas Day, and suddenly I need to know it all. I want to know why now. What exactly are you here to tell me?"

Hannah was taken aback; she hadn't really thought of this meeting from her sister's viewpoint. She'd thought that it would be uncomfortable, that Holly would be angry, but she hadn't really thought of anything but her need to see Mason, and even that thought had to compete with her constant impulse to drug herself. "Well," Hannah said, trying to sort through her thoughts. "I guess I am here to tell you that in a couple of months I'll be ready to take Mason home. If . . . if you can hang on that much longer, that is."

Holly stood up so quickly that she hit the coffee table and knocked over Mason's sippy cup. In two strides she was at Mason's side. She snatched him up and held him tight, using her hand to press his head to her shoulder. "You're not taking him." Her voice was shaking.

Mason started to squirm. "Down," he said. "Down!" But Holly buried her face in his neck.

Hannah gaped at her sister. She was not prepared for this—she'd never dreamed Holly would want to *keep* Mason. She struggled with her own thoughts and emotions—disbelief, anger that Holly would presume to keep her son, sympathy for her sister—when Wyatt calmly walked into the room. He put his hand on Mason's back. "No one is taking anyone anywhere today," he said to Holly, and stroked her arm. "Take a breath."

He slowly peeled her hand away and took Mason into his arms. He touched two fingers to Holly's chin and gazed in her eyes a moment.

And then he said to Mason, "Let's go see what happened to that fool dog," and carried the baby out of the room.

Holly waited until he'd gone before she sank down on her knees and splayed her hands on the coffee table, staring at them.

Hannah was holding her breath. She felt dizzy. She didn't know what to say, what to do. She wished she'd taken Rob's advice and brought him along. He'd know what to say. "It looks like I've botched this," she said apologetically. "I didn't mean to say it that way. I didn't understand . . . I mean, obviously, I want to do what works for you—"

"What works for *me*?" Holly snorted. "Look, the bottom line is that I can't let Mason go until I know you aren't going to do this again."

"I'm *not*."

"That's what you say," Holly said, then stood up and moved to the mantel, where she fidgeted with one of their mother's figurines. "You can't have him, Hannah. I won't let you waltz in here and just take him after all he's been through. Mason has stability here. It would be irresponsible of me and grossly unfair to him to put him in that situation before it is abundantly clear that he will be safe."

Hannah's pulse began to race. "That's my son," she said as calmly as she could manage.

"You gave birth to him, that's true," Holly said. "But that's where it ends, for all intents and purposes.

The few months you had him you were on drugs. Then you dumped him. You voluntarily gave him up. Now you've come out of intensive drug treatment and you think you're ready to be a mommy again? If you think I am going to hand him back after all that, *especially* to a drug addict, you can forget it. I'm looking out for Mason here. Are you?"

Hannah flinched, inwardly and outwardly. Holly made her sound so ugly, so vile. "I am not going to use anymore."

"Be real," Holly scoffed. "Do you know what the relapse rate is? I've known a dozen people like you— the first time you have issues, you will drink or take a pill. It's a slippery slope, you know that, I know you do. And if you fail, what happens to Mason?"

Hannah had not expected this. She felt strangely adrift, without answers. Mason was her reason for staying clean; he was the end all and be all. He was what got her up in the morning and tamped down her temptations during the day. She'd never dreamed, not once, that Holly would try to *keep* him. *Be calm. Breathe deep.*

She stood up. "I admit that I have done something very wrong. It was awful, and believe me, I will spend every day for the rest of my life feeling like shit for it. But, Holly, why do you think I did it? Why do you think I brought him to you? Because I knew I needed help. I knew that giving him to you was my only hope of getting help and getting well so that I could come back to take care of him like I should have been doing all along. I told you I'd be back."

Holly's eyes widened. "Are you insane? You were so

high when you came to my apartment, it's a wonder you didn't slam right into the moon!"

"Let's not do this—"

"So you think you can wreck my life and then come home several months later and it's all over? Just because you say so? No way, not this time, Hannah. I won't give Mason up. I was with him when he learned to walk and to talk. I have *devoted* myself to him!" she cried, throwing her arms wide. "You can't just come in here and rip out my heart or his on top of everything else!"

"Oh . . . oh, Holly," Hannah said sadly. She understood completely, understood exactly what her sister was feeling, because the heart had been ripped out of her, too.

"We were having Christmas," Holly said stiffly. "I am respectfully asking you to leave."

"Okay," Hannah said, and put up her hand. "I will go. But I want to say good-bye to Mason, and I want to start seeing him regularly."

"Then get a lawyer."

Hannah gaped at her. "You don't mean that."

"Like hell I don't," Holly said. "I will do *anything* to keep him safe. Especially from the self-centered parents who dumped him like he was nothing but a baby doll."

"Okay, I get it!" Hannah snapped. "You're angry—"

"I am beyond angry," Holly said calmly.

"Enough!" Hannah cried. "I can't say I am sorry enough to suit you, that is abundantly clear. But I am not going to give him to you, Holly. We'll work something out, I promise you, but get the idea that you are keeping him out of your head. He is *my* son!"

"I'm not the same person I was, either. You can get that out of *your* head."

This had been a huge mistake. Hannah didn't say more; she walked to the door. She paused there, looking out at the wet day. She'd thought it was impossible to feel any emptier than she had in the last year, but when she looked back at Holly and saw the pain in her sister's eyes, the way her chest lifted with each deep breath, she felt more alone than she'd ever felt. "I don't expect you to believe me, but I am truly very sorry, Holly. Just know that I will spend the rest of my life making it up to you."

"Good-bye, Hannah."

Hannah stepped out the door.

Wyatt was there on the porch with Mason, who had a little watering can and was using it to water some empty pots. A black dog was lying on the porch; his tail began to thump when he saw Hannah. Hannah looked warily at Wyatt. "May I say good-bye to him?"

He nodded.

She could feel him watching her as she picked up Mason and held him close. "Lala," he said.

Hannah kissed his cheek. "Mommy loves you, Mase. Mommy loves you more than life."

"Down."

Hannah smiled sadly, kissed him once more, and put him down. Mason picked up his watering can.

"Holly loves this kid with everything she's got," Wyatt said quietly. He seemed to think he was telling her something she didn't know.

"Obviously," Hannah said. "But so do I. And he is

my son and I will not give him up. It was nice to meet you, Wyatt."

Wyatt said nothing, but his gaze was steady on hers.

Hannah turned to leave.

"Bye-bye," Mason said. "Bye-bye."

Hannah didn't look back. If she had, she would have lost her fragile hold on her composure. And if she had stopped walking, she would have collapsed with grief and regret. She kept walking, but Hannah felt strangely confident that it would be one of the last times she ever walked away from her son.

Chapter Twenty

O ver the next several days, Holly felt like she was shrinking. Fear filled her up and squeezed the life from her, squeezing a little more out of her each day.

In the week between Christmas and New Year's Eve, she dreaded every ring of her phone, every knock on her door. The anxiety of waiting for the proverbial other shoe to fall made her heartsick. Holly loved Mason more than anything or anyone. She'd had him almost five months, and sometimes she marveled at how quickly she'd gone from complete despair to having him inserted in her life without her permission, to despair that she might lose him.

Oh, but despair she did. It almost felt as if she were waiting for an executioner to come and lop off her head; it could be no less painful than losing him.

Two calls from Hannah pushed her fear into full-blown anxiety. Not that Holly could bring herself to answer the phone. She could hardly bring herself to listen to the message, but then again, she couldn't bear not hearing it, so she snatched it up and played it back both times.

The first message was very simple and cordial, like Hannah. "Hello, Holly. I hope your day is going well. I called to check on you and Mason. Will you please call me when you get this message? Thank you."

"Like a robot," Holly muttered, and erased the message.

The second time Hannah called, she did not sound quite as cordial. It was New Year's Eve morning. Holly was at Wyatt's house with Mason while Wyatt and Jesse worked. She and Wyatt had made plans for the evening; fireworks for the kids, and after they went to bed, Wyatt had a bottle of champagne chilling for the two of them. "We're going to celebrate," Wyatt said. "Where we've been and where we're going."

Holly didn't feel much like celebrating, but she smiled and nodded all the same when Wyatt suggested it. He'd tried very hard all week to buoy her spirits. She'd tried just as hard to be buoyed . . . but it wasn't working. There was a sea change coming; she could feel it in her bones and was completely distracted by it.

She was making a stew for Wyatt; the recipe was one she'd found in a drawer in her mother's kitchen, written on a yellowed index card in ink that had faded. She could hardly make out some of the instructions and was trying to read the last step when her cell phone's cheerful little song startled her.

Holly threw a dish towel over her shoulder and grabbed the phone. When she saw the number, she dropped the cell phone as if it had stung her, and turned away, letting it ring. The moment it stopped ringing, she picked it up again. Holly debated whether to listen to the message, but it had the allure of a car wreck—she didn't want to listen, but she couldn't stop herself. She punched in her pass code.

"Holly, it's me. You can't avoid me. I want to see Mason and I will drive out there again if I have to, so you might as well pick up the phone and call me back and arrange a time like a sane, rational adult."

Holly clicked her phone shut and tossed it across the kitchen table. It hit Wyatt's computer and spun off, falling to the ground.

"Mine," Mason said, and picked it up.

Holly was prying it from Mason's hand when Wyatt and Jesse walked in.

"Whoa, cowboy, what's wrong?" Jesse asked cheerfully, and squatted down, poking a bawling Mason in the chest.

"He had my phone," Holly said.

"Who wants a phone when you've got a truck this cool lying around?" Jesse asked, and distracted Mason with the truck while Holly freed her phone.

She shoved the phone into her pocket and walked back into the kitchen.

"Hey," Wyatt said.

Holly avoided his gaze. "Hi," she said, and began to stir the stew.

"We just stopped in to get some coffee. You know where the pot is, Jesse."

Jesse picked up a coffee tumbler and poured a cup. "What about you, Happy Jack?" he asked Wyatt.

"No, thanks."

Jesse doctored his coffee—lots of cream and even more sugar—screwed the lid on his tumbler, and smiled at Holly. "Happy New Year, Hollyhocks," he said, and walked out of the kitchen.

Wyatt put his coffee tumbler in the sink. "Everything okay?" he asked Holly.

"Great," she lied. "I'm not sure I have all the spices I need."

He eyed her skeptically. "I'll see you later?"

"Yep."

When Wyatt left, she picked up the place and had Mason nap. Then she sat at the kitchen table, her emotions churning. She didn't know what to do. She tried to think of how she could meet Hannah halfway. A bargain, some agreement to share him. Joint custody. Something. It made sense to her—they'd both been a mother to him. Why couldn't they be a blended family? It was the only thing that was fair to Mason, wasn't it?

Later that afternoon she was still sitting there, watching Mason move his cars around the living room, when Wyatt came in. "Hi," she said as he walked into the kitchen. He leaned over and kissed the top of her head. "You don't look any better this afternoon than you did this morning. What's going on?"

Holly shook her head. "Another message from Hannah. Only, this time she is demanding to see Mason."

He did not seem fazed by that. In fact, he shrugged. "I think you should let her."

Holly stared at him. "You do?" She thought she should, too, but wanted Wyatt to be on her side, to have her back on this.

He squatted down beside her, put his hand on her knee. "I think you're being unreasonable."

"Great," Holly said, and looked away.

"Baby, listen to me. She's in no position to take him. You're going to talk to Jillian in a couple of days, and she'll make sure Hannah can't drive out here to claim him like some forgotten piece of property. But I don't think you should refuse to let her see him. It won't hurt, and it won't make Mason love you any less."

Holly caught a painful breath in her throat.

"And in the meantime, you're making yourself sick stressing over something you don't need to stress about."

"You don't understand," she argued, and moved her knee from under his hand and stood up. "You don't know what it feels like to believe you might lose the most precious thing in the world to you."

Wyatt slowly rose up to his full height. "I don't?"

She winced. "I'm sorry. Come on, Wyatt, I don't want to argue with you. Honestly, I don't want to do anything but get in my car with Mason and drive to Mexico or Canada—any place she can't find me."

Wyatt gave her a sympathetic smile and said, "It's going to be okay, Holly."

For once, she didn't believe him. And his assurances weren't helping.

Neither did the envelope that arrived at the homestead that week.

It so happened that Jillian Hunter was still on vacation, not expected back until the following Monday. Holly didn't hear from Hannah after the message on New Year's Eve, but she expected her sister to come rolling up in that black BMW in some designer suit and demand her son.

Hannah didn't come, but the demand from a lawyer did. It was a letter signed by someone named Rob Tucker. It proposed a visitation schedule "with the expectation that these visits will result in a permanent reunification of Mason with his mother."

Holly showed it to Wyatt, expecting him to dismiss it. But Wyatt read it and then folded it up and put it back in the envelope. "I think you need to speak with Jillian."

"She can't do this, right?" Holly said. "I mean, I should have some say in it."

Wyatt said nothing.

"Why are you being like that?" Holly asked, but even as the words were tumbling out of her mouth, she knew that she was wrong. She just couldn't admit that she was. Admitting she was wrong made losing Mason real, and she couldn't bring herself to do that. She was trying. God knew she was trying. "You don't think she can do this, do you?"

Wyatt gazed at her with a strange look of pity and impatience. "I don't know if she can or she can't. But you should be prepared in the event that she can."

"What happened to all the 'Don't worry, be happy' talk? I don't need to prepare myself for anything, and I would appreciate it you would be more supportive."

"I've tried to be—"

"No, you've tried to convince me that nothing is wrong, and now you are telling me to give Mason up."

"Holly . . . ," he said in a voice full of rebuke.

Wyatt went home that night. They needed some space.

Holly apologized to him the next day. "I am sorry," she said stiffly. "I know I was being ridiculous to you, but I can't seem to help myself. I am so worried about what's going to happen to Mason. It's not fair to insert him into yet another life and take him from what he knows now. He's attached to me, too, you know."

"I know he is," Wyatt said. "But you have to acknowledge that even though Hannah went off the deep end, she's made every effort to right herself."

"She could relapse," Holly argued. "Something could happen and she could relapse."

Wyatt smiled sadly and put his arms around Holly. "I understand," he murmured, and kissed her temple. Then the bridge of her nose. Then her mouth. They made up without words, sinking into each other, each needing reassurance and comfort.

But something felt different to Holly. It wasn't the same magic. She could hardly admit it to herself, but the little fantasy she'd been living in—Wyatt, Mason, Grace, and her—was unraveling before her very eyes. There was no light at the end of her winter—it felt as if her winter hadn't even begun.

Jillian Harper met Holly a few days later. Holly let her read the letter from Rob Turner, Esquire, and then explained everything more fully than she had on the phone.

Jillian listened, taking notes, nodding thoughtfully. When Holly had finished, Jillian put down her pencil and pressed her fingertips together. "What exactly do you want to see happen?"

"Well, obviously, I want to keep Mason safe—"

"Not going to happen," Jillian interjected matter-of-factly, and Holly's heart dropped to her toes.

"What do you mean? She *dumped* him on me. She

is a drug addict. Who's to say she won't do it again?"

"What she does in the future is another issue entirely. When she left him with you, did she tell you she was coming back for him?"

Holly frowned. "Well, yes, but she didn't say when."

"Was there any abuse in the home prior to that? Any signs of neglect?"

"Not that I saw, but obviously, if she was doing drugs—"

"Listen, Holly, I don't disagree with your assessment of what happened or your sister's fitness to raise her child. But what you're wanting is a very tough legal hurdle to jump. Here is what you need to know," Jillian said, and folded her arms on her desk, looking at Holly over the tops of her readers. "The laws in Texas favor the biological parents. Period. Hannah has not been charged with a crime, and she is not under the monitoring of Child Protective Services, and given that she is out of treatment and putting her life back on track, I don't imagine they'd do much more than watch her for three to six months to make sure she's not going to add to their caseload."

"She's not on their caseload, but she should be. I could have called them, you know, but I didn't—"

"No, you didn't," Jillian said, and held up her hand to halt any argument Holly wanted to make before she could make it. "Again, I don't disagree with you. I am just telling you the legal practicalities. It is very difficult to take a child from a parent, even when they aren't working or paying for their child and are living off the state. Listen to what I am saying: Even if you turned Hannah in today, the fact of the matter is that she took the necessary steps—the *same* steps the state would require her to take—to get her son back. She is demonstrating that she is stable by maintaining a job—she has a job, right?—and a place for Mason to live. Is that right? So the most the state would do at this point is perhaps add on a parenting class and a twelve-step program if she's not already in one." Jillian sat back in her chair and picked up her pencil. "As for her husband, other than the cheating, is he into drugs that you know of?"

Holly snorted. "Is that the standard? If he's not an addict, he's okay?"

"It's the reality, Holly," Jillian said with a shrug. "The state has so many more children in much worse circumstances. They triage like everyone else. It is not okay to abandon your child, in Texas, but if you leave the child with a relative, and you say you'll be back, and you maintain some sort of contact and support, well . . ."

"I can't believe this!" Holly said angrily. "Those two people abandoned their baby with me!"

Jillian gave her a pitying look, the same sort of look Wyatt had given her a time or two. "I'm not saying you can't fight it. What I am saying is you would end up spending a lot of money—and I'm talking tens of thousands—and you still probably wouldn't get what you wanted in the end. The court may even agree that you are a better mother to him than your sister, but your sister has the law on her side. You have the burden of proving that she is somehow unfit—which I don't imagine she is, because if drug use made you an unfit parent, half the children in Texas would be removed from their homes. Do you understand what I am saying?"

"Yes," Holly said. "You are saying that I lose. Hannah gets to go on like nothing ever happened, and I get to pick up the pieces. I understand that clearly."

Jillian smiled sadly. "I can't imagine that her life is proceeding as if nothing ever happened. If you think about it, she had to make some pretty tough decisions."

Holly knew that, of course she knew that. Sometimes she'd thought about how hard it must have been for Hannah . . . but her sympathy for her sister began to disintegrate when Holly thought of Mason. She couldn't see past her love for that little boy, and on some level Holly knew she was blinded by it.

"My advice is that you respond to this letter with some sort of visitation agreement that favors you, as well as with a plan to transition Mason back to her so that he's not abruptly removed from his secure environment and you. We need to impress on them that this should be as painless as possible for Mason. I can draft something and present it to her if you like."

Holly didn't answer immediately; she was trying to find her breath.

Jillian looked up from her notes. "He is a very lucky little boy that you were there for him, Holly. And you will continue to be there for him. We will make sure of that."

No, Holly was the lucky one in this equation. The last months with Mason had been the best of her life.

"It's not fair," Jillian said. "But I'd guess you've been around enough to know that life is seldom fair. Shall I draft the papers for you?"

With her gaze on Mason—her view of him blurred by the angry tears that had been burning the backs of her eyes for over two weeks now—Holly nodded.

Chapter Twenty-one

It was happening again.

Wyatt had tried so hard to guard himself against it, to erect steel walls around his battered heart, but in spite of it, it was happening again.

Goddammit, for two years he had avoided people and all their entanglements, because he didn't trust them, because he couldn't bear the thought of losing himself again. He'd moved out to this ranch in the middle of fucking nowhere, but then Holly had moved into the Fisher place, and he'd gone and fallen in love—hell, he'd even *admitted* it to her—and now . . . now he was here again, feeling a distance growing between them that he did not know how to bridge.

Even when she was smiling and trying as hard as she could—oh, he had no doubt she was really trying—he could see the pain in her eyes, on her face, in the way she held one hand in a tight fist. He could see the way she looked at Mason, as if she were counting every moment. He understood, perhaps better than anyone on this earth, how gallingly unfair the situation was to her. Yet, even having stood in her shoes, he could not summon the right words to help her. Words seemed so trite, so meaningless. He knew from his own experience that there was little anyone could say to ease her pain. So he did what he could. He tried to be there for her when he thought she needed him, and he tried to give her space to confront her feelings.

He tried.

Their lovemaking was still pretty spectacular—for him, anyway—but he noticed a subtle difference in it. It almost seemed to him that Holly was someplace else, losing herself in the moment as she always did, but detaching from him at the same time. He wanted to bring her back, but he didn't know how to do it any more than he'd known how to bring Macy back to him two years ago.

Holly had been terribly despondent when she returned from Jillian's offices with the news there was nothing she could do. Wrapped in her father's barn jacket, she'd walked out onto the porch and stared at the sinking sun until Wyatt finally made her come in. For a few days she hadn't been able to look at Mason without tearing up.

"You're not losing him," Wyatt had reminded her. "You'll still be part of his life."

She'd given Wyatt a blank look. "I won't be there when he wakes up. I won't be there when he goes to sleep. I won't be there to see what he learns every day. I won't be there, Wyatt. He's given my life a purpose like nothing else ever has, not even music, and I don't know how to give him up."

"I'm not there every day for Grace, either, but it doesn't make me any less a part of her life," he'd said.

Holly had dipped her head, and her shaggy hair had covered his view of her face. "But it's different when you're a mother."

He couldn't argue with her. He didn't want to argue with her. God knew he'd had those feelings about Grace. Sometimes, in the space of a few days, she would seem to grow and change and learn so much. But it was for Holly, as it was for him, a reality that had to be acknowledged.

As he'd privately guessed, Hannah was more than happy to agree to a visitation schedule for Holly and a transition plan for Mason. The attorneys had decided the visits would begin at the Baby Bowl, where Holly and Wyatt took the kids each Thursday, until the parties agreed that Hannah could see Mason for longer periods without Holly hovering over them. No overnight visits would be allowed until Hannah graduated from her stint at the transitional house at the end of February.

The first time Hannah came, she arrived in the company of a big, barrel-chested guy. He shook Wyatt's hand and introduced himself as Rob Tucker. "I'm her sponsor," he said.

"Hello," Wyatt said.

"Thanks for bringing him," Hannah said when Holly handed Mason to her. Holly avoided her sister's gaze and kept hers on Mason.

"Bye-bye," Mason said, waving at Hannah. Wyatt knew he wanted down and inside the little gate so he could play. Grace was already inside, climbing over a big cushy dinosaur.

Holly ran her hand over Mason's head. "He likes

the big blocks," she said to Hannah. "He likes to put them together and make a train."

"Okay," Hannah said, and smiled into the face of her son. "Let's go make a train, Mason!"

"Train," Mason said, and Hannah turned away from Holly and took him inside the play area.

Holly sank down onto the edge of a chair, watching.

Rob Tucker grinned at Wyatt. "This is your standard awkward situation, isn't it?"

Rob Tucker looked to be a talker, and Wyatt had to suppress a sigh of tedium.

"I wish it hadn't come to this, but I can understand Holly's concern," Rob said equably.

Her concern? Was this guy serious? As if Holly were some distant observer who thought perhaps Hannah needed a little more time to be sober. That was a concern. Holly wasn't concerned; Holly was heartbroken.

"But Hannah, she's worked really hard," Rob continued, as if Wyatt had asked for an explanation. He must have given the guy a look, because Rob said, "I've known Hannah a long time, and I know where she was and how far she's come."

Wyatt shrugged. It was pretty clear to him that ol' Rob had a thing for Hannah. He kept looking at her, smiling a little when he talked about how great she was doing. Wyatt wondered if he himself did that when he talked about Holly. He looked at Holly now; she was worrying a nail, her gaze still locked on Mason and Hannah. Mason was showing his mother some blocks, his face upturned to hers, handing them to her and then watching hopefully as Hannah exclaimed over each one. Gracie was terrorizing some poor child by trying to kiss her. Wyatt half stood, prepared to go and stop his child from spreading her love indiscriminately, but Gracie chose that moment to spin around and run to the wheels and buttons and levers mounted on the wall.

He slowly resumed sitting.

"I know she is going to make it," Rob Turner continued. "I've never known anyone like her, to be honest." He chuckled. "She's a perfectionist, if you know what I mean. I was joking around and told her that she even was perfect in being an addict. Went right from zero to sixty. But she's working really hard at sobriety, and I know she won't have any trouble staying sober in the long run. The fact that she wants her son back worse than anything is the carrot, you know? But she has to prove to me and everyone else that she's ready."

"*You?*" Wyatt asked curiously. "Why do you get to decide?"

Rob shrugged. "That's what a court would require of her, if we're being honest. I guess me because I am her attorney and we are hedging our bets in case her sister decides she wants to make a bigger deal of this than it already is. Hannah could walk into a court today and demonstrate that while she made a mistake, she has done everything reasonably possible to correct it." Rob smiled proudly, as if he'd done it all himself.

"Just out of curiosity," Wyatt said, "when you were propping Hannah up to look like a little treatment star, did you think of Holly?"

Rob looked confused by the question.

"Holly. Her sister. Did you ever once think about

what she's been through? What she's done for that kid?"

"Of course," Rob said. "I mean, we were going to propose a really generous visitation schedule after Mason is reunited with his mother, but Holly came back with one that we're going to use. Yes, we thought of Holly."

"You didn't think about her, you thought about Hannah," Wyatt said calmly. "And frankly, Rob, I'm not sure you thought that much about Mason."

Rob smiled. "Honestly, I'm not the villain. Look, I don't want that little boy ending up with his dad. Trust me," he said with a slight roll of his eyes. "I've known Loren Drake for a long time, too, and he's a piece of work. But he's also an attorney and a damn good one, so I wanted to get this locked down with the sisters and make sure we've all got a united front against Loren."

"Okay," Wyatt said. "But just so you know, I am not on the Hannah bandwagon."

Rob looked unsurprised. "Wyatt, I understand this sucks for everyone. But you're wrong about Hannah. She's really a good person who made a terrible mistake. It happens."

He'd left it like that with Rob, letting Rob think he'd convinced him that Hannah had done a complete three-sixty. Wyatt didn't care if the pope made Hannah a saint tomorrow. He only cared about Holly, and Holly wasn't dealing with this situation very well.

A few days later, Holly called him while he was working with Jesse and said she wouldn't be over that night.

Wyatt put down the chain saw he was using to

cut brush and walked a good distance from Jesse. "Why not?"

"I have a splitting headache, and Mason's kind of fussy. I think maybe he's got a little cold."

"I could come and check on you."

"Oh. Sure." She didn't sound that excited by the idea.

"Can I bring you anything?"

"No," she said quickly. "We're good. Just . . . just resting. I'll talk to you later."

She hung up before Wyatt could say anything else. He slowly closed his phone and shoved it back in his pocket, then walked back to where he and Jesse were working.

Wyatt rode Troy to Holly's later that afternoon with Milo loping along. In his saddlebag, he had a cigar box with crayons for Mason, and the biggest chocolate bar he could find for Holly. As he crested the hill, he heard the music.

He pulled up, listening to the tune. Holly wasn't resting. She was working. And the song she was writing was heavy and dark, the chords as gray as a winter day.

He sent Troy down the hill.

Mason was standing at the door when he'd tethered Troy to a tree and walked up onto the porch. "Doggie!" he cried.

Holly opened the door a moment later and Milo dashed through, toppling Mason in his haste. Mason laughed and got up, waddling after Milo.

"Hey," Holly said, and pushed her hair back from her face. She smiled.

Wyatt kissed her. "What was the song I heard?"

"Oh, that," she said, and shifted her gaze away. "That's the song I wrote for you. 'A Light at Winter's End.' I decided to change the melody. What did you think?"

"I think it sounded kind of sad."

"Really? I didn't think so. It's a love song."

"A sad love song, then."

She sort of laughed and walked back into the living area. "Do love songs need to be cheerful?"

"I always thought love was happy," he said. "Unless it's gone south."

Holly looked at him then, her gaze resting lightly on his face. "I think love is more complicated than that."

"Do you?"

"Don't you?"

"I love you, Holly," he said. "There's nothing complicated about it."

She smiled and looked down. "That's really sweet, Wyatt."

"I didn't say it to be sweet—"

Holly waved a hand at him. "I don't mean to cut you off, really, but I . . . I am not feeling well and I don't think I can have this conversation right now."

What conversation?

"Listen, could you do me a favor? I've been cooped up in here all day. Would you mind watching Mason for a few minutes so I can take a little walk? I need to clear my head and my lungs."

What conversation? If Wyatt wasn't so afraid of hearing exactly what conversation, he would have asked her, but he stood there paralyzed with dread, a

cigar box full of crayons in one hand and a big chocolate bar in the other. "Sure," he said, and put the things
on the console near the door. "Take all the time you
need."

He walked across the room and picked up Mason.
"Little Buckaroo, how are you today?" he asked, and
when he turned around again, Holly already had a
jacket on.

"I'll be right back," she promised.

"Lala," Mason said, and pushed against Wyatt's
chest. "Down," he said.

Wyatt obliged him as Holly walked out the door.
"Lala!" Mason cried, and ran to the door after her,
then stood at the screen, staring out. Milo wandered
over and sat beside him.

Wyatt reluctantly followed and stood behind them,
watching Holly's arms swing as she marched down the
long drive, away from the three of them.

It was only a walk, but he could feel her slipping
through his fingers like so much sand, and he could
not stop it. "Come on, bucko," he said to Mason, and
picked him up, shooed Milo out of the way with his
foot, and closed the door. "Let's go drown our sorrows
with some juice."

Chapter Twenty-two

It was fascinating to Holly on some remote level that she could fall in love with someone one day and not know what to do with him the next.

She knew she was hurting Wyatt. That was heart-breaking to her—she would sooner hurt herself than him. The weird thing about it was that she needed his comfort and support, yet she couldn't seem to stop herself from floating away from him. It was as if the tether of her little balloon had snapped, and no matter how hard she tried to get back to earth, the force was greater than she was and was carrying her off.

She had never, in all her life, faced such a deeply personal crisis.

She'd begun to accept that she was losing Mason. Even she could see that Mason's affections were turning back to Hannah. She'd watched it happen as the weeks had unfolded and he'd spent more time with his mother, and she'd marveled at the strength of the bond between mother and child. That it could sustain such turmoil and still be as strong was remarkable to her. She wasn't certain she could ever forge as deep a bond with him, even if she had him for the rest of his life. It seemed to be something that was bigger than her love for him, something so primal and instinctual that she couldn't touch it.

Holly couldn't compete with Hannah. It didn't matter that Mason had now lived five months under her care, or that she had to interpret much of what he said for Hannah because Hannah didn't understand him, or that she had to tell Hannah that Mason hated peas but he liked green beans, and that he loved Thomas the Tank Engine but was indifferent to Barney. It didn't matter because Mason called Hannah Mommy and Holly Lala. He smiled brightly when he saw his mommy coming and giggled when she kissed him. His mother had been physically absent from Mason, but she'd been there all along in his little heart.

Holly could see all that, but that did not dampen her feelings for him. She'd done something she hadn't known she was capable of doing—in fact, she would have argued with anyone that she was incapable of doing it. But she had taken in a child, a baby, and she'd loved him, and she didn't want to give up, no matter how many signs were pointing to Mason and Hannah. *She did not want to give up.*

Holly studied Hannah for any signs of drug use, anything that indicated she was less than perfect in her trek back from addiction. Holly desperately wanted to find something, a fissure, anything she could wedge a stake into and widen. But there was nothing. As in all things she did, Hannah excelled at recovery. She went to twelve-step meetings. She told Wyatt she was mentoring a young woman at the transitional house, and they were using the buddy system to stay clean and sober. She'd started running, apparently, for she was late one afternoon and breathlessly reported she'd been delayed training for the Capitol 10K race at the end of March.

Holly and Hannah didn't really talk much. The tension between them was thick and hard; no knife could cut it, no blowtorch could make a dent. Frankly, Holly had no idea what to say to her sister. She didn't hate Hannah, but she couldn't bear her just now.

Nevertheless, Holly was struggling to accept the inevitable, that Mason was going home to his mother. She knew that she had to think beyond that, to how she would pick up the pieces of her life and move forward. The ticket to Nashville burned a hole in her thoughts. All these years she'd been afraid to take a step like that, convinced that her family was right, that her passion for songwriting would lead nowhere. Now, suddenly, it seemed like not only the logical thing to do but the only thing she could do for the sake of her sanity.

Once she was certain Mason was settled and didn't need her, she'd just get out. Just get out of here so she didn't have to watch Mason growing up with Hannah.

Holly was acutely aware that she did not know what to do with Wyatt. Her heart hurt for him. He was trying so hard to be all things to her, but God help her if Holly knew what she needed him to be. She'd tried to explain it to him. "I fell like I am living in a bad dream, pretending at being a mother, but then being asked to give a child I love over to someone who is just back from the land of using drugs."

Wyatt had nodded but not said anything.

"It's not fair," Holly had said.

"I know," Wyatt had agreed patiently.

"There's a *but* with that, isn't there?"

He'd smiled a little and touched her hand. "I guess the but is that I understand Hannah, too."

Holly had been shocked that he'd said it aloud.

"Not the drug use," he'd been quick to amend. "I will never get that. I know it's a disease and all, but I . . . I don't understand that."

"Then what?" Holly had pressed.

"I understand how she feels about Mason. I see her side of it." He had sat up on the couch, leaning forward, as if they were about to have a very serious conversation. "I don't know her, and I don't know what all she's done, but I do know that you could convict me of mass murder and I'd still do everything in my power to keep Grace with me. That's something I would fight to the death for, and I think Hannah . . . I think she's fighting to the death."

"Yeah," Holly had said solemnly. "That's part of my bad dream."

Holly didn't disagree with him, but she was surprisingly hurt. She'd wanted Wyatt to be at least as ambivalent about Hannah as she was. She'd wanted . . . things she couldn't even put into words. Holly could not bring herself to admit to him that, in a way, he was part of her bad dream. All of it—the homestead, the happy little family they'd formed, the whole thing—it had all been a lie. She'd allowed herself to play make believe, to avoid reality as she was so famous for doing, and now it had all blown back in her face.

"Do you understand what I am saying?" she'd asked

Wyatt carefully. *I am saying I can't do this anymore. I have to get out.*

He'd looked at her for a long moment, his gaze studious. "I hear what you are saying, but I am not sure I understand it. It hasn't *all* been a bad dream."

"No. Not all of it. Not you."

Not Wyatt. Just the situation with Wyatt.

Thinking about it all, sorting through the complexities of her emotions, made Holly crazy. At night, she would sit on her bed after she'd bathed Mason and given him a little bit of milk and read him a story. She would sit with her legs pulled up to her chest, staring out the bay windows at the darkness, rocking back and forth, wishing, and praying. But the days kept rolling by, and the executioner kept getting closer, and Hannah kept rebuilding her life and her relationship with Mason, while Wyatt kept trying to be there for Holly, and January turned into February, and Holly could not find peace.

She wanted peace. She wanted to feel good about everything again. She wanted to feel like she had the world by the tail. But how did she grab onto it?

Chapter Twenty-three

The only moments when Hannah felt whole were those she spent with Mason. That little boy with the big smile and the curly hair had brought her back to the land of the living, and her determination to atone for her behavior during the first year of his life grew stronger each day.

It had not been easy, obviously. When she'd returned to Austin after her stint in treatment, Hannah had felt so fragile. That was several weeks ago, and now she felt entirely capable of reclaiming her life.

She had to thank Rob in part for it. Rob Turner was not the most handsome guy Hannah had known, and he could, at times, be annoyingly cheerful, but the man had the biggest heart of anyone she'd ever met. For the first time in her life, Hannah was seeing a man who really cared about her.

She hadn't intended to date Rob. She hadn't really wanted anything from him, but Rob would not step back. "I've seen you this far, and I'm not going to let you down now," he'd said with all the confidence of a partner in a big law firm, which he was. As time went on, Hannah began to find him attractive in a big teddy bear sort of way. But what really drew her to him was the way he cared about her. He took her success very personally, and he was there for her worst moments and her best.

One night, before Holly had agreed that Hannah could see Mason, and Hannah had feared an awful, protracted fight with her sister, she'd felt such despair that she had walked down the street to a little café with the intention of having a drink.

Just one drink, she'd told herself. One stupid drink wasn't going to make her undo all the work she'd done in the last several months. She had had the wine list in hand when Rob had strolled in and sat down at the table with her. He had taken the napkin from the plate and whipped it open, spread it across his lap, then smiled at Hannah. "Feeling down?"

Hannah had blinked. "Really down," she'd admitted. "How did you find me?"

Rob had shrugged as he'd taken the wine list from her hand. "I had a feeling."

Hannah had sighed wearily. "You're always there to save me, aren't you?"

He'd smiled wryly. "I care about you."

"But it doesn't seem fair. You're there to save me and I . . . I don't have much to offer right now."

"I don't care," he'd said in his usual cheerful manner. "I'm not here because of what you can offer me. I'm here because I care about you and there is a little boy out there who needs his mother."

It was the nicest thing he could ever have said to her. She'd slid her hand across the table and covered his. "Thank you. From the bottom of my heart, thank you."

With Rob's help, she was slowly working her way back to normal.

There were obstacles, of course. One was Loren. He'd harbored a crazy idea that they would get back together again. As if nothing had ever happened—as if he'd never cheated and she had never been an addict— he had thought they'd just go back to what they were. Even when Hannah had finally told him that would never happen, he'd been resistant. "You act like there was never anything between us."

"Loren, listen to me. There was never anything between us. We married for all the wrong reasons."

"Give me a break. Did you learn that from some shrink?"

When Loren had finally understood she would never take him back, he'd threatened her with Mason. "There's not a court in Texas that will give him to *you*," he'd said angrily.

"What will I do?" Hannah had tearfully asked Rob later, convinced that her stay in rehab would shift the court's favor to Loren. It was a nightmare—Loren didn't care about Mason. He'd seen his son only about half a dozen times over the last several months, but he had no trouble using his own child to get what he wanted.

"No offense, but he doesn't want you," Rob had said to Hannah. "He just doesn't like to lose. I've known Loren Drake a long time—longer than you have—and I promise you that is what this is about. He does not like to lose."

But Loren had lost. Rob had had a talk with him, and Loren had conceded on the issue of Mason. "You can have him," Loren had angrily informed Hannah. "But you can't have that house. Got that, Hannah? You are not going to milk me for the worst years of my life."

Hannah could not have cared less about that stupid house. It had been Loren's from the beginning. Hannah had never wanted the house and its furnishings; she'd just followed along behind Loren, drinking her wine and nodding in a blurry haze. "What did you say to him?" she'd asked Rob over dinner that night.

Rob had grinned and shrugged. "*Anh,*" he said with dismissive wave of his hand. "Loren has a few skeletons in his closet that have no bearing on you. But they are useful in negotiating. So was that house. He thinks it is worth something."

"It probably is."

"I am sorry you gave it up," Rob had said.

"Not me. It's a part of my past I don't want to remember, much less have to deal with." Hannah wanted a new beginning, free of Loren, free of the person she'd been then.

Her second obstacle was work. Hannah was intimidated by her return to the office, convinced that everyone knew about her fall from grace. One of the things she'd learned in therapy was that she and Holly had been raised to believe that appearances to others mattered more than anything else. It was what drove Hannah to be perfect and, she suspected, what had made Holly turn away achievement for fear of failure. Rob said it didn't matter what anyone thought, and that they were too busy thinking of themselves to think about Hannah.

Nevertheless, Hannah felt entirely conspicuous. She tried to suppress memories of things she'd done at the office when she was high—losing checks, letting things fall through the cracks. Vomiting in the ladies' room after a drinking binge the night before. But the memories were like roaches—ugly little things that snuck in through the cracks in her resolve.

And then Tamara, her second in command, the woman who wanted her job and, Hannah was certain, thought she'd have it, sidled into her office one day and said, "Did your sister ever find you?"

Hannah had looked up from her work. "Excuse me?"

"Your sister," Tamara said. "She called one day last year looking for you. She didn't know where you were."

Hannah blinked. She smiled. "Yes, she found me. Thanks."

"No problem," Tamara said, and slid out.

It was time, Hannah thought, to find a new job. A new start. When she had Mason, she would find a new job.

But the hardest, most gut-wrenching aspect of Hannah's recovery was Holly. Holly had obviously accepted that Mason would come back to Hannah. Yet Holly was Hannah's little sister, and no matter what had passed between them, Hannah's heart ached for her. She couldn't begin to imagine how painful this was for Holly, for it was clear how much she loved Mason.

The guilt Hannah felt for having put Holly in this

horribly untenable position was stifling, but Hannah couldn't turn back the clock. She could not make this better for Holly, short of giving Mason up. But she could spend the rest of her life trying to fix what was broken between them. It was her silent promise to her sister. It was all she had.

In the third week of February, springlike temperatures arrived, and so did Hannah's release from the transitional house. She moved her few things to the condo she'd bought with her savings. It was close to the Montessori day care, where she'd managed to reserve Mason a space in the toddler program. The condo had a backyard that was perfect for a small dog, and there was a playground across the street.

Hannah had furnished the condo with items taken from the Tarrytown house, and she was happy with it. But she wouldn't spend her first night of freedom there because she was going out to the homestead. She thought she ought to come and spend a few nights with Mason and Holly, so that Mason would not be surprised when he left with Holly and moved with Hannah to his new home. To Hannah's great surprise, Holly agreed. Hannah had expected an argument, but she got none.

"That will be fine," Holly said.

"Seriously?"

"It's best for Mason."

"Right," Hannah said. "It's best for Mason."

Holly was waiting for her when Hannah pulled up to the house. Mason was playing in the yard, happily chasing after a litter of barn kittens. When he saw Hannah, he said, "Kitty!"

Hannah's heart opened up like a flower. "I see him!" she said, and squatted down to give Mason a hug. But when Mason squirmed to get away and run after the cat, Hannah stood up and looked at Holly. "How are you?"

"Fine," Holly said. "I've been staying in your old room. You can stay in whichever room you want."

"Thanks."

Holly turned around and walked up the porch steps and into the house.

Hannah sighed. She was under no illusion that this would be anything less than three days of torture for her and Holly both. "Mason!" she said brightly, and held out her hand for her son.

"No!" Mason shouted, and ran from Hannah.

When she'd corralled Mason and brought him inside, she set him down in the living room and glanced around. Holly had left the house as their mother had had it, but now there was sheet music, a guitar case, and toys everywhere. She guessed her mother would not be happy with the clutter; she used to ground Holly for spreading her life around her room and not picking it up.

Hannah could hear Holly banging around in the kitchen, opening cabinets and then shutting them, and followed the sounds after she'd made sure Mason was occupied.

Holly looked up when she entered. "Where's Mason?"

"In the living room. Something smells really good," Hannah said.

"Roast," Holly said, and opened the fridge.

"Roast? Where'd you get it?"

Holly shut the fridge. She was holding a can of biscuit dough. "I made it."

Hannah smiled at what she thought was a joke, but Holly did not. "You *made* it?" she repeated incredulously.

Holly's gaze flicked over Hannah. "Yes, I made it. I've been teaching myself to cook." She nodded toward the bar, and Hannah saw their mother's old cookbook. It was open, and bits of paper and index cards stuck out from between the pages.

"Wow," Hannah said. "That's great. Surprising, but really great."

Holly shrugged, cracked open the can of biscuits, and began to lay them out on a cookie sheet.

"Is there something I can do to help? Set the table?" Hannah asked, and turned around to see that the table was already set. For three. "Oh," Hannah said. "Is someone coming?"

"Wyatt."

"Ah." Hannah was actually relieved. She liked Wyatt, what little she knew of him. Frankly, she'd welcome anyone. This was uncomfortable. Holly obviously didn't want to be alone with Hannah, and it left Hannah feeling wobbly . . . and a little despicable. "Looks like you've got it all under control," she said uneasily. "I'll just put my stuff away."

"Wait," Holly said, and Hannah felt almost hopeful as she turned back to her sister. Holly picked up a dish towel and frowned down at her hands as she wiped them. "I don't know how to ask this."

"Ask me anything," Hannah said. *Anything, Holly. Anything.*

Holly drew a breath. "Okay," she said. "I found the pills in the toilet. I got rid of the wine bottles that were in the closet. I need to know if there is anything else in the house."

The blood drained from Hannah's face. She shook her head.

Holly considered her for a moment. "Okay," she said. "I'll take your word for it." She turned back to the stove.

Holly would never trust her again. Never. Could she blame her? Hannah made herself walk out of the kitchen, away from the air of disapproval and distrust. In the living room, she picked up her bag, then her son, and whispered to him that she loved him as she walked up the stairs. She went to the nursery first to change him. She looked around the room and felt a wave of nausea. In those weeks after her mother died, Hannah would bring Mason out here. She'd put him in his crib, then go downstairs and drink. He would cry when he wanted out, and Hannah had had the ability to ignore him. *God have mercy on her soul.* Hannah shook her head and looked down, blinking back tears.

"Doggie," Mason said, and held up a plush dog toy.

Holly was right not to trust her. Hannah could hardly trust herself. But they were still sisters, and somehow Hannah had to find a way for them to be sisters again, in spite of all that had gone between them.

Chapter Twenty-four

Holly could hear Mason's laughter drifting downstairs and into the kitchen. He was squealing happily, having a grand time with his mother.

She went through the motions of making dinner. She felt like a fool cooking like this. It was like she still had one foot in the little fantasy she'd created. Holly, a cook? Hannah had been shocked, and really, what a laugh! Okay, so she could heat up a roast with the best of them and open a can of biscuits. Holly wasn't a cook. She was a glorified oven operator.

Holly heard a vehicle pulling up to the house and leaned over the kitchen sink, peering out the window, squinting in the waning light of the day. She saw Wyatt get out of his old truck with Milo and reach into the bed. She smiled as he heaved a big sack of something onto his shoulder. She loved him. No matter what else, she loved Wyatt.

Holly tossed the dishrag off her shoulder and went out onto the porch. "Hey," she said as Wyatt walked across the yard.

"Hi baby," he said, and smiled up at her.

"What have you got?"

"Fertilizer. I am determined to bring this yard back to life this spring."

God, she did love him—so why was this so hard? "Jillian called today," she said. "The will has been probated."

"Oh yeah?"

"I can sell this place now."

"That's good news. Are you still willing to sell it to me?"

"Of course."

Wyatt grinned and dropped the bag of fertilizer on the ground. He put his hands on his waist and gazed up at her. He was such a handsome man. A kind man. A great father to Grace, a hard worker . . . *So what was her problem?*

"Are you okay?" he asked.

Holly tried to smile, but somehow the smile came out as a shake of her head, and Wyatt mounted the steps, wrapped his arms around her, and held her tight. He kissed her temple, but he didn't say anything. He just held her. It felt good to have him hold her.

Holly drew back and smiled up at him. "Thank you, Wyatt. For everything."

"Whoa," he said, and arched a brow. "That sounds like you're going to give me my paycheck and send me home."

She laughed. "I just want you to know how much I appreciate you."

Wyatt's smile faded; he kissed her. "The feeling is mutual."

The sound of Mason's laughter reached them, and

Holly slipped her arm around his waist. "I should get dinner." They walked in together, their arms around each other's waist.

Hannah was standing inside with Mason in her arms. She looked nervous, Holly thought. It was so strange to see Hannah nervous and uncertain.

"Are you sure there isn't something I can do to help?" she asked Holly.

This was bizarre. That was usually Holly's line, and then Hannah would give her a look of impatience and say no, it was taken care of. "No, thanks," Holly said. "It's all taken care of." But playing Hannah in this bizarre little play didn't suit Holly at all. "You could help keep Mason occupied. He likes to help."

Hannah nodded. "Hello, Wyatt."

"Hannah."

Holly put the food on platters. She carried the food to the table, filled glasses with water—she'd taken all the wine from the house and given it to Wyatt—and then looked around. There was nothing left to do but eat. "Okay," she said. "Dinner is served."

And what an interminable dinner it was.

They sat down after making sure Mason was situated. Holly had put his chair next to Hannah. She could hardly bear to do it—not feeding him seemed the last act of surrender—but she had to do it for Mason's sake.

She sat across from Hannah and kept her focus on her plate. Wyatt was at the head of the table, and he tried very hard to lighten the mood. "How are things going for you, Hannah?" he asked.

"Oh. Good. All things considered," she said, and self-consciously tucked a tuft of hair behind her ear. "I, ah . . . I reserved Mason a spot in a Montessori school near where I live," she said, looking at Holly.

"Oh, that's great," Wyatt said. "I hear those are good schools."

"Yes, I think he'll really like it there," Hannah said. "And there is a playground across the street from my condo."

Holly forced a bite of roast down her throat. Her throat was dry, as dry as the inside of her. "That's wonderful," she said. For all her anguish, she was trying too.

"The roast is delicious," Hannah said.

"Thank you," Holly said.

No one said anything for several moments. Mason babbled about his food and tried to fit carrots on his little spoon.

"My attorney called today," Holly said, looking at Hannah. "We can sell this place now. If it's okay with you, Wyatt has expressed an interest in buying it."

"Oh." Hannah put her fork down. She glanced nervously at Wyatt, then Holly. "It's hard to think of selling it, isn't it? But sure, whatever you want to do, Holly. It belongs to you."

Holly put down her fork too. "I know Mom left it to me, but I told you I would share it all with you. Do you remember that?" She meant it sincerely. She guessed that someone who had been as addicted as Hannah must have forgotten things, being too stoned to know what was going on around her.

But Hannah clearly bristled. "Yes, I remember, Holly. Unfortunately, I remember most things. But Mom left it to you. It's yours. And I want you to have it."

"You want me to have it?" Holly repeated disbelievingly. "I don't feel right about it. This is *our* inheritance. Not just mine."

Hannah gave a little self-conscious laugh as she stopped Mason from throwing his food off his tray. "Holly, honestly. I don't *want* it. I would much rather you have it. That seems to me the right thing to do."

The right thing to do? If Hannah remembered most things, as she said, then she would remember that she'd felt slighted by their mother leaving everything to Holly. Hannah had never thought it was the right thing to do. Suddenly, Holly understood. "Oh, I get it," she said disbelievingly.

Hannah did not look at her.

"You want me to have this house and this land as my pay-off for taking care of Mason."

"Holly," Wyatt said softly.

"No, it's true," Holly said to Wyatt. "Isn't it, Hannah?"

Hannah shook her head. "Don't be absurd. That is obviously not what I meant."

"Then what *did* you mean? Because before you left, you were pretty incensed that Mom had left it to me when you had done so much for her. Do you remember *that*, Hannah?"

"Yes. I remember that too," Hannah said stiffly. "But I am thinking a little more clearly now, and I don't *want* it because Mom left it to you. She was very clear in her wishes and I would like to honor those wishes."

"Bullshit," Holly said, and stood up from the table. Wyatt tried to take her hand, but Holly yanked it away.

"God, Holly," Hannah said angrily. "What is the

matter with you? You act like you gave birth to Mason and have to give him away to a total stranger. I don't want what Mom wanted you to have, okay? But even if I did, would it really be so bad if I *did* want you to have it as my way of thanking you? Am I not allowed to say thank you, or I'm sorry, or anything else?"

"You can say whatever you want," Holly said curtly. "God knows, you always have." She walked away from the table.

"She's not herself," she heard Wyatt say, his way of making an excuse for her. That was the problem: Wyatt thought she needed to be excused for being frustrated with her sister. Holly kept walking, out onto the porch. Milo was there, lying beside the door. His tail started thumping against the porch; he lifted his head to her, waiting.

She ignored him, folded her arms tightly around her, and stared out at the brown yard, the old windmill that didn't squeak anymore, the barbed wire fence that she guessed Wyatt would take down once he bought this place.

She heard the door open behind her, heard Wyatt's footfall. "This has to be getting old for you," she said flatly.

"What?"

Holly glanced at him over her shoulder. "This drama. *Me.*"

Wyatt looked sheepishly guilty, as if he'd been caught with his hand up her skirt.

"That's what I thought," Holly said.

"I understand this is really hard for you—"

"Could you please stop being so understanding?"

Holly exclaimed. "Please stop! Yes, this is hard for me, but I don't need you to make excuses for me. I know I am making it harder on everyone. I *know* that, and I can't seem to stop myself, but I don't think that means my feelings or my . . . my issues," she said, gesturing to herself, "are any less valid. There is a lot of stuff between me and Hannah, Wyatt. A lot of stuff you don't know about. My problem is that I don't know how to work it all out. I know I have to, but I don't know how to do it, and right now . . . right now I can only manage to focus on handing Mason over to her. That's it."

"Okay," he said. His expression was wary; his blue eyes were locked on hers, as if he were afraid he would miss something significant if he looked away.

Holly took a deep breath. "I need . . . a break."

Wyatt's brows rose but he did not speak.

"I need some time on my own to . . . to cope with what is happening. And it's not just Mason, I swear to you, it's not that. I have come to terms with it, I really have. But there is more. All these feelings have bubbled up inside me and I need to figure it out."

"You mean . . . without me around to be understanding," he said coolly.

Holly ached with regret. The hurt on Wyatt's face was devastating. "I love you, Wyatt," she said desperately. "I do. I love you with all my heart. But I don't want to ruin what we have, and I will if we continue like this. I know myself, I know that I will blow it, and I don't want to do that. Can you . . . do you see what I am saying?"

"No," he said. "That's not the way I do things. When

the going gets tough, people who love each other circle the wagons. They don't go out to fight battles alone, because they are usually outnumbered."

"Wyatt . . . I just need some time."

He looked skyward. He pushed both hands over his hair and locked his fingers behind his neck for a moment. "I can't believe this," he muttered. "So, what are you saying? That all we've been together, all we've become, is gone?"

"We've been playing at a fantasy," Holly said softly. "We were pretending to be a happy little family."

"Jesus, Holly, we *are* a family. And we can still *be* a family."

"*You* can be that. *Grace* can be that. But Mason and I *can't* be that, not anymore. And now I have to face up to the fact that I don't really understand who or where or what I am, because of all of *that*?" she said, gesturing to the house. "That happy family we've been? It was a smoke screen."

"A smoke screen," he repeated, and pressed his lips together. "A fucking smoke screen." He dropped his gaze to the ground, folded his arms tightly across his chest. Holly moved to him, put her arms around him and rested her cheek against his shoulder. Wyatt stood stiffly. She kissed his cheek and stood back. "I don't want it to be like this, but I need some space."

"Take all the space you need, Holly," he said through a clenched jaw, and stepped away from her. "Milo, come," he said, and walked away without looking back. Holly watched him as he went around the side of the house, Milo trotting behind him. She wanted to call him back, but she couldn't make herself do it. She realized, as saw he got into the truck and drove away, that she was silently weeping. Her heart, having suffered so many fine fractures with the blow of losing Mason, now shattered completely into tiny pieces.

Holly stayed outside for a long time, sitting on the porch steps, shivering in the cool night air. She wished for a beer, but of course, with Hannah around, she had none. She could hear the sounds from inside, heard Hannah cleaning the kitchen, heard Mason babbling happily, Hannah speaking to him softly.

Holly gritted her teeth against the pain of her loss.

A little later she heard Hannah in the living room. Then moving upstairs. She guessed it was Mason's bedtime. More time passed. More numbing, blank minutes. Holly had no idea how much time had passed when she heard the door open behind her, heard Hannah come out, and felt the jacket she draped on Holly's shoulders.

She sat beside Holly on the steps. "It's cold out here."

"I guess," Holly asked dumbly.

"Did you break up with him?"

"More or less."

"Why?"

"Because I need to figure some things out," Holly answered honestly. "A lot of things."

Hannah sighed. "I hear you. Me too. What things?"

Holly was suddenly reminded of another night the two of them had sat on their porch. It had been summer, and the sun was beginning to set. Bobby Briggs had broken up with Holly after two months of "going out," which was all that Holly had been allowed to do at the age of fifteen. Holly had been crushed by Bobby's abrupt brush-off.

"I'm glad he broke up with you," Hannah had said that evening.

"Thanks a lot."

"No, seriously. I heard he's been hanging out with Gretchen Moyer. Plus, I had him in Algebra II, and he's an idiot. You can do way better than him, Holly."

"He's really a great guy, Holly," Hannah said softly now.

"I know," Holly said, sniffing. "The best. But I need some space. I've been thinking a lot about where I am going in life the last few days, and it's not fair to drag him through all my baggage."

"I know the feeling," Hannah murmured. She leaned over her knees and grabbed her toes.

"How, Hannah?" Holly blurted. "Why did you get hooked on drugs? I mean, you had everything going for you. I've tried to make sense of it and I can't."

Hannah snorted. "Do you think *I* can? It's really complicated."

"Tell me," Holly insisted.

Hannah regarded her a long moment, as if she were debating how much to confide. But she nodded. "Okay. I'll try my best to explain. But can we at least go inside? It's cold out here."

They sat on the couch in front of the cold hearth, facing each other. Hannah spoke in a very calm way, as if she'd repeated the story a thousand times. "I was never one of those people who could stop with one drink," she started. "Even in high school, when we'd get beer on a Saturday night and drive out to the old silo, remember? I couldn't really stop with one beer. I liked the way it made me feel, and the more I liked it, the more I drank."

"You drank in high school?" Holly asked. "I didn't know that. You were so . . . perfect."

"I drank," Hannah said with a shrug. "Then I went to college and I didn't drink. I was working and going to school, you know, and I didn't have time. Every once in a while I'd go out with friends and I would just . . . binge," she said, grimacing a little. "But I never felt addicted. I would stop for weeks, then do it again."

After college, Hannah said, she'd begun her working career, and the drinking had worsened with the introduction of Friday night happy hours. "It got to where I could drink more each time, and it took more for me to get drunk, but when I did, I was wasted." She confessed to Holly that she'd had blackouts, and once ended up in bed with a man she'd met only that night. She remembered nothing about the sex they'd had.

"Oh my God, Hannah!" Holly said, horrified. "You could have been killed!"

"I know. That's when I stopped drinking. It scared me to death, and I didn't even realize I could drink that much." She smiled ruefully. "In true Hannah fashion, I just made up my mind and stopped. No pain no gain, right? It never occurred to me to get help. Just do it."

"Mom," Holly said.

"Yeah, Mom," Hannah said with a shake of her head. "Remember what she used to say? 'No crying, no whining. Just do it.'"

Holly couldn't help but smile. "Then what?"

"Then I blew my knee out skiing, remember? And I

had my first taste of pain pills." Hannah told Holly that her knee had hurt so badly that if the prescription said take one, she took two. She confessed that she'd gone to two different emergency rooms to complain of the pain, just to get more. But she hadn't gotten hooked on the pain meds then, because she hadn't known how to get them.

"And then I met Loren," Hannah said with a sigh, and shook her head, glancing away. "You were right about him, Holly. From the beginning you were right about him, but I was too blind and in love to see it. Loren had a way of making me feel like the brightest, most beautiful woman in the world. Can you believe it?"

"But you were," Holly said. "You didn't need someone like Loren to tell you that, did you?"

Hannah's laugh was sour. "I guess I did. I didn't feel that way at all. All my life, I tried to measure up—"

"To *what*?" Holly exclaimed disbelievingly.

"I don't know. Something. Whatever I did, it wasn't good enough for Mom. She always thought I could have done more. According to her, I was too smart, too pretty not to be out conquering the world. But the more I conquered, the more I achieved, the more she raised the bar. It was never good enough."

"Good God," Holly muttered. "I was never you. That was my crime. I never shone as brightly as you at anything."

"I know," Hannah said sadly. "But I guess, in my case, I was good enough for Loren. And he was a drinker."

She said the drinking had started up again when they

became engaged, and neither of them thought much about tying one on Saturday night and being hungover the next day. "We thought that was just life. But Loren would lay off after that. Me? I was a firm believer in taking the 'hair of the dog.' For days." She grimaced; the memories were obviously painful. "I knew it was growing beyond my ability to control. I knew it. But I convinced myself I could handle it. The only time I didn't drink was when I was pregnant."

"What about the pills?"

Hannah's face colored. "I started with some pills Loren had after his back surgery. That's when I found out about his first affair. That killed me, Holly. It made me feel so small and unattractive and stupid. But his pain pills made me feel like I could float along and not think about it. Pills on top of booze. If that doesn't make you feel good, nothing will. And then . . . it got really bad when Mom got sick."

Hannah told Holly how she had borrowed pain pills from their terminally ill mother—had even convinced the home nurse that their mother was losing them or throwing them away. "I thought I could quit the pills whenever I wanted, but from time to time I felt like I had to have them just to be *normal.*"

She told a silent Holly how, after their mother had died, she needed the pain pills just to function. The days of getting high were fewer and farther between. She was taking twenty pain pills a day, supplemented with Xanax and Valium and Ambien, pills she had been prescribed at different times in her life and had abused. She described the lengths she had had to go to get them—doing things that made Holly cringe—just to feel like herself again. But what had finally precipitated her cry for help was the time she left Mason in his crib to go get pills and then was involved in a fender bender.

"That did it," she said. "I knew then that it was really bad, that I needed help. And still it took me another couple of weeks to actually go to treatment. All my life had been building to that point, all the pressure to succeed, all the disappointments, all the things that made me feel good . . . I turned into an addict without knowing it. All that time I thought I could stop . . . until I had to stop and I couldn't."

"I don't know what to say," Holly said.

"There is nothing *to* say," Hannah said. "But now you know."

Holly considered her sister, so beautiful, so accomplished. So tortured. "I felt so stupid when you called me from Florida," she confessed. "I couldn't believe you could be an addict like that, and I didn't know. I felt so self-centered and useless."

"Oh, Holly, no," Hannah said, and touched Holly's arm. "You have to understand that I was a master at hiding it. A *master.*"

"Still, you are my sister. How could I not know? And now I worry that you will relapse."

"I have the same fear," Hannah confessed. "All I can tell you is that I have two amazing guys in my corner. Mason most of all. I will spend my whole life regretting what I have done and trying to make up for it. If I ever think of a pill or a drink, I think of Mason, and the craving goes away. And then there is Rob. He's been there for me. He understands. He's got my back.

That's the best assurance I can give you. I know it's not much, but it's my word."

Holly nodded and picked absently at her jeans. "I don't know how to forgive you, you know," she said softly. "I want to forgive you, but I can't seem to do it."

"I hardly blame you," Hannah said wearily. "I can't forgive myself."

"Keeping Mason has been the best thing to ever happen to me. I love him, Hannah. I can't imagine a day without him in it. It's a cruel joke the universe has played on me, because I can't tell you how hard it is to give him up."

"But you're *not* giving him up," Hannah said. "You will still be in his life, as much as you want. You can come every day if you want."

Holly shook her head. "Thanks for that. But it's not the same and we both know it. I can't be his mother. No matter how hard I try, I cannot be his mother."

Hannah didn't dispute it.

Nevertheless, Holly thought they'd at least made some progress that night. They'd laid their cards on the table, and it was a beginning. But it was not the end. They had a long way to go to find their place as sisters again, but they agreed on two things: They would sell the homestead to Wyatt. And they would check in with each other once a week, every week, so that they could at least attempt to rebuild their relationship.

The next two days flew by. Holly didn't feel quite as awkward because Hannah seemed more like the sister Holly had known all those years ago when they'd lived under the same roof, and less like the sister Holly had come to avoid in the last few years.

Hannah kept things superficial by making small talk: Mason was growing like a weed. Wouldn't it be great if the windmill actually worked? Remember how Dad used to plant tomatoes that grew as big as softballs? Holly had the feeling that her confession had taken a lot out of Hannah. She sympathized—it had to have been very difficult for Hannah to admit all that she'd done. Holly had been appalled by Hannah's confession, but she admired Hannah more than she could say for having the courage to tell her the truth.

Holly kept busy with work. Quincy was in the recording studio, and she was working on "A Light at Winter's End." It was different from the country swing tunes she usually penned, but Holly liked it. She talked to Quincy about meeting his manager, and Quincy was more than happy to facilitate that. Holly kept the plane ticket to Nashville on her dresser and looked at it every day.

She kept busy, but every waking moment she thought about Wyatt. She wondered what he was doing, if he was sad, or if he was, in hindsight, relieved. She expected to hear his truck on the road, but he did not come. She wrote Wyatt a long letter explaining, as best she could, why she needed to take a little time. It sounded as lame on paper as it had when she'd said it aloud, and she didn't send it.

She kept that on her dresser too.

On Thursday morning she heard the sound of a truck and caught her breath. She jumped up from the piano and ran out onto the porch. It was Wyatt's old pickup barreling up the road, and Holly's heart surged with relief. He was coming to be understanding once more. He was going to let her take her break and tell her that he would be waiting for her. He was going to forgive her and promise her everything was okay.

But it was Jesse Wheeler who got out of the truck and made his way up the walk. "Hey, there, Holly-hocks," he said cheerfully.

"Hi, Jesse. You're alone?" she asked, peering past him to the truck.

"Yep. Just me and my good mood," Jesse said. "Wyatt's stomping around like an old bull this morning. I came to get a tiller. He said he left it over here in your barn."

"Oh. Sure." Holly walked with Jesse to the barn.

"World treating you right?" Jesse asked, throwing his arm around her shoulders and squeezing tight for a moment.

"Yes. You?"

"Lucky to be here," he said, and opened the barn door. It had been used as storage for what seemed like centuries. There was the Oldsmobile her father had never wanted to part with. Junk had been piled on top of it—clothes and coffee cans that her mother had always saved, and boxes of papers and odds and ends. Beside the car were old dining room chairs that no one wanted, and plastic crates full of generations of a family's belongings. Holly couldn't imagine what they'd do with all this stuff when Wyatt bought the place. She'd asked Jillian to negotiate the sale.

"Oooh, I'd be *delighted*." Jillian had said. "I always did enjoy wrangling with Wyatt."

"There it is," Jesse said, pointing to the tiller. He

pulled it out, tipped it back on its wheels, and started pushing it to the truck.

"So, what are you guys doing today?" Holly asked, skipping to keep up with Jesse.

"You guys? You mean me and Attila the Hun? He's going to till a garden and I'm going to go down and cut some brush from that hot spring on the west end." He glanced at Holly. "Maybe you two can do some skinny-dipping after I've gone home. Or maybe we could all—"

"Jesse."

He laughed. "So, are you and the Mason Jar coming over later?"

Clearly, Jesse had no idea that she had pushed Wyatt away. That was just like Wyatt, to keep everything close. "Ah . . . not today," she said, her step slowing. "My sister is here."

"Oh, yeah?" Is she as pretty as you?"

"Prettier." Holly watched him load the tiller into the truck.

"Well, then, tell her I have a natural spring I'd like to show her." He closed the tailgate and winked at Holly. "That is, if you're going to stick with Sourpuss."

Holly smiled. "See you, Jesse."

"Later," he said, and climbed in the truck, honking as he drove away.

Nothing. Wyatt had said nothing. There was nothing.

Holly turned back to the house and was surprised to see Hannah standing on the porch, watching. "Seriously, Holly, are you going to let him go?"

Holly frowned and started up the steps. "I am doing him a favor."

"That's ridiculous," Hannah said. "He's a wonderful man and obviously crazy about you."

"He was crazy about the little family we had. He was crazy about a fantasy, Hannah. And he still has his baby!" she exclaimed, and gasped with painful surprise when she uttered the words. She hadn't even realized it . . .

"Holly—"

"I really don't want to talk about it," Holly said, and hurried past her sister and went inside.

The sooner she went to Nashville, the better. She was making herself crazy.

Chapter Twenty-five

Wyatt, I am just worried sick about you," Linda Gail said on the phone. "I haven't seen you in town for two weeks. Are you alive?"

"What do you need, Linda Gail?"

"Well, besides the usual signature on my paycheck, I need to know you are okay."

"I'm fine. Jillian Harper is going to call you about a sale. We've agreed on price and need to get it to closing."

"Jillian? What piece of property is that?"

Wyatt suppressed a sigh. "A ranch. She'll fill you in. Is there anything else?"

"Nothing that a few manners wouldn't cure," Linda Gail said crisply, and hung up.

Wyatt didn't worry about Linda Gail's snit—he had been no less and no more rude to her than he normally was. But Linda Gail sensed something was up, and she did not like to run into brick walls when she was ferreting out gossip.

Jesse was another matter. It had taken a week or so, but he'd finally figured out that Wyatt and Holly weren't seeing each other anymore.

"Oh no," he'd said, marching into the kitchen one morning. "No, no. Don't tell me you *blew* it."

Wyatt didn't have to ask what he was talking about. "Would you please go back outside and work for the money I pay you?"

"Good God, Wyatt, I feel like I need to follow you around and supervise." He started marching toward the door, but he stopped and pointed at Wyatt. "And she was perfect for you, you stubborn jackass."

Wyatt wouldn't argue with that. But apparently, he wasn't perfect for her. No, *he* was too understanding. Damned if you do, damned if you don't, and it hurt like hell. It kept him up at night, made him impossible to live with during the day. He was beginning to wonder where he could go to hide from his pain now; he was running out of real estate. When his groceries began to run low, he even thought about living off the land. Pecans and wild berries seemed preferable to going into town and seeing the looks.

Oh, he knew he'd be getting looks. Macy wondered why he hadn't taken Grace to the Baby Bowl. Jillian asked some sly questions, such as whether or not he and Holly had discussed a price or terms. No, he'd said. *Huh,* Jillian said.

But what really galled Wyatt was that Holly's sister kept calling him. "Wyatt, please call me. I need to speak to you."

Well, he didn't need to speak to her.

"Wyatt, this is Hannah Drake. I would really appreciate it if you would call me back."

He was not interested. The only person he wanted to call him was Holly, and when she had in fact called, he'd had that asinine moment when he had decided she could just leave a message and wonder where the hell he was, like he wondered about her with every breath. He had let it roll to voice mail.

"Hi, it's Holly," she said in her message. "I just wanted you to know that I am going to Nashville. Well. Okay."

Well. Okay. That about sealed the deal, he figured. There had been no invitation for him to go along. There was no apology, no hint that she wanted to see him. Wyatt had lost the most important person in the world for a second time, and the only way he could cope was to cover himself up with hard, physical labor and burrow deeper into his little ranch.

His routine returned to normal. Up with the sun, check the Word of the Day and the sports scores, go and saddle Toby to ride around and look for something hard and punishing to do. Avoid Jesse. Avoid Linda Gail. Avoid himself, if he could figure out just how to do that.

Wyatt didn't like to think. He didn't like to analyze why he kept falling for impossible women. He would much rather ruminate on the possibility of being alone all his life, a burden on Grace in his old age. That was cheerier.

After a few days, Hannah stopped calling. He assumed that was the end of that little drama. But one afternoon, big, heavy rain clouds drove him back to the house, and there Hannah was on his drive. Mason was running around and she was just standing there beside her car.

"Wy-wy!" Mason said. "Wy-wy!" He pointed at Wyatt.

Wyatt hadn't realized until that moment just how badly he'd missed that little kid. He hauled him up and held him high overhead. "Little Buckaroo," he said, bouncing him and smiling at Mason's giggling. He put Mason on his hip and looked at Hannah. "Usually, when someone doesn't return your calls, it's an indication you shouldn't drive all the way out to see them."

"Usually. But in this case I won't take no for an answer," she said, and smiled.

"I'm going to help you out here, Hannah. There is nothing you can say to me that's going to change anything. And since that is the case, you might as well save your breath and go home."

"I thought you were in love with Holly."

"Hey," Wyatt said, his voice full of warning. He wasn't about to let her lecture him or remind him how he felt.

"Well, I did. Do you know she is leaving for Nashville?"

"Yep. She left me a message."

"And?"

"And what? She's going to Nashville."

Hannah groaned skyward. "I swear to God, I have never known two more recalcitrant, stubborn people."

He didn't need her to tell him that, either. "What do you want? If you came to tell me she's leaving, I already know it. Go home."

Hannah sighed. Her shoulders sagged. "May I just tell you one thing?"

"No."

"Our mother would not have won any Mother of the Year awards," Hannah said, undaunted.

Wyatt got the sense that this was going to take a little longer than he liked, and reluctantly put Mason down.

"She was awful in a lot of ways," Hannah continued. "The way she was awful to Holly was to belittle her. She made Holly believe that she was lazy, that she'd never amount to anything, and that she didn't deserve good things to happen—like you, Wyatt. Deep down, Holly doesn't believe she deserves a guy like you."

He rolled his eyes. "Sounds like someone's been in therapy."

"Please don't do that," she said softly, and Wyatt instantly felt contrite. "I am very serious. Holly is very much in love with you. But she is trying to piece things together and she has convinced herself that she has done you and Grace both a favor by cutting you lose, and now she is leaving for Nashville, and I am afraid that she will lose the best thing that ever happened to her. So I have come to beg you—*beg* you, Wyatt—to take the high road here and go to her. Give her the opportunity to ask your forgiveness. Because she will do it, I know she will."

"It's great that you have found some compassion for your sister," Wyatt said. "But you aren't her. I know what she said. And I have to take her at face value. If she wanted to apologize to me, if she wanted to try and make amends, she'd be standing here instead of you."

Hannah's face fell. "You are making a huge mistake. Holly is great. She's fun and creative and she . . . she is so caring. Much more caring than I could ever hope to be. And when she loves, she loves completely. But your feelings are hurt, so . . ." She shrugged and picked Mason up.

"It's a little bit more than that," Wyatt snapped.

Hannah's eyes narrowed. "Oh, I'm sure that it is," she said. "Your hurt is so much grander than hers, right?"

Wyatt's pulse was starting to race. "You don't know what you're talking about," he said tightly. "Holly is the one who ended things, not me."

"Yes, and that was a really dumb thing that she did. But we all do dumb things—*all* of us. And all of us could really use someone who can forgive the dumb things and still love us." She dipped into her car to put Mason in his car seat.

Mason started to cry. Hannah stood up and looked at Wyatt. "I was really hoping you were that for Holly. Good-bye, Wyatt." She got in her car and revved the engine.

Wyatt stood on the drive long after she'd gone, wanting so badly to forgive Holly. But he really needed Holly to do the asking.

Chapter Twenty-six

Two months later

Holly stared at herself in the full-length mirror in the condo she rented in Nashville. She hardly recognized herself. She was wearing a sleek lavender satin dress, the hem mid-thigh, the décolletage cut very low. Quincy's record label executives had hooked her up with a stylist for tonight, and they'd dressed her and done her hair and applied her makeup. Holly looked like a star in this dress, like someone who had a right to be in Nashville.

The car they were sending for her would be here in thirty minutes.

Tonight was the launch of Quincy's album. But the single released ahead of the album—"A Light at Winter's End"—had done amazingly well, hitting the *Billboard* charts and getting some phenomenal play time on radios around the country. Holly had made the melody a little more melancholy than had been her initial instinct, and Quincy had added texture to the song that had awed her. It was a runaway hit, and now the album looked like it was going to launch Quincy into stardom. To celebrate, the record label was hosting a big launch bash, and some of the biggest stars in Nashville would be in attendance.

Everything was working out as Holly had always dreamed it would. She'd been in Nashville two months now and, thanks to that song, she was in demand. Artists were calling to find out what else she had. Quincy had made good on his promise that she would meet his manager, who had not only signed her but landed her a contract. She had actual work, and for really good money for the first time in her life. This was the moment she'd been waiting for all her life.

She should be happy, but Holly felt empty. So dull.

Holly glanced outside: The clouds were thickening, and the temperature was dropping, but it was spring. Winter had finally ended.

Mason loved the Montessori school. Hannah sent videos of Mason every week. He was growing so fast, and he seemed, from all outward appearances, to be thriving. Holly had been able to get back only once since she'd left, and she missed Mason so much. He was a constant presence in her thoughts, but there was something comforting in knowing he was happy.

Mason wasn't the source of her emptiness. That was a deeper, broader hole that Wyatt had left in her. Especially tonight. He was the one who had believed in her talent, had given her the ticket to Nashville, and here she stood on the threshold of something big without him.

How had that happened? How had she lost not only

Mason but also the one man she had ever truly loved beyond measure? She thought of him often, dreamed about him, wondered what he was doing. She'd written him a long letter two or three weeks ago. *I hope you are well. I think of Grace all the time. I wonder if she misses me or Mason.*

Saying good-bye to Wyatt meant saying good-bye to that little girl, and Holly ached with regret.

I am so sorry for ending things like I did. I still don't understand why I did it. I guess I wasn't in my right mind, I was just so blinded by what was happening with Mason. But I am so sorry, and Wyatt, I've been missing you so much. So I'm telling you I need you. I love you. You once told me if I needed you in Nashville, you'd come. I need you in Nashville. I need you everywhere. Can you ever forgive me?

She'd checked the mail every day, hoping for a response—anything, even a letter asking her not to contact him again—because at least then she'd know, she wouldn't be wondering if there was still a chance.

He had not written her back.

"Girl, you screwed that up," Quincy had said over coffee one day when she told him what she'd done.

"Tell me about it," Holly had moaned. "What do I do?"

Quincy had mulled it over. "Send him a plane ticket and a pass to the launch party."

Holly had thought about Wyatt, how he hated those sorts of things. "That's not his style," she'd said.

Quincy had shrugged. "That's the best idea I've got," he'd said, and smiled sympathetically. "Buck up, Holly. You're about to be a star. There's plenty of fish in the Nashville sea, especially for you."

But Holly didn't want any other fish. She wanted Wyatt.

She'd kept what Quincy said in the back of her mind, however, and just last week, in a moment of desperation, she'd taken his advice and sent Wyatt the launch party pass.

Quincy's label is hosting a big launch party for his album and my song. Please come. I'd love for you to come. I'd think I'd died and gone to heaven if you came. I would tell you how much I love you and how sorry I am and how I promise to never flake out on you again. Please say you will come.

There was no response. Holly had told herself she had to face up to it: She'd loved. She'd lost. She'd thought she couldn't continue in the world she and Wyatt had created, and she'd been a fool for thinking that.

Quincy had tried to hook her up with his bass player for tonight, but Holly had politely refused. She was going to the launch alone.

At half past six, her phone rang. "Car service, Miss Fisher," the man said. Holly picked up her beaded bag that matched her shoes, checked her reflection once more, and went downstairs.

"Good evening Miss Fisher," the suited gentleman said, and held open her car door.

"Hello. Thank you," she said, and climbed into the backseat of the Lincoln.

When they reached the venue, she could hear music pulsing out the open doors. There was a red carpet; several country-western stars were posing for pictures. The driver helped Holly out, and she began walking up the carpet. How she wished Wyatt was here to see this! How she wished he was standing next to her, his hand on the small of her back, reminding her in a whisper that she was the reason this party was happening.

"Holly!"

She turned; Quincy was there in a red suit, grinning from ear to ear. "Can you believe this? Look around, Holly—these people love your song. Come on, let's get pictures," he said, and put his arm around her waist, dragging her to a spot on the red carpet. The flashes of the bulbs blinded her and she wished again that Wyatt was here to see this. Who would have believed it? Who would have guessed Holly Fisher would be standing on a red carpet?

And yet, she felt so hollow.

When at last she got inside, she made straight for the bar and asked for a glass of wine. Holly hadn't drunk since Hannah came home. She hadn't wanted it around Hannah, having seen what alcohol had done to her sister. But tonight she needed something to take the edge off her nerves and her sadness.

"Holly Fisher, right?" a man said, sticking his hand out. "Mark Vaughan. I'm with RCA records. Love your song," he said, pumping her arm. "Who's your manager? Grif Lewis, right? I'd like to talk to him. Maybe we can collaborate on a couple of projects I've got in mind."

"Sounds great," she said.

"This is your night," Mark said. "Can't wait to hear Quincy perform."

Holly smiled. She was thinking of Wyatt on Christmas morning. And how she'd performed for him, an audience of one. She was thinking of the expression on his face, and how she'd known he loved her by the look in his eyes. *How she wished he was here!* She looked around for him, her hope surviving on a weak pulse, but of course she didn't see him.

There was dancing, and an elaborate buffet with an ice sculpture in the shape of a guitar, which Holly gazed at, wondering how on earth they had carved it. She wandered about, talked to some new acquaintances, and was introduced to a dizzying number of people by her manager.

An hour or so later, Quincy took the stage.

"Thank you all for coming!" he said to the crowd. "I know what you want to hear, and I am going to get right to it. A special shout-out to Holly Fisher, who wrote this song for me," he said, and strummed the first chords.

"No," Holly muttered to herself. "I didn't write it for you."

He began to play; Holly sighed and turned around.

She saw him then. He was standing with one arm on the bar, watching her. Wyatt's gaze slid over her, lingering on her décolletage, on her legs, and Holly's heart started to beat. He was wearing a tux coat and shirt, jeans, and highly polished boots. His black hair was slicked back and in a little tail. He was clean-shaven and his eyes, his blue eyes, were as penetrating as ever. There was not a sexier man in attendance.

Holly was frozen in place. People were moving past her, trying to get closer to the stage, but she was mesmerized. She couldn't believe her eyes. He'd come. *He was really here.*

Wyatt pushed away from the bar and walked toward her, his head down, his gaze locked on hers. He stopped just before her. "You look like a million dollars, baby. You look like a star."

"You came," she said breathlessly.

His gaze slipped to her cleavage. "You said you needed me. And you sent me a pass."

Holly drew a shallow breath. "I didn't think you'd come."

"I almost didn't," he said, his gaze dipping lower.

"Wyatt . . . I don't know how to apologize. I want to apologize in a big spectacular way and beg you to forgive me but I don't know how to do that."

"No need. I forgive you," he said, and lifted his gaze to hers.

"Just like that?"

He smiled a little. "I had to think about it. But I've missed you, Holly."

She couldn't take her eyes from his. She couldn't speak. A million thoughts rushed through her head, the first and foremost that she loved him.

He moved closer. "All right, then, you said you needed me. So, what is it you need?"

"You," she blurted roughly. "I need *you,* Wyatt. I need you like I've never needed anyone or anything.

More than Mason. More than music. I need you more than that."

"If you need me more than that," he said calmly, his gaze now on her mouth, "why did it take you so damn long to say it?" He slipped his hand behind her neck, tilting her face up to his. "Why did it take you more than a month to reach out?"

"Because . . . I was afraid to hear that you might not need *me*. And I wouldn't blame you. I mean, really, you've had firsthand experience with how flaky I can be . . ."

"I like flaky," he said, and kissed the corner of her mouth.

She wrapped her hand around his wrist. "I'm sorry, Wyatt. I am so sorry. I was so stupid . . . You were the best thing that had ever happened to me, and I was babbling about all these issues—"

"Legitimate issues." He kissed the other side of her mouth.

"Legitimate, I don't know. Now that time has passed and I know that Mason is okay, I look back and think, *Why? What was happening to me?* And I think maybe I was really afraid of losing you, too, and I wouldn't be able to bear that, not with everything else, and then there was Grace, and how would she feel without Mason—"

"I get it," he said with a slight grin, and kissed her on the mouth. His hand found her bare thigh. "Do you have any idea how much I've missed you?" he murmured in her ear.

"Yes," she said, nodding adamantly. She was vaguely aware of Quincy singing the refrain: *She was his lover and his friend / She was his light at winter's end.* "I know exactly how much."

Wyatt moved closer, slipping his arm around her waist. "I am going to lay down the law here and now, Holly Fisher. I don't ever want to miss you like that again. Do I make myself clear?"

"Yes," she said. "Perfectly."

"And if I want to be understanding, you're just going to let me."

She couldn't help smiling. "You can understand as much as you want. Or not at all."

"And you're going to be part of Grace's and my family, and I am going to be part of yours and Mason's, and we'll build *our own* hodgepodge of family. Got it?"

"Got it," Holly said smiling. "I love you, Wyatt."

"Maybe as much as I love you," Wyatt said, and started to sway with her.

She was his lover and his friend, / She was his light at winter's end . . .

"One last thing," he said, and kissed her neck. "The moment this song is over, and you hear the crowd roar for your song, and you bask in the knowledge that you did it, that you wrote a hit song, and that you're a damn good songwriter, we're getting the hell out of here to make up for the time you've cost us. Right?"

Oh yes. Yes, yes, yes. "Right," she said, giggling.

Wyatt pressed his cheek to hers, dancing with her.

Maybe, Holly thought as they slowly danced to the melody she'd created, she and Wyatt would have a dozen little Masons to run around with Grace on their little ranch. The two of them and a bunch of little kids, a couple of dogs, and songs running around in her head. She could think of nothing better in life than that.

Contentment. In a state of peaceful happiness. As in, *at the end of winter, they found the contentment they deserved.*